Miss Boston and Miss Hargreaves

RACHEL MALIK

PENGUIN BOOKS

PENGUIN BOOKS

UK | USA | Canada | Ireland | Australia
India | New Zealand | South Africa

Penguin Books is part of the Penguin Random House group of companies
whose addresses can be found at global.penguinrandomhouse.com

Penguin
Random House
UK

First published by Fig Tree 2017
Published in Penguin Books 2018
001

Copyright © Rachel Malik, 2017

The moral right of the author has been asserted

Printed in Great Britain by Clays Ltd, St Ives plc

A CIP catalogue record for this book is available from the British Library

ISBN: 978-0-241-97609-8

www.greenpenguin.co.uk

MIX
Paper from
responsible sources
FSC® C018179

Penguin Random House is committed to a
sustainable future for our business, our readers
and our planet. This book is made from Forest
Stewardship Council® certified paper.

PENGUIN BOOKS
Miss Boston and Miss Hargreaves

Rachel Malik was born in London of mixed English and Pakistani parentage. She studied English at Cambridge and Linguistics at Strathclyde. For many years Rachel taught English Literature at Middlesex University. *Miss Boston and Miss Hargreaves* is her first novel.

Prologue

A woman standing at a window, looking out at the fields beyond. The window is open and the cool of the morning and cold of the room meet on her face. Outside, the morning is coming clear, another good day. The woman leans out to get a better view. If you were passing by the house, you might see her in the casement window. If, for no one comes up here on a whim. There is a track, narrow, cut through a wood, but it peters out before it reaches the gate. The cottage has the name of an old mine – Wheal Rock – of which only the brick chimney remains. Very occasionally a stranger comes up the track, curious, having seen the chimney from the road, but they rarely linger – it feels like private land.

But if you did get as far as the cottage you would see the figure of a woman at the upstairs window, looking out, half a shadow; the light catches her thick, springy hair. You might notice the black cat sitting in the window like china and the neat, well-stocked garden.

Closer, and you would see that she is waiting. There is something of that slightly fidgety intensity, that unwilling patience. A good deal of her life has been spent waiting, one way and another. She'll carry on waiting, but from today the waiting will be different. And this bedroom window is her lookout too, because she's also watching. Her eyes scan gate and hedge, searching for anything untoward or unwelcome: trespasser, stranger, animals out of place. It's an old, old habit – there is always the possibility of incursion, danger. She is on her mettle, steely.

Her face has been called pretty, but more often pleasing and fine. She has been called soft too, but with her head in mind. She has also been called a fine figure of a woman. This seems to describe her better. And yet. Few would dispute the fineness and match of her features, but there is something about her expression, the way she looks at things, people too, that gives you pause to wonder if any of these phrases really describe her at all.

* * *

A second woman with a cardboard suitcase, standing alone on the cobbles. The door in the great wooden gate has already shut behind her, a London morning rushes by ahead. The clock has just struck eight – symbolism – and she smiles to herself. She doesn't need to be told this is a new day.

She starts to walk briskly towards the road, struggling a little with the case; it is clear that she isn't expecting anyone to meet her. Almost ready to cast off into the moving street, she turns to look back at the building behind her, how big it is. The thick stone walls, the narrow windows, the great wooden gate with the little door – all this time and she's never seen it from the outside. She takes a deep breath, turns left and strides onward into the morning, thankful there is no one to see.

She used a map to memorize the first stage of today's journey: a half-mile walk to the station on the Holloway Road. Everything about her looks grey, streaky, apart from the buses; it isn't much of a prospect. She swaps bag and suitcase and continues, there is an edginess to her; she is excited but she wants to keep it bottled up. She passes a cafe, busy, steamed up – one of the guards told her they did a good breakfast – but she doesn't want to linger here, not while she is still so close. She turns right with relief on to another, busier road, the wires thick above her, lots of shops, so many commands to see and read – Sylvia's Dresses, Woolworth's, Abbotts Shoes, Parr's Stationers. She feels green and light-headed from all the space. A tube train rumbles somewhere below her. She pauses, looks into a shop window and finds herself – shallow, faint, all angles. Bare-headed, she feels exposed, but many of the women walking past, and men too, seem to have given up on hats; if anything makes her stand out, it won't be that. She carries on looking into the glass, watching the people on the street as they stride or dawdle, paying careful attention to what they are wearing. It's a good thing it's a working day: her dark jacket with its neat collar and buttons is like a dozen others. She looks back at herself again, more carefully this time – it isn't vanity, it's just possible someone might remember her from the papers. She doesn't wish to attract sideways glances. She

2

straightens her collar – in other circumstances she would be quite pleased with her appearance. This is the first time she has worn her own clothes in nearly two years.

★ ★ ★

The first woman is still standing at the window, watching, waiting, remembering.

'I liked Wheal Rock from the first,' she had said. This was recorded in her police statement. 'I liked it because it was quiet, because it reminded me of a place where I lived for a long time, the place that I grew up.' The young WPC who wrote this down was uncomprehending, but she wrote it down anyway.

Starlight

I.

Seeing Double, June 1940

She stood at the window, looking out at the fields beyond, her fields. The calves were up by the gate, nosing each other, waiting for her – still unsure of their new routine. The great horse chestnut tree was swaying, she could hear it from here, feel the cool of its shade. In Fair Field, the oats were just starting to pale – her oats. The rest of the view was blocked by the tallboy. She had dragged it in last night. It was badly splintered at the back, but at least it was empty. She carried on standing at the window, looking out, waiting.

Tomorrow this view wouldn't belong to her – not quite. It would belong to the girl: for as long as she was here. The girl was arriving this afternoon at about three. Elsie was dreading it.

She looked slowly, carefully, around the room. The walls were bare, but she'd found a strip of matting and brought in the blue jug and basin. She'd even put some flowers on the mantel. The changes made the room more homely, but she wasn't sure she wanted that. It wouldn't do for the girl to get too comfortable. She wondered which bed the girl would choose. All four beds remained, and the drawers and wardrobe were crammed with clothes (the wardrobe reeked of lavender when you opened it). Well, the girl would have the tallboy and that would have to do: she couldn't be bringing so very much with her. The land girl.

Elsie had seen them in Lambourn in groups, walking three or four abreast, primped, on their half day she supposed. Uniforms unpicked and resewn far too tight. Old Cole had half a dozen now and she'd heard them too, hollering one to another, across the fields. Now one was coming here, it was all arranged. Only one, just one. One couldn't be too bad, and she needed the help. She had made the request.

Elsie looked out across the fields again. The calves were still waiting, a little restless now. The new postmistress cycled slowly up Sheepdrove – she wobbled as she went by the house. Elsie blinked and turned away from the window all of a sudden; she felt shy being in here.

On the landing she closed the door carefully and went downstairs; downstairs still felt her own. She made herself some tea – she couldn't eat anything – wiped the table and mashed up some scraps. Then, instead of sitting in the kitchen, she carried her cup through to the sitting room so she could listen in. Since the war had started, it seemed that there was much more music on the wireless, all those songs, all those oboes and clarinets played by Millicents and Joys. The voices that came through the wireless were the only ones in the house now, apart from her own. For they were all gone: two sisters married and the third moved away; three brothers, dead such a long time ago – their names engraved on the memorial to prove it; her mother and her father as well. Sometimes it seemed that her sisters were ghosts too, and not glimpsed since the war started. This war.

The voices called her back – the news had started, and as so often these days the war wasn't going well. Those quiet, clear voices from the Home Service tried to put on a good shine, but she knew. Foreign names she had once read and stumbled over – Arras, Armentières – spoken smoothly now over the wireless. They echoed in the sitting room, half familiar, along with other names she didn't know or had forgotten, just recently Dunkirk. Our brave boys had been brought home safely. Triumph seized from disaster's jaws. Sometimes Elsie thought she could see those jaws.

This war was simpler than the last, she thought. Poland was a friend, as were Holland and Norway – Norway was such a good friend that Elsie sometimes heard the news in Norwegian very early in the morning. A lot of Britain's friends were in trouble. Germany of course was an enemy, and now Italy. France had been a friend but now she wanted to be friends with Germany, or a part of her did. France was unreliable. Elsie didn't have friends, but she had a neighbour who was rather like France: untrustworthy and too close for comfort.

And now a stranger was coming, a stranger who was supposed to help her; perhaps she would. If only she wasn't coming from so far away. The land girl was coming through London and she was being picked up by car at Newbury. Elsie knew that London wasn't much more than sixty miles away, knew it could be reached by trains that ran quite frequently, but to her the city was another world, quite another being: dark, ferocious. Once you'd been there, you could never quite get free of it, it would keep trying to suck you back. After Moira returned from London that first time, she'd never sat down properly again, always restless.

She hoped the girl wouldn't be like Moira, or Brockway. Brockway was bringing the land girl in her car, and if the Land Army was a real army, Brockway was in the senior ranks. Elsie hadn't liked Brockway, hadn't liked her jaunty manner, thought she held her nose too high. She very much hoped the land girl wouldn't be like Brockway. Elsie had asked, rather tremulous, if the land girl came from London. 'Oh no, Miss Boston, you mustn't worry, she's been with the force for over a year.' And then, as an afterthought, 'I think she comes from Manchester,' and Elsie, still tremulous, had said, 'Oh.' But she certainly needed the help, and Elsie felt sure she could teach the girl perfectly well as long as she worked hard and was willing to learn.

They had all worked so hard in the early days. The boys outside with Dad, cutting a path through Yellow Field and clearing out the pond, the girls trying to make the house comfortable. Everyone's hands and feet permanently splintered, the rain running through the attic like a tap. Oh, how they had worked. Except Moira. As long as the land girl wasn't like Moira. Elsie switched off the wireless and carried her cup back into the kitchen. If only she didn't have to stay in the house, sleep in the room directly opposite hers. They would be eating their meals together, every day. These things terrified her, quite literally. The door to Starlight opened, left ajar, a string pulling; it felt as if someone was tugging already – there would be letters, cards, the girl would take off to Reading for the pictures, she might ask questions. Elsie wasn't at her best with questions.

There were people who thought she would give up as soon as old Alfred had died. All on her own on the edge of the Downs with no money to speak of, you'd have thought she'd have had that much sense. But Elsie didn't have that kind of sense. Besides, no one in Lambourn had ever believed the Bostons would stay when they arrived – and that was thirty years ago. And yet here she was, cows milked, calves at the gate, still here, holding on. It had never been easy. Once there had been Bert and they were going to work the farm together, brother and sister, when everyone else had gone. They just had to wait. Now everyone had gone and Bert too; his foot had been blown right off. But she was still here.

She pulled on her boots and went out. In the garden, the vegetable plots were neatly marked out and full of good food; the beans waved on their poles like flags. The house didn't look so bad either with its soft red brick. There were a few cracked chimney pots and some broken tiles (they could be put right easy). No sign of Smoke, who was probably still asleep in the barn – fine guard dog he was. She tied up a few stray shoots and crunched some snails briskly with her boot, then she slipped easily over the gate and across the new tarred road to where the calves were waiting; the ones at the front rested their chins on the top bar of the gate. They all pushed forward when they saw her, greeting her with their soft calf moos and twitching ears. 'Silly things, what are you waiting for?' She patted them before she pushed them off. 'I've nothing for you, off you go, go on.' They turned finally and ambled away. Pickwick was drinking at the bath trough; he raised his bony head to look at her and whickered, but quietly, as if to himself. The animals were looking well and there was still plenty of grazing.

But in the orchard, half of last year's apple crop had rotted on the grass and the abandoned glasshouses were a sorry sight. She usually tried to avoid this view. She and Dad had done all right with the marketing for a while. It had kept them busy: tray after tray of salad, all those tomatoes and strawberries, just the two of them. But now the ivy had got everywhere and the vine had reared into a monster, cracking the roof of the biggest glasshouse. Her sister Moira had persuaded Dad to buy the vine, one of her notions: *Vitis vinifera*, expensive, fancy. Dad was so soft. 'Moira doesn't even live here any more,' Elsie protested, but he hadn't taken any notice.

She found Smoke by the gate of Yellow Field. He barked delightedly then lay down, front legs stretched out, his nose deep in his paws, bashful. 'Silly dog. Where were you, silly old dog?' He thumped his heavy tail. Elsie slung the leather tool bag over her shoulder and set off up the field. Yellow Field reached its highest point almost exactly in the middle, and Elsie liked the gusty breeze that followed her up the slope. At this time of year the field justified its name, thick with buttercups. Smoke trotted beside her at first, eager to prove himself, but Elsie's pace was demanding and by the time she reached the gate to Cob Field he was distracted and lagging far behind, snuffling out butterflies and lacewings in the damp grass. It was the long, eastern hedge of Cob Field that brought her up here. This hedge marked the boundary between Elsie's land and Fern Farm, which belonged to Phil Townsend, and last week some of Phil's hoggets had got into her field. It wasn't the first time. She (and Smoke) had sent them back – it had taken most of a morning – and she'd stopped up the gap with old planking and gorse. Today, she wanted to make sure that there was no way back.

Elsie didn't like sheep: she didn't like the dim disregard in their eyes when they looked at you, or their moments of sudden growling anger; she particularly didn't like the way that some of them were dedicated to getting places they shouldn't. Cows were so much easier, so much friendlier.

She made her way slowly along the hedge, checking for signs of weakness. The repair was holding well, but the shreds of wool lodged on her side seemed like an affront. In the past Phil had kept his hedges and his fences well, but he didn't seem to be taking much care these days. The war had made her wary of incursions. The little planes flew over most days; our boys, she'd been told, but it didn't make her feel much safer.

She whistled and then paused to wait for Smoke, retying her scarf, watching the clouds – the sky was everything here. Phil had thanked her for sending the sheep back, but he hadn't done anything yet to secure his own side. He was often out and about these days, slow but steady with his stick. He seemed to especially like the edge of Cob Field – well, it was his boundary too. Sometimes, early in the morning or at dusk, she had been up here and got a sense of someone close by, on the other side of the hedge perhaps, or in the shadows. It gave her a shiver. She had caught the smell of sweet tobacco, his tobacco, but when she called out, there was no reply.

Elsie knew that traitors could live close by. Only last week she had read that an ice-cream parlour in Windsor had been shut down, the electrical equipment seized, the owner taken away. Phil didn't seem to Elsie like a man who would know German – or Italian, come to that – he didn't speak his English too well. No, Phil Townsend wasn't an alien, but he was up to something, she was sure of it. But why would he want to hide on his own land, hide from her? It was the sort of thing a poacher would do – except a poacher wouldn't smoke.

Elsie continued very carefully along the edge of the field, alert to signs of possible ingress. Years ago they had dug this very ditch, the whole family trudging up the hill with lamps and shovels. She remembered nothing about the digging, only the ditch full of muddy water after a torrent of spring rain. Someone had pushed Bert into the ditch, everyone laughing and shrieking. Her mother had been so angry.

Smoke was still dawdling, so she carried on without him. The slow pace was tiring and her hands were clammy. She rubbed them dry on her long shirt, then retied her scarf again – she should have brought a hat. More than halfway there. She had reached the stile and Fern Farm came into view – it was a natural stopping place, but she took a deep breath and pressed on. She didn't need to see how well it all looked, how big and shambling. Phil always managed to make money. Just now he had all manner of schemes going with the Land Ag, to do with the war. In the past he had given them sound advice, friendlier than other locals: told them to grow oats for the horses, tips about choosing stock and farm sales and where to buy guns cheap. It was Phil who had fixed up the strawberry picking that very first summer. Squashed into the cart in the middle of the night, the pony's hooves ringing in the dark – the first memory Elsie owned to – then making her way through row after row of plants with her basket and blistered, bloody fingers.

Phil had stayed close, too close she often felt. 'I promised your dad,' said Phil, whenever he offered her the hand of friendship, as he called it. Last spring, he'd asked if he could graze one of her fields. He would have paid her, it was only what farmers did, but she had said no, sensing encroachment. Elsie was walking faster now. Here most of the hedgerow was thick with hazel and blackthorn, but there were places where the ditching had crumbled and been scratched away, quite enough room for a sheep to get through if it was so inclined. Somewhere upfield she could hear the quick, rusty tune of a yellowhammer; she whistled back. The wind had dropped and the sun warmed her. She spied a pair of Small Coppers flopped on the hawthorn, such pretty things with their dark, velvety edges. Soon she'd be turning for home; she was even starting to get hungry. She pushed on, nearly at the end, and then, all of a sudden, the hedge of bright hazel ended and there was a burst of flowering spindle, all pink petals and orange hearts. She stopped still, her feeling of dread returning. Yesterday she had cut a big bunch of spindle for the land girl's room – she didn't usually bring flowers upstairs. Silly, silly. She took a deep breath and walked on briskly, calling again to Smoke, 'Come on now, come on.'

Back in the kitchen she sat down at the table, pulled off her boots and poured more tea – lukewarm and stewed, but she didn't mind. She still didn't feel ready to eat breakfast; the walk hadn't settled her at all. Outside the chickens were scuffling – Sally and Jones it probably was – she waited to see what would happen. Sally could be a dreadful bully. The squawking increased then subsided; all was well. Smoke barked cautiously, confirming. Elsie hoped the girl wasn't frightened of dogs. City people were often scared because of the strays – that or too soft. She hoped the girl wouldn't be too soft.

She leant back. The tap drip-dripped in the sink, dripped steady and cool into the deep bowl. Usually she loved this sound, and the quiet that let her hear it, but today it made her think of the heat in the room upstairs – the girl's room it was now. She had closed the window; that bedroom could get very stuffy in the late morning – should she leave it? Oh. She was seeing everything double and she didn't like it, it put her all at sea. She pulled off her scarf and rubbed her hands through her hair, trying to clear her thoughts.

Yes, she would go up and open that window, and that would be it. Elsie stood up with decision and just then she heard something. She listened, not quite trusting her ears.

It sounded like a voice. She couldn't hear what it was saying, but she could tell that it was close, very close, somewhere in the house.

For a moment she froze. Had the girl come early? Who might she be talking to? Elsie put her ear to the door between the kitchen and the hallway and listened. It was a lowish voice and it sounded like a woman. Elsie crept out into the hall. The voice grew louder; it seemed to be coming from the sitting room. She paused at the door and took a deep breath, her grip growing tight on the handle.

And then she knew who it was.

Silly, silly, Elsie said to herself. She had forgotten to turn the wireless off. Of course. The words came clear on the instant. Diana Linnington, 'an English traveller in the East'. Last year Elsie had half followed her about Greece – so many boats. This time she had travelled further to Persia, and Elsie was enjoying this more. The streets of Persian cities were full of mules and donkeys and, Elsie didn't doubt it, camels. Well, that didn't sound so bad. Unfortunately, the streets were also full of people. Miss Linnington had watched from her hotel room in Baghdad as crowds of people streamed through the Northern Gate every morning. Silly. Elsie switched off the radio and went upstairs to the window.

2.

The Girl in the Porch

> . . . Already,
> Mothers tell stories of animals
> That drew cars, called horses . . .

>> Bertolt Brecht, 'Of the Remains of Older Times',
>> *Poems, 1913–1956*

'Hargreaves? Pleased to meet you. I'm Brockway. How was your journey?'

The other woman nodded and smiled briefly but she did not speak. They shook hands, a little awkwardly, and waited by the luggage car.

The guard brought down a smallish navy trunk and they each took one of the narrow metal handles. They had the task in common, there was no need to say anything more. It wasn't so very heavy, but the metal dug harshly into their hands.

Behind them the doors slammed and the train was whistled out of the station. 'Hargreaves' bit her lip.

They were both wearing the Land Army uniform and wore it well, no mischievous re-stitching; and yet. There was the difference in ages – Brockway was young, twenty-one, twenty-two – but it was not dramatic. Something else.

'You must be hot. Why don't you put your coat in the back?'

Brockway had an ease that Hargreaves lacked. Hargreaves had confidence, but something about her was on edge.

Again she said nothing, just nodded, took off her coat, folded it quickly and laid it on the back seat of the Ford. She had put on her whole uniform this morning to help the packing, but it had turned into a hot day.

'That's better.'

They hoisted the trunk into the boot, then Brockway slammed it shut and they got into the car.

'The drive won't take long, it's about eight miles. There's some tea in that flask if you want.'

The car turned off the road and into a narrow lane. The village was a good two miles behind them now. The hedges were high, the sun was hot and they were climbing fast. The lane, for all the new tar, was bumpy.

Brockway had clearly enjoyed the drive, and she braked more sharply than the road demanded.

'Here we are.'

There was honeysuckle in the hedge, Rene could smell it.

They both got out of the car and carried the trunk up to the little porch, then she hurried back to get her coat, feeling excited.

Just a small house really, two-up two-down, square with scrimping windows; soft red brick, a few tiles missing from the roof, some others missing corners. The house had a pretty wooden porch though and the vegetable garden was well kept. A fruit tree grew against the front wall – she thought it might be a pear.

Rene climbed the gate and called into the yard. From somewhere round the back a dog barked, shaking its chain. Over by the tap there were two big hutches, full of rabbits, sensing her and already shivery. She splashed her face and drank a little of the soft water, lovely water but too soft for rinsing your hair. She had quite a look at the dairy with its cool tiles and great white sink, so clean after the ragged yard, then she went back to find Brockway, who was waiting in the car.

'No one home.'

Brockway was eager to be away. She had made a point of saying this was her free afternoon.

'You might as well go. She's bound to be back soon.'

'Are you sure? It should be all right. Miss Boston was certainly expecting us this afternoon.'

'It's fine. She can't be far away.'

'You're sure you don't mind?'

'No. Not at all.'

'I'm sure she'll be pleased to have you, she's all on her own. There was someone here till quite recently, I think. Mrs Tranmer from the committee will be round early next week, just to see everything's all right.'

'I'll be fine.'

'Bye then, Hargreaves.'

'Bye.'

'Good luck,' Brockway called as she drove back down the hill.

She dragged her trunk out of the way so that it didn't block the path and put her other bag on one of the benches in the porch. She called out again just to be sure, and again only the dog replied. She didn't mind that Miss Boston was late – she rather liked being on her own. There was a Fordson tractor, quite new but filthy, and a fat pony munching in the paddock with ten – she counted – calves. The smallest one came over and ruffled its muzzle softly, wheezily, in her hand.

Her experience of animals was greater than her experience of tractors, but she was more than willing to learn, sure that she could, eager. She didn't like to wander round too freely, so she sat down on the little pew in the porch. Even in uniform she felt half a trespasser. Another half hour passed. Perhaps Miss Boston had forgotten she was coming. She found it hard to imagine a woman, or a man, living here on their own. It seemed a little strange. Yet she liked the soft red brick of the house, and the orchard with its shrunken fruit trees.

She rolled up her coat and leant against it, and her eyes were caught by the picture hanging in the porch. It was a photograph of the house. It had been taken from quite far back, the track perhaps; you could see the whole house, even the chimney pots. The same fruit tree was growing against the wall, more neatly pruned. But it wasn't just a picture of the house, there were four girls sitting in the porch, two on each bench. Three could be seen quite clearly, but one was just a face. It was an old photograph: the girls were distant in their white blouses and long skirts, they all looked young. She wondered which one of them might be Miss Boston, her Miss Boston. Underneath the photograph in neat copperplate was written: *Starlight Farm, Sheepdrove*.

She sat in the porch quietly humming, one of those silly cheer-up songs from the billet – Brockway had been singing it in the car. She didn't particularly like the song, she hadn't especially liked Brockway, but she kept on humming, tapping her finger lightly on the wooden pew of the porch.

★ ★ ★

Elsie had spent a useful few hours in Newbury, shopping for things she couldn't or wouldn't buy in Lambourn. The meeting with the bank manager had gone better than she'd expected. The mention of the impending land girl seemed to raise his spirits, though without the cash from last month's stock sale he might have been less cheery.

If only she didn't have to travel with George Townsend. If Phil was untrustworthy, at least he and Elsie could talk, farmer to farmer. His nephew George was different, young – younger than her anyway. He was supposed to be married but it didn't stop him acting up. She wished there was some other way, but the Townsend car – now the pony cart was beyond repair – was difficult to resist.

'And to think, I could have been making this journey on my own-e-o. What a day you've made for me, Miss Boston, what a day. What a treat.'

She had managed to fend off his invitation to lunch, but he had kept her waiting by his car a whole hour before they started for home. It was as if he were paying her back. He was certainly the worse for wear, and it only seemed to make him more talkative. She felt horribly pressed.

'A quiet one you are, Miss Boston. May I call you Elsie? I always knew you'd open up. Just needed the right key. I've found the key to Elsie. Ha ha. A song. The right key.'

He kept offering her cigarettes, blowing the smoke from his own right into her eyes; he didn't seem to mind if she said no, but he kept on asking. It was the same with his questions: how many sisters do you have, Miss Boston, and do any of them live close by? He knew not to ask about her brothers. He spoke more than enough for both of them; she felt quite dizzy with it. She wished she'd sat in the back with her packages.

They were going to be late for the land girl. Elsie particularly didn't want to meet her with George Townsend – she didn't want the girl to get any ideas. She didn't want George to meet the girl – they'd never have a moment's peace – but of course he would insist on driving right up to the gate.

* * *

She heard the car, caught a glimpse of its long grey bonnet slowing. It wasn't quite what she was expecting: she had thought Miss Boston would appear at the gate, or perhaps she would glimpse her in the distance, approaching across the fields. But the car had stopped just outside on the lane and she heard a man's voice, she couldn't make out what he was saying – he was the driver and she could see the jaunty set of his cap. Miss Boston, she assumed it was, was sitting beside him in the front passenger seat. She was huddled tight against her door, as if she wanted to keep as much distance from the driver as possible. The man took off his gloves, still talking; Miss Boston seemed unwillingly caught. On he went, would he never stop, but finally Miss Boston turned her head awkwardly towards the house and must have seen her sitting in the porch.

She jumped up, fumbling with her hat, and hurried to the car, wanting to be helpful, afraid of looking too much at ease.

She reached out her hand. 'Miss Boston? How do you do? I'm Rene Hargreaves.'

Miss Boston said nothing – perhaps she smiled – so Rene opened the door of the car carefully, then reached on to the back seat and started retrieving the various packages.

An hour later they were sitting in the kitchen, drinking tea and eating bread and butter.

'It's so nice and quiet here,' Rene said. 'The billets are mad. Four girls to a room, six in some.'

Miss Boston had shown her the yard and the animals. Get up at five. The six remaining cows were brought in and fed and milked. Chickens fed and eggs collected. Phil Townsend came at half past six for the milk. Then the cows were put out in Back Field, out of the way of the calves and Pickwick, the plump pony. Then it was time for breakfast. And so it went on. It was just the two of them and it made for a tight routine, but Rene liked to be busy, liked to be quick. Miss Boston paused while she poured them each another cup of tea, dousing both heavily with sugar. Rene said nothing, it didn't matter really. Miss Boston carried on with the routine, and Rene wondered how one person could ever have managed it all.

'Miss Boston, where does the milk go, who buys it?'

'Oh, oh, call me Elsie, please.' She looked quite flustered for a moment. 'I don't rightly know – Phil arranges that. Before the war it went to Huntley and Palmers.'

'And Phil's the man who was driving the car?'

'Oh, no. That's George, his nephew, he's not a farmer.'

'Looks like a spiv,' Rene said.

'A what?' Elsie looked awkward and Rene wished she hadn't spoken.

'What did you call him?' Elsie asked again. She looked both curious and wary.

'A spiv, a chancer,' Rene said.

'He's certainly that.'

After tea, they lugged Rene's trunk upstairs to her room. It smelt starchy and damp, but the window was open and there was a slight rattling breeze. She wondered at all the furniture and the over-stuffed wardrobe, but there was plenty of space, she thought. A room to herself was a luxury.

She took in the blank walls and the picture shadows, but it was the great sticks of flowers in the jug that caught her: the colour blazed in the afternoon light.

'Thank you. Thank you so much.'

She wanted to say something else but decided not to.

There was no blackout upstairs but she wasn't going to mention that either. They stood there for a moment and then Elsie went over to the window and they both looked out at the half-view of the fields beyond. 'These are my fields,' she said, and pointed out the boundaries.

Those first few mornings she waited for Elsie's promised knock at the door, before calling, *Down in a minute* – even though she'd been awake for an hour or more, dressed and staring out of the window, into the dark. In the evenings, she went up as soon as she'd washed the dishes, leaving Elsie to her house and her wireless. She could see Elsie was used to her own company. Upstairs, Rene was asleep within moments. In between times, she worked, throwing herself into every task. After they'd seen to the animals that first morning, she drove the tractor to Fox Field (under Elsie's guidance) so they could finish harrowing. Elsie walked beside her, talking her on: *a little faster, that's right, whoa there.* And through the day, the talk was nearly all like that, of the task, of the moment, mainly from Elsie. *Hold that,* she said, or *Watch your hands* (said quite often), or *Shall we have a few minutes?* and Rene would fill in with *Thanks* or *Yes* or a nod, and from time to time a question – it seemed to suit them both. And when they did pause to eat their sandwiches, Rene suddenly self-conscious in her uniform and overdressed for the heat, Elsie supplemented with long silences and little pieces of local knowledge. The northern edge of Fox Field was the boundary between Starlight and a big farm owned by a man named Cole. They were Cole's fences and he kept them well, but she didn't have much talk with him. Rene couldn't catch from Elsie's tone whether this was a good thing or not. She was aching long before they drove home, her palms blistered under her gloves, but she was surprised at how quickly the day had passed. Elsie seemed pleased with what they'd done. She was late to be harrowing but still hoped to get the potatoes in – 'You'll finish the field tomorrow?' Rene said she was sure she could.

If the first day was a test of sorts, Rene passed it and after that she was on her own a good deal of the time, tidying up the orchard, clearing out the pond in Yellow Field – there was an awful lot of clearing. No one needed to tell her to work hard: she wasn't one to shirk on the sidelines. On her land-girl training she had always listened carefully to instruction. Other girls might get a milky, far-away look in their eyes, but Rene would only see what was in front: this field, this choked-up pond. Don't look back.

And while Rene worked, Elsie worked too, spending most of her day on rickety ladders, fixing the barn roof. Once the roof was done, it was time for the rats. Smoke and the sour-tempered cat, Missy, were locked up while the traps were laid in the barn. Elsie did the setting – you could mangle your hand or worse – and then the barn doors were locked. Two days later they opened up and went inside, armed with shovels and sacks. Elsie had warned her that the rats died horrible, but Rene wasn't prepared for the bloody mess that greeted them. Some were still alive and they had to finish them with shovels. Rene wobbled and nearly lost her balance. She was too ginger to do anything more than make them squeal and jangle her nerves, but when Elsie wielded her shovel deftly, with such a hard, fast crack, Rene found herself admiring.

When work gave her time to wonder, she wondered about Elsie. There were many things she liked: her soft way with animals, the stripy curtains made out of shirts in the parlour, her love of the wireless. She enjoyed Elsie's food too – the pies full of garden vege-tables, the peppery potato bread, the rabbit stews – but she didn't make too much of it. After all, it was only what Elsie might cook for herself, and she sensed that compliments made her nervous. This was as obvious to Rene as it was obscure to George Townsend. Rene found herself thinking back to that first afternoon. She had offered her hand to Elsie, and Elsie had reached out hers but it wasn't a greeting – Elsie had reached out as if she were trapped and needed to be pulled out, pulled free. And Rene had opened the door and quickly, carefully, started to take the packages out from the back, babbling quite foolishly about nothing at all. (George, mean-while, had hoped to be introduced but, finding himself forgotten, eventually turned the car round and drove back down the lane. He didn't beep.)

They had both stood for a moment at the gate, saying nothing, Elsie still flustered and clenched, and then she had picked up her packages and Rene, behind, had watched the awkward figure walk down the path towards the porch. It wasn't a long path, it couldn't have been more than thirty feet, but to Rene's eyes it seemed much further for, as she watched, Elsie started to unstiffen and grow taller. It was such a change to see how she smoothed and straightened, such a change and quite remarkable. The hunched and frozen creature in the car was suddenly a woman who walked ahead, tall and loose. It happened in a matter of moments before her very eyes, the same woman who showed her round the farm, who fixed roofs and smashed the skulls of rats, the same woman who had made such pretty curtains and didn't use blackout upstairs.

3.

Elsie Unked

Unked, unkind, uncanny – now dialect
unknown, strange – from ME
awkward or troublesome, from unfamiliarity or novelty,
    against the grain (1634)
unfamiliarly lone or dreary, solitary, forlorn, lonely –
    Cowper (1706)
uncanny, eerie, weird – Rosetti (1866)
uncouth . . .

Oxford English Dictionary

When Rene cycled to Lambourn to do her shopping, she soon realized that she wasn't the only one wondering about Elsie: *So you're working up at Starlight with Miss Boston? Is she all on her own now? Are all her sisters gone?* Other questions and the same ones she was asked, over and over, and Rene could only be glad she didn't have the answers.

'She's lucky to have the help. I'm sure she's grateful.'

This odd remark came from old Mrs Morris, who was taking an age to measure out Rene's tea and sugar.

'I've known her since she was just a little thing. She and her sisters came into the shop when they first arrived. That was before the first war; my husband was alive then. Did you say you wanted the rashers?'

Rene didn't but she took them anyway. She'd been a land girl long enough to know that the stand-out uniform was a goad to some.

The shop was dark and smelt of leather and linseed oil – you could have called it cosy – and Mrs Morris seemed very eager to be friendly.

A few weeks later she went in to find her drinking a cup of tea with another old lady, a Mrs Blyth, tiny and withered and whip-crack sharp. Once she knew who Rene was, Mrs Blyth looked at her very carefully through blurred, cataract eyes.

'Oh, so you're up at Starlight, are you? Mrs Boston named it Starlight, did you know? I always thought it was a pretty name.' She paused and raised her cup to her mouth with an unsteady hand, keeping her eyes on Rene all the while. 'Some people in the village said it was fanciful, Starlight. We're very plain people here, Miss Hargreaves.'

Rene smiled politely and kept her attention on her stamps.

'Poor Miss Boston, what a time she's had. We all thought she'd give up when her dad died.'

'I never did,' Mrs Morris said, with some satisfaction. 'She were always very independent-minded.'

'Well, Phil Townsend was sure she wouldn't stay. He said she was going to her sister in Reading.'

Mrs Morris said something which Rene couldn't catch, and Mrs Blyth wobbled the cup to her lips again.

Rene moved back from the counter.

'Came from London, the Bostons. Did you know?'

'No, no, I didn't,' said Rene and immediately wished she hadn't spoken.

'Where are you from, Miss Hargreaves?'

It was Mrs Blyth who spoke.

'Manchester,' Rene said and pushed open the door, the bell sing-ing shrilly. She was glad to get outside. There was something heady in the atmosphere – she didn't want to hear any more. And what did Rene know anyway? What did it amount to? That Elsie was a farmer – not a farmer's wife, not a farmer's widow. That her sisters had all gone and her brothers were on the memorial. That she was struggling and proud and would not give up. Rene didn't need to know any more than that, certainly not from Mrs Blyth and Mrs Morris.

If Rene had been willing to listen, she could have heard quite a story about her Miss Boston. Everyone agreed that Elsie was an odd one, unked since she was a little girl. The way animals attached themselves to her was the best of it. It was said, a little grudgingly, that she could gentle any animal, and as she got older she got quite a reputation for bringing sick creatures round. Old Jonas the herdsman remembered a warbler singing in her hand when she was just a little girl, and the rough black cat she kept for a shadow, it would claw anyone else to shreds.

There were the stories about the examination of course, always told with relish, for she had been the star pupil. Elsie was going to be a teacher, it was as good as settled that she would replace Miss Davenant when she retired, but when the day of the examination came . . . no two stories were exactly alike. One girl said she had frozen when the papers were handed out and wrote nothing but her name in the whole two hours; another that she had torn the examination paper to shreds and stormed out of the schoolroom; another had her scribbling away like billy-o but it was all just loops and squiggles – little Vincent Crozier, who was practising his numbers, had seen it all. The only thing everyone agreed on was that Elsie had left school that day and never returned. No one could understand it, and Mr and Mrs Boston were so upset.

There was also the tale of Tanner's pond. The boys from Woodston, back late from a nature walk with their teacher, had come to an awkward halt on the other side of the pond, a nudging quiet. It should have been a laughing matter for the boys at least, but it wasn't. They had stood and watched the girl who was lying in the shallows of the pond, her hair rippling in the pondweed, her body ruffled by water and light: green, pink, white. The teacher thought there had been an accident or worse. He gulped and readied to call across the water, but thankfully there was no need, for just then her hand came up to stroke the paw of the ruggy dog that sat beside her, guarding the neat pile of over-clothes. The girl didn't stir again but the dog raised its muzzle and looked across at them steadily, as if willing them to be on their way. There were at least a dozen versions of this story – one for every boy and more, some saw a good deal more than others. When she grew older the boys and young men who liked her looks were bewildered by her manners. She was not unfriendly, you couldn't call her high, but she wasn't quite like other girls – she didn't soften.

But there was also Colonel Pinkie, who had bought one of the new villas further down Sheepdrove. In good weather he sat out much of the afternoon, reading, watching, popping inside at five to mix himself a gin. Even from the road, the colonel's face was pink. Close up he was handsome and even pinker, his face and neck permanently reddened by the Mespot sun. He always called Rene over for a chat. He was watching for planes and birds with his binoculars and kept notes on unusual sightings. *Would you tell Miss Boston I saw the goshawks again today? They must be nesting close by.* And Rene felt a rush of warmth for the colonel with his handsome pink face. *I'll tell her.*

Elsie wasn't quite like other people, but that didn't matter to Rene. Elsie, who had been to the pictures only twice, so long ago, and hated it; Elsie, who didn't know how to gossip, who had never been to a dance or ever seen the sea: none of it mattered to Rene one bit, because she had fallen hook, line and sinker for Elsie's lonely power.

* * *

By August, a slightly different routine had established itself at Starlight and though the two women still spent most of the day apart, the evening was shared. This change was of Elsie's making. She invited Rene to sit with her, listening in to concerts and sometimes plays. Sometimes after the wireless ended, they played Patience. Elsie sat at the old desk beside the open window, the faint breeze making up just a little for the dull of the blackout; Rene sat in the armchair with the round japan tray on her knees. Rene only knew Clock and Soldiers but she was eager to learn. She didn't quite ask Elsie, but she would go and stand behind her, watching – *Do you mind? Oh, no* – and quickly picked up Elsie's favourites: Aces and Kings, Ladybird and Castle.

As the population of Starlight had dwindled, Elsie's determination had grown – *No thanks, I can manage* – but as the weeks went past she sometimes found herself saying to Rene, *I'll come and find you if I need any help.* She rarely did – her own habits were so hardened – but she rather liked thinking that she could. She also found that she wanted to explain to Rene that Starlight didn't use to be like this, that she worried things might have fallen too far back, that she was frightened for the future. There was a word Elsie had heard a good deal on the wireless in the past months in talk of allies and allegiance. The word was *staunch*. She liked the word, liked its sound and had an urge to use it, and then, one afternoon, she heard the sweep, scratch, sweep of Rene's brush in the yard. She went to the kitchen window, looked out and saw Rene pausing to survey her handiwork, stroking her hair neatly back behind her ears. Well yes, yes of course, Rene was staunch and Elsie smiled out of the window, thinking she couldn't be seen.

She remembered little enough about the day that Rene had arrived. That awful journey back from Newbury, George Townsend. Rene had taken her hand, nice and friendly. Helpful, that was her first thought, or perhaps, not so young. Small; neat and wiry with her hair cut quite short. *I'm Rene Hargreaves.* She didn't look comfortable; she didn't have the high tones of Brockway, or look like Moira. Her worries had seemed to fall away. And they had sat in the kitchen quite easy, drinking tea and eating bread and butter. Older than she'd feared, quiet and polite, she did what she was asked. She always seemed to listen carefully, the quick nod, the serious eyes. A good listening sort of girl. Elsie also liked the occasional bursts of laughter, none of the chatter she had feared; even before the week was out, before Mrs Tranmer's awkward visit, Elsie knew that Rene fitted. A stranger to be sure, but one who didn't make her feel strange. The only odd thing was being called Miss Boston. *Please call me Elsie,* she found herself saying.

She didn't know much about Rene, only that she was a widow from Manchester. Her husband had died very recently, his name was Phillips – that was all. She didn't think to ask why Rene called herself Hargreaves, she couldn't know that she'd been told more than anybody else. Elsie didn't ask many questions, but she did think that Rene sometimes worked too hard. Not showy work – Moira had been prize at that. Rene's work was different: some things done too long, a yard brushed harder than necessary, the dairy tiles scrubbed and rubbed over and over – unwilling to give up the rhythm of the task.

'You're good with horses,' Elsie said, matter of fact.

They were standing by the stable door late one evening. Rene was rubbing the rough hair on Pickwick's cheek with her knuckle and he whickered gently, happily. Elsie had brought the pony in because he looked lame; now she suspected he might have been shamming. He leant his head against Elsie's then nodded it free and went back to his hay. Rene liked the warm smell of the pony in the stable. She had forked him out a deep straw bed; it was probably extravagant and she hoped that Elsie wouldn't mention it. Rene slid the smooth bolt across the stable door with a jolt of memory for the great heads of the dray horses in the yard beside the Blue Elephant. Such gentle creatures but ghostly in the field on summer nights.

They both paused for a moment, looking into the dark of the stable.

'We had a lovely pony when we came here first, black nearly all over. He was called Prince. My dad bought him and a cart together at a farm sale. He had the kindest nature.'

Elsie picked up the lantern but she didn't move.

'Where I grew up, there were brewery horses,' Rene said. 'I don't remember their names now. The man in the yard used to pay us to brush them down. They were big – my friend Lily and I used to stand on chairs. But they were so gentle, never gave us any trouble.'

'Big horses usually are.'

'They had brown stains on their feathers and we tried to wash the stains out with soda.'

Elsie laughed.

'I can't remember if it worked,' Rene said.

Elsie started to come in from the fields a bit earlier on Friday afternoons. It was Rene's half day and the day she cycled to Lambourn to do her shopping (now taking Elsie's ration book with her too). She enjoyed Rene's return, the packages, the little bits of talk . . . *no wheat flakes today . . . the bacon's good and streaky . . . I didn't get the gloves in the end . . .* She enjoyed it all the more because she hadn't had to run the gauntlet of the shops herself. There was quite a little routine on Fridays. Sometimes Elsie would be back before Rene returned from Lambourn and she would make the tea. Sometimes, and Elsie rather liked this, she would come in to find Rene already there: the tea made, the biscuits, which she would once have thought wasteful, laid out so neatly on the willow plate. And there was always the newspaper to read, if she so wanted. In the evening, once they had eaten and all their jobs were done, they would sit up quite late: first with the concert or the play on the wireless and then more tea and on with Patience, and the shuffle and *slip-plat* of cards on desk and tray would get slower and sometimes stop altogether as they talked about this and that. Rene had seen Colonel Pinkie up on Barrel Hill with his binoculars; Elsie had been talking to their other neighbours, Miss Troughton and Miss Lyle – they had asked her advice about their goat. And then Elsie was telling Rene all about Miss Troughton and Miss Lyle, who lived in the first of the new villas on Sheepdrove; retired schoolteachers, they kept a little car which was always breaking down, but they took it in good cheer. Over the weeks the never voluble Elsie found herself talking about all sorts, about Starlight and the land around, the other farms and her creeping fear of the Townsends, about Bert dying, and just a bit about Moira: a little Moira went a long way. Rene didn't have much of her own to say, but Elsie did notice how carefully she listened, how much she remembered, and yet she never pressed her nose in too deep.

No sign of Rene today, but she must be back because the water was heating on the stove and there was the *Courier*, open on the table. It was opened in the middle, a spread of advertisements which took up the whole two pages. Elsie walked round to the other side of the table to look. She could smell the print, strong and heady, as she read the slew of names: Gaumont, Savoy, Pavilion, Electric. Strong and heady in another way: items in a long list of places that Elsie didn't want to visit; busy, crowded places she didn't want to know. The cinema halls were suspect. *I'm meeting him at the Electric*, she could hear Moira say.

A sound from upstairs – she nearly jumped. But then Elsie recognized Rene's footsteps on the stairs, light and quick.

Elsie looked down at the paper again: ALL NEW PROGRAMME FROM SATURDAY. *Laugh It Off*, *A Window in London*, *Somewhere in England*.

She turned to see Rene watching her, smiling.

'We used to go every Friday at the billet,' Rene said. 'Sometimes we went Sundays too. Is it very far to Reading? Could I get there and back in an afternoon?'

Elsie busied herself at the stove, poured the water into the pot, looked around for the lid.

'You'd have to leave early,' she said, 'to get to Reading.' Where was that lid?

But Rene had it. She passed it to Elsie without saying anything. That little bubble on the rim always made it difficult to fit; she got it finally and then stood facing the stove, not knowing quite what to do.

All at Sea.

Rene folded the paper away, out of sight, set down the cups.

They both moved to sit down. Rene smiled, quick and tentative.

'I don't especially want to go to Reading,' she said. 'I certainly wouldn't want to go off early.'

Elsie looked down; maybe she smiled very slightly.

She took a biscuit; they tasted like sawdust.

'The biscuits aren't getting any better,' Rene said.

'I don't know why you get them, it seems wasteful.'

'I don't know either. It feels like a treat to buy them.'

Elsie said nothing but she definitely smiled.

'There's a play on tonight . . .'
The Girl Who Forgot.

* * *

Elsie didn't see Rene's letter till lunchtime. A little surprised, she took a moment to admire the handwriting before she opened it. It had been a long time since she'd seen her first name written out and here it was again inside, *Dear Elsie* – she liked that too. She sat down at the kitchen table with her cup of tea to read.

Only last night there had been bombing, heavy enough, far enough away to have them rush out into the dark. They had climbed to the very top of the hill and, turning their backs on Lambourn and the valley, they had watched the bright come and go and heard the rumbling and spitting of the bombs, like distant weather. Unable to do anything but stand and wait, they watched as a glow built slowly on the horizon – Portsmouth or Southampton, Colonel Pinkie thought, for he was out there too. They had felt jittery and oddly excited, but then a plane shrieked over Inkpen Hill.

'Close shave, close shave,' called Colonel Pinkie.

'Whose is it?' shouted Rene.

'Don't know, doesn't matter.'

And then Elsie and Rene had rushed into the dark, into the house, frightened but laughing all the same.

'Goodnight,' Rene had called to the colonel. It sounded wrong somehow.

Dear Elsie,

I'm sorry to write and not speak. I have wanted to tell you, I've planned to. Only last night I nearly did but my nerves gave out at the last. So I decided to write to you instead. You have been so very kind and I haven't told you about my life before I came here, before I joined the Land Army. I should have explained.

I told you I was a widow and it's true. It's what I told the Land Army too when I joined, but when I left Manchester, Alan, my husband, was still alive. He was sick, though no one knew it then, but I didn't leave

because he died. It was more the opposite – not because of him exactly,
but because I could not cope with being married. I ran away.

But it's worse than that, much worse . . .

Elsie paused for a moment, forced herself to look up and away from the letter. She mustn't rush. Smoke's blanket was folded on the chair beside her – Rene must have tidied up before she went out. Last night they had let the old dog in to sleep in the kitchen – it didn't seem right to leave him outside on his own. Rene had been pleased. Elsie took a slow breath and went back to the letter:

But it's worse than that, much worse . . .

I have three children. Can you believe it, Elsie? They're lovely and I left them all. The youngest, Mikey, was just a baby when I left. He's hardly more than a baby now. But that's not the worst bit. I planned everything out so carefully. I sent Jessie and Stevie, the two eldest, to stay with their nan in the country – that's what I told Alan too. I put them on the train, they were so excited. That was the worst bit, the cunning, the cold of it. The baby, Mikey, was too little, so I left him with a friend to look after. It was before the war.

I joined the Land Army just after. I didn't think I was running away at the time – I told myself I had to be on my own for a little while. And then the war started and everything seemed to go a long way away. I should never have got married, Elsie, and I can never go back. I realized that quite soon, because of what I'd done. The older two know that I left them, that I lied – just a little journey, I said, a holiday with your nan. I could never face them. The baby's still with my friend. She has no children of her own and she's raising him. It's so good of her, but I hate it. Jessie and Stevie are with their aunty now, Alan's sister. They're still in the country, safe from the bombs, but I never liked Alan's sister. I wish I could explain it better – I thought a letter would help. I miss the children – I can't say how much – but I know I can never see them again. Elsie, I'm sorry to write and not to speak to you. You have held out such a kind hand to me. I wanted you to know.

Rene

Strings that pull, ties that bind. Elsie read the letter again, sitting quietly at the table. Upstairs a window was banging: it was Rene's room – there was a problem with the catch. She found some nails and a hammer and went up, glad of something to do. It was a fiddly task and took a while, but the catch was fixed finally and she lingered at the window, staring out at the road. She could see the new postmistress cycling slowly up Sheepdrove. She still wobbled a bit.

Back in the kitchen, Elsie sat down again and read the letter a third time, sipping her tea. It was bitter and dry on the back of her throat but she drank it anyway and, as she drank, she remembered Celia Marshall's wedding cake – such a long time ago – the yellow rose, the little white bows and curls. Such a long time ago, but she remembered it all so clearly: the rough sugar of that yellow rose, slowly melting smooth; the paler yellow of the marzipan, concealed like a shock between the cake and the icing.

'I always wonder what happened to her, where she went – Celia Marshall. It was just after the first war. I read your letter, Rene, I read it three times. It must be dreadful to feel you can't make things right . . .' She dried up. Rene was watching her, wondering what she would say next.

'You are not hard-hearted, Rene, I can see that. You are kind to me, even though I am nearly a stranger. If you had to leave, then you had reasons – even if you don't know quite what they were. I don't know what else to say.'

Rene carried on looking at her; her face, for all the summer heat, was pale.

Oh yes, of course, the cake. The dry burnt raisins and the sour edges of peel. She had never tasted such a beautiful cake, and she couldn't understand why it came with shaking heads and sly murmurs – crocodile smiles, Moira said.

'Celia Marshall, she lived in the village. She was going to get married too and then she ran away.'

Everything was ready, everything was planned. Moira and Cally had been full of glee.

'What?' said Rene, she was confused.

'Celia Marshall. She ran away on the day of the wedding. No one knew where she went. She never came back.'

Everyone had had a slice of that cake. The sweet bright taste of the decorations – ribbons and curlicues of sugar plaster that melted to nothing. And Elsie had never understood, till now. Now she understood Celia Marshall's cake perfectly.

(Celia Marshall's mother didn't stop screaming for three weeks. 'If anyone asks, tell them that I never had a daughter.')

'They called her the runaway bride,' Elsie said. 'She didn't want to be married either, did she?'

'No.'

'But she found out more quickly.'

'Yes.'

For a moment Rene looked as if she was going to cry, then she bit her lip and burst out laughing. Elsie laughed too. And then for a while they couldn't stop.

The cake had been handed round the village, like a rumour, like a mocking, a beautiful cake and Elsie had never understood it.

'Thank you,' Rene said, when they finally stopped laughing. 'No, Elsie, I mean it, really I do.'

For Elsie had already stood up, brushed down her apron.

'Goodness, how late it is,' she said.

* * *

They didn't talk about Rene's letter in the days that followed, most things continued as before, but there was a slight change to Rene's movements, an uncoiling. Not visible to Elsie, but she did notice that there was more of the laugh she liked, more of the quick words and quick wit she didn't always follow.

They spent more time together. The workday reasons that drew them into step – a check on the oats, another incursion of Phil's errant sheep – multiplied. These joint undertakings took their place alongside events which had no precedent, such as when Rene carried a chair out into the front garden one warm evening and sat down to read the paper while Elsie was busy with the plants. When

Elsie thought about it afterwards she couldn't be sure why it had been so pleasant. She hadn't wanted help, for she trusted no one else in her garden work. And yet, how nice it had been, getting on with her usual pulling and trimming and trailing with Rene sitting there, and then Rene had brought out tea and cake and a second chair and they had sat together till Rene got cold and they both went inside.

A 'we' was creeping into their talk, sometimes an 'us'. *Shall we take a walk up Inkpen Hill? Let's go back through Cole's wood, it's lovely in the rain.* This 'we' belonged to Elsie first, and was usually a question; not an old habit, but a placing of the two of them side by side. And Rene, quick and cautious, took it up, sometimes in questions but more often to reprise – *This is where we saw the hawk with the rabbit* or *We should tell Colonel Pinkie about that bird we saw – do you think he'd lend us his binoculars?* – so that the couple of months she'd been at Starlight, quick in some ways, slow in others, grew thick with incident and memory.

'Who used to lived there?' Rene asked.

It was the middle villa, the one between Colonel Pinkie's villa, with its veranda, and Miss Troughton and Miss Lyle's, with its black and white angles and round rose-glass window.

'Oh, there were lots of different people, none of them stayed very long. Most of them came from London, I think.' The connection with the capital made Elsie wary.

They were coming back up Sheepdrove after a long walk. Rene had never taken much notice of the house before: the door was boarded up. It was the only one of the three with a name, recorded in a small wooden plaque on the gate, Orchard Rest. What a silly name. Rene looked through the gate and up the path. There were red curtains in the windows.

House and garden were minimally maintained by the owner – Phil Townsend. One of his schemes, Elsie said.

'He advertised for tenants in the paper. Not the local paper. Colonel Pinkie showed me. He described it as a "weekend getaway" in the advertisement. What do you think that is?'

'I don't know, it sounds a bit silly. How long has the house been empty?'

'Oh, a good while. Three or four years. None of the tenants lived here continuous. I remember one coming and asking if I had a telephone in the house. Fancy!'

Rene smiled. She could just make out a clutch of pictures on the wall above the mantel.

'Oh yes,' Elsie was getting into her stride now, 'I think one of them was an actress.'

'An actress?'

'Oh yes, yes, she kept the place up quite well. Mrs Cannell at the butcher's told me. Quite a . . . quite . . .'

'Famous?'

'Yes.'

Elsie turned to look back for Smoke, who was dawdling as usual. All of a sudden, it seemed, she had reached the limits of her interest.

Close by, a bird was calling, bright and insistent – a blue tit, Rene thought, but she couldn't be sure. The bird's call sounded like an announcement. *Here I am*, it seemed to say. Another replied with the same song moments later from somewhere behind the villa. *Here I am*. It sounded to Rene as if they were looking for each other. She should ask Elsie what the bird was – she would know what it was saying. How silly it all was though. An actress on Sheepdrove, between the sunset colonel and the spinster teachers. And Phil Townsend for a neighbour. And Elsie. She'd been here long enough to appreciate the strangeness of it.

'Can you remember her name?'

'Her name? Oh no.'

Elsie seemed to find Rene's interest surprising – surprising and not very welcome. She turned away from Rene and the house and carried on walking. 'Smoke, come on, come on now.' The dog looked up briefly from his sniffing and barked happily. After a moment Rene turned too and followed Elsie, but Elsie was walking fast and she didn't catch up with her long stride till they reached Starlight.

Elsie relented later. She couldn't recall the name, but she thought that the actress was from the pictures. It all came back then. The place got quite packed out sometimes. Mrs Cannell at the butcher's had been run off her feet, and some deliveries came direct to the house from London in liveried vans. Too many comings and goings. They had a gramophone as well, and it could be noisy. And then Elsie seemed to have forgotten the middle villa and was talking about the walkers. Phil Townsend had talked about setting up a ramblers' tea room at the weekends, but he never did anything about it. Groups of walkers, occasionally they ventured up to the gate to ask about eggs and butter. And Rene could see the ramblers, see them coming up Sheepdrove in little clusters, heading for the very top of the hill where the track became a shadow and faded to nothing on the Downs. She could see them so clearly, see them striding out with quiet vigour, grouping and regrouping as they went, sometimes pausing to check their way, pulling out a big map, good-humoured, talking. She could even see Elsie watching them from the gate, smiling perhaps and wondering.

4.

Rene, Vicky and Pearl

I should like to mention one little point with regard to the film which, I have no doubt, would be a great improvement in the eyes of the audiences in our picture houses . . . My suggestion is this. That after each film of any importance, a few feet of film be used to show the chief actors and actresses as they appear in real life. I have mentioned this point to several of my friends and they approve of it . . . If, in any way, we could influence the taking-up of this idea, I'm sure it would improve the kinema greatly.

Letter from a film fan to *Picturegoer*, December 1924

Vicky McCrane first came to prominence in the silent age as Mona Verity, a name she always insists she chose herself. In those days she was sometimes spoken of as the British equivalent of Pearl White, the American Serial Queen, a comparison she now laughs off. She has never been one to seek out the attentions of movie fans or photographers, slipping back into the shadows as soon as the furore about her latest film has died down . . .

Interview, *Film News*, March 1936

Rene peered through the dirty glass of the window – the looped red curtains seemed to give her permission, though she didn't like the idea of Elsie finding her here. Elsie, she thought, would not approve of her interest in Orchard Rest. She couldn't make out any of the pictures on the mantel wall, except that some of them looked like photographs. There was a big comfortable armchair by the fireplace, covered in a shiny fabric – it didn't look like Phil Townsend's choice – and beside the chair a round table with an ashtray: a swirl of thick blue glass. On the windowsill was a pile of *Picturegoer* magazines; the top one had a cover of Bonita Granville, Nancy Drew – she remembered it from a few years back. Rene stood there looking through the grey glass; there wasn't much else to see but she lingered, trying to make more of the photos on the wall, hoping to catch something she had missed. If only Elsie could remember the name of the actress. For Rene adored the pictures. She carried on looking through the glass as she remembered her trip to the Imperial all those years ago. The Imperial Picture House, the papers had called it a wonder. She'd been to grander since, but no visit had ever been so exciting. Her first and only proper visit to London, staying with her aunty Nora. She'd travelled down from Manchester all on her own, not much more than seven – it was just before the first war. The big house was covered in plaster, white and high as a cake. She and Nora slept in the basement – Nora was the housekeeper – and Rene could hear careful footsteps and long silences above her head when she was lying in bed. Up on the second floor lived a princess, Vicky; she even had golden hair. It was Vicky who took Rene to the Imperial.

They had arrived there just after lunch, and Vicky had bought nuts and a syrup and soda in the foyer. Then into the dark and half out again as they made their way towards the screen. As they walked down the aisle, a man in an absurd bathing suit waded out of the sea right in front of them, legs wobbling. The audience roared with laughter, and she and Vicky paused to watch. Clearly exhausted, the swimmer was quickly wrapped in blankets, the screen flickered a stitch of white and he'd gone.

They found two seats next to each other and there was a fair now, on the prom, and all manner of hairy-scary things in a sad little caravan museum. And at the end of the pier, the sea again – 'Can't you smell the sea,' Vicky said, laughing, and poured the caramel nuts into Rene's hand, and Rene was quite sure she could hear the sea, hear it splashing out of the doors of the cinema on to the street outside. The screen cycled on – Rene thought it would never stop. The man in the absurd bathing suit appeared again; this time he strode into the sea firm-legged – he was going to swim the Channel, no wonder his legs were wobbly afterwards – she never caught his name. The woman next to Rene was peeling potatoes into a bucket. Some children pressed past on their way out and she caught the smell of lemon sharps among the sweat and potato peelings. 'Again?' she asked, squeezing Vicky's fingers, and they settled back into the crowd to watch Pearl White in *The Perils of Pauline* for the second time. This time, Rene knew that Pearl would escape the man with long and frightening moustaches. As soon as he locked the door of her attic room and went downstairs to set fire to the house, Pearl would pull out the knife she kept hidden in her sleeve, cut her feet free and jump out of the window. Yes, Pearl would escape again: she would always escape. And on it went till they returned at last to the swimming man. 'It's getting late,' Vicky said.

They had lingered in the foyer, getting used to the light. Vicky bought Rene a present, a little picture-card of Pearl White, 'the Serial Queen'. They walked back along the streets, the dipping light still strong; it was very quiet. Back at the Imperial, that silly man was still swimming, still puffing his way across the Channel.

* * *

She had run down to the wall at the end of the garden – it was a big garden – and scrambled up on to it somehow. 'Come on,' she'd called to Vicky. She crawled along for a few moments, hands stinging, before she stood up and started to walk, gingerly at first, but soon she was bold again, striding and hopping, arms out. This way and that she went – she wasn't afraid of falling. This way. This way. But it was tiring all the same, her legs felt heavy and her arms, held out like a tightrope walker. She stopped and crouched down, noticed a tear in her pinafore and remembered what she was supposed to be doing. The cat, she was looking for the cat. 'Tibby,' she called, but quietly. A plaintive mew, she was sure of it. 'Vicky, this way, Tibby's here.' She jumped down into the back of a very overgrown garden; the ground was soft under her feet. Some way behind she could hear Vicky but she didn't look back. She pushed her way through bushes, then the bushes ended and she found herself standing by the remains of an old building of some kind: a little stone ruin with no roof and an empty hole of a door. There was rubble round her feet and she had to tread carefully, eyes to the ground. Once she stumbled and nearly fell, grabbing at a tall, thin stone to balance herself – her hand came away from paper-dry ivy, powdery white. There were sounds ahead, of water and chatter and, some-where further away, children playing. There was a strong smell of paint. Then, quite abruptly, the dusty world ended and she saw a young man sitting in a deckchair, filing his nails. He had the blackest hair she'd ever seen, and there he was sitting on a deckchair. He was in profile and a mass of dark leaf behind him exaggerated his sharp nose, like a silhouette, like the pictures. Suddenly she was closer. Had she stepped forward? His lashes were thick and impossibly long and quivered occasionally on the white, white mask of his face. Sadness surrounded his face like an aura, but when he looked up at her, it seemed to float away into the air behind him. He didn't seem at all surprised that a little girl had stepped out of nowhere.

'Hullo.'

She watched him raise his eyes and felt Vicky's arms come to rest gently on her shoulders.

'And hullo.'

'I'm glad you didn't arrive any later,' he said, smiling, 'we might have been frightened.'

Rene turned and looked back the way she had come. Behind her was a churchyard, a cluster of headstones and white dust every-where, like snow. Vicky was veiled in dust, her own arms – brown from the summer heat – had been shocked pale: a pair of ghosts.

('Goodness, where have you both been?' said Aunty Nora later, looking at Vicky.)

Rene and Vicky had found their way on to a half-dismantled film set. The young man's deckchair was posed on a station platform, a fragile wonder; the sign above him read LONDON NECROPOLIS (the film was *Murder on the Funeral Train* – Rene had seen a poster). To Rene's right was the platform edge with a shallow dip to a track that ran for no more than fifteen feet. The track itself was a sunspot; bees hovered lazily around the flowers that sprouted from the platform and there, between the rails, lying in the sun, licking her paws, was Tibby.

A loud clap of laughter took her eyes deeper into the garden, towards the house, and Rene walked to the end of the platform where she could take it all in. Two bathers with pink hairnets were sitting at the edge of a small, square, marble pool, their bare legs quivering in the water, fish-like, insubstantial; one was ruffling the water with her hand and they were talking, close, confidential. The house, still far away, in what seemed an enormous garden, was merely a backdrop, a windbreak for the garden and its worlds. There was a tiny orchard that started just a few feet from the pool, the setting for a tumbledown cottage. She reached out to clasp Vicky's hand and found it reassuringly warm, then pulled her on through the garden and towards the house.

There was a group of people sitting at a table on the terrace, next to a glass extension, and suddenly the man stood up and waved them forward with a flourish as if he was the ringmaster in a circus, some kind of magician.

Vicky started to explain about Tibby; she sounded worried, but no one seemed to be listening. The man did most of the talking. He had an odd name, foreign – Rene didn't quite catch it – and a slightly odd voice. She was more interested in the woman who was sitting next to him; her name was Estella Blake and she was an actress from the pictures. She was quite beautiful, draped in all manner of scarves and shawls; one had a shiny black fringe that trailed around her chair. Estella was also wearing what Rene didn't recognize at the time were sunglasses. She offered them tiny fancy biscuits from a tin, her voice very slow and significant. There was an old lady too, very smartly dressed and sitting very upright, who refused the biscuits but in a foreign language – this was Madame something and she was the man's mother. Vicky didn't want any biscuits either.

The man, whose first name was Eric, asked Vicky a lot of questions, but because she was sitting on Vicky's lap, Rene felt awkward, too close to the attention. It was Estella who asked her name, and everyone exclaimed at Rene's accent. Estella in her scarves and shawls actually squawked, 'Why, she's from Manchester!' For a moment Estella sounded like her mum, then the likeness was gone, wrapped away in the slow voice and the scarves. The talk carried on, but after a while the young man with the long eyelashes – Freddie, he was called – came over and took her to meet the girls by the pond; they pointed out the carp, bright orange, sleepy and stately. 'Something's going on,' Freddie said, to no one in particular, 'mark my words.' Soon after, Vicky called her – she was standing up now and clasping Tibby. They were shown out through the front but they were coming back tomorrow.

Rene barely slept that night. After the two girls arrived home, to be scolded and hugged by a round-eyed Nora, they were sent upstairs to wash and change. 'Say nothing,' Vicky said to Rene, dramatic and excited. Vicky's mother was away and Nora was in charge. Vicky got the worst of it: 'You'll be sixteen in September, what were you thinking of staying out so late?' They were sent off to a warm white bathroom that Rene hadn't seen before where they rubbed the dust off hard like a ritual. Then Vicky disappeared upstairs and Rene was put to bed with a story from Nora and drifted off to sleep.

When Rene awoke, her feet, for all the summer warmth, were cold. Nora was in bed, deeply asleep, with her hair in what Rene delighted in calling 'crispy papers'; Tibby had colonized the pillow space between them. Fully awake, and half thinking it might be morning, Rene got up, went along the narrow passageway to the kitchen, and out into the garden by the side door.

Night, but it didn't stop her; perhaps the afternoon's adventure had opened a vein. The grass was still warm and crackled slightly under her feet. She walked slowly down to the end and climbed once more up on to the wall. It was not especially quiet or particularly dark. She went in the same direction as before, but with no firm motive of return. She just wanted to walk on the wall and see, and see. A few of the houses were shut up for the summer, but from others came sporadic sounds: a stranded clatter, the thud and squeal of shutters being closed against the cooling air, once a piano, never voices, she was never close enough. Many of the gardens followed the same pattern as the McCranes': a pond close to the house, set in a lawn banked by shrubs. Some had a few fruit trees, newly planted, towards the back. To the edges: coal stores, sheds, neat rows of salad and onions, glasshouses, most packed with shoots and seedlings. At the back of one garden she saw a big cage, just like at the zoo, and peering in, she glimpsed a monkeyish creature with a long striped tail. For a moment they looked at each other, and then it sprang silently away, landing impossibly on a perch at the other side of the cage. One garden, larger than the others, was almost wholly taken up by a tennis court. Beyond this house was nothing, just churned-up ground. Turning back towards the gardens and the houses, she quickly discovered she had lost her way. The walls felt different to her bare feet, rougher, and the familiar smell of cement which had followed her earlier was gone. For the first and only time she panicked, so many times far from home. But she quickly adapted, crawling along the walls now, trying to find handholds in the sharp twines of ivy that had sprung up and spread before her. After the first moments, she didn't really doubt herself. Finally, and tired, she reached a junction where four walls met and the ivy had been cut back, a reassuring crossroads.

So Rene sat and dangled her legs over the wall, wondering whether to jump on to the soft clay below. Beside the wall, on a small table, were two thin-stemmed wine glasses, forgotten. Reaching down, she carefully picked up one of the glasses by the stem – it wobbled briefly in her grasp. Then she brought it to her lips, sipping, practising; the actor Freddie's mask-pale face and long lashes flickered in her mind. She could smell an invisible residue captured at the bottom of the glass. Moving the glass away from her lips again, she saw the faintest stain of lipstick.

In just a few days she would be going home, but she was as far from homesick as it was possible to be. Tomorrow they were going back to the strange house, the young man Freddie had promised to find her some clothes to dress up in and Vicky, Vicky was going to star in a picture, she was going to play a girl called Phoebe, such a beautiful name. Estella was the star of the picture, and Vicky got to play her maid. The film was called, and Rene would never forget it, *Lady Audley's Secret*. Rene raised the glass to her mouth, more slowly this time, and smelt the musty sharp residue.

The following morning the two girls climbed the stairs to the front door of the house and Vicky, giggling, asked Rene to pull the bell. The man with all the questions came to answer it, but she knew his name now, Eric Stoller. He was more smartly dressed than yesterday and he directed them through the house to the studio (the glass extension of yesterday: Eric pointed out a thick curtain rail running right round the room and heavy drapes).

Maybe to indulge Vicky, or maybe to dispel his marked attention to her, Stoller decided that Rene should play Lady Audley's abandoned son, Georgie – they were roughly the same age. So when one of the girls took Vicky away to be dressed as Phoebe, Rene went along too and was togged up as little Georgie. The black velvet suit was a great success – just a little big – and everyone congratulated her, apart from Estella. When all the petting and smiling was over, Estella took Rene's hand, smiled brightly and shook her head. 'Oh no, Eric, oh no. This little girl can't be my little Georgie.' Estella shook her head again slowly, almost regretful, and stroked out her own bright locks to make the contrast: 'She is so very small and dark.'

It was an awkward moment. Vicky looked down at her feet, Freddie raised his eyebrows, and Rene looked up at Estella, uncertainly. But Eric decided to be indulgent – 'Whatever you think, my darling, whatever you think' – and Estella went off to change, humming sweetly, clearly well pleased with herself. Freddie took care of Rene and Vicky. He and another young man had been setting up the drawing room of Audley Court, where the main action of the film occurred. They were in high spirits, posing a strange stuffed animal in various attitudes. 'Mongoose,' explained Freddie, 'from India.

They eat snakes.' He didn't look quite as pale as yesterday but his eyelashes were just as long. He had taken a shine to Rene, though he was uncertain of Vicky or her consequence.

Stoller hadn't yet decided whether he needed a piano for Audley Court.

'Pray not,' said Freddie, 'it's on the second floor.'

'Freddie's stronger than he looks,' said the other young man, and they both laughed.

Out in the garden the scene was more or less unchanged from yesterday: the two bathers were now fully clothed and sat at the table sewing, still deep in conversation. Somewhere nearby people were playing tennis.

Still togged up as little Georgie, Rene watched Vicky's first steps in cinema, sitting on a heap of black velvet curtains. She had found Estella's attention a little unnerving: used to being indulged or ignored by adults, attracting hostile attention was a novelty. But she didn't wonder for long. She sank into the dark curtains, they smelt of smoke and home, and she soon fell heavily asleep. She was woken by Freddie to eat lunch – sardines on toast (never forgotten) – which they all ate together, sitting outside. She and Vicky were the only ones who did not drink wine.

And then she was looking through the glass and her face was cold and stinging from the window of the train. Vicky and Aunty Nora standing on the platform. Always trains, she thought, always trains and stations.

'Tell your ma I can come up and help her in December, I've got a bit of holiday owing.'

'Yes,' Rene mouthed and nodded vigorously. The train jerked forward.

'I'll write,' Vicky called, and her hand scrawled and flourished across the air, Rene was sure she could hear her. *I'll write*. The train pressed on out of the station.

She remembered nothing else about the journey. Next thing, she was pushing on the heavy double doors of the Blue Elephant with all her strength; miraculously she squeezed through.

And there, at the bar, was Dad. She rushed over and he leant towards her, hoisted her up and over the counter and into his arms. 'Rene, we've missed you so. You're never going to believe the surprise. You've got a little brother.'

Rene didn't understand.

'A baby,' he said.

'There's a baby here, upstairs?'

'Yes, your mam's had a baby, a little brother for you to play with.'

'Can I go and see?'

'Of course you can, but go up quietly, tiptoe.'

Everything was just the same, except that there was a baby in a crib in her parents' bedroom.

'We'll have a big party, Rene, to celebrate, when your mam's a bit stronger. We're going to call him Leo.' Her father was so happy it made her dizzy. 'I'll get you a new coat. Would you like that, Rene? What do you say?'

* * *

Vicky wrote, though it was nearly two months later, breathless, exuberant – her life was moving at speed.

> *Dearest Rene,*
>
> *It seems such a long time ago since I waved goodbye to you at the station and so much has happened.*

Rene, sitting on her stool in the bar of the Blue Elephant, didn't doubt it.

> *I'm going to tell you all about it. I hope this letter won't be dreadfully long.*

Rene's stool was a little high and she enjoyed rocking it back and forth as she read; it was precarious, but she never got seasick. As they came through the door, regulars called to her, half friendly, half distracted, and their voices wheeled like gulls through the huge, high room. So cold in winter – Siberia blew in when you opened the door.

> *At the restaurant with Eric last night, we drank champagne. I only had*
> *two glasses and it went straight to my head! I was so excited I hardly ate*
> *a thing.*

The words were simple for the most part and she was a good reader, but the letter, with its thick paper and hurried hand, brushed a strange dust. Sometimes it made the words shine out, bright and gleaming, like the silver box her dad had given to her mum at the christening, but the dust could make the same words fade and wobble. She went back to it over and over, shining up what she could.

> *Eric took me to watch 'Lady Audley's Secret' last week with Freddie, just*
> *off the Tottenham Court Road. It was just the three of us and it was so*
> *odd to see myself – Freddie said I had the perfect face for pictures. Please go*
> *and see it, Rene, I do hope it will be in Manchester! We'll be starting the*
> *next picture soon, and this time I will play the heroine. It's such a terribly*
> *sad story, you'll cry when you see it and I think I may die at the end. Oh*
> *Rene, it's so exciting, I can't think of anything else that I want to do*
> *apart from make pictures, for ever.*

Rene couldn't wait to go to the Palace with her best friend Lily and see Vicky, Freddie and Estella in the TALE OF MYSTERY AND BETRAYAL. That's Vicky, she would say, that's my friend from London, she's called Mona Verity. For Vicky had a new name, especially for the pictures. Rene rocked to and fro on her stool, but gently now, musingly. It was getting late and the stories around her were getting taller and slower. Her mother glanced over at her from the bar, and Rene held up her hand, begging five more minutes.

Upstairs, baby brother Leo slept too, watched over by her mum's new friend and general help, Bertha Lane. By day Bertha managed the rooms and the commercial travellers who came and went with their heavy cases: Mr Skeat with his cutlery; Mr Frank with his sink fittings; Mr Cromartie with his measuring tapes and scales. In the evenings when her mum and dad were working in the bar, she took over the minding of Leo. Just a few years younger than her mum, somehow Bertha seemed years older – except she had all the energy poor Annie-Maria lacked. Bertha was also a marvel with the needle; she had sewn up bundles and bundles of baby clothes and now she had started with her knitting needles. When Rene went upstairs she could hear her needles click-ticking; she could hear them in her bedroom when she was trying to get to sleep.

Rene, by the time you receive this letter I won't be in London any more . . . but I will try to write to you as soon as I can. I'll send you a card with a picture – it's a big secret and I haven't told anyone but I think we're going to the South of France. Wish me luck.

* * *

She stood up and brushed herself off, looking down at the Blue Elephant, stately and marooned at the point where the Chester Road ended. She and Lily were going to see the new picture show at the Palace – she'd be late if she didn't hurry. Rene started down the hill, running, Stretford below and the city beyond. The hill pulled her forward, taking over her legs, a tangle of trees rushed past her, an old man, a dog barking. At the bottom she managed to pull up and paused to catch her breath; the light in the sky was changing. She pressed on, puffing. As she turned into Nelson Road the sun stretched out to meet her. Past the mission, with its rickety *Jesus is Lord* sign, it was uphill again. Mustn't slow down. Lily was quite capable of flouncing off on her own, but she had a stitch and needed to catch her breath. Mustn't stop. And suddenly there was somebody behind her. She was running along a railway line, pursued by a man with frightening moustaches – he came right out of *The Perils of Pauline*. And she was Pauline, racing now through a narrow canyon; the man in his cape was just behind her on a galloping black horse. And now she could hear the badly played piano and the whole audience draw in its breath, blotting down the music. Faster.

Rene found a final burst of speed, turned the corner and there was Lily. 'You're late, Rene Roberta,' she shouted, chin in the air, mocking. Rene hated being called Roberta, and Lily knew it too, but she bit her tongue because Lily was still here, she had waited.

At the Palace, Lily and Rene clutched hands. The film they'd been waiting for was about to begin: *Lady Audley's Secret*, a full seventeen minutes long. There was Lady Audley – Estella – impossibly pretty in the dark, wooden grandeur of Audley Court; the parkland view from her window wobbled a bit. Tense with secrets, she wasn't who she said she was, she wasn't what she seemed. And there was Freddie, his eyelashes even longer; he was playing the detective hero. And just out of shot of Audley Court was the main road with its trams, the smart street where Vicky lived, and Rene was the only one here who knew. A couple of minutes later, Lady Audley pulled a veil over her face and stepped on to a train. A couple of scenes later, she stepped down on to the platform and pulled it up, gasps, for it's Vicky's face staring out of the screen. Rene clasps Lily's hand tighter, sitting on her knees to see. Vicky looks older, paler, impossibly different. She is playing the maid, but she is still a princess.

Safe at last, reads the final intertitle.

That's what the hero says – he's had Lady Audley locked up in a madhouse. You could see her in the final shot, looking down from a barred window. Estella looked sad, Rene thought, but no one thought the hero had done anything wrong.

* * *

'Rene?'

It was Elsie. She looked ghostly in the dusk. All that evening she'd been busy, up and down ladders, twining the pear carefully on to the new trellis she'd set the day before. Rene had tried to help at first, but she had known that Elsie wouldn't want it – *No thanks, I can manage*. So she had retreated to the grass with the newspaper, drifting, reading. Now Elsie wanted her view.

Was it straight, was it even? How did it look?

It looked very well. Still a little awry, but Elsie explained that the training, as she called it, would take some time. Rene walked down to the gate and looked back. From here it looked even better, so neat and flat, like a child's drawing of a tree on a blackboard.

'Come and see it from here.'

Elsie came to join her. Now the two of them stood together, examining the shape of the tree. Oh yes. It might fruit again next year. The pears had never been sweet but they'd made chutney, very tasty, and wine – once or twice. There was a bird singing close by, a blue tit, maybe it was the one from the middle villa. Only one tonight, so bright and clear: *I'm here, I'm here*, it called, unwilling to give up the evening. Perhaps the other was close by or perhaps it was already sleeping.

5.

At the White Horse

A month passed. September, a busy month, the air was heavy with smoke and stubble and Elsie's harvest was in. She had worried the oats would be past their best by the time the thresher got to Starlight (they seemed to be last on the list for harvest help, Rene noticed, but it did come in the end and all was well). The last week, Rene had been apple-picking at a big fruit farm on the other side of Lambourn. They had seen next to nothing of each other, spending their evenings tending to Starlight, digging up produce and filling up the old troughs for the cows in Fox Field, bucket by bucket – the piping had cracked long ago and the summer weather had left everything parched. But finally there came a lull and one evening they finished before nine and were settled together in the parlour before the news started. They listened in without comment, and presently the concert started. Rene started to play Patience in a rather desultory way; she didn't really mind how the 'clock' turned out but she enjoyed the sound of the cards. She was tired – she'd ridden to Newbury that afternoon to the pictures. She went every Thursday, always Thursday, it was part of her routine. She hadn't tried to tempt Elsie again, she sensed that Elsie didn't quite approve, but she wouldn't give it up and Elsie made no attempt to stop her. Rene yawned; it was nice having nothing to do for once. Elsie was a little distracted. There was a fly buzzing around the window seat; it crawled over the cushion before banging itself, *tap-buzz*, against the window. They had closed the window for the first time that evening.

'Elsie?'

'Yes.'

'It's a quiet day tomorrow, isn't it?' Rene knew she had no obligations at Pool Farm but she didn't like to presume.

'Um.'

'I wondered . . .' Rene paused, still careful, eager not to press '. . . if we could go and see the White Horse?'

'Yes, oh yes, we must. Didn't I say so? Psst, psst.'

Elsie was still distracted. Missy was maddened by the fly's antics and was trying to claw her way up the curtains.

'It's my birthday tomorrow. Nearly today.'

'Your birthday! But you didn't say. Oh, I wish you had told me. I would have made a cake. I'll make one tomorrow.' She was excited all of a sudden.

'Could we go and visit the White Horse?'

'Isn't it too late?' Elsie paused for a moment, but the question was just her thinking. 'Oh, why not, why shouldn't we? We could go as far as Woodston on the bikes. It's a bit of a climb from there, but it wouldn't take long. We could be there for your birthday.' She looked up and smiled. 'And be back in time for the morning.'

And suddenly they were going to see the White Horse, that night.

Not exactly Rene's suggestion or Elsie's proposal, not quite, but they were going now; the decision had slipped out of their hands.

Elsie went to check the bikes and Rene made sandwiches and tea. To Rene's surprise, Elsie also produced a half-bottle of brandy.

Only when they were just about ready to leave, only then, did Rene dare to say, 'Is it too dark?' For it was pitchy outside.

It was certainly late, so late there was no one to see them. They'd both had a shot of the brandy and it went straight to their heads. Once they'd dragged the bikes out of the yard, they fairly streaked up the road, and the speed and the dark released them. They could barely see each other, just the half-dimmed bikes. Rene rode ahead at first, though she didn't know the way. Just by the Townsends', she swerved to avoid an animal fleeing across the road – a fox, a weasel? Elsie, who was as good as teetotal, shrilled with laughter from some way behind.

'Better luck next time.'

'One weasel down, sir. Might have been a fox.'

'KNOW YOUR ENEMY.'

'I think I can safely report that there are no enemy planes flying over England tonight.'

'Famous last words.'

'But BE VIGILANT.'

'Famous last words.'

They sped on, laughing, gasping, into the night.

Rene was wearing an old jacket of Moira's, dark grey with faint lines of red and blue, and it suited her. Perhaps Elsie would have liked it on anyone but Moira, but it gave her an odd pleasure to see Rene wear her sister's things.

A little out of Woodston, they left the bikes by a stile and began the climb. The exhilaration of the ride and the effects of the brandy were temporarily suspended. To Rene it felt like a long climb, not steep – Elsie had assured her – but the combination of the deep dark and the uneven ground made her fear for her balance; the little torch only seemed to make it darker. Elsie didn't seem to need the torch, she pushed ahead – it was the first time they had walked for any length together – and Rene sensed her sure-footedness in the steady pace she kept. Not for the first time, she was thankful for the boots; broad and flat, they made her feel fractionally more stable, more secure. Elsie hummed quietly as she walked, sweet and soft in the night, but distant too. Rene, left alone with her own thoughts, half wished they'd waited till tomorrow. Perhaps it was Elsie, who seemed to be striding ahead, oblivious, caught up in her own adventure. It was a foolish scheme coming up here in the middle of the night. It was so dark, there'd be nothing to see, and the horse was covered up anyway – that's what Elsie had said – because of the war. She was cold too, blowing on her hands, rubbing her arms and face. Buttoning the jacket, she felt something in one of the pockets: cigarettes and matches, old ones probably, forgotten by the errant Moira. Well, they could always try and light a fire; she smiled to herself. And then Elsie stopped humming and turned back to her and asked if she was all right. 'Not far now.'

Like many national landmarks clearly visible from the air, the White Horse had been covered so it wouldn't become a signpost for enemy aircraft – Jerry had his Ordnance Survey too. If Reading was going to be bombed, it wouldn't be the horse's fault.

Abruptly Elsie came to a halt.

'We're here.'

Rene was underwhelmed, but any disappointment she felt soon dissolved because they could sit down quite comfortably in a flat protected niche – the horse's ear, Elsie said. They ate some of the sandwiches and drank more of the brandy. And Elsie babbled – very unusual. She told Rene about the horse, how he had four legs, two ears but only one eye – he might have lost the other in a battle long ago, he was a very old horse after all. Colonel Pinkie had said that a man from the university had paid a pilot to fly him high over the hill and that he'd seen the outline of a far bigger horse from above. Well, she didn't know about that. People used to come and clean him from time to time, she said, so he shone his chalk-white best, 'but not for ages'. She'd never been to one of these scourings, as they were called. She didn't tell Rene about the women who used to come here because they wanted babies.

It was Elsie's idea to unpick the turf, so they could see him properly.

'We can't come all this way for nothing,' she said. 'Who knows when you'll get another chance to see him.'

Rene wondered whether this was a comment on the likely length of the war, or her stay at Starlight. How could she possibly hope for the first? But she did.

Elsie was different tonight, no quiet *thank you, I can manage.*

'We haven't got all night!' she yelled, already some way down the hill. 'Come on.'

Rene was shocked to find Elsie so lawless, like an outlaw from the westerns. With a few headline exceptions, Rene had always thought the law was what most people did. She was pretty sure that what she and Elsie were doing now was not what most people did.

Soon the two of them were clambering all over the hillside. It wasn't difficult, there was no puzzle in the pieces or the placing: just dry, rough squares of turf, scratchy to the touch. They hadn't been put down with much care; many were curled at the edges and the turf bumped awkwardly above the ground. Rene tripped more than once. They piled the turf up neatly, like cushions brought inside when there was a prospect of rain.

It wasn't stealing. What would they have done with the turf anyway? It wasn't an act of sabotage: Elsie had every intention of putting back everything exactly as found. She perfectly accepted the logic of the horse's concealment. It was certainly not an act of treachery in dangerous times, opening a way for an enemy incursion. It was not trespass, or not of the usual kind. This wasn't Mr McGregor's garden after all. It was common land, if not common ground.

'Keep clear of his feet,' Elsie shouted, 'he might kick!' Rene didn't know where his feet were. Something had got hold of them both. They panted and giggled, and at one point Rene nearly cried off she was so tired. But Elsie simply ignored her, so they carried on; another bit and another, till they thought they'd uncovered it all and collapsed back into their niche. Around them everything smelt like summer-mown grass.

It was still stubbornly dark, so there was little to see. The torch picked up indifferent patches of white – nothing more. They were flagging now but warm, still excited. They drank more brandy and their heads got lighter and Rene remembered Moira's cigarettes.

'I've never smoked,' said Elsie, looking at the packet.

'I've never smoked either,' said Rene, not quite truthfully. 'Shall we try one each just to see? I will if you will.'

They wasted four matches, even though it was so still. Rene inhaled too deep and coughed; recovering herself quickly, she posed like one of her dark movie stars and the torchlight turned her into a crazy shadow. Elsie laughed and inhaled carefully, managing not to cough. As soon as they'd finished one, they each lit a second, feeling dizzy and faintly sick. Rene's eyes watered so she closed them tight. She opened them briefly to see the smoke coiling around them. Elsie coughed and smiled. Their lips were burning.

They awoke within moments of each other; it must have been about six. The sun was already up, the grass already warm, buzzing and itching. Elsie sat up immediately, stretched, tried to smooth her springy hair, but Rene lay still, remembering last night's climb, and wary. The cuts of turf about them looked surprisingly neat, but forlorn. How breathless they had been last night, quite light-headed, running, skittering over the hillside, not sure what they were doing. Rolling carefully on to her stomach, she saw above them the chalky-white line of the horse's cheek. The light came quickly, rolling out around them, spreading everything out. They were safe, thought Rene, just as Elsie had said – they could never have fallen. Echoing the thought, Elsie turned back to look at Rene, smiled. They said nothing. It was good perhaps that they had the horse to distract them, but from where they were, there wasn't much to see.

Rene reached for the cigarette packet, dewy, slightly damp; one last cigarette. Elsie was rubbing her palms together, smoothing away the ridges and dents left by the grass and stones. So they looked out across the hazy flat beneath them – stretched out like a faded map – and for a few moments everything seemed to lie within their ken.

They followed one of the bright, dusty paths down the hill, so they could see the horse properly – it was what they had come for, wasn't it? They needed to get much further away to see him stretched and smooth, to see his great leap, as Elsie put it. If they could have summoned last night's confidence they might have run down the hill, or at least stridden down, but that moment had passed, the morning-side contours uncertain.

But they hadn't come all this way for nothing, and they carried on, walking further down the hill. Rene kept turning back, but Elsie, walking in front, tall and loose, never faltered till they reached the bottom.

★ ★ ★

Close up, his white dusty shapes are abstract, aleatory, but that's because you're too near, crawling among his dusty bones. Halfway down the hill is where he starts to emerge, short-backed, more dog than horse, his ear exaggerated by the angle; he is compressed, caught in a half-clenched fan. It is only when you get to the bottom of the field that the ground's canvas flattens, and you see him stretched and smooth, 'making his great leap': long-backed, certainly no dog or dragon (the dragon sleeps just below, you can see his glacial claws). You could walk all the way along the bottom of the hill and watch him slipping in and out of sight, growing bigger-smaller, stretching and contracting. If you were quick enough, he would gallop unsteadily on the spot like an old film.

★ ★ ★

They replaced the turf piece by piece; it was grinding work after the walk back up the hill. No sandwiches left and neither of them could face the last of the brandy. The day was pulling them now but they were trying hard not to feel it. The huge, grassy oval mound below was the strangest thing Rene had ever seen. A great flock of rooks emerged from the valley beneath. At the bottom of the hill they stopped and looked back again. They'd made a pretty good job, but you could still see him through it, or so it seemed.

'Make a wish,' said Elsie. 'I forgot to say that last night. You're supposed to make a wish.'

'I hope Reading wasn't bombed last night,' said Rene.

They both laughed and it was all suddenly vivid again – it was safe to go home.

6

Battle of the Atlantic (Starlight Front), 1941

Rene moved quietly about the kitchen, taking her light with her – sometimes she still forgot. She had boiled two eggs last night for the sandwiches (this much she had to let on to Elsie). Now she mashed them with damp-cotton cress and salt. In the queasy light, she spread too much butter on the bread but she didn't care. Maybe it was childish but she wanted this picnic, this half-surprise, to include as many different things as she could muster. Two thick slices of the cheese, two pink apples, a clutch of crumbling cream crackers, the little bar of chocolate. She didn't care too much for chocolate and nor did Elsie, but the stamps told her it was special.

Elsie would be over in the feeding shed by now. As soon as she went outside, the yard came suddenly and briefly to life: the shudder and throb of the tap in the yard, the single bark, then Elsie's voice – soft and secret – an instant charm on Smoke, who would then lie down again quietly in his box. Oil lamp in hand, Rene rummaged in the larder, as she had done at least a dozen times over the past few days, and found something she hadn't noticed before: a big jar of what looked like raspberries. Nervous and inspired, she prised open the jar – she could smell them now – and spread the soft fruit on to more slices of bread, squished it together and wrapped it all up in the thin paper. She hoped it wouldn't leak. Elsie would be back soon.

Everything was ready. She washed her hands, dark-stained from the fruit, and peered out of the window, just a glimmer of light in the sky. She fancied she could hear footsteps, the click of a coop opening, muffled clucking. She put the kettle on for tea and moved the lamp over to the table; she sank into what had become her chair with a calm satisfaction, Elsie's was opposite. Her hand ran over the picnic bag, remoulding the shapes under the canvas. Marooned in the surrounding dark of the kitchen, the flickering in the stove was the only other beacon, a friendly outpost. Through half-closed eyes, a tiny suitcase swam into view. *I'm running away, Mum.* Back in her childhood bedroom, on the high bed that seemed to float in the dark, were all the things she was going to take with her: a map and a torch, a pair of gloves left by a guest, her own copy of *Treasure Island* and, inside it, an envelope, with Vicky's letter, the two cards. The book was tied with brown ribbon.

'I'm going tomorrow, really I am.'

Her mum was sitting on the chair by the fire, feet up, hugging her knees. No sign of baby Leo – Bertha had taken him out in the pram.

'Couldn't you wait a while, perhaps till next week?'

There was a trace of a smile in her voice, surely.

'We're so busy over the next few days, I do so need your help.'

'All right, but I will need to go soon.'

'Of course. I understand, but don't go yet.'

Her mum had leant forward and squeezed her hand.

Physically settled at her island table, her mind ran here and there in the diminishing dark. She had been worrying at this memory recently, it kept coming back. Elsie's step – she would hear her soon – and the coming of the dawn seemed to set a limit on its promise; already it spread and thinned in the lightening.

Waking to Leo's crying in the middle of the night. Everyone said he was good as gold, but oh, how he cried, and sometimes he just wouldn't stop. The next thing she remembered was standing in the doorway of Mum and Dad's bedroom, the door wide open. They were sleeping peacefully, her mother's hair spread dark over the pillow; everything was quiet. She stepped forward to close the door and saw that Leo's crib was empty. There must have been terror but she couldn't remember that, just standing frozen in the doorway. Then it was later and she was sitting at the kitchen table, watching Bertha by the sink, filling a pan; Leo was clamped to Bertha's hip and bawling.

'I didn't want him to wake your mam. Jiggle him, will you, while I get the milk.'

The water had puffed and squealed through the pipes.

Later, it was Rene's task to carry Leo back to Mum and Dad's bedroom. She put the baby back in his crib as if he were a changeling.

The kettle was tapping and whistling. Out in the yard she heard the pony whicker. Elsie would rub his neck vigorously, *Silly old thing, would I forget you, silly old thing.* She was soft about Pickwick, whatever she said.

Tea made, bread sliced, jam put out. She tried again to pan for something to complete the little girl sitting on the bed with her suitcase, getting ready to run away. She hadn't run away of course, not then. But now she wondered where she had been planning to go all those years ago with her map and her torch and her oversize gloves. To the station of course, always the station.

'Rene. Rene, dear.' It was Elsie's voice, calling her back.

'You were so still, I thought you must be asleep. Do drink your tea, and then we must go, or we'll miss them.'

* * *

On 10 April 1941, a sharp exchange occurred in the House of Commons between the MP for Southport and the MP for Eye about the calibre of the nation's farmers.

Rene and Elsie, meanwhile, spent the day idly, taking a long walk along the more salubrious parts of the old Wilts and Berks Canal. It was Elsie's birthday. As is common when fates are being decided, the two women had no sense of gathering storm clouds.

Mr Robert Spear Hudson, MP for Southport (Con.) and Minister for Agriculture and Fisheries, was bold about the pain that lay ahead. Britain's agricultural economy was neither efficient nor productive, by wartime standards. The challenge had not been faced square, not yet. And it had to be, as a matter of urgency.

Mr Robert Spear Hudson had been made aware of numerous sensitivities. He knew that farmers did not represent a single interest. Smallholder and landowner, big farmer and small, old and new – all had their axes to grind, their furrows to till. There were too many kinds of old, too many kinds of new. Elsie would have agreed with some of this; she had a good memory for the changes. Elsie and Mr Hudson might have agreed on a whole range of matters, but Mr Hudson had no time for soliciting opinions, for niceties; these were new times.

Hudson had put his faith in the Agricultural Executive Committees – a challenging central vision, embodied in local know-how: his ideal. Men who knew what was what and who was who in the county – an enduring category when so much else had gone up in smoke. The membership was composed of locals for the most part: the people best placed to decide. Many of these committees ended up looking like the local hunt at work, and that was reassuring to many, certainly to Hudson. In Lambourn, Phil Townsend had squeezed his way in, not liked but tolerated, though some of his fellow committee members blenched at his manner, among them Harris and Cole, the two biggest landowners. Once bitter rivals, they were discovering more and more in common; new times. These committees had real power: they could lend a tractor, organize you a bit of labour, even stand security for a small loan. Controversially, they had the power to intervene if they decided the land wasn't being put to best use. In extremis, they could evict occupiers.

But war didn't change everything, not overnight. If Harris or Cole, or Hudson for that matter, had taken the bridle path running east of Sheepdrove early one April morning, a familiar and stirring sight would have greeted him: a string of horses, plunging across the gallops. As dawn broke, Rene and Elsie had taken that very path, continuing to the summit of Inkpen Hill, where they had watched. A magical sight. Thirty or more horses, paired and in various shades of dark, trotted down the slope to where the gallop began in earnest: a slow-rising curve of six furlongs. Too far away to see the minute adjustments of reins and stirrups, or hear the barked commands from the stunted trainer, Rene and Elsie moved closer, pausing at a newly fitted five-bar gate. The hooves drummed somewhere beneath their feet, and both fancied they could hear the steady light puff of the horses' breathing in the cool air. Soon the horses were out of sight. Elsie called out something to Rene and strode on, past the gate.

Rene was still not used to this land; its hard-rutted intractability tired her. It had been dry all winter, the ridges and crackings of the ground looked delicate, but she was wrong, and drained already. They reached a stile and Elsie was up and over it in a moment; it looked as if she would just carry on, but then she turned. 'Come on, keep up.' She sounded brisk, but she stretched her hand back at the same time and Rene grasped it, tried to hop across deftly, nearly fell, recovered. Through it all and her final rueful laugh, she kept on holding Elsie's hand, a casual gesture perhaps – many might reach a hand out to one tiring and ill-prepared. But one of them, perhaps both, kept the grip, till the path ran narrow once more: the approach to the canal.

At about ten, they paused at an old lock, resting briefly on the chill powdery wall while they took a drink of tea from the flask. Rene produced the chocolate bar from her pocket. The chocolate itself was disappointing, but the unwrapping, the *occasion*, the give of the thin wrapping, were pleasures enough.

'Happy birthday again.' It was the day's chorus.

The canal used to run right through the valley, pressing close to the Kennet and the Avon. Parts of it were now beyond derelict, and dangerous besides: clotted and marshy, or treacherously slippery. At times, both water and mud were disturbed by various chemical foamings that usually settled into a yellow-grey milk, rumoured to be the residues of Huntley and Palmers. Other parts of the canal had sunk into oblivion: spun by ivy, dried up, tumbled down. There had been periodical protests to the papers about the dangers. Only last year a little girl had fallen from an old lock gate and drowned in the mud. Yet there seemed nothing to be done about it.

Between towns though, there were pleasing routes through the reedy stillness, passages where the water flowed freely, borrowing the natural current of a river or a busy stream.

On the powdery wall, they paused and drank their tea, trying not to shiver in the thin sun.

Elsie had known the canal all her life. It was already falling into disrepair when the Bostons came to Starlight. Now, for long stretches, the canal was a memory, an imprint: some overhanging branches whose shape suggested a curve below, a patch of bricked walkway or a sudden uneasy flatness in the view ahead; Rene could pick out the weeping willows. And then you came upon the soft red curve of a broken bridge, a sudden half-punched hole of black water, visible only for a moment.

In the early days, if the stream in the upper field ran dry, Elsie and Ruby would drive the cows along a short stretch of the towpath – a shady, slow walk in the summer heat – and over a narrow bridge to a marshy, half-forgotten, half-common field. In those early days, much of the land beside the canal was still open. Later came rumours of another railway, and although the speculation came to nothing it brought claims and boundaries. And one spring Sunday, soon after Alfred died, Elsie took a walk and found new fencing and a stile. Upset, and a little disoriented, she had turned for home immediately. She had been back since but it was never quite the same.

There were so many ways of owning the land: it was too symbolically rich, too literally empty. Governments turned to it time and time again as saviour and soother; and now, well now it was the national interest: the nation at war in full sacrificial cry.

Back in the Commons, Mr Hudson, the Minister, was getting into his stride:

'Mr Granville has asked how you define a bad farmer. It is very simple really. There are three categories of farm, and three categories of farmer.'

The categories were always the same, good, fair and poor, and these judgements had consequences. The survey was already under way. In Suffolk alone, eighty tenancies had been terminated; evictions would follow.

And Rene and Elsie were neglecting their duties. They had paused again to eat their picnic, leaning over the bridge, watching the water. The raspberry bread was a great success: bright pink and soft and just a little tart. Spring pudding, Elsie called it.

Hudson wasn't going to let pity intervene:

'The only time a man is turned out is when, clearly, he is the sort of man who will not do the work, who will not obey the orders given to him, who will not make use of the resources. He is the hopeless fellow and rightly he is turned out.'

Hudson found, as many do, a ruthless pleasure in what emergency made possible. This was no time for elegant acres and picturesque groupings of deer. What was called for was the reassuring, patriotic and above all indifferent marks of plough and tractor in the monotonous turn of earth. More personally, Hudson also enjoyed the accessories of urgency and danger: telegrams (which he had once derided as a waste of time), special telephone numbers, authorization codes, the accessing of documents via silent processes of multiple special signatures, ringing heels, darkened corridors (he had not participated directly in any such ritual as yet). An older language also fed him and he took up the banner of a Burkean vision: the national landlord, however embodied, must bring his tenants to order. If they were found wanting, if needs must, they must be 'turned out'.

Rene and Elsie had finished their leaning lunch; they were both watching a moorhen trying to tempt her chicks into the water. A marsh hen, Elsie called it, but it was the same bird: neat and dark with the bright red beak and stalky legs. The grey chicks were still fluffy, watching their mother from the bank, curious, as she glided this way and that, circled and returned. The chicks would not follow, but continued to observe her, till one lost interest and trod away, as if on stilts, in search of food. The charmed circle was broken, the group began to dissolve.

'They like snails, you know, to eat,' Elsie said.

'Oh. Whole?'

'I think they break them open on stones.'

There was a long pause, then she continued, 'I remember reading once that the French like to eat snails.'

'Whole?' Rene was laughing now.

The chicks caught the sound; they looked up and huddled, curious.

'No, no. They cook them on metal trays, with little dents for the snails. There was a picture. They give you a special fork, and a little pair of tongs to pull them out, and you eat them with butter and parsley. I always wondered what they would taste like.' She laughed too.

'Like cockles, like oysters.' Southport. Out on the prom in the yellow-grey fog, Alan laughing, she laughing. So cold, hair scratching her face, the vinegar made her eyes water. Taste of the seaside.

'But they're pickled,' Rene added.

'No, I don't like the sound of that. I don't like vinegar.'

Elsie had never tried cockles or oysters anyway. She had never been to the sea.

'But you like the sound of snails?'

They both laughed.

'It's different. They're cooked, with butter, and you have a special plate and fork.'

'You don't like them in the garden.'

'It's my revenge.'

They started to pack up the remains of their lunch. Rene smoked a cigarette. The chicks had disappeared, only the hen remained; she swam up and down the bank a couple more times and then hopped back on to her nest in the reeds. The two women stood on the bridge watching, caught in the sunlight. The last few days had been warm, even the stone on the bridge seemed to feel it.

And then out of nowhere and without a glance in her direction, Elsie said:

'Was your husband a bad man?'

Rene didn't know quite what to say.

'No, oh no, Elsie. He was very kind, very gentle.'

Elsie kept on looking down into the water. There was a long pause.

'And you wanted to get married?'

'At the time. At the time, yes, I did, but in the end I couldn't make things suit.'

Cally and Ruby had been lucky to marry, Elsie had been told – because of the war.

They clambered down the steep bank, doing their best to avoid the nettles – it was the only way on to the path from here. They went quietly, trying not to disturb the moorhen in her empty nest. From here the water looked darker, oily. The path was very overgrown and they walked single file.

'He had a good nature.'

Elsie sensed that a good nature wasn't quite the same as good. She had worried that Rene's husband wasn't gentle. There were men with violent hands, women found with their necks bruised blue or broken at the bottom of stairs. She knew this from headlines.

Rene could hear Elsie thinking, wondering. She wanted to help but she didn't know how.

'He was very kind. He didn't hit me, Elsie, never, never. And he didn't rage. And he didn't drink, not like that.'

But they were still in trouble.

'He was a train driver.' Rene didn't know what else to say.

'Oh.'

Someone else, another woman, would have asked what happened or what went wrong or even do you have a photograph, but these weren't questions that Elsie knew to ask. No one had ever asked her, do you love him?

Quick he was, always quick, he came running along the street to help her when she skidded and fell in the snow. She had taken his hand, wary but so tired, Christmas Eve, too many packages, gloves lost, hands stinging, Dad dead and the tears pricking her eyes. His hands were so light and soft when he wrapped his scarf around her neck. He was going to whisk her away.

'It was a good job, a good job in bad times. He worked hard. We were lucky. He got good money. We should have had enough . . .'

'Was he a spiv?' Elsie asked, turning back to look at her.

'Oh no, nothing like that. Not like George Townsend.'

And Elsie smiled and Rene too; it wasn't such a bad guess.

They walked on, still single file, but quicker now, the way familiar.

Not a spiv, but Alan had had his patter too, he could be funny, he could do the cheer-up talk – she had liked it at first. He brought flowers to the pub that first time, Bertha had nudged her, how she had blushed. Soon they would be leaving the airy cold of the Blue Elephant for Bertha's little house in Judd Street. 'You mustn't think of getting a job yet, Rene, remember your mam, she can't be left on her own, not now.' Oh, Bertha thought of everything. When Alan arrived that afternoon with his flowers, Rene couldn't wait to be away. She had promised her mum that she would return a book, so they took the tram up to the Free Library. The big reading room was full of people trying to get warm; she and Alan had wandered along the shelves, Alan twisting his head sideways to read the titles. They were nervous, giggling, an old man in one of the aisles shushed them loudly and they had rushed off, laughing the louder. The corridors smelt of carbolic; the library had been a hospital first, and Alan said he was sure he could smell ether.

Elsie had reached a wider part of the path. She paused for Rene to catch up and they continued side by side. Still warm but the sky above them was thick with cloud – it seemed to muffle the sound about them and the water so still. When Rene spoke again her voice sounded muffled too.

'It's not easy to explain about Alan. He never shirked, he was lovely with the children.'

Elsie said nothing but Rene knew she was thinking, listening.

'He was a gambler.'

'Oh.'

For a moment Rene wished she was talking to Lily or her old neighbour, Hilda – oh, Hilda knew exactly, three children, just like her, a gambler for a husband, just like her. But this was Elsie and she so wanted Elsie to understand.

'Horses?' asked Elsie. 'I never knew anyone who gambled.'

'Mainly horses, yes.'

Alan's horses were just slips of paper with silly names, Glow in the Dark, Jim of Diamonds, three to one on. So different from Elsie's horses: the crotchety Pickwick, the handsome black Prince of her childhood, the White Horse, running down that hill. She must try harder.

'Oh Elsie, things are so difficult to explain. He was a gambler. It sounds like something you do, doesn't it?' He's a train driver, he's a butcher, he's a gambler.

'Did he lose a lot of money?'

'Yes, but he won a lot as well. He was lucky more often than some. (*You have to say that, don't you, Ren? I'm luckier than most, aren't I?*) It was his whole life . . . I never knew where I was. I could never be sure what was going to happen.'

'Oh Rene.'

Something had struck a chord.

'Sometimes, when I came back home, I'd wonder why the room looked different and then I'd see – something was missing of course, the lamp or the clock, all manner of things, things from the kitchen, even the wireless.'

'Oh Rene.'

'We got a good part of it back. He was always to and fro to the pawnshop but we lost a lot outright. It was so *tiring*. I was quite run-down with it all and the children.'

And of course Alan was hardly ever there when the bailiff came – he was at work. She was the one who had to let things go, the one who took receipt of the endless slips of paper from Mr Lemster – such a polite man, such a sad, regretful face. The children running rings, her head running circles. Half the original contents ended up in the surrounding streets, but she could never quite grudge the neighbour who had their carriage clock – a wedding gift from Bertha – or old Mrs Grey who had her mangle.

'I'm sure there were people who thought I should have worked harder to keep him at home. But no one blamed me, not to my face.'

Bertha had blamed her at the beginning; Lily had defended her and now here was Elsie.

'But you do work hard, very hard. I've seen how hard you work.'

Lily would have raised her eyebrows at that, but Elsie was struggling, tired of this talk.

They turned away from the canal now in favour of Cole's wood, and Rene was glad to get away from the stillness.

Here all the trees were shooting green and everywhere birds were twittering, darting, things rustling in the leaves.

'Oak,' Rene said hesitantly. She couldn't think of anything else.

'Oh Rene,' said Elsie.

For it was a beech wood, with the usual errant fruit trees. A spindly, springy branch had sprouted low from a stubborn scar and Elsie pulled off a leaf: bright yellow-green with little hairs all round.

'There used to be deer, lots of them, but they've nearly all been poached.'

'Since the war?'

'Oh, well before that. There are still a few left, if you know when to look, if you come very early in the morning. This way . . .'

Rene followed just a little behind. Lily would have giggled at Elsie – not at the time, but afterwards. *Oh Rene, really, you can't be serious*. But Rene didn't want Lily now. Lily had got rid of her swimming cups when she got married. She would carp and grumble plenty, but that was it: you'd made your bed. They'd all made their beds when they got married. Lily was no use, nor was Hilda. She would much rather have Elsie's ghosts: Moira with her jacket pulled tight around her, complaining about the mud, never in the right shoes; Bert falling into the ditch; Moira coming back from a dance, sitting in the cart, singing while everyone else slept. The cart passed on; everything floated away.

They came out into a clearing finally full of sunlight where the trees stretched and soared and Elsie, all loose-limbed and easy, pointed out the clutch of trees that had been struck in a summer storm. Still dying, she said, and sometimes she could still smell burning, and the blackberries were the best for miles for the storm had let the light through.

'Look!'

Rene had seen something hanging in the trees above.

Elsie looked up.

'It must be a parachute . . .' Rene's voice was a whisper, dry.

YOU MUST NOT BE TAKEN BY SURPRISE.

'Are you sure?'

It was hard to be sure, something white or perhaps grey – it looked like a big white sheet hanging lankly in the branches high above. BETTER SAFE THAN SORRY – that didn't sound right.

'What else could it be?'

Rene's mind spun – someone falling, jumping, out of the sky. The surrounding woodland was suddenly alive with Germans, caught, concealed in the trees. Enemy agents, spies. TELL NO ONE, NOT EVEN HER. Elsie didn't have blackout upstairs. LIGHTS OUT IN THE BLACKOUT. Elsie didn't have light upstairs. Take a deep breath.

'A sheet,' Elsie said.

'What?'

Elsie had her neck craned back at a near impossible angle, shielding her eyes, staring up. 'Somebody's washing, I don't know. It was that blowy on Monday.'

YOU MUST NOT BE TAKEN BY SURPRISE.

Or an English airman flying home, now lying injured, lying dead. She didn't want to find a body.

'We should look around, in case there's anything else.'

They looked around on the ground underneath the trees, uncertain of what they might find, what might count. If this were a film, Rene thought, there would be a pair of cracked flying goggles, a map, foreign cigarettes and German writing, yes, somewhere there would be German writing, but all she found was a blunt penknife with a rusty blade. That sustained their search but they found nothing else and started to lose interest; it was getting cold and late. They stared up at the fabric one final time. There was no sign of strings, but maybe that was just the angle: it was forty foot up at least.

YOU MUST NOT BE TAKEN BY SURPRISE.

Rene was calm again now. Elsie smiled at her.

'If there was a crash or something, Colonel Pinkie is bound to know. We can ask him when we get back.'

IF THE INVADER COMES, KNOW WHAT TO DO AND HOW TO DO IT.

That night, after Elsie had gone to sleep, Rene got up and went downstairs, clutching the tin box where she kept the remains of her other life. Her most precious things were still folded into the old copy of *Treasure Island* and tied with fraying ribbon. This she left well alone, but she tidied up the other bits and pieces, read a letter from her dad to her mum – *Oh, my darling* – and stared at her wedding photograph for some time. She wasn't quite sure why she had kept it, except that it was a reminder. Just a small group: she and Alan in the middle, her mother and Leo, with a silly smirk on his face. And on Alan's side, his mother – such a nice woman – and his sister with her fox collar limp round her neck. And then there were the cuckoos in the nest: Bertha and her fiancé, just announced, Mr Ernest Massey (surely they're too old, Leo had said). It was only the second time she had met him, short and sturdy with his barrel chest, and smart that day in a borrowed suit. He stood beside Bertha, the proverbial spinster, pencil thin – no wonder Leo smirked. Rene had never quite recognized herself in the photograph, eyes down as if she were shy; she had thought she was clever that day, had thought she was escaping.

* * *

Phil Townsend came up to Starlight the following evening, not something he did very often these days. Very friendly he was: did Elsie know he was on the Land Ag now; any help you need, just say the word. Full of it. He brought a copy of *The Times* with him, with a report of yesterday's debate. *The Times* came courtesy of old Harris. It wasn't Phil's usual reading, but he said there was something Elsie should see.

For Elsie, reading the paper was part of being a farmer: it was what old Alfred had done. The *Newbury Advertiser*, the *Berkshire Gazette*. Rene made a habit of bringing her back one of these when she went into Lambourn on Fridays. But other, more specialized press also fell into Elsie's hands. There had once been a subscription to the *Farmer*, and when Elsie went to the mart, or to the forge to get the pony shod, there was often a copy of something. Local, parochial in so many respects, untravelled, she knew nevertheless that before the war most of her cow cake came from South Africa and Canada, about the grand empire beef conference, about the farming of ostriches and emus for meat, and of trade fairs, in London and Paris. Rene was quite amazed by some of the things that Elsie knew; amazed too that this knowledge didn't seem to make the prospect of visiting the town of Reading any less frightening. Elsie read and Rene took it up too: reading her way into Elsie's world. They took it in turns to read aloud – taking turns to be the wireless, Elsie called it. The war made it a duty of sorts and so, after Phil had left, they had sat in the parlour, taking turns to read the report of the Commons debate from *The Times*. Imagine Rene's soft rising rhythms, the faintest unattributable lilt from Elsie:

> The debate was bad-tempered in parts, and there was much righteous anger that no one from the war cabinet saw fit to be present . . . It is certainly reassuring to know that the House can still muster the redoubtable qualities usually associated with more tranquil times. Readers of these pages may well have wondered if the member for Caernarvon Boroughs' oratory has been too frequently praised of late, but yesterday, he spoke 'with wizardry and magnetism' . . .

Lloyd George had a strong suspicion of these Agricultural Committees, too much stroking self-interest. This struck a chord with Elsie, who was inherently suspicious of the Land Ag – just wanted to line their pockets. Above all, said that most famous MP for Caernarvon Boroughs, an army was needed to grow the food that would fight this war. Stirring stuff.

Lloyd George, how old must he be now? Rene, hearing him broadcast in Elsie's soft tones, found it easy to respond, 'A war indeed.' She had learnt very quickly during her training it was best to be at the front of the field, to see only what was in front. Irritated by interruption, by foolers, always the first to volunteer, front-of-the-queue Hargreaves (a good-natured jibe, that), she was fighting, no mistake; and didn't everyone have a bit of their own war mixed in with the rest?

* * *

The letter arrived two weeks after Elsie's birthday. It was another 'letter from no one', as Elsie called such communications, to Rene's initial amusement. There had been a slow and steady stream of these, mainly from the Ministry of Agriculture, since the mid-thirties. She had read them all, acted on some, ignored others, crossed her fingers, hoped, feared and forgotten. Each letter carried the possibility of the past, a sin of omission, a link in some obscure, tightening chain. There was no such thing as a letter from no one: she knew that really.

'Why do you call it that?'

They were sitting at the table, lingering over breakfast, the first shift of the day done.

Elsie placed the letter (one page, official, spun with acronyms) very carefully in front of Rene, pointing at the inky squabble of a signature.

'See.'

'Yes, yes, the writing is dreadful.' She stole a glance at Elsie, who nearly smiled. 'But look, it says *Robinson*. It comes from Robinson, oh no, wait, a Mr M. *Sealy*-Robinson from the Ministry of Agriculture. No wonder he can't sign his own name.'

'I don't know anyone called Robinson, Sealy-Robinson.'

They both laughed at that, but Elsie soon turned mutinous.

'I don't like it. He knows me but I don't know him. What does he want with me?'

'He doesn't know *you*, but he knows you're a farmer. And farmers are fighting the war. Like the land girls. You and me, we're fighting the war. These are our orders, our instructions. This is the Lambourn front, the Starlight front.'

Rene found this line of argument easy, natural. She'd heard a good deal of it on her training. It was speech that talked itself and she had filled up on it.

She was right about orders, but they didn't come in the form expected. The letter, with its unreadable signature, announced a survey: 'designed to obtain a complete picture of the current state of agricultural production in England, Wales and Scotland with the aim of increasing productivity . . .' It announced, within the next few weeks, the arrival of a field recorder, a complete stranger who would, with their assistance, complete the above-mentioned survey on the condition of Starlight, its current and future 'productivity'. They should be ready to expect the arrival of the recorder on the morning of Wednesday 4 May and be prepared to make themselves available to assist him. He would expect to be shown all over the farm, alone or accompanied. He would inspect the condition of all the buildings, including the house; the state of all walls, gates, fences, ditches and water supplies. He would record details of all stock, foodstuffs, seed, machinery and equipment.

The birthday card still sat on the parlour mantel: pale yellow tulips in a willow-pattern jug. It was a long time since anyone had remembered Elsie's birthday. It was a lovely picture, but the real interest was inside: Rene's writing, a looping ribbon: writing you could look through, spun and swirled. She had found the pen and the dark green ink in the drawer of old Alfred's desk. Elsie had been amazed. Her own hand was a clear, easy copperplate, but this, her name like this, was beyond anything. She was a picture; her name like icing piped on a cake.

* * *

They spent the next ten days working all hours, trying to put things to rights. Some of the fencing mended, much of it a patch-over job. The cowshed scrubbed down, a gate painted and its rusty catch fixed, the two furthest drains cleared. Rene took it upon herself to bleach the walls of the cowshed, found some white paint for the rotting window frames and whitewashed the walls of the yard. The little vegetable plot at the edge of the orchard was already budding with greens; they were eating well. The old field of glasshouses looked terrible, but there was no time to clear the glass and no money to replace it; in the end, Elsie could only secure the gate. At least it was a field that could be offered up to the plough.

The diminished livestock were intrigued by the sudden activity. Penned into the small paddock while Rene scrubbed out the cow-shed, the Guernseys watched, pretty, golden brown, with their soft dark eyes. Periodically, they rested their heads on the wall. Inside, she darned and patched curtains, and sewed up all the coverings one bright morning when Elsie said the sky was promising wind for later. In the kitchen she scoured the old deal table. She cleared out the larder and scrubbed that too, put down new paper, threw out the contents of a few jars and boiled them clean. She ranged them by the sink, a shining mass of waiting glass. They were ready for anything. She wondered if this man, this field recorder, would want to look upstairs. There was a leak in the bedroom when it rained heavily, and the paper on the ceiling was tea-stained.

★ ★ ★

Alan Ainsley, the young field recorder who was conducting the survey in Hungerford and Lambourn, wasn't sure what to make of the 'two maiden ladies', as he called them in the survey. Harris, his host, was openly hostile.

'A woman, a woman running a farm on her own. What utter foolishness! Can't be done. When her father died, everyone thought she'd go. Only sensible course. But no. Decided to stay put. Even her sisters thought she was mad. Farm's in a terrible state, according to that chap Townsend.' Harris paused; he had slid into gossip, rather like the kind his wife brought back these days with the shopping. Nevertheless, Harris thought it was important young Ainsley should have the full picture.

'It's all hare-brained if you ask me. Now, she's got a land girl to help her. You'll see her. You'll see them both, I dare say. Well, she's not going to complain about that. But farms that size just don't make sense. Especially not now.'

Ainsley smiled politely, and waited for Harris to continue. Each was sure they had the other's measure. Harris thought Ainsley was all very well with his talk of nitrogen and variegated leys, and you didn't get much company these days. But it wouldn't do to load him up with too much responsibility: just a young chap, must be feeling the pressure. Besides, this was county business, and for Harris, county and country were one. When the two diverged, he chose not to notice. He knew where the war was being fought and where it would be won.

Ainsley's vision did not preclude the small farm. He took pride in his scientific approach. He was no iconoclast, but he could see the future: a chain of white coats, great concentrations of fowl and pigs, milking factories, artificial insemination. There was no need to shout, and he was not without sympathy for yesterday's man. His picture wasn't monochrome, no indeed, it was full of nuance and delicate variety, but for the most part it came in packets: each a combination of leys perfectly matched to a different soil type. He never got into an argument. His tomorrow was assured, its exact date of implementation the only uncertainty. Ainsley's war was a great opportunity. He was more than willing to be out gathering evidence, to see what he was up against, and occasionally, if conditions seemed right, plant the proverbial seed of his vision.

Yet when he arrived at Starlight, Ainsley didn't find the farm as he expected, as Harris had led him to believe. There was no struggling lady farmer; there was no land girl. Not any more. There were just, as he would write in his report, 'two maiden ladies who . . .' They were both waiting for him by the gate. They were both wearing trousers, but he was quite used to this by now. Miss Hargreaves, who was very slight, wore her hair very short. Miss Boston, who wouldn't leave, invited him into the farmhouse for tea before he made the inspection. They were friendly and welcoming, and he was relieved about the land girl. Ainsley had become quite used to land girls, though their numbers varied across the country. Like Elsie, he remained frightened of these startling brown Amazons, with their hands on their hips and their sharp-seeing eyes. Like Elsie, his fear was far stronger when they occurred in groups (his definition of a group was conservative rather than scientific).

It fell to Rene to show him the farm. He noted the stile (recently fixed), the cracked pipe, the cheap repairs that had been done to the fencing. He saw that the glasshouses had been abandoned and that the oats were green and strong. They walked the boundaries. Miss Hargreaves was the easier one, he thought: quick, chatty, interested in what he had to say (he wasn't used to flattery). But here on this land, in this fresh blow, she sounded so foreign, you could taste the smoke. It was she who asked about the categories and their consequences: A, B and C; good, fair and poor.

They ended up at the farm gate, waiting for Elsie to come out and say her goodbye. Rene had planned everything out very carefully: Ainsley would get a last view of them together, polite (that would make a change from a lot of places), serious, willing. It was a good day for showing off the farm, she thought, early May, just the suggestion of summer.

'What happened to the land girl?' asked Ainsley.

Rene said nothing.

'Mr Harris told me that Miss Boston was sent a land girl.'

'Yes, that's right.' Rene looked at him straight.

'Did she not stay?' And then, because this might have sounded rude or intrusive, 'Some of them don't really fit the task, or so I've heard.'

All in all, Ainsley decided to take the rough with the smooth where Starlight Farm and the two maiden ladies were concerned. In his report, he noted the signs of recent work and responded to the willingness both women displayed. *Eager to take advice*, he wrote, *no reason why they shouldn't do well with a little assistance*. Fair enough, he thought. Fair. B.

How utterly foolish, Harris thought when he saw the report, but he said nothing till the next meeting of the Land Ag and Ainsley was long gone by then. The committee all agreed that he was a fine chap with an interesting future, but very young. He hadn't made too many mistakes, considering. It was probably best if they sorted these out among themselves. Phil Townsend agreed.

* * *

It was nearly a month later when Phil Townsend came with the news. Only Elsie was at home, and she invited him into the kitchen (her father had always taken him to the parlour). He left his stick by the door and limped over to the table, where he sat down in old Alfred's carver. Elsie, flustered by his visit and wondering why he had come again so soon, sat down too. He had no newspaper with him this time.

It didn't do to delay: he was here about the farm. Starlight. The Land Ag had met, the Land Ag had decided . . .

'They can't give me orders after all this time,' said Elsie. She felt sure of her ground. 'It's my place. I know it. I know it best.'

'Miss Boston, I don't think you understand.'

'Yes I do. You want to tell me what to do.'

And him most of all, she thought. No one sat in that chair now, not even Missy.

'Miss Boston?' He wanted to get on.

But she wouldn't look up, she was too busy thinking. She stared down her nose at her hands, fingers crossed and clenched together.

'Miss Boston, it was a C they decided on.'

At the end, he couldn't quite blame it on Ainsley.

She looked up, uncertain, trying to understand.

'A C?'

Did Elsie even know there was a C? Had Rene told her?

'Poor.'

Townsend's hands slipped awkwardly from the table on to his lap.

'Look, I'm sorry. I know this is a big shock. C means poor, I'm afraid. They didn't think you could make the farm work. No one blames you, I'm sure you did your best. It's a tough job for any-one . . . In an ordinary situation it wouldn't have mattered, but this is war, things can't be left to run on. You're being asked to leave.'

Like Elsie, Phil wasn't used to making long speeches, but once he made his mind up about something he somehow managed to get it out.

There was a silence.

'But this is my farm.'

'Not now, not in wartime. They have the right to take it over, to own it.'

There would be a letter soon, he said, official, but he thought she would rather hear it from someone like him.

'After all, your dad and me were quite friendly like.'

'He never trusted you.' She flashed him a look and then her eyes were back on her hands, crossed and clenched.

'It's a shock, I can see that. Look, I won't stay.'

'No,' she said, and stood up. She wouldn't look at him again and he took his cue.

It hadn't gone too badly, considering. He paused in the doorway. She was still standing by the table.

'The Land Ag thought it best if I took over. It's handy me being so close, and I know the land.' He didn't want her to hear this from anyone else, not yet.

She looked at him properly then but dully; he hovered in the doorway.

'I'd be happy to take any stock off your hands. Not that pony, mind, but the rest. I'll give you a fair price.'

'No,' she said.

'Righty-ho. Fair enough. Better be on my way now. Let me know if you change your mind about the stock.'

* * *

Poor farmer.

When Rene got back from Lambourn and didn't find Elsie in the yard or the kitchen, she called out briskly, but thought little of it when she got no reply. She untied Smoke and filled his water bowl, splashing soft water over her face and neck. The old dog wagged his tail gratefully and tried to follow her inside. She wouldn't have minded but Elsie was strict, so she shut the back door. Inside, she unpacked the shopping and sat down with a big glass of squash. It was then that she heard noises from next door. Rene stood up on the instant.

'Elsie?'

No reply.

Too much noise for Missy. An intruder?

The noise again: rustling – she hoped it wasn't rats. She opened the back door quickly and called Smoke, who trotted across the yard with unexpected energy. Next door, more rustling – Smoke's ears were pricking – then she heard the crash of something heavy falling.

The parlour door was closed, which was odd, but Smoke started to squeal and scratch at the door.

As soon as Rene pushed the sticky door open, Smoke rushed in, then stopped and sank to the floor, whimpering.

Elsie was sitting on the floor beside Alfred's old desk; hardly sitting – huddled into herself, hands across her knees; she seemed to be staring at her clenched fingers. She was surrounded by paper. She was paper-pale too; her thick springy hair had been sunk by the heat and lay lank around her neck; strands of it were streaked across her face.

A great moat of paper surrounded her, cutting her off. Most of it was yellowing newspapers and magazines, part of Alfred's 'record' – kept so lovingly by Elsie in the boxes behind his desk. These had all been turned out, shaken out with force. They were mixed with official correspondence, typed and acronym-heavy: the letters from no one – not a single one had been thrown away. There was loose paper too, handwritten: letters and notes and charts. Rene could make out what looked like a map or plan of the farm; pages torn from an account book, sketchily filled in. These had been shaken on top of the yellowing print, like an afterthought of angry confetti. But perhaps Elsie had thought better of all her turning out; some of the papers and magazines had been coaxed back into precarious piles – how long had she been here? What had happened?

'Elsie.'

In the late-afternoon sunlight, the room swam with dust. Elsie wasn't paper-pale at all but dust-pale and ghostly. A few feet from Rene, she seemed so far away.

'Rene, I'm a poor farmer.' She didn't look up. 'Do you know what that means, a poor farmer?'

'Yes,' Rene whispered.

Smoke whimpered and inched forward.

'After all this time, it turns out I'm a poor farmer, all my life . . .'

'You're not a poor farmer.'

'Yes I am. It's what they said. They're sending a letter to prove it. You said it would be all right . . .' She looked up for the first time, looked straight at Rene. Her face was so empty it was worse than crying.

'I'm sorry,' Rene said.

'You said.'

'I'm sorry, it's what he said – Ainsley. B: fair. It's what he said.'

'I'm not a fair farmer.'

'Oh Elsie, I'm so sorry. Is there anything we can do . . . to stop it?'

But Rene knew the answer to that already.

'We can't do anything. It's the war; the war owns Starlight now . . . and Phil Townsend.'

Smoke whined and slithered forward. Rene stayed where she was, uncertain.

'I can't find it,' Elsie said, after a pause.

'Can't find what?'

'My board exam . . . they sent a letter. It was a letter. I've been looking for a certificate all this time, but they sent a letter because I failed.'

'Elsie? What are you saying?'

'I failed the school board exam – everyone wanted me to be a teacher but I didn't. It would have taken me away from Starlight. Rene, you must help me find the letter.'

'Yes of course.' If there was any way she could make amends.

'That bastard Townsend.'

Elsie never swore.

'That's what my dad called him. He was right . . . That bastard Townsend,' Elsie said again, more slowly this time, more distinctly. 'He said there'd be a letter. Rene, will you open it when it arrives? I don't want to see it. I don't want to see.'

'Yes,' said Rene, 'anything, anything.'

Elsie reached out her hand to Smoke and burst into tears.

7

The Changing View

Elsie was calm after this episode, directing all her energies towards the disposal. She sold the Guernseys to a farmer on the other side of the valley, she sold them cheap, but they were going to a good home, well away from the Townsends. Elsie's eyes pricked as she urged them up the ramp, but there was a biting pleasure in knowing Phil Townsend would see the trailer and its cargo, bumping back up Sheepdrove.

In the evenings, they made and remade lists and piles of what to wrap and scrap. Elsie was determined that as little as possible got into enemy hands, and for now there was only one enemy. Objects, long forgotten and uncared for, made her suddenly, painfully, tender. She would not have them picked up clumsily, fingered by the Townsends. What couldn't come with them would be safer with strangers. And so, although Elsie flinched at the idea of a proper house sale, Rene quietly put the message round that they were leaving and soon there was quite a line of traffic up to the house and all manner of people, who left with bedsteads and mattresses, chairs and chests of drawers, some strapped on to carts and others on to trolleys and backs. Carriers sometimes coming away with a jacket or a couple of old jumpers for good measure. Slowly and carefully, Starlight was dismantled.

Calm as she appeared after the outburst, capable too as she made her lists and did her sorting, Elsie could make no grasp at what had happened. If a great tidal wave had come in over the Isle of Wight and Hampshire, sinking Starlight and the rest of Berkshire, Elsie would have borne it better; a flashing September storm that set the downlands alight after a tinder-dry summer, a plague of slugs, even an earthquake – any of these would have made more sense to Elsie.

Starlight was hers and it always had been hers. How could the Land Ag take it away?

It was up to Rene to secure a future and she was nervous: it had gone so badly wrong with Ainsley. They were to leave as soon as possible – it didn't do to linger, she was sure of that – and she was in charge of making it happen: dates, times, transport, destination. Elsie showed no interest in any of it. It made matters easier for Rene in some ways, but the stakes were very high. One Friday morning she took the early bus to Newbury where she bought a notebook and a pencil along with writing paper and envelopes (she had borrowed old Alfred's pen). On the notebook cover, she wrote, simply, *Arrangements*. She had her whole day planned out: library, train station, back to the library again to write her letters, and then to the post office. Any time left over and she'd buy a few things they needed for the journey. She'd told Elsie she'd be back by the end of the afternoon.

She had already decided they would go north; now it was a matter of where, and she couldn't afford to be too choosy. In the library she searched through magazines, registers and maps. She chose a farm from a map only if it was on a named road near a town; for the rest she searched through all manner of articles and advertisements and made a list as best she could, filling in here and there with what she hoped were sensible guesses. Anywhere they went had to be easily reached by train, and whatever she arranged, it was a leap in the dark. Leaps in the dark were not something that Elsie was used to, so many of the farm names came as some relief: *Top Farm, Hill Farm, Fern Farm, Drove Farm, Home Farm* – names familiar from the valley, names Elsie had known all her life.

She was back at Newbury library by quarter to twelve (not a patch on the Manchester Free), still plenty of time to write her letters and get them to the post office. When she started writing, though, things didn't happen so easy. Her handwriting was the same as usual, the handwriting that Elsie admired; perhaps it was the words. *We are two maiden ladies, two spinster ladies . . . one has worked the land all her life, the other . . . All reasonable work considered.* Some parts just looked awkward, wrong: *independent accommodation required, such as a cottage . . . Please write care of . . .* But eventually she found her rhythm and the words came quicker. After a time, her hand even started to ache and it was a relief, the side of her little finger smudged with ink, but then the tears were pressing into her eyes, remembering the last time she had made plans.

She wasn't running away, not like Manchester, not like before. She and Elsie weren't running away. But they must leave soon, leave before the Townsends came knocking, before they had to. This rush to look free when you weren't – perhaps that was why it felt like flight. It was very quiet in the library; for all that she was busy, the big, empty room made her feel idle. She wrote out the farm names on to the envelopes in very clear capitals – *TOP FARM, HILL FARM, FERN FARM, DROVE FARM, HOME FARM* – and as much of the addresses as she knew or could guess.

After she had finished writing, Rene folded each letter neatly into three and slid it into the envelope; how thin the paper was. She licked each envelope, aware that the woman at the desk was watching her. What kind of letter did she think she was writing? They made quite a little pile – twelve in all. She would get stamps at the post office.

Those mornings at the park in the hot August days before the war started. Jessie would skip ahead and Stevie would try to keep his hand on hers. Along the dusty gravel path, *the woods are lovely, dark and deep*, past the refreshment shed and the bandstand – the banner *Homeless and Unemployed* drooped lifelessly around the railings. The words had run so you could hardly read them, but no one would take it down. Her fingers hot and sticky from the pram. Every day the same. Push and up on the swings and whee on the slide and then off to the pond where they always stopped. And that was where little Mikey would wake up and start bawling and Jessie would try to distract him, throwing bread for the ducks. *Here, Mikey . . . Look, Mikey . . . Look.* Trying to hear without listening too carefully – that was the trick with children and she didn't have it. *Silly baby, stop crying, look at the duckie. Look! A RAFT of ducks* – Rene had been teaching Jessie her collectives – *a FLOCK of seagulls, a DRIFT of swans*, but it was something else when the swans were flying, she couldn't remember. Out of the park on to Kingston Street, Stevie banging his sand bucket like a drum. And not to be outdone, Jessie would start her reciting:

> 'The woods are lovely, dark and deep,
> But I have promises to keep,
> And miles to go before I sleep,
> And miles to go before I sleep.'

Wirelesses on everywhere, in all the shops, smart London voices, *a PRIDE of lions, a PARLIAMENT of owls*, everyone waiting. The sweat trickling down the back of her neck and Stevie and Jessie squalling, *But you said*. The tears brimming in Stevie's blue eyes, Jessie grabbing her hand, *He's a liar, Mum, he's a liar*. And somewhere inside she was being tuned up high and tight. Mikey's little face all flushed in the pram and thank God they were nearly home and here was Alan waiting at the door, such a sweet smile, leading her into the sitting room, over to the settee – a little more tattered than the last time she'd seen it, some four months ago. The two uncomfortable armchairs Bertha had given them were back too, and her wireless – last spotted two weeks ago in the window of Silver's Pawnshop. A big win then, he had a rose in his buttonhole. Swings and roundabouts, but it felt more like the deep blue sea. Jessie and Stevie squealing on the carpet – so happy and quite made up – and Mikey sleeping through it all. And still strung so tight inside. She knew what was coming. There would be food, a feast. Roast beef and fondant cakes and jam tarts and ham with a marmalade crust – he had surpassed himself this time. Peaches on the japan tray and a huge, orangey-brown pineapple. The children would eat too much and get excited, she would try to settle them, and finally she would go upstairs. A big win, she knew the drill: his light tread on the stair, his light cough (that was more recent), the pause outside the bedroom door. He had come to stroke her out of uncertain humour, bring her back to safer ground. He could calculate her like he calculated odds – he was usually very good at it. And the money was hers of course, all hers. And there was a lot of it, she had to admit . . . *Spend it, hide it if you want, buy Jessie a new coat, treat Stevie for his birthday. Save it. All yours, I don't want a penny.*

Never trust a gambler bearing gifts.

Oh Ren, he used to say. Just *oh Ren*, which meant 'I'm sorry' and 'I'm such a fool' and 'please don't kick me when I'm trying', and 'aren't you just a bit impressed?' No one else ever called her Ren. A charm of finches. A string of ponies.

Two days later it was gone. She'd hidden the notes ever so carefully in the old copy of *Treasure Island* and the book at the back of the crock cupboard in the kitchen. Vicky's letter was still folded neatly inside, with Pearl's card and the other card, the card that Vicky had sent her. He had even tied the ribbon back. A temptation of greyhounds, a glitter of gamblers.

There was a long queue in Newbury post office. Rene was glad she wasn't wearing her land-girl uniform, she would have stood out. Besides, she had resigned from the Land Army – another letter – they would want the uniform back, but she hoped she could keep the boots. The queue waited patiently; they were a girl down behind the counter and everyone wanted their money's worth when they reached the front – no one wanted anything as simple as postage stamps. Across the road from the post office was the Majestic; the programme started at two: *Three Girls and a Boat* and then the main feature, *The Black Cat*.

Those last weeks in Manchester had gone by at such speed, but at the very end everything slowed right down and separated and each bit was perfectly, painfully clear – even now she didn't understand how they fitted together.

She was standing outside Bertha's. How helpless she must have looked, and Bertha poised on her spick-and-span doorstep. 'Take the whole afternoon, don't you dare come back before six. Are you going to the pictures?'

Sitting on the tram, Rene wondered about Bertha. Today Bertha had set her free, looking after the children, cooking a meal for Alan that Rene would carry back home, wrapped in a towel. She couldn't have been kinder, and Rene was grateful but there was always a rub. 'Do you need money?' she had asked. 'I can always help you out.' And Bertha was too careful not to tot it all up. Somewhere, Rene thought, everything was reckoned and it went back years. Did she do the same with Ernest, she wondered, would he one day receive a bill? He was a good few years older than Bertha – he might die before he could settle up. What did Bertha make of married life? She and Ernest seemed to get on perfectly well in their way. She was meek with Ernest, careful, but it didn't quite ring true. Oh Bertha, Bertha. The problem with having your hands free for a couple of hours, thought Rene, was that it freed up your head in ways you didn't want.

At the Belmont, Rene sank gratefully into the smoky dark. A film was just ending, a young woman standing on the deck of a great ship, looking out to sea, anguish in her eyes. She crosses to the other side of the deck and looks down, not at the glassy water but at the busy quay – for the ship hasn't left harbour yet. There she stands, poised between port and starboard, till the great ship honks. The woman drops her bag, rushes down the ramp and through the crowd, runs to a man, his arms outstretched. The music told her this was happy.

The next picture started. Rene stretched out and settled more deeply into her seat, only half-aware of the antics on the screen. If her life and Alan's were a film, it wouldn't be a comedy, she thought, more of a 'women's picture'. The marriage a series of struggles and disappointments, she would be on the brink of something and then, out of nowhere, a terrible accident would leave her hovering between life and death. He would take a solemn oath never to gamble again and she would wake up in a white hospital. He would squeeze her hand, and she would smile, his reward. A new start.

The next picture was better, a western: a great train of covered wagons travelling west. There were plenty of dangers – snakes and Indians and fast-running rivers – but it was a small price to pay for a better life. Joan Bennett was the heroine, with her new dark hair and a no-nonsense manner. She had dyed it for another film, but

Rene had read in *Picturegoer* that Miss Bennett enjoyed her life much more as a brunette. She liked Joan Bennett. Vicky had written a film for her, *Look Away Now!*

In Vicky's film, Joan witnessed a horrible murder and had to go into hiding. She had cut her own hair, dyed it dark and disappeared. She couldn't remember what happened at the end, except that Joan escaped. Scenario by Mona Verity. For Vicky was no longer an actress, her face had disappeared. Now it was only her name on the screen – script by, story by, Vicky's stories, Mona's words – to Rene this was just more magic.

But the next picture had started and she was losing track. This was the one that had been playing when she arrived – she recognized the girl. It seemed to take an age, but finally the girl reached the quay where her ship was waiting, with its far horizon. She strode up the steep ramp, brisk and assured. Rene stood up. The girl took a deep breath, walked across the deck and looked out to sea – how wide, how possible, her cue. Rene turned away from the screen and strode up the aisle, came blinking into the light.

'I love the ending, don't you?' the usherette said. 'So romantic.'

Rene didn't answer.

It was only four o'clock when she came out of the cinema. She didn't want to go back yet, Bertha would be annoyed.

So she wandered about the streets. Everything seemed very loud, very bright. Eventually she found herself at the entrance of the indoor market. Her head was like tangled wool. Sweet-bitter: she spied the stall where she'd bought the cufflinks that Alan had sold, the milk bar with the high stools where she had brought Jessie and Stevie. Next to the milk bar was a new stall, a table, covered with oilcloth and a banner tied around it: WOMEN'S LAND ARMY. There were two girls talking to another girl, older, sitting behind the table. The two girls were giggly, silly, the type Rene had no patience with these days. They were in light summer dresses, the kind she used to wear. The Land Army girl was wearing a smart green V-neck jersey over a shirt and matching green tie. She'd taken off her felt hat – her only concession to the heat – and it sat beside her on the table, still part of her uniform. The girls giggled and Rene walked past – she felt pushed out. She walked down to the end of the market, past the stall that had the pies Alan liked. Then she turned and walked back up the aisle. The Land Army girl was on her own now; she looked up and smiled.

'Would you like a cup of tea?'

Rene hovered, uncertain, strings beginning to pull.

'You'd be doing me a favour really. I'm dying for one. Go on, sit down, I'll be back in a minute. Don't worry, I won't try and recruit you.'

The girl jumped to her feet on the instant, leaving her felt hat behind on the table. She was wearing what she and Lily used to call bicycles and Bertha called bloomers. They looked pretty silly but the girl didn't seem to mind.

'Can I help you, er, miss?'

She had finally reached the end of the post-office queue, and now here she was, standing at the counter, looking at the man through blotchy glass. Gradually, as if someone was turning up the wireless, she became aware of the noise behind her.

'Miles away,' he said, half under his breath, but Rene's quick hearing caught him and she smiled ruefully.

'Sorry. Just stamps.'

Letters posted, Rene treated herself to a bun and a pot of tea, did some bits of travel shopping and managed to miss the bus. The next one wasn't for an hour and a half.

She'd still be back at Starlight by the end of the afternoon, but she didn't want Elsie to have any reason to wonder or worry. Then she remembered that Miss Troughton and Miss Lyle had a telephone, the only people on Sheepdrove to do so. She found a box and gave the address to the operator.

'Lambourn 8274?'

She felt nervous all of a sudden and shy.

'Oh, Miss Troughton?'

'Yes. Who's speaking, please?'

'This is Rene Hargreaves. I work with Miss Boston at Starlight.'

'Oh, hello. Yes?'

Perhaps Miss Troughton was wondering where she was.

'I hope you don't mind. The thing is I'm in Newbury and I've missed my bus. I won't be back till quite a bit later. I wonder if you could . . .'

'You'd like me to pop along and tell her.' Miss Troughton was quite at ease. 'Of course I can. I'll step out just now. What time shall I tell her that you'll be back?'

'Half past five, maybe quarter to six. Thank you.'

'No trouble at all. If you don't mind me saying so, I think it's such a shame about the farm.'

'Oh, yes,' Rene said.

Rene sat at the back of the bus going home. She tried to look through the steamed-up window; thinking of Elsie at Starlight, she wondered if Miss Troughton had knocked on the front door or climbed over the gate into the yard.

She found Elsie waiting for her, quite excited. 'Miss Troughton came with your message, how kind.' So she was pleased then. That evening they took a break from the sorting and the lists: they listened to a concert and played Patience after – it was the first time in weeks. And Elsie seemed less far away and Rene was less fearful of what it might mean to take her somewhere else, to dig her up. 'I want to leave now, Rene, as soon as we can. I don't want to wait for the Townsends' (Phil was keeping his distance). And then they were back to their sorting and packing and eating chicken and more chicken. 'We are eating chicken recklessly,' declared Elsie, and even Smoke and Missy grew sick of it. Miss Troughton and Miss Lyle were delighted to take a dozen chickens. They also took Pickwick. Elsie warned them about his bad temper, but they were not to be daunted. 'We have a goat,' said Miss Lyle, and no one could say fairer than that. The two ladies insisted on giving her £10 for Pickwick, which paid for all the trains and more besides. 'That's the first time he's ever helped with a journey,' Elsie said, and they laughed together for the first time in ages. Smoke was too old to come with them, Elsie said, and it was Rene who tentatively suggested they offer him to Colonel Pinkie. 'He's a bit like me, isn't he?' the sunset colonel said, making the joke Rene didn't quite dare to.

He bought the wireless too and paid well over the odds. They could take Missy with them though. A cat could be put in a basket, fitted in, accommodated; besides, she was a Starlight cat, a link, Rene thought. For Rene wasn't light about moving on either. She had settled here and time ran thick. Elsie and Starlight had given her years of memories.

*　*　*

The station was crowded and full of uniforms.

There was far more than they could possibly eat and the children were confused by the profusion. Jessie had peeked inside the greaseproof packets and seen that some of the sandwiches had paste: warm, fishy, delicious. There were apples and shortbread, there were even cherry lemons in a crumpled, airy paper bag and, as a special treat, Rene had bought ginger beer in the kiosk by the platform. They were early of course. Jessie and Stevie took it in turns to gallop little Mikey down the platform on his reins. Though he tottered and staggered he was getting pretty fast. He was squawking and far too excited, but Rene didn't have the heart to stop them.

She found a compartment where there was just one passenger – a smart elderly lady – and Rene asked haltingly if she would be kind enough to keep an eye on Jessie and Stevie. The old lady looked rather fiercely down her long nose at them, as if her nostrils might smoke, but if she was a dragon, she was a friendly one. Certainly, certainly, she said, where were they going?

She was travelling a good deal further. A sensible idea to get the children out of the city; she was sure that they were very well-behaved children. 'We're very well behaved,' said Jessie, eager to be helpful, 'aren't we, Mum?' Rene settled Jessie and Stevie at the two window seats and tried to tidy up the bags and jackets. Mikey was really struggling now and she had to put him down on the floor; he made a lunge for the door and fell heavily. For a moment he was quiet, then he started to howl. Rene scooped him up and got a tight grip on his kicking legs; in reply he started pulling at her hat and her hair. His cheek was hot and soft against hers, tears trickled down their faces, and she licked at them, trying to make him smile.

The children had a piece of paper with Granny's address, just in case there was a problem with the train.

'What kind of problem?' asked Jessie.

'There won't be. It's for just in case.'

'What kind of problem?' said Stevie.

'Mum said there won't be,' said Jessie, helpfully.

'Oh,' said Stevie, still looking confused.

Rene wanted to laugh, just for a moment – weren't they funny, weren't they clever? She was full of pride, but the words wouldn't come and she kept licking at Mikey's tears.

'Why's he crying?' asked Stevie.

'Because he knows you're thirsty,' Rene said, leaning forward and pressing Mikey's wet face against Stevie's. But Stevie didn't like this, and roughly rubbed his own face dry. There was still too much time.

'Mum, what about the bottles?'

Rene had promised to open them once they were settled on the train, and had brought a bottle opener with her for this very purpose. Nothing had been forgotten or left to chance.

Inside her head words gushed, like the cool fizzing of the overflowing bottle, but they died on her lips. All around them, it seemed, energy was pulsing, but it was waiting too, everyone was waiting. A pair of shrill girls clattered up and down the platform, peering in at the windows of the train, looking for someone. A whistle went somewhere, far up the other end of the station.

'Mum, Mum, you must get off now. The train will go.'

'That's not our train, dear,' said the dragon, kindly, 'our train doesn't go till quarter past, you've a few minutes yet.'

But Jessie wouldn't settle.

'I think you should get off now. Please, Mum.'

'Get off, get off. Time to go,' said Stevie.

On the platform, she waved Mikey's pudgy hand for him.

'Come on, Mikey, wave bye-bye.'

Again she licked at tears. Her and Mikey's faces were slippery, stinging.

The doors slammed and the whistle went and she waved Mikey's pudgy hand for him. 'Say bye, Mikey . . . say bye-bye.'

And then she was standing outside Bertha's house again, and Bertha on her doorstep. Her arms reached out to take Mikey.

Bertha thinks that I need a bit of a change.

And then back home to scrub the house and leave the letter for Alan. She had written it last night, everything explained, so tidy, except that it was burning in her pocket: *I'm not sure how long I'll be away but I will write again.*

* * *

It was the first time they had ever been in a car together, and they were squashed apart by the luggage and the sharp angles of Missy's basket.

Once she got in the car, Rene didn't look back, she didn't wish to trespass. Elsie looked – how couldn't she – and saw for the last time the square house with its scrimping windows. In the porch were a white space and a hook where the photograph had been. Elsie kept looking, she didn't blink. There was the gate, off-kilter, with the hard, dry tracks beneath, the wallflowers growing high and wild over the hedge. She looked back till they reached the end of Sheepdrove and the taxi turned away from the Townsend place. It was only then that she turned away and came to face forward. Her eyes were full of tears, but in her mind was a picture of Rene: the first time she had seen her, sitting on the bench in the porch. She held the image in her eyes like a charm.

Moving On

8

Peripatetic

The pig is a friend, the cattle's breath
Mingles with mine in the still lanes;
I wear it willingly like a cloak
To shelter me from your curious gaze.

R. S. Thomas, 'The Hill Farmer Speaks',
Collected Poems 1945–1990

At Heathwater, Cumberland, 1943–7

PLAN YOUR FUTURE, SAVE WITH A PLAN. *I Know Where I'm Going!*

'All the way from Berkshire? That's near London, isn't it? Why d'you come so far?'

The woman sounded suspicious, or that was how it felt.

'I used to live . . . in Manchester,' Rene said.

'Oh. Well, I don't know . . . cities, places like that.'

Rene thought everything had been settled by letter, but now it seemed there was another test.

'But you know farming?'

'Yes, we know farming.'

Rene did the talking, by agreement. She was good at reassuring echoes.

'We're farm workers.'

This was the formula they'd decided on, not so far from the truth of before. No deliberate deception; CARELESS TALK.

'I don't want to talk about Starlight,' Elsie had said.

'We don't have to.'

'I wouldn't like to have to explain.'

99

So Elsie sat quietly and wondered about Mrs Parks's hair: so red; she'd never seen anyone with hair that colour before.

All reasonable work considered. They were taken on till the end of the summer – better than nothing. Muriel Parks was from Yorkshire, and perhaps there was something in Rene's voice – neighbour if not friend – that recalled a familiar antipathy.

They got a cottage: two rooms, one bed, tiny and filthy, but it was *independent accommodation.*

The journey to London had been dreadful, squashed tight in a corridor all the way from Reading, and Rene trying and failing to cheer Elsie up.

IS YOUR JOURNEY REALLY NECESSARY?

Coming into Paddington there had been a shrieking complication of tracks, blackened buildings bearing down, gaps like sudden ghosts between. Then they had to travel halfway across London to catch the other train. Rene had kept this part of the journey to herself till they reached Paddington, and Elsie didn't thank her for it. As they criss-crossed the city, she said nothing, keeping her attention entirely on Missy, who was sulking in her basket. She hated the thought of another train journey, ever so much longer.

In the event, the northern train was half empty and Elsie sank with relief into the seat by the window.

FOOD, FUEL AND MUNITIONS MUST COME FIRST.

Rene couldn't lead Elsie into the unknown, but Cumberland wasn't exactly somewhere she knew. Leo had worked up at a big hotel on Windermere the summer after Dad died; Bertha and her mum had gone to visit him. It was better than nothing. Rene thought she'd be grateful for landmarks, but she hadn't realized that the names of places could be so painful. You could change for Manchester anywhere, or so it seemed, and worse was the slew of other names, part of the unexpected stuffing of her old life. The whiskery guard's voice rang out unexpectedly clear and the train beat them out, over and over: Nelson, Blacko, Foulridge, Coppull, Ribble Valley, Nether Valley, Bolton-le-Sands. And there were so many stations.

She had settled them on the train and waved goodbye, but the children were waiting for her on the platforms now. Usually it was just a glimpse in a waiting room: a girl with big eyes and neatly tied hair peering at her through the murky glass. But once she saw the three of them quite distinctly on the platform opposite, sitting on a bench, the two older ones flanking Mikey. And then another train came in, blocking her view, and she forced herself to focus on Elsie, whose nose was now pressed to the other window, totally absorbed, the journey to London for the moment quite forgotten.

LET US GO FORWARD TOGETHER.

At the end of the summer, Muriel asked them to stay on till the spring, and she was glad to have them: both her husband and son were fighting, and though the news was improving no one knew when the men would return. They made an odd pair, but no one could say they didn't pull their weight: they'd done up the cottage and Elsie had worked wonders with Muriel's garden.

For Rene and Elsie, there was little more than relief at first, but it was good hard work and they did well with the sheep and the long distances, often together, sometimes apart. They liked the dark scarring rocks, the sudden falls and streams; they liked the houses beside the lake that seemed to eye each other sidelong, so cool and white. In time, they even learnt to see the smirks and rages in the faces of the tors. At Heathwater, field, hedge and farm stretched out comfortably, like a cat enjoying the sun. Parks Farm occupied 150 acres of mainly flat and verdant grassland; lucky land – no wonder the sheep skipped, danced and multiplied. Rene saw it through Elsie's eyes: so different. The comparison was there, faint and melancholic: no dreamy, still chalk pools; no dry field paths among the grasses. But there was also much to like, most of all their Sunday walks and occasionally rides (from somewhere Muriel found them two old bicycles, suitable only for ladies of twenty years ago, so heavy and sedate). At a brisk pace, and if they set out early, they could make Coniston Water by midday. A longer journey, by bus, for Rene to get to the Regal in Ulverston, but she still tried to go every week.

A new kind of life and it wasn't easy. They had to plan and didn't dare, they wanted to feel at ease but couldn't risk it and there was no way back. On their last but one night at Starlight, they had raised a big bonfire, Elsie's idea: all manner of papers from the backs of drawers, her father's farming magazines, Bert's letters from the first war and hers, a copy of *David Copperfield* – won for her reading – a half-dozen cheap romances discovered behind the dresser (Moira's?). It was a kind of ending. If there had been wires to cut, Elsie would have cut them. If there was ever a time for sabotage, it was then. The Townsends would never have full possession. What Elsie kept of her past and took: her chequebook (never used again), the *Smallholder's Handbook*, the uncut Bible, given to her the year before she failed the exam – she couldn't burn that, any more than she would leave it for Phil and George. These things she took, along with her card and her ration book and her gun, the photograph from the porch and all her clothes and boots stuffed into a navy tin trunk. The trunk was so heavy but she still felt hollow inside.

Elsie, for all her pride, had known she was not a free agent. Weather of course, weather above all, but it didn't do to forget the man at the bank, the weekly mart, they could all pull her strings. Sometimes the strings were slack, but it didn't do to forget them. Now, it seemed, they were also subject to the whims of Muriel Parks. Their time here was always going to come to an end; it was hard not to be waiting.

'It won't be for a while yet.' Rene didn't want Elsie to worry, but she couldn't make promises – the memory of Ainsley was still too strong.

'And besides, there are other Muriels, lots of them. They need us.'

'A row of Muriels.'

They both laughed at that. What a thought, for Muriel seemed to Elsie quite extraordinary, with her purple-and-green plaid scarf and her soft boots. No farmer, no farmer's wife, come to that, with her tortoiseshell slides and bright red hair.

'There'll always be plenty of work. Round here too, if we like it.'

'Yes.'

They were out together that day, checking the sheep. The neighbouring farm had been losing a lot of lambs to foxes. It seemed to get worse every year. Old Mr Latimer had been out with his gun and his grandson night after night, but with no success. Muriel was on the brink of having all her sheep brought back in, and sure enough in one of Latimer's fields they found a recent kill. Damson had whined and whimpered.

It was a horrible sight, the little lamb's legs were still running, a collar of pinky red around its neck. Rene turned away blinking, but over the past couple of months Elsie had also softened. They had bottled some of the weaker ones in the cottage – much to Missy's annoyance – set them to sleep in a basket beside the stove, wrapped in old scraps of flannel. The lambs made such a funny noise when they sucked at the bottles.

'Poor little thing.'

They walked on through the soft drizzle and clambered over the ditch that took them back on to the Parkses' land. Damson stayed close to Rene's side; his big brown eyes gleamed wet and sad. They were pretty high up now, and from where they stood they could see the lake. Elsie paused, stayed very still for some moments, looking, listening. From somewhere in the distance came the sound of a hawfinch – Rene knew it well by now, it sounded just like scissors cutting through fabric. Across the lake the wind was getting up – the clouds were on the move – and the light was starting to fade.

'It's the right time,' Elsie said.

'What for? What are you going to do?'

'I'm going to send the foxes away.'

'Send them away?'

What could she mean?

'How are you planning to do that?' Rene asked.

'An old remedy.'

'What?'

'You'll never believe me if I tell you.' Elsie smiled briefly but she was serious. 'You need to stay here and keep hold of Damson. I won't be long.'

'But what are you going to do?'

'Shhhh.' Elsie was already off up the field, 'I'll be back soon.'

So Rene sat down on the grass and waited quietly. She smoked a cigarette and tickled Damson's ears till his dark eyes filled up with happiness. 'Silly dog,' she said, and he whined his approval and lay down in the grass, oddly patient. She listened out for the hawfinch, but he had stopped with his scissors. It started to get colder, the sheep turned darker, the lambs slowed. Rene waited, the dog still and sleepy beside her; she teased out some shreds of wool and plaited them idly, brown and white and brown. Then, from some way away, she thought she heard singing; it sounded far away but she couldn't be sure, and she couldn't tell from what direction it came.

'Elsie?' her voice called quietly into the dimming.

But there was no reply.

She stood up and looked around but there was no sign of anyone. The song stopped, and after a few minutes began again. It was not quite singing, she thought, more like chanting. An incantation? She felt sleepy then, for all that it was getting chill, and, like Damson, she lay down patiently in the grass, sure that Elsie would soon be back.

There were no more problems with foxes that year. It didn't go unnoticed. A year passed. A good year, they could approach the coming winter with a little more confidence. They were saving, just – coin and coupons. They called it the Christmas jar, but it was insurance really. Damson lived with them now, not officially their dog, but he had made his choice. Muriel had doted on him, had soaped and rubbed him in her tin bath to bring out the purple in his dark fur. He had never liked that. Now he curled up by Elsie's chair and tried to slink into their bedroom when no one was looking. A good year. And on Christmas Eve they stayed up late and spiced pears and roasted chestnuts.

If Muriel was resentful about Damson, she said nothing, except that Elsie was a wonder with animals. And sometimes people came up from the village on Saturdays now with limp, furry creatures wrapped in towels, children some of them, or Elsie was asked if she could come and have a look at a cow or a pig or a pony.

Slim pickings for the Christmas jar, but she often came back to the cottage with a nice big ham or a round of cheese. 'I'd rather have the wireless,' she said, for she missed her old friend terribly and they were trying to save up for another.

Muriel brought them their news now and it wasn't the same: her voice seemed to echo and vibrate. They missed the bland tones of the man in London, speaking so carefully, so clear.

'You know, I think she's lonely,' Rene said, after one of Muriel's visits.

Less easy-mannered than Rene, Elsie found Muriel's presence trying. 'Why does she come *here*? She's so friendly with Josie Rogers and Ivy whatever her name is. But she doesn't spend half as much time with them as she does here, with us.'

'She's the one who calls them friends,' said Rene. 'Anyway, I don't think it's that. Josie and Ivy are like her, aren't they?'

'She doesn't seem very like them.' Elsie was in a good mood but she was rarely concessionary. Oh, that red hair.

'No, I mean they're on their own too. I know Josie has the land girls, but they're in the village and she's not one to mix with people she doesn't know. No, I think they're all a bit lost. We're not like that.' Rene had maybe run on a little further than she intended.

It was easy to be lonely at a busy table. Elsie knew that.

'No, we're not like that.'

'We have each other.'

'Yes, we have each other.' Elsie had caught Rene's echoes and suddenly she was bold: 'I'm glad.'

'*I'm* glad.'

Elsie made a show of carrying on with the clearing-up. For all that she had spoken first, it wasn't easy to hear the same words said back.

WE WILL GO FORWARD TOGETHER.

The lake pulled them, as it pulled everyone. In Coniston there was a place that called itself a museum but looked like a shed. On the front door, there was a framed picture of a man in a blaze of spiky orange sunlight. Under the picture, covered in plastic, was a notice about opening times. They stood by the lapping, slopping shore; the lake was sleeping, waiting, waiting for the war to be over. The patrols, regular as cat's cradle, only touched the surface, though there was still talk about the German airmen, just boys really, whose bodies had been washed up three days after a spectacular night-time crash.

And there was a disorienting familiarity to be found in some things, the big low skies reminding Elsie of the valley and Starlight. She saw the farm from a distance now, as if she were standing at the bottom of the track that dipped and rose in a ribbon up the hill. Many less painful things were familiar, for they knew the rites and figures of war from elsewhere; here too were the ugly pill-boxes, the ration queues, the late-summer lanes suffused with groups of children and later still with the shrill of land girls. Here too, it seemed, women were steady and enduring and men arrived and left with little warning. Muriel told them how the Coniston hedgerows had grown the whole nation's children strong with rosehips. In the cottage, they ate patriotic 'perchines' from Windermere, canned by wild girls rumoured to swim naked in the lake.

On a bright May day in 1945, Rene and Elsie climbed through a wood full of bluebells, in search of High Light Tor. At the top, the views were spectacular, but the wind soon had them huddled in the tor's shadow. A little while later, a small troop of walkers bobbed over the crest of the hill. Politely, they coughed their presence and settled at a distance. Elderly, practised with their sticks and map; no war was going to stop them, no wind either.

The ramblers were not proprietary – if asked they would have declared that the countryside was for everyone. Nevertheless, they made the two women uncomfortable and they soon stood up, Rene gave up her hard-lit cigarette, and they half nodded a goodbye before returning the way they'd come. As Rene looked back, she glimpsed three small shadow children clambering over the tor – only Mikey grew bigger – still the fear of them falling.

As the two women disappeared from view, a horde of rooks rose, cawing and cackling. Some little time later, one of the ramblers followed Rene and Elsie's path to the edge and looked over. No sign of the rooks which had spun away, but he did catch sight of the two ladies who had been by the tor. They had reached the trickiest part of the hill some way below. The taller of the two was slightly ahead. She paused, then turned to help her companion, reaching out her hand. The shorter one grasped it, but she must have been a little nervous for she kept hold of it as they continued down the hills. Not an experienced walker, clearly.

'A gloom of rooks, isn't it?' said Rene.

'A murder, I thought.'

On VE Day, they sneaked off before daybreak to avoid Muriel and spent the day by the lakeside with sandwiches and beer and powdery biscuits. They found a grand place on a little grassy promontory, just outside Coniston, not too close to the excitement. They caught the happy mood and waved and helloed the tour-boat as it came and went, quite a set of calls back and forth, back and forth. Sailboats always looked like a festival. They cheered the boats as they went by – Elsie needed a little encouragement – decorated with streamers and flags. Boys leapt from the pier, knees to chest, shrieking at the dark, cold, cold water. And they cheered them too. The kingfisher, always promised by the tour-boat captain but rarely seen, chose this day to appear. Flitting close by Rene and Elsie, apparently casual, he stabbed at the water and disappeared, reappearing, moments later, with a silver, shiny fish. How they cheered; it would feed them for hours.

Good news at last for Muriel: Mr Parks and her son would soon be on their way home. Muriel was hoping her son would settle in Cuthbert Cottage – it could be a new start for him. As evening approached, Rene and Elsie sat on by the lake, not sure what to do with themselves. They didn't want to leave, not yet, but the scene was no longer so pleasing. Everything had looked so gay, but there was no one over at the pier now and the flags and bunting were forlorn, just a few boats left on the water, someone singing.

> *When the lights go on again all over the world*
> *And the boys are home again all over the world*

Their own settlement with its remnants of picnic and mackintosh squares also said that the party was over. Earlier they had taken turns to read the detective aloud to each other, Rene had a real gift for it, but now it lay cover up, silent and limp. Elsie was buttoning her cardigan, hunched against the cold.

> *When the lights go on again all over the world*
> *And the ships will sail again all over the world*

So many men were coming home, women too, but there was no going back for Rene and Elsie. Rene tried so hard to look back with Elsie to Starlight, but sometimes the farm melted into mist and there was nothing, nothing behind her at all. Then she felt so heavy, as if her legs were made of lead, and there was no going forward either.

A flurry of letters, two for Rene, one from Manchester – Elsie only found out because Muriel mentioned it and even then she didn't ask – the other from her brother Leo, from Burma of all places. The ways war takes you, thought Rene. *And, you'll never believe it, Rene, but I'm married, to the prettiest little Burmese girl.* Same old Leo: he was planning to settle, there was money to be made, chances to be had. He sent a photo of the wedding with the letter: four rows of brown people and Leo sitting among them, looking thin and sly. She was a very pretty girl, Ruchee, tiny. Were these people her family now?

Rene left Heathwater first: she had to be sure of their next place before Elsie saw it – knew how hard she found leaving. Elsie was left behind to pack up – pain of its own – but Rene reckoned it was better that way.

Cuthbert Cottage
Parks Farm
Heathwater

Dear Rene,

It seems funny writing to you. I don't think I've written to anyone since Bert was in hospital. Well, everything is packed up now and I think I've made a good job. I'll be sad to leave, but as you said, we have to accept that everything is going to be a little topsy-turvy for a while.

Muriel will be sorry to see us go, after everything. Although she's happy to have her boys home, I think she's found it all a bit of a shock. She says she's busier now than she was during the war!

I had a letter from Moira. She sounded as if she was in a bit of a state. I do wonder if she mightn't be ill. I don't know how she traced me here – perhaps it was the colonel. I wrote back to her and gave her our new address. I didn't want to but I felt I had to. I do hope she doesn't want to visit.

I have been thinking so much about Starlight these past couple of weeks. I know you said that I should not look back and I agree, but at the moment I feel upset by it all over.

Missy had her kittens – only three in the end – on our bed! Two girls and a tom. I chose the tom. His name is Silas. I do not particularly like the name, it was Muriel's choice. I feel sorry leaving Missy, but she's too old to move again. I'm not sure she ever forgave us for bringing her here.

The van is arranged now and I will see you next week. I should be with you by the late afternoon.

Elsie

Elsie read the letter back to herself very carefully before she sent it. She always checked the letters she sent. There was still a trace of that girl who had done so well at school, that girl who had written to Bert all those years ago, near the end of another war. Those letters were gone now, burned to ashy nothing in the bonfire. She kept the letters Rene sent to her though, so bold, she thought, so full of news and plans.

Half an hour from the Harrogate Gaumont by bike, uphill most of the way.

DON'T WASTE BREAD.

Home Farm was much bigger than Starlight, or Parks Farm come to that; there wasn't the interest of the lakes, they missed that, but everything was fair. That was how they summed up the Laceys. The Laceys were very steady, very correct; you always knew where you were with them. You couldn't call them slave-drivers, for they slaved themselves first and foremost. There were cattle here, a small herd of doe-eyed Guernseys for the cheese – Elsie took special care of them – but mainly it was sheep. They had their own sheepdog now, Tomkin. They'd paid a guinea for him as a puppy, but Mr Lacey did most of his training; this included some training of Rene and Elsie, which they had all found difficult. Home Farm was deep-tiring work, as Elsie said, but there was satisfaction in that, and it was steady. The two women settled well enough into their new bungalow cottage. It was situated at the top of a steep hill, reached by a narrow, winding lane. The Guernseys were wary coming down the hill; from behind they seemed to tiptoe on their skitty little hooves, their golden bellies swaying.

And then Leo came to visit. *April Showers, He Walked by Night.* Since he'd returned from Burma, he'd been on their tails half a dozen times with letters, wheedling, coaxing, pleading. Rene had tried to put him off. He was too curious about Rene and her friend, and how they were placed; she suspected it was money he was after. Yet there was old affection too and she was susceptible. She was nervous he would ask questions she didn't want to answer, nervous Elsie wouldn't know how to handle him; he certainly wouldn't know how to manage her, shades of George Townsend. She kept putting him off, more and more feebly. In the end she asked Elsie direct.

'I couldn't have said no to Moira,' Elsie said.

And so it was settled.

Thin and left oddly pale by the Burmese sun – 'God, Rene, the heat was something' – Leo was otherwise unchanged, quick-tongued, slippery, still conjuring. (Before the war he'd bought an act lock, stock and barrel from an old magician; now he was hoping to start over.) He'd fallen out with his father-in-law. Ruchee and the baby had been left in Manchester with Bertha, just for a little while, till he found his feet. It must be crowded in Judd Street now, with Mikey there too and Ernest. He waited till they were alone before he told Rene about the children. Mikey was a quiet boy, loved the football, City. 'I should have got a photo' – Rene felt more doors closing. 'Cheer up, Rene.' He hadn't seen Jessie and Stevie – they were still with Alan's sister in Ludlow. Jessie was working and Steve (as he was now) was getting excited about doing his National Service training. That was all. Nearly grown. Rene bit her lip and wondered about the children who waited for her at stations and passed by on trains, glimpsed in windows, so small, so who were they? Her eyes burned, and she picked up her cigarettes and went out into the garden to find Elsie.

He worked hard to be a good visitor at first, he even cooked them some curry – he'd brought a tin of red powder with him. It made their eyes water and Rene sneeze, but they ate it with cold beer and potatoes, and goodwill. He spent part of each day writing letters, at least one a week to Bertha, written at the kitchen table, always with a message for Ruchee and a kiss for the baby, Susan. 'You can't call a baby that colour Susan,' Elsie said to Rene after he showed them a photograph. He wrote other letters too, which came downstairs licked and stamped. He always had stamps, that and tobacco and change for the kiosk. Elsie noticed he didn't have Rene's fine hand-writing. He gave them fifteen shillings a week for his keep at the start.

But it didn't take long for Leo to outstay his welcome. The money dried up, he was never out for any length of time and he got in the way of their quiet evenings. While he was about, they never shared the sofa. Often Leo sprawled there, other times it sat empty – lonely, thought Elsie, like the detectives that lay unread, for Rene was shy of reading aloud when Leo was there. Once or twice, Rene, with Elsie's agreement, gave him money for the pub in Occanby and he was happy to oblige. It was splendid to be back to themselves, hard to forget he wouldn't be gone for long. And when Leo did return from the Duck that first time, he had news they didn't like. They were quite a talking point in the pub, he told them, the ladies at the top of the lane. Elsie looked uncomfortable and Rene wondered about the ladies; Leo clearly enjoyed their discomfort.

And then one day Elsie came back to the cottage and found Leo by the coop. He'd been feeding the chickens, he said, but when he stood up and brushed himself off she thought she heard the clink of something. She followed him back to the cottage, wondering.

Elsie hated thinking quickly, it wasn't her way. She had been going to make a pot of tea, but she didn't want to risk turning her back, so she stood watching him as he sat down at the kitchen table and pulled his chair in close. She heard the clinking sound again, noticed his hand awkward in his jacket pocket. He didn't seem to want to look at her, just started humming a tune.

'You've been stealing,' she said. Her voice sounded loud.

'No, no!' he exclaimed, quite put out. 'It's just a loan, a little loan. I know I should have asked first but I was in a hurry, sorry.' He smiled and shrugged, looking far too comfortable.

Elsie foundered. She didn't know what to say to that.

'Rene wouldn't mind,' he said boldly, looking at her straight, claiming his priority.

Well, she wasn't having that.

She looked back, just as straight. She'd always found it hard to smile at men, especially if they were her age, or younger.

'How much have you taken?'

There was a pause. Elsie sat down at the other end of the table and wondered if he was going to bolt.

But Leo had realized his mistake.

'I don't know,' he fumbled, and started to take the money out of his pockets.

She knew exactly how much was in the tin, to the ha'penny.

He knew pretty well because he'd taken it all.

He continued, nervously, a mass of pockets and patches – there was a guinea in each of his socks. The money made a surly pile in front of him.

The little table had never seemed longer.

He pushed the pile to the centre in a gesture Rene would have recognized. Steadily, Elsie began to draw the coins towards her with a careful forefinger, separating them carefully as she did so. She'd always been good at arithmetic. Before she'd finished counting the coins, he'd got out his shabby wallet and taken out a £5 note, handing it to her directly.

His things were all packed. He'd been planning to get the Knaresborough bus at four. He'd even written a letter for Rene, explaining about the 'loan'.

Slow, quick, slow, slow, quick. Elsie's head was banging. Moira had given up trying to teach her to dance. *You could do it perfectly well, you know . . . you just can't be bothered.* Quick, quick, slow.

When Rene got back to the cottage that evening, Elsie was nowhere to be found. Instead she saw a letter from Leo resting against the stone-cold teapot. There was no sign of him either. She tore it open, half suspecting something.

In writing far tidier than his usual scrawl, Leo explained that he'd had to leave for Manchester that afternoon, something about his magic act and a touring show, and then Rene saw Elsie's name. Elsie had given him £1 for his expenses. He'd write properly soon.

Kind of Elsie. If Rene hadn't been so relieved, she might have wondered about Elsie's generosity or Leo's sudden liking for Elsie's name, but she didn't wonder because she was just so happy that he'd gone.

'Three pounds – that was a lot, Els.'

'He won't make much of a magician,' Elsie said. 'And where's he going to find rabbits for his act now there's mixy everywhere?'

And that should have been that. Except that the following day, the Laceys came up to the cottage, both of them. Leo had broken into the house and Mrs Lacey had caught him trying to steal a pair of antique pistols. He'd been sent off with his tail between his legs, no need to call in the police. The Laceys didn't want any trouble, any unpleasantness, they were sure that Rene and Elsie knew nothing about it. But they couldn't see how the two women could stay on in view of what had happened. Rene and Elsie couldn't see how either.

Cant Farm, St Minver, 1950–52

A brisk cycle to the tiny, cramped Rex in Wadebridge. The programmes didn't always change on time.

BRITAIN CAN MAKE IT.

Their first journey into Cornwall took them to the north coast; their cottage was a direction – past the white cottage – halfway between the village and a cove with wonderful bathing.

Sheep, apples, a bit of this and that. Good people, the Carnes, but struggling, shades of Starlight. A brave new world was supposed to be unrolling: horizons growing, wartime in peacetime, but the message hadn't got through to Cant Farm. Not enough work for the two of them most of the time, and Rene was often away, 'loaned out' for weeks, sometimes months, at a time. Nearly two years of this, and in the end it didn't last. Despite Mr Carne's pledge to die on his own land, he and his wife sold up and moved to Torquay. The new owners were not farmers; they needed the cottage but not Rene and Elsie.

Crew Farm, Coldridge, Crediton, 1952–3

A four-mile walk to Copplestone to catch the bus for the Exeter Regal.

Out of Cornwall, back east to Devon and it felt like another country. Tom Crew, a young man, lame and yellow from fighting in the East, with wandering sunken eyes. His mother had salted some money away and he used this to buy more cattle and, with a careful loan from the bank, invested in the new milking machinery. MODERN WONDERS. For all that Tom Crew tried to look to the future, his eyes couldn't stop wandering: the enemy were everywhere. There was an upset over the rent book and they had to move on. SPIES ARE LISTENING. *The Man Who Watched Trains Go By*, *Trent's Last Case*. Their last farm-cottage: the link in farm-cottage was coming untied.

Back into Cornwall. There had always been daffodils at Lintern, the farmer told them, as they spread and boxed the limp, pale stalks, trying not to touch the flowers, their fingers numb under the gloves. Rene received a letter from Alan's sister: *You may be interested to know that both your children have left my home. It would be better if you were forgotten – you are certainly not forgiven.*

Gull Cottage, Cywednack, St Keverne, 1954–8

Rene loved the ferry that took her across the Helford, then on to Falmouth and the Arden Picture House, once second to none, now growing tatty.

'It's a very small cottage. The second bedroom's just a box room really.'

'Thank you. We'll manage.'

'You're sure you'll be able to manage the rent? We've tried to keep it down but it's not easy these days.'

TELL HER NOTHING. SHE MIGHT BE AN AGENT.

In the years immediately after the war, they were still familiar figures in the landscape – there were so many women without men. Many didn't ask, they just assumed, and the ones who did ask were easy to lead, very slightly, astray.

'So many people who've lost people.'

'Yes.'

'I don't know a soul who didn't lose someone special.'

'You're right about that.'

'Sometimes it still feels like wartime.'

'I know just what you mean.'

In the fields they stayed camouflaged longer than they might have elsewhere. *Timeslip. Tiger in the Smoke.* Over time, though, the questions started to come a bit sharper.

'So are you both on your own?'

And:

'Will you be working or do you have something coming in?'

'Both.'

Both – not quite the truth.

Gull Cottage was not so very different from Heathwater, or Crediton, or Budock. It was the nearest they had ever lived to the sea, and everything was greyish-green and bleached by the salt and wind. The first house in the village, or the last – from the front door you could see the village spread neatly along the road: Mrs Wallace's house with the palm tree in the garden; the general shop, as it was called. From their patch of garden at the back, you could look out across the marram grass to the slaty glimmer of the sea.

Elsie gave up regular farm work now: she wanted to be in walking or cycling distance of the cottage. But if she wished to stay close to home, Rene had to go further afield – there wasn't enough work close by. Often she was away the whole week, coming home dead tired on Friday evening. In St Keverne, Elsie worked as a gardener for an old army man, Major Veesey. A chance meeting in the post office: the major had a beautiful terraced garden at the other end of the village that sank deep into the valley. From the top of his garden you could just see the sea, but by the time you zigzagged down to the bottom, it had vanished out of sight. The major was exacting and inclined to the experimental; Elsie borrowed books from Boots and spent lonely evenings in the cottage, thinking over his proposals. Sometimes she talked to Rene about this and that and the major's plans when she wasn't there. At some point during these years, she had become 'Bert'. Rene had never liked her middle name, but Elsie was very taken with Roberta. And Roberta became Bert. 'Like your brother?' Rene asked. 'Oh no,' said Elsie, 'you're not like him at all.'

'You're a wonder,' the major told Elsie. He wasn't quite sure what to call her – if she'd been a man it would have been her first name, and he couldn't do that. But he was a plain-speaker and 'Miss Boston' was a little fancy. A fine figure of a woman. The major offered Elsie all manner of things from his overstuffed house: a barometer, a nest of prettily inlaid tables he'd brought back from India, a glassed forest scene with a red squirrel. They had no room for such things in Gull Cottage, but she always thanked him carefully. Then came the day when he offered her his old wireless, and she accepted so quickly they were both startled. 'See,' he said, showing her a drawing in a catalogue, 'this is the new one I'm getting. I'll be able to take it to the bottom of the garden. Now that really is something.' Elsie agreed that it was. When Rene came home the following Friday, the wireless had already found a home on the windowsill in the front room. Within a month, Elsie had memorized the schedules and rearranged her early-evening chores to fit with *The Archers*. No Norwegian any more, but Warsaw and Moscow; when she reached them on the dial, she didn't know whether to speed up or linger. Once or twice Elsie heard a programme in the afternoon for older children. It was called *I Want to Be* . . .

Elsie still had her gift, her knack, for growing. Pigs-might-fly gardening, she called it – but the pigs did fly, with good strong wings, in the most unlikely of places. Soft buttery lettuces, spinach and nice fat cucumbers through the summer months – all from a bed that rarely got full sunlight and couldn't be protected from the wind. The cucumber they pickled, to eat with pilchards and mackerel through the winter. Their late-summer treat was tomatoes, ripened on every ledge and sill. All their gardening was aided by generous helpings of Corry's Slug Death. 'You should put up a card in the post office,' said Rene, but Elsie didn't like to be that public. She did any other local work that came her way – the major didn't take up all her time – and she started to breed chickens and, after an interval, rabbits, in larger quantities to sell.

They had no visitors and not many letters. Muriel wrote from time to time and Mrs Carne sent a card at Christmas. The only person who wrote reasonably regularly was Bertha. Sometimes Rene left the letters open on the table; more often they disappeared into her bag and were never seen again. They heard nothing from Leo, but Bertha kept Rene informed. The magic tour had not been a success. She had put her foot down about Ruchee and Susan, and Leo had come to take them away; since then, she hadn't heard a word.

Nothing from Lambourn: there was no one to write to them and Elsie wouldn't like the news. The valley was changing. More stables, more horses, fields opened, hedgerows scorched, the less recalcitrant downlands reclaimed. Ainsley had been right about

Berkshire at least: modern methods were thriving. The Townsends were bought out, the cuckoos ousted. Another miserable seaside retirement: Phil slow-stepping, with a stick in one hand and George on his arm. George, resentful, furious, still hoping, wondering if there was any money he didn't know about, still looking about himself, as he crawled along beside his uncle. Elsie's revenge.

Good years for Rene and Elsie, hard but good. The only thing it seemed to be difficult to grow was money. PLAN YOUR FUTURE. SAVE WITH A PLAN. Sometimes they would take less than they were owed just to have money – but the jar and later the tin, an old black tea-tin patterned with pink and yellow flowers, remained stubbornly half empty. They rented themselves to the harvest, joining the mesh of locals and strangers. With the other hired hands, they enjoyed the work, left to themselves, trusted to get on with it, part of the fizz and buoyancy, hearing little eddies of talk and laughter as they worked late into the night. A rich pleasure for Elsie, deep and uncomplicated. But Rene, seeing her fellow workers' faces up close, found a heavy mirror. So many were no longer young, some were struggling with the work, and yet she could see they would never settle to the comforts of the new council houses. At the almshouses in Heathwater, Rene gloomily remembered the sign ALL VISITORS MUST REPORT TO THE WARDEN. At best, old age was a room in a boarding house owned by the council, tea at five, cocoa at half past eight; two rooms – she doubted they'd be allowed to share. There would be other rules, inspections probably. Living under other people's eyes, she and Elsie would become strangers. She found herself getting to an ending like this far too often. It cast her very low and she found she could say nothing about it to Elsie.

Travelling to and from Gull Cottage on bus or bicycle, in and out of the shops, the post office, there were more and more signs, more messages, far more than the war. Some of them spoke so direct – CLEVER YOU – and you were sure they must be talking to you especially, but then you looked closer and realized they couldn't be – CLEAN YOUR TEETH. Occasionally she felt the person they were talking to was standing just beside her – WIVES! She couldn't really justify the cost, but she still bought magazines when she could. Many of the stars she had known as a girl had died – she hadn't seen mention of Vicky – of Mona – for years.

Rene and Elsie knew better than to get too comfortable at Gull Cottage, but that didn't make leaving any easier when it came. The owners could see the future, holiday lets were the coming thing, they were going to clear a path down to the beach, a driveway for a car.

Major Veesey was very sorry to see Elsie go. 'Will you come back in the autumn to help me tidy up?'

In the event they didn't go far. Rene kept her dairying job.

When I was a young girl, I went to live at Starlight Farm, Lambourn, Berkshire, with my parents. When I was about thirty years of age my father made the farm over to me by deed of gift.

In June 1940, Miss Hargreaves came to the farm as my land girl and I have known her ever since.

In 1958, we came to live at Wheal Rock, Rosenys . . .

9.

Wheal Rock

The cottage was a ruin when they took it.

The agent drove them over from Falmouth in a rickety old Ford. 'No one's lived here in a while,' he said, as they bumped up the lane. As he got out of the car he flourished the key, but it turned out to be unnecessary: the door was set a little ajar. It was stiff too and wedged into hardened sludge; Rene and he had to prise it open.

Inside, the kitchen was sticky and dark with grease, and in the little sitting room the walls were dappled with mould. There was a coat of reddish hairs on the sofa, and a dense smell which led with an animal reek and ended in damp.

The agent directed them up the tiny staircase – there wasn't room for three. Elsie led the way. Upstairs, she walked straight across the bedroom to the tiny window and looked out at the fields beyond. Rene lingered in the doorway, staring at the fantastical map stains on the bed; a stack of mouldering linen had been left, forgotten, on the floor.

'You can't see the chimney from here,' Elsie said, pushing the window open and sticking her head right out. There was a heavy, fluttering sound of birds disturbed from the eaves.

Rene watched her.

Elsie craned her neck sharply to the right.

'Oh yes, I can see it now. It's so tall. I wonder when the mine closed, it must have been a long time ago, there's no sign of any-thing recent. Did you see how the ground was red from the mine?' She was babbling.

'So you like it then?' Rene said, smiling.

'The chimney? Oh, you mean the cottage? Oh yes.'

Elsie withdrew from the window and turned to Rene. 'What about you, Bert? Do you like it? Should we take it?'

She was excited and it fell to Rene to sound a note of caution.

'Did you see the state of those walls? And the kitchen?'

Elsie nodded but she didn't look downcast. 'It's a lot of work,' she said. 'I know it's a lot of work and we'd have to make do with the furniture.'

'Which is dreadful.'

'Which is dreadful.'

'And probably rotten.'

'Yes.'

But Elsie had set her heart on the place, that was clear.

'I'm sure we can set it to rights,' Rene said. There was something here that reminded her of Starlight – the sky, neat fields that gave way to wilder ground. When the new villas were being built on Sheepdrove, all those years ago, the chalk had fought back and the dust had turned everything white. Elsie had told her how her hair went white, how the cows had coughed and faded. Old Alfred, he had been alive then, had wheezed, everything frosted with dust, the edges of the house faded like an old picture. She could see Elsie standing at the gate, young with her white hair.

LET US GO FORWARD TOGETHER.

When they came down to tell the agent, he seemed surprised that they'd reached a decision so quickly; he had two other places to show them, one was in Helston and . . .

But this was the place they wanted.

'The second bedroom's just a box room,' he said.

They hadn't even noticed the other bedroom.

'You'll have your work cut out.'

Elsie walked past him into the sitting room. Rene still did most of this type of talking.

'We'll soon bring it right,' Rene said.

'It's a bit isolated. You're a good couple of miles from the village here.'

But they knew that, he had told them already. Perhaps he was put out by their resolve.

'Oh, we're used to that.'

'Yes, we're used to that,' chimed Elsie from the window.

They made him nervous, his clammy hand when he said good-bye confirmed it. Hardly more than a boy, but it didn't stop him being curious: his eyes travelled between them, uncertain of their relation and uneasy.

The owner agreed to replace the windows and supply a stove; the rest was up to them. They went to work quickly, cleaning and painting and mending and fixing as they tried to secure another out-post. They salvaged most of the furniture, scrubbing and scrubbing and sanding it on the flattish ground beside the house – it was a good thing the summer was so warm and dry. They had to take the bed apart, and Rene wondered – as they wrestled the frame down the stairs – if they'd be able to set it back together. But they did. They always managed – well, nearly always. They turned a rickety cupboard into some slightly less rickety shelves. They took the little sofa completely to pieces: there was nothing to do about the springs, but they replaced part of the wooden frame, and Elsie made new cushions which they stuffed with horsehair. It would never be com-fortable, said Rene, but at least it looked nice, and they could sit down together in the evenings. Most of what was in the kitchen was unusable though, and scant savings had to be spent replacing pots and pans and crockery.

Vinegar, then bleach for the mould, and then they rubbed at the walls with the bristle brush till their backs and shoulders ached. ADD BRIGHTNESS TO CLEANNESS. They tried the same medicine on the floor and the walls of the kitchen, with less success. 'At least we can paint the walls,' Elsie said, but the kitchen resisted most of their efforts. It was clean but it still looked filthy. The whole place smelt of vinegar and bleach. The vinegar prickled at throats and eyes, the bleach went lung-deep. CLEAN AND CLEAR. Nib, Elsie's little black cat, sniffed her disapproval. She spent the sunny days basking in an old trough by the gatepost. But in time the smell of chlorine faded and Nib came inside and spent her afternoons on the sofa. The days were getting shorter, but it was still sunny and the rain stayed off. The cottage came to smell of paint (with an undertone of damp). The paint made Elsie heady; it reminded her of Starlight all those years ago, before the field recorder came. Then, the smell of paint had crept into the house and she had disliked it; now, it wafted out through the windows, vital and pungent – a sign of new life.

And Elsie was making good progress. She was on her own now in the days as Rene was working away at a big dairy farm the other side of Helston. But though she missed Rene, there was such pleasure in showing her what she'd done in the evenings: a new board on the stairs, another set of ingenious curtains made of old shirts and sheeting, the shine she eventually got on the tin bath, inside and out. And Rene, exhausted as she was, from the early rise and the long cycle ride, never failed to enjoy it all, even if she sometimes had trouble keeping her eyes open.

She had borrowed the bike from Mrs Cuff, who owned the post-office shop in Rosenys. And it was through Mrs Cuff that she and Elsie had got the big sack of horsehair for the sofa. Rene had met her when she first walked into the village. She went in search of carbolic and white spirit. She came back with her bag bulging with more indulgent provisions, a good number of them donated by Mrs Cuff, free or cheap because she had ordered too many or because people hadn't taken to this, that or the other in the way she'd hoped. She was a good-natured woman, and she and Rene hit it off from the first. Rene soon started helping Mrs Cuff – Margaret – with deliveries at the shop, and occasionally delivered parcels in and around the village. It made things easy if there was a letter for her or Elsie – she could just pop it in her pocket.

It remained mild well into November, but by the middle of the month Rene and Elsie declared a temporary halt to all their improvements. They had been working all out since May. What was undone would have to wait till the spring. They spent their evenings quietly now, playing Patience – separate, together – and dominoes – Mrs Cuff had found an old box in her attic. On Sundays, they got up later and took long walks in the morning, armed with a flask of tea.

They found a lovely old wood, all fern and oak, and this soon became one of their favourite places.

On the first Sunday of December, they woke to a world all muted and white. From the bedroom window and the kitchen too, the usual landmarks were obscured; only the chimney stood out, though it looked further away than usual. They were up and out quickly: Elsie wanted to see the wood. Heavy-footed, they made their way along the track and the road. There was no one else about and just the sound of a bird here and there, that and the sound of their boots in the snow, so crisp they could almost hear them squeaking. They drank their tea as soon as they reached the wood, tired and hungry, but it was worth the effort. The ferns looked like they'd been iced for a cake, and everywhere there were the little prints and marks of the creatures that had been there before them. Soon they were completely enclosed in the white, branching quiet and Rene remembered the poem:

> 'Whose woods these are I think I know.
> His house is in the village though;
> He will not see me stopping here
> To watch his woods fill up with snow.'

In the silence she thought that she heard Jessie, her feet beating out the rhythm.

'What's that rhyme?'

'I don't know what it's called. I just remembered it.'

'I like it,' Elsie said.

'It came back to me just now. I don't know if I can remember the rest.'

'Is there more? Will you try, Bert? Please do.'

She looked so eager, standing there with the flask in her gloved hand, ready to wait or to carry on walking. Rene found to her surprise that she remembered the whole thing:

> 'My little horse must think it queer
> To stop without a farmhouse near

Between the woods and frozen lake
The darkest evening of the year.

'He gives his harness bells a shake
To ask if there is some mistake.
The only other sound's the sweep
Of easy wind and downy flake.

'The woods are lovely, dark and deep,
But I have promises to keep,
And miles to go before I sleep,
And miles to go before I sleep.'

'Oh, but that's lovely. Will you write that down for me, Bert? Will you?'

Still so eager. Her eyes were pricking.

'If you like. Yes, of course I will.'

They found some wonderful holly with great bunches of bright, hard berries, snow-iced. Elsie cut and gathered up as much as she could in her arms. There was mistletoe too, with chill, waxy berries. Rene filled her arms, distracted by the poem and the cold. She paused to stamp her feet and saw that a little way in the distance there were three figures. They were standing still, a woman flanked by two men; she could tell from the way they stood that they were young. They were all dressed warmly for the weather. She couldn't be sure if they were watching her, it felt as if they were, and then the young woman leant over and said something to one of the men, and the three of them turned and walked quietly away.

Rene and Elsie walked on too – it was time to start for home.

'What a lovely morning, what a lovely wood,' Elsie said. '"Lovely, dark and deep. And I have promises to keep. And miles to go before I sleep . . ."'

But I have promises to keep, Rene thought, that's how she remembered it, such a long time ago, but she said nothing. It sounded better Elsie's way. Happier.

That same afternoon, Elsie began her Christmas baking. On Rene's suggestion, she made a cake for Mrs Cuff with a fat coat of yellow marzipan, and Rene made a card for her and her daughter Belinda, her looping script as bold as ever. As Christmas approached, a few cards arrived for them. The first to arrive was from Bertha (and Ernest), duty dispatched (Ernest never wrote his own name, Elsie noticed). As 'Miss Boston', Elsie received a card from Major Veesey. It was a postcard of the Shalimar Gardens in Lahore, all water and arches; not very Christmassy but a kind thought all the same. As 'Miss Boston and Miss Hargreaves', they received a card from Muriel Parks, as they did every year. They put the cards on the little cupboard in the sitting room around the wireless. It was a bit of a huddle, but they looked nice enough and Elsie put up sprigs of holly and mistletoe anywhere she could.

There was also a letter, addressed to Rene, which arrived about the same time every year. When she received it from Mrs Cuff, she glimpsed the writing and thrust it in the pocket of her coat, out of sight.

It was a letter from Bertha about the children. Never a long letter and punctuated with other bits of Bertha news. Steve, as she must remember to call him now, had a job in Glasgow working for the telephone service, good money; Mikey (still Mikey) was on National Service in Germany, now he was gone she rather missed having him about; Jessie had gone to work in London. Bertha was a meagre correspondent, but Rene pored over these letters, spinning all manner of stories: some mild and modest, others full of triumph and disaster. If Bertha knew more, Rene would never ask; she must accept what she was given.

Once she had read the letter, it was folded back carefully into its envelope. There was quite a collection of them in the top drawer of the tallboy – kept in a tin box now along with the older relics, Vicky's letter, the two faded cards, none of them shown to Elsie – the book and the brown velvet ribbon were long gone.

That first Christmas they bought candles, tall and tapering. Rene got them at cost from Mrs Cuff, but Elsie still thought they were an extravagance. They ordered quite a few things from her post-office shop: tinned grapefruit to eat with sugar and ginger; a large round of Cheddar; dates in a narrow box saying *Eat Me*; and a bottle of port. They also bought a ham and some sausage meat from Mr Marrack at Yew Farm. Rene tended to the mildly reckless; Elsie would always try and temper. Unusually, they chimed with the times, the new plenty still offset by a reassuring austerity (Mrs Cuff's shop was filling up with new comics and cleaners and all manner of packets and tinned things, but there were no sightings yet of fresh bananas and pineapples). Elsie was sure the Spar at Helston would have been cheaper, but said nothing on this occasion.

They took their ease on Christmas Day. After lunch, they settled on the sofa by the fire and listened to *The Moonstone* on the wireless, they roasted chestnuts, and shivered at the Shivering Sand. They forgot tea and had another glass of port and Elsie started to talk about Starlight, softly, quietly, something in her tone sounding almost like the wireless; Rene liked the idea of Starlight on the wireless. It was a story that had stuck in Rene's mind as it had in Elsie's, the first time they went to Newbury market. Rene could see them arriving in their new cart with Prince. They'd all gone to the market that first time except Moira, who had twisted an ankle. She found it hard to picture Elsie in the jostle and fray of brothers and sisters, thick hair combed and pulled, things borrowed and broken, but Elsie always seemed to hold her own.

'We had pasties and treacle cake in a big, steamy, smelly tent and Mum bought us all ribbons.'

The boys begged and shared a jug of ale which left eleven-year-old Tom with glassy eyes and hiccoughs that wouldn't go away. They had all laughed at that, and then Alfred took Elsie off to help him choose the cows. Five toffee-and-white Ayrshires – Rene could imagine Elsie as a little girl, looking at the cows gravely. Each of the girls got to name one. So: Betsy (Cally), Agatha (Ruby), Caramel (Moira), Bell or Bluebell (Elsie), and Mum called the smallest one Snowball. A rather grand name, Agatha, but the cows were going to live like queens. In winter, soft beds of litter and bracken would keep them warm; in summer, they would munch cake and crushed oats along with their grass. Pea princesses, Bert once called them, though they always ate their peas.

Just before they left, Elsie, Bert and Ruby made a last visit to the tent to buy more treacle cake for the journey home. A dark-skinned man came over and started talking to Bert. Elsie thought he must be a fortune-teller with his black eyes and earring, but he had no futures to sell, only puppies in a carpet bag. Part fox terrier, part something long-legged and lanky – 'They'll make good ratters,' he said. Bert went off to ask Alfred and they bought two. 'Bloody gypsy,' Bert said, but he petted the puppies readily enough.

A long, slow journey home that first time with the Ayrshires. 'I'm sure I was the only one who was awake the whole time.' Cautious of his new stock, Alfred insisted each cow was haltered and led. Ruby, George, Thomas and Cally did the leading. It was quiet once they left the market revellers behind, just the odd drunk rolling homeward. Much later, they passed a man, followed twenty or so yards later by a woman and child, a girl of about Elsie's age. The man stared ahead though he didn't seem to see the horizon, and the woman looked steadfastly down at her boots; only the girl looked up and at them as they passed. She smiled, straight and sad, into Elsie's eyes. 'They were together, the three of them, though you'd never have known it. I remember them so clearly, Rene. So clear, so many stars, and still a late-summer warmth in the air, and the smell of hay.' Rene remembered how the high hedgerows along Sheepdrove twitched and crackled. She could feel the start of the steep climb out of the valley, the sky was thick with stars, on and up the hill they went, and then Elsie picked out one more light winking and wavering in the thick dark at the top of the hill: they were home.

'Bramble and Flossie were such lovely dogs, Rene,' Elsie said, sipping at the last of her port, 'but both of them were terrified of rats.'

It grew dark, and they drowsy, and then Rene lit the long, tapering candles and put out the lamps, while Elsie fed the animals and the fire. For supper they had chicken sandwiches, too much pepper, even Nib woke from her cushion and sneezed. Then they watched the fire and listened to a concert from Manchester, the Hallé orchestra, and found themselves falling asleep.

★ ★ ★

More than a year later, and observed from outside, from the lane perhaps, the success of the Wheal Rock venture still appeared doubtful. Rene and Elsie had built a couple of skittery extensions, one on each side of the cottage, and painted them white. (There was a plan to whitewash the whole cottage but they hadn't got round to that.) Behind the cottage was a makeshift yard with hutches and runs for chickens and rabbits. They had fenced off the flat ground at the front and found a new gate for the gatepost. But the 'garden' was improvised at best. Elsie had never done without a garden, and in the past she had coaxed the most refractory ground to yield and behave. But at Wheal Rock, the ground nearly defeated her. The old mine had soured it, poisoned it in places, and when it was wet, the earth bled orange from the copper. Nevertheless, she had, with immense effort and a great quantity of compost, secured a small vegetable patch to one side of the cottage which was beginning to flourish. In the rest of the 'garden', she found a flimsy trail of honeysuckle nearly choked by ivy and other wispy shades of forgotten plantings. She did her best to nurture these, bringing home cuttings from her walks to make more friendly company. But for all Elsie's efforts, the front continued to look bedraggled, temporary.

At dusk though, the exterior began to change: the chimney smoke wreathed and twisted against the darkening sky, the rickety extensions turned opaque and the dishevelled garden grew blurry and indistinct. By the time it was dark and the lamps glowed orange in the windows, the cottage seemed invulnerable. Rene loved returning when it was dark, her first sight of the lights through the trees as she cycled up the lane. Coming home: Elsie in the kitchen window, standing at the sink, washing, waiting. Sometimes it felt to Rene as if they would always live at Wheal Rock; it was foolish, but sometimes she couldn't help herself.

129

In the kitchen now was an old but effective oil stove; a leaved dining table they had 'borrowed' from Margaret, which couldn't be opened because of the space; and two chairs. In the sitting room, the wireless had the place of honour on the little cupboard and a rug with a flaunting peacock lay in front of the uncomfortable sofa. It didn't keep the draughts out – nothing seemed to do that – but it made a change from the flagging. Nib had colonized the window seat with its new green cushion, and on sunny mornings she curled into a fixture of carefully wound fur. By the fireplace was a smart set of fire irons that Rene had picked up at a house sale. The furnishings were sparse, but it was the way they preferred it. Upstairs, the second bedroom remained a box room, full of plans prospective and abandoned. In their bedroom, they now had a dwarf wardrobe to complement the skinny tallboy with its carefully allocated drawers. They had put a board under the bed to try and bolster the mattress, and Elsie had made a new cover and curtains for the window. Everything was kempt, clean, lived-in, though very little was comfortable. From the window of the bedroom, the fields stretched across to Rosenys and beyond.

Elsie didn't seem to mind her age – she was now sixty-three; vigorous, healthy (Rene was troubled by her chest), Elsie looked good years younger, and not just to Rene's eyes. It wasn't getting older that worried Rene, it was THE FUTURE. When they were together, 'next year' was the acknowledged horizon, the point of reference for things that would be done differently or the same: *we should get the holly from the wood a little later next year, let's make another cake for Margaret next Easter.* It was a comfortable measure belonging to Elsie first, but Rene had adopted it for her own. LET US GO FORWARD TOGETHER. But they were not always together, they couldn't be, gaps could open up. Working away as she did, and with Elsie spending more of her time at the cottage, Rene was made aware of different currents. There was another future, and it wasn't next year, a future of rockets and bombs, and everyone, everything, was in such a hurry to go faster and faster, running, driving, flying. Margaret Cuff's Belinda wanted to be an air hostess; Jessie was working in London, living in London. Imagine. Now that was a future, and Rene hoped it would be a good one. Bertha's letters were getting more frequent but it was all little details about this or that neighbour, and Ernest. Increasingly, it seemed, Bertha's letters included rather a lot of Ernest. He was getting old, she said, as if she wasn't, or perhaps as if she was seeing him in a new light. And when Rene's mind started to run on in this way, her future and Elsie's was not next year at all but a bad ending, inseparable from the new council houses, or the almshouses on the edge of Heathwater – so pleasing to the casual motorist. The old home was the most likely outcome: no privacy, separate bedrooms, meeting on the landing, on the stair. ONLY MARRIED PERSONS MAY SHARE A BEDROOM. Trying to save a place for each other at the lunch table: ambushed by others – some vague, some familiar – and hovering trays. All this so vivid, and still never a word to Elsie.

* * *

Rosenys was six miles from Helston, that was what the signs said, but Rene was certain it was further, especially when she was cycling home tired on a Friday night. From Helston, it was a slow, steady climb to a crossroads some way out of Rosenys. She always paused there because after that the incline got much sharper. It was a bleak spot, not a house in sight and the usual rumours of hangings and hauntings, but Rene wasn't easily frightened. To the left was the stony track that snaked to Tregoran and the sea; to the right was a steep, sharp turn to Upper Rosenys. Ahead, up a steep, straight hill, lay Rosenys. She always took the hill with gusto, though it fought back against her knees and the fronts of her thighs; at the top she would pause again, a little puffed. High up now, the sound of the waves rushed out as if from nowhere, buoyed by the wind; and there, below, was Rosenys, a scant but distinctive pattern – part plough, part jug. A glorious slope followed, you could fairly fly down to the village if the wind was with you. But Rene always slowed down before she entered the village – she didn't want to be spotted shooting through at top speed, it didn't look friendly. 'They'll think you're a harpy,' Elsie had said, when she told her.

Harpy Hargreaves, thought Rene, nearly at the top of the hill, nearly giggling, a little out of breath and exhilarated by the wind that was boxing her from behind. It was only September but there was already a chill in the air, charging her up. She was looking forward to a smooth sail down, but she came to a stop too fast, too heavily. Earlier the bike had been sluggish but she hadn't bothered to check the tyres; now she realized that the bike had a puncture and a bad one too. She climbed off to check – and sure enough she could feel the damage. There was no chance she'd be able to cycle home.

It was at least another two miles to Wheal Rock – not an emergency, but she didn't fancy the walk in the wind with a dragging bike. She lit a cigarette, inhaled slowly and considered her position. If the bike had been hers, she would probably have left it where it was and gone back the following day – the chance of theft was pretty small – but to do this with somebody else's bike seemed casual. She stood beside the bike, glad that the rain had finally stopped; but the wind was still strong, it took turns at circling and pushing her about. Noisy too, so she didn't hear the engine till it was quite close, and even then she wasn't sure where the sound was coming from. But then she saw the van come chugging up the hill. She dragged the bike further back from the road, but she had already been spotted; the van was already slowing to meet her. It came to a halt expertly a couple of feet in front of her. The driver's window was wound down and she was face to face with a woman, a little younger than herself, with short fair hair.

'You look like you need some help. Back door's open. Shall I help you with the bike?'

Just moments later, it seemed, Rene was settled in the front of the van, the bike safely stowed.

'Where are you headed?' the woman asked.

Elsie worried when Rene was late in the evenings. In daylight, things took the time they took, but once it got dark, mantel clock and wireless took over with their relentless measures. In the new year, they were going to be connected to the telephone service, an innovation that left Elsie unmoved, except in this one respect. Tonight Rene really was late – it was already after seven. At first Elsie had plenty to distract herself with: she fed Nib and gave the puppy some milk, then she coaxed the fire and tried to settle to some sewing. She delayed putting out the tea things and tried to avoid going to the kitchen window too often. Sometimes when she was waiting, she caught a glimpse of Rene's bike through the trees. Not tonight.

At half past seven she went out to feed the chickens and the rabbits (usually she waited till after they'd eaten). The rabbits were hunched, even more flat-eared than usual, quivering miserably from the rain. She fed them quickly, and the chickens, and built up a bank of straw around the meshing of the hutches to try and keep out the wet. The rain had come on again and she was soaked by the time she got back in. She hung her jacket carefully out over a chair, stuffed newspaper in her boots and made herself a pot of tea. More things to keep her busy. Quarter to eight.

She turned the wireless off – it was some light programme she didn't find funny, and all it did was tell her it was late. Normally by now, she and Rene would be settled in the sitting room, or as settled as they could be on the sofa. They both savoured Friday nights. Eight o'clock. She went to the window again, knowing how little there was to see in the dark.

* * *

It was nearly half past eight by the time Rene got home, and Elsie had worked herself up into a fine old state. Switching ever more frequently between the kitchen table and the sitting-room sofa, her senses had quite taken flight. First, there were images, wonderings: Rene, wincing with a turned ankle, limping slowly towards home; or lying concussed in a ditch, knocked unconscious; or worse, in a mess of mangled metal under a bus. But then a story forced itself through the possibilities: a knock at the door; a policeman accompanied by Mrs Cuff to soften the blow; Mrs Cuff going with her in the police car to the hospital, holding her hand; her first sight of Rene, varnished with the special stillness of the dead; Rene's cold hand hanging down, unreachable.

It was all so clear that when she first heard the sound of the vehicle outside, she was sure it must be the police (how she hoped Margaret would be with them). She stood up and clasped the edge of the table for balance, her legs heavy as pond-wet clothes. Her heart thumped. Outside was the noise of doors opening and closing, and then she heard Rene's voice – ordinary, light – a criss-cross of thank-yous and goodbyes. It was unmistakably her. Elsie sat back down, unsure of her legs, unable to adjust. Even when the door opened and she saw Rene standing there in the doorway. All there; alive; unhurt; her face just a little flushed.

'Everything's all right, nothing to fret about.'

But Elsie couldn't speak, she just went on looking at Rene.

'Look, look, I'm all here, nothing missing.'

Elsie flinched and huddled into herself.

Rene wasn't usually one for silly jokes, but nerves could make her foolish sometimes.

'Elsie, I'm sorry, such a silly thing to say. Please don't be upset.'

Elsie stood up slowly and went to the stove, put the pan on to the heat, looked around for the pepper, found Rene's face again.

'I shouldn't have joked, I'm so sorry. I'm fine, really I am. I had a puncture (and of course I didn't have the pump). I thought I'd have to walk home, all the way from the crossroads. Luckily a van came by and I got a lift.'

But it was after half past eight. There must be more to it than that.

Elsie busied herself unnecessarily with the soup, trying to avoid looking at Rene, trying to avoid thinking, but it was no good.

Rene took off her coat and smoothed her hands over her trousers, then she sat down and lit a cigarette, but she was fidgety and after a few moments she got up and went to the window. Dark, dark, dark; nothing could occupy her there. She sat down again, briefly settling her attention on the new puppy asleep in the basket, but soon her fingers were drumming and she was looking around for something to do. Elsie watched her all the while, she could tell that Rene was excited and trying to hide it, her eyes were very bright in the dull of the room.

'Could you light the other lamp,' Elsie asked, 'and set the table? It'll be ready in just a minute.'

Rene sprang to it, recognizing the request for the bridge that it was. She lit the lamp, got out bowls and spoons, cut some bread and laid the table. She rinsed out the cups; the carrot peelings were still in the sink and she rubbed the earth into the drain.

So they had their supper: after the soup they had cheese and some apples that Elsie had been saving, juicy and sharp; and finally a bit of talk found its way to the table, about the weather and the puppy and Nib's latest antics. It was only then that Rene got up to make some tea.

'Bert, are you all right?'

'Yes.'

There were things Rene kept to herself alone, like the letters she slipped quietly into a pocket and never mentioned to Elsie. She had decided long ago that it was better like that, better for her and better for Elsie. But sometimes, when she closed the top drawer of the tallboy, she wished she could say something. There were things she had told Elsie that had left her feeling lonely. They were not the deep things – a funny turn of phrase she'd heard in a shop, a copse of white bluebells she came upon unexpectedly, near the big dairy farm where she worked – but Elsie did not seem very interested. Words brought back from Rene's weeks away could light up the distances between them. Rene knew that what had happened to her tonight, her adventure, could easily be misunderstood.

Once her bike had been safely stored and she had got in the van with Kat – for Kat had volunteered her first name as she briskly shook Rene's hand – they had reversed and then made the steep U-turn for Upper Rosenys.

'I'm happy to drive you home,' she said, 'but I need to drop these crates off first. You don't mind? It won't take long.'

Kat pushed the van to surprising speeds along the narrow, winding lanes and the crates rattled merrily away behind them. Rene found it exhilarating, but her hand clutched the strap all the same. Kat didn't notice, talking away, non-stop, but it was all very friendly, for all the smart southern vowels. There were no sidelong looks, no curious glances, and Rene felt – despite the speed – strangely at ease. Kat told her about the van – she was clearly proud of it – it was a Ford Thames 300E and only a couple of years old. It was just the thing they needed, she said. She begged a cigarette ('Don't tell Jude, she hates me smoking') and got Rene to light it for her. Just moments later, she screeched to a halt to avoid a large animal in the road: a badger. She swore royally as it finally trotted away.

'You're not a local either, are you?' Kat said.

'Manchester,' Rene said, 'but that was a long time ago.'

And thankfully Kat asked nothing else and she was soon rattling on again. Rene listened quite rapt, only half understanding the family she conjured, 'so stuffy', and the school that had taught her nothing worth knowing. When Kat got to the war, things made a lot more sense. She'd been working in London and made some great friends – it had all been 'fantastically exciting'. Soon after VE Day she'd come down to Cornwall for a holiday, Upper Rosenys of all the luck, and . . .

'Is there someone waiting for you? You can use the phone in the pub if you want.'

Rene didn't like to say that she didn't have a phone.

Upper Rosenys was tiny, smaller than 'their' Rosenys, though better lit.

'It's just one house deep,' Kat said, having slowed to a crawl, 'like a stage set. We don't have a shop, or a post office, but we do have a pub and our very own recluse.'

'Recluse?'

Rene didn't think she'd ever heard that word.

'Oh yes, but she's harmless, quite friendly really. Ah, here we are. This is us.'

Kat swung the van into a small car park and came to a stop. They both got out and Rene looked up at the brightly lit sign: *The Fox and Hound*. A fox stood improbably on the branch of a tree, its tail twirling in the air. It was looking down at a hound that seemed to have lost its way.

'I like the sign,' Rene said.

'Nice, isn't it? A friend of ours did it. It's a boring name but we didn't like to change it – some people think it's bad luck.'

Kat was already round at the back of the van, opening the doors. She pulled the bike out and rested it against the side of the van.

'It'll be fine here. I'll get you that pump. You don't mind helping with the crates, do you?'

They stacked most of the crates in a storeroom that was also an office; it was a mix of things, most of it bottled: beer, lemonade, ginger. There were another couple of boxes of what looked like household shopping. The first was all soup tins and biscuits; the other box was, to Rene's eyes, decidedly fancy, for it included tins of olives and sardines and two bottles of red wine.

Once they'd finished in the storeroom, Kat picked up one of the crates.

'Come on,' she said, 'come and meet Jude, she'll get you a drink.'

Rene followed her to the bar but slowly: the bubble of noise ahead made her uncertain – she was a stranger after all, for all Kat's friendly talk. Hovering in the doorway, she watched as Kat went up to the woman at the bar and touched her gently on the shoulder. She turned to Kat on the instant with no trace of surprise, the briefest of smiles. It was just a moment but it was slow motion in its clarity.

'So here you are again,' the woman said. She and Kat smiled at each other and Kat laughed.

'Jude, this is Rene, she had an accident with her bike up at the crossroads.'

'Hello,' Rene said.

It was strange hearing her name like that from a stranger. She didn't know what else to say.

'Are you all right?' Jude asked.

She reached forward and stretched out her hand. Like Kat she was friendly on the instant and interested.

'I'm Jude. Pleased to meet you.'

'Rene. Rene Hargreaves.'

Kat explained what had happened and Jude didn't seem at all surprised, more amused, as if Kat often found stranded cyclists and brought them back to the pub. Rene found herself smiling too.

'At least have a drink before Kat drives you back.'

It was awkward. She wanted to stay, but she was also thinking of Elsie.

'Is there someone at home like me who'll be wondering where you are?'

'Yes, but . . .'

'Would you like to use the phone?'

'We're not connected yet.'

'Oh dear, well, you better drink up quickly then. Whisky?'

And they had all laughed and she was handed a big glass of whisky, no mention of water, and that had settled it. Jude and Kat fell into talking quietly, and Rene sipped at her drink and lit a cigarette. For all that she looked cautious, she was rather enjoying herself. It was so long since she'd stood on this side of the counter. It was a nice place, the usual country things on the walls, recently painted, spick and span. She looked out across the bar to the busy tables beyond; nearly a full house – a small place compared with the Blue Elephant. It was all so familiar, her elbows on the bar, the heavy ashtray beside her. She looked again at the tables, one by one, and then she looked again – in one way it wasn't like the Blue Elephant at all.

It had all happened so quickly, Kat pulling up in her van, reversing, the drive to Upper Rosenys and then there she was, standing in the bar . . .

'Rene? Rene? Are you all right?'

It was Elsie and she was back at home, at Wheal Rock.

'Are you sure you're all right? You look like you're in a dream.'

'Sorry. I was making tea, wasn't I?'

'I've done it. Are you sure you're all right?'

Rene looked down and saw her cup on the table, and made an effort to listen. There was a play on later, Elsie was saying, but it didn't sound like their kind of thing. They could start the puzzle if she wasn't too tired. Dear Elsie. Rene nodded and smiled but she was still distracted, her eyes were still too bright and her fingers tapped at the edge of the table; she wasn't quite ready to come back. Eventually she went and got her big brown bag – always a heap – that was sprawled over the mat, took out a fresh packet of cigarettes and then found what she was really looking for, smooth and cold at the bottom of the bag. She paused before bringing it out.

'Do you want some beer? They gave me a bottle.'

'Who?'

'The people at the pub where I got the pump.'

'At the Boar? People?'

Elsie was confused. There weren't 'people' at the Boar. There were Matt and Tillie Boulter; they ran the pub in Rosenys, which Rene and Elsie knew only by repute.

'No, it was Upper Rosenys.'

Rene knew she was making a mess of things but she couldn't stop now.

'On the house, the landlady said. It was her friend who gave me the lift in her van. They were really friendly, chatty. Asked if I lived nearby.'

'Upper Rosenys?' Elsie said.

It was only a few miles away but it could have been across the border.

'Elsie, you know there are an awful lot of women in Upper Rosenys. I haven't seen so many since the war.'

Elsie said nothing; it might have been a warning, but Rene was headstrong, she wasn't going to take any notice. She had gone too far to stop now.

'Women in the pub, I mean; they were just there together. I wondered if it was some kind of meeting, or a party, but it wasn't. I don't think there was a single man.'

There hadn't been a single man.

There was a pause. Rene could hear the window in the sitting room rattling.

'Lucky him if he's passing by.'

There was a silence.

Rene didn't know quite what she'd seen but she didn't want to be on her own with it.

'Elsie?'

But she was looking down at her lap and didn't answer.

So that was all Elsie was prepared to say, not even her own words, more like a comedy voice from the wireless.

The bottle of beer lay cold and explosive at the bottom of Rene's bag.

'Could you live together like that, in a place like that, with other women?'

Elsie stood up. 'I'll see to that window.'

But Rene didn't want to change the air, not yet.

She had half wanted to stay for another drink – they had asked her, Kat and Jude, pressed her really.

'And to think you live in Rosenys,' Jude had said, when she said her goodbyes. 'Fancy that. You're nearly a local. You'll have to come back, you know. And you must bring your friend with you next time.'

Kat had begged a cigarette as soon as they got back in the van and they had driven out of the village. It was a tiny place – one thick, as Kat had said – but just past the cottages was a long high wall.

'The big house,' Kat said.

'The recluse?' Rene still wasn't quite sure what that meant.

'She's not really a recluse, it's a bit of a joke. I mean she'd never come into the pub, but she's perfectly friendly. We go and have lunch with her sometimes.'

'She lives on her own?'

'Oh yes, quite alone. I'd hate it, but I think she rather likes it. There used to be a group of them living there – I think they came here before the war. Very bohemian, if you know what I mean. No one quite knew who was who, or who was with who.'

Kat laughed and Rene smiled.

She was hopelessly lost now, fascinated, confused: the casual way Kat spoke her feelings so direct; the exotic world she conjured so carelessly.

'We do some shopping for her but she gets most things delivered. She's pretty well off. Oh, look, here's the turning for . . . I do love driving in the dark.'

And they had turned down the hill towards the main road.

Before she got out of the car, Kat pressed her again to come back to the Fox and Hound, 'and your friend. Both of you must come.'

She knew it was a real invitation but she wasn't going to mention it to Elsie, not now. She wouldn't mention Kat and Jude again. Elsie was probably right, it wasn't really them.

Elsie was still standing there, watching her, curious, uncertain.

'I think I'd like to make a start on that puzzle,' Rene said.

Later in the evening they were nicely settled on the uncomfortable sofa and Rene was meticulously turning the puzzle pieces over, looking for sky, looking for corners, still a little bit shaky.

She and Kat had left the pub by the front and, as she went, Rene couldn't stop herself casting a last look back at the busy tables – just a small place, but it looked so comfortable. 'Don't you miss the war sometimes?' Kat had said. It was a curious thing to say, but Rene knew what she meant.

Ernest

IO.

The Visitor

A week later, Belinda Cuff walked over to deliver a letter. It was a Sunday morning; she didn't stop for tea – she was in a hurry, she said.

Elsie took the letter. It was addressed to Miss Hargreaves and Miss Boston, Wheal Rock Cottage, Rosenys, Cornwall. Elsie liked 'Miss Hargreaves and Miss Boston'; they received very few letters like that. Then she saw the Manchester postmark. They usually got cards from Manchester – on Rene's birthday and at Christmas. The Christmas card came addressed to Rene but 'and Elsie' was written inside the card, always below Rene. She passed the envelope to Rene without saying anything.

Rene saw the postmark first; about to tear the envelope, she paused for a moment to look more carefully at the handwriting – it was not the handwriting she was expecting, nor was it handwriting that she knew. She said nothing and dug her fingers into the envelope.

The letter came from a neighbour, Mrs Smith, Bertha's neighbour, and she was writing because Bertha –

She'd been taken off by ambulance to Withington General late one night and had died just two days later. The pneumonia got her – that was what the doctor said.

The funeral was set for two weeks' time – Ernest's nephew was doing the arranging. Mrs Smith hoped the date was convenient for Rene, hoped she'd be able to come. Ernest had taken it very hard, Mrs Smith said.

Rene passed the letter to Elsie – she had never given her a letter from Manchester to read before.

Elsie started to read, almost as quickly stopped.

'Bertha!'

Elsie went back to the letter, reading slowly and carefully, as was her way.

Bertha's name hung in the air – a pencil shadow but fainter than before. Rene finished her cold tea and sat, shivery and light-headed, drumming her fingers on the kitchen table. It was certainly a shock. She lit a cigarette and looked around the little kitchen, still dark, despite the paint, yet homely with the tangle of jackets and scarves on the door and Jugger lying in his basket, watching her. Unwillingly, her mind started to fill with train tickets and dark clothes and whether she'd be able to borrow a hat from Margaret and then, as the first shock began to wear off, she wondered if she'd remembered to close the sitting-room door last night because the puzzle was on the floor and she didn't want Jugger to spoil it before it was finished. She got up and went to check. It was a splendid puzzle too – 'August Holiday, Windermere' – and it was taking them an age: such an amount of blue water and sky and crafty reflections. As she returned to the kitchen, Jugger looked up hopefully and banged his tail and she reached down to stroke his long, silky ears; Elsie was still reading and Rene knew better than to interrupt.

* * *

Just a year ago, Rene had visited Judd Street. Bertha had asked her, it was a few months after Mikey left for his National Service training. She remembered very little about the visit except the strangeness of being in Manchester after so many years, but she remembered saying goodbye very clearly, standing on the street beside Bertha's blue door. Bertha had taken up her old place on the step – which didn't gleam as brightly as it used to.

Bertha always knew how to save the best till last. 'I worry about Ernest, Rene,' Bertha had said. And Rene hadn't understood. He looked all right to her: she had left him sitting serenely on his new chair, nursing a whisky, a blanket over his knees. Why should Bertha worry?

'I worry about Ernest, Rene. Oh, he's fine when I'm here, I give him the guidance, but I worry. I don't always feel so well. What if I was taken poorly, Rene? What if I was taken?'

'Bertha!' Rene had been shocked.

'I fret so,' Bertha said. 'Sometimes I wake up in the middle of the night and it's all I can think about. The other night I got myself into such a state, my heart was quite banging.'

Rene didn't know what to say, but Bertha reached forward and clasped her hand.

'How would he manage if I wasn't here? He couldn't look after himself, he's never been that kind of man.'

'Bertha, you mustn't upset yourself like this, it'll make you ill. Properly ill. You mustn't worry. You don't have to worry.'

Rene needed to get away. She wasn't late for the train but she had a sense of approaching danger.

'But I do worry,' Bertha said. 'I can't help it.'

Bertha always knew how to insist.

'You shouldn't worry,' Rene said and then stopped.

Bertha said nothing. She knew how to stop too, she could do it better than Rene.

'You know you shouldn't,' Rene said feebly.

'I can't hold you to that. That was a long time ago. Such a long time.'

Rene said nothing. Bertha squeezed her hand, shook her head, smiled.

'You mustn't worry,' Rene said again. She felt chilled, her voice mechanical. 'He'll be looked after.' It was all she could say; it was far too much.

'Oh Rene, that was a life ago, the war was barely started. You were in such a state . . . I feared for you that day, I really did, I didn't know what you might do. I should never have asked.'

'You didn't ask.'

For the first time, Bertha looked uncomfortable and Rene couldn't stand it.

'I promised,' Rene said.

It wasn't what she wanted to say. It didn't sound right. But Bertha had something on her hook now and she wouldn't let go.

'It can't have been what you were expecting. You thought it would be me who would need the looking after, when the time came. It's what I thought – it's what I still think some of the time. It's usually the women who are left, isn't it?'

'Bertha, I don't want to talk about it any more. I promised then and it still stands, whatever happens.'

She couldn't bring herself to say the exact words.

But it seemed enough for Bertha, who squeezed her hand and nodded.

'Hurry now, you'll miss your train . . .'

'Thank you.' It was Rene speaking.

And that was the worst – *thank you* – as if she had signed something, something binding.

Rene had promised and now Bertha had been taken by the ambulance and the pneumonia. But first there was the funeral, there was no escape from that. Elsie didn't like her going to Manchester – funeral or not, promise or not – a door had opened, strings were stirring, beginning to pull. It was only when Rene was waiting to go, in the dark skirt she had borrowed from Margaret with her hat in a box – oh, why had she waited? Rene looked so different and distant too, chin up, mouth set shut. It was only then that Elsie said very quiet, almost timid, 'Rene, do you think about the children – often, I mean?'

Rene had been looking for something in her bag. Now she stopped and snapped it shut with a click.

'All the time.'

Elsie didn't know what to say.

'I don't mean there's nothing else,' Rene said quickly, 'of course I don't. I mean that whatever else I'm thinking, they're there too.'

The taxi was waiting and Rene squeezed Elsie's hand, a quick smile, sweet, but it only seemed to fill out the distance between them.

Even though Ernest told her that Mikey wasn't coming to the funeral, Rene was frightened that he would. Ernest showed her the letter from Germany with a postal order for flowers – he couldn't come because of 'special manoeuvres'. Ernest seemed to like this phrase, but Rene wondered about compassionate leave. In the event there was no need to worry about Mikey, but Ernest's nephew drew her aside at the pub after the service to tell her how worried he was about Uncle, didn't think he was managing.

Couldn't manage was the euphemism everybody used, but Rene wasn't so sure about the *couldn't*. He did look fragile – there was little sign of the broad, barrel-chested man Bertha had proudly introduced all those years ago. Nevertheless, he was alert enough. She realized how little she knew him; awkward in his manners, he was difficult to read, even though she was a good reader. Yet he knew her and greeted her familiarly as Rene. *Good girl, Rene, good girl*. And now she was here to tidy everything up, while Ernest sat in his chair, nursing his whisky, taking it hard.

Bertha would have been mortified to see the fallen state of her home. She had carried on cleaning till near the bitter end, but her failing eyesight (never acknowledged) and fading energy had done their worst. The red doorstep, Bertha's pride and joy, was now dull and whiskery with spiders, the kitchen floor was filthy and the nets were yellow and set. Did ghosts ever come back to clean? Rene wondered. For the week after the funeral she was driven on by a rage of energy, cleaning, scouring pans and tiles, scrubbing steps, settling bills, sorting out jumble, her fingers drumming, *tap, tap, tap*, while Ernest sat on his chair in the sitting room, reading the paper and taking whatever was given him: tea, pie, toast, cake, another paper, another pint pot. The house remained gloomy for all the cleaning: the hall mirror showed her up all sepia and hollow-eyed. The furniture was shiny with elbow grease, but that didn't put the dark off; any sunlight that had found its way through the double defence of shutter and net was quickly sapped. In the parlour, the piano lid made a shelf for Bertha's many sewing boxes.

Rene had dreaded the sorting out because of what she might discover, but Bertha's habits of collection were frugal and all she found of Mikey was a single photograph, taken in Germany – he was wearing his uniform – *Dear Aunty B.*, he had written on the back, *don't I look smart* . . . She found the photograph in a drawer in the bedroom and thrust it into her bag, her throat suddenly hot and swollen.

And all the while Ernest sat on his chair, nursing his pint pot, reading the paper. *Good girl, Rene, good girl.* And she had to call him 'Uncle'. She didn't want to call him that, now they were in such close proximity, now and for the foreseeable future. Uncle was coming to live with them at Wheal Rock. She didn't like how that sounded at all, but she had promised. It wasn't quite what she had promised, it wasn't what she'd expected, but there was nothing else to do.

She kept only a few of his things. In the end it was just the clock, a fancy candle stand, and the portable shaving mirror – nearly new, his last birthday present from the ailing Bertha. These things could be squeezed into his room at Wheal Rock. She also decided to take his chair. It was a comfortable chair, recently re-covered – she didn't know where they'd put it and Elsie wouldn't approve but she kept it all the same. She sold the rest, though it was hardly worth it. 'No one's interested in this kind of stuff any more,' the dealer said.

On the second to last day she telephoned Elsie, by arrangement, at Mrs Cuff's shop.

It was only the second time Elsie had spoken on the telephone, and it sounded like she was reading a letter, a neat little paragraph about the garden and the new family of birds that were nesting in the chimney; but presently she ran out of news.

'How is . . . ?' Elsie couldn't say Ernest. And Rene, lonely at the end of the phone with only 'Uncle' for company, felt ever so far away.

'He's not the best. The change of scene will do him good.'

But after a little while, once they had talked about travelling plans, Elsie started to sound more like herself.

'Jugger's missing you, he's in a real mope.'

'It won't be long now – I'll be home in a couple of days.' Saying that made Rene feel better.

'I'll tell him that, I'm sure it'll cheer him up. Are you eating properly?'

And suddenly she really was the old Elsie.

'Are you?' Elsie was not giving up.

'Oh Elsie.'

'Sure?'

'Yes. Promise.'

'You're smiling.'

Elsie was getting the hang of the telephone now.

'Isn't that good?'

'Yes, I suppose so.'

'It's only two more days.'

Only two more days.

Elsie knew that Rene had promised Bertha. As the years passed and Bertha got older – no one was sure exactly how old Bertha was – they both knew that one day, if Bertha was no longer able to live on her own, she would come to live with them. It had never occurred to Elsie to challenge Rene over this. Bertha had taken Mikey, she had let Rene leave. From this perspective, Elsie had much to thank Bertha for. She knew that Rene felt a deep debt, but she also knew that nothing could ever weigh the same as the children. Whatever Rene did for Bertha, things would never be even. You can't compare apples and pears, butter and honey, people said – though Elsie didn't see why not. But Bertha and the children, these you couldn't compare, that she understood. It would have been like comparing Starlight with money. She still saw advertisements. FOR SALE BY PUBLIC AUCTION: ONE HUNDRED AND TWENTY ACRES, AMPLE BUILDINGS, VACANT POSSESSION, TWELVE DAIRY COWS. No, some things could never be matched.

Over the years, Elsie had caught a little of Rene's dread of Bertha, knew something about her sticky webs and her ruthless housecraft. If she thought about it, she hadn't liked the idea of Bertha coming to live with them at all. But Elsie didn't usually think very far ahead. Now it turned out that Bertha wasn't coming. Ernest was. Rene had never said much to her about Ernest, he had remained a stranger, insubstantial. Imagining this vague presence at Wheal Rock didn't seem to change much, not for her and Rene. In a way, she was happier that it was him, relieved too that he was a man; he would be easier, she was sure, than Bertha. She couldn't have been more wrong.

* * *

Rene and Ernest arrived at Wheal Rock just after six. Elsie, who had been standing at the kitchen window on and off since half past five, saw a faint flush of lights in the woods. She rushed upstairs and opened the window: a few moments later, she saw the taxi. Elsie couldn't help feeling excited – Rene was finally home – and relieved: there were too many strings in Manchester, pulling her, holding her. She came downstairs and hurried outside.

At first it was only Rene; she waved from the cab window, then she was getting out of the taxi, opening the boot, helping the driver with the luggage – she always did that. Elsie thought she looked thinner, after just a week, but she was home now. Suddenly it seemed they were standing on either side of the five-bar gate.

'You could have opened it for once,' Rene said.

'There's a cow loose, one of Ronan's.'

They stood smiling at each other; everything was quiet in the twilight and all the distance between them gone. And then Jugger came charging out of the cottage, barking, hurtled past Elsie and squeezed under the gate. He threw himself at Rene and she reached down to pick him up. He licked her cheek and squealed with delight before wriggling out of her arms and bounding back into the garden. Elsie fumbled with the bolt on the gate and the driver piled the luggage up on Rene's side.

'Do you need any help with the old fella?' he asked.

They had quite forgotten Ernest.

Rene and the driver helped him from the car, and Elsie got her first sight of him. He was smartly dressed, coated, hatted, gloved (Rene had layered him up to save on packing). Once out of the taxi, he leant rather heavily against Rene (Elsie didn't like that at all). But for all his tidy, neatly buttoned clothes, he looked confused, floppy;

his eyes drifted though they kept coming back to his shiny black shoes. They all stood where they were for some moments and then Rene urged him forward. It was quite a shock when he started walking: it was as if he came to life, unhooking himself from Rene's arm and walking towards the gate, jaunty and brisk. She knew at that moment he was trouble.

'We're here, Uncle,' Rene said. 'Home.'

The gate was open now. Elsie knew what was coming next: Rene would introduce her, that's how it would be, and they would shake hands. Until now he had been a stranger, somehow kept at bay; she had never even spoken his name.

'Uncle, this is my friend Elsie, the person I've been telling you about.'

They both mumbled and then he reached out his hand, took hers and looked at her, so very carefully. She didn't like the squeeze of his hand or his look. It was so different from the drifting eyes of a few minutes ago. He smiled and nodded, friendly really, she had to admit. But there was something else, something she couldn't put her finger on, something she didn't like.

'Elsie,' he said. 'That's a lovely name.'

The first couple of months were all right. He would wake at about eight, and after breakfast he usually took a walk down the lane; sometimes he ventured into the little copse. The weather was fine and dry that autumn and he seemed to draw some strength from the morning blue. Back at the cottage, he divided his time between his chair, which had been squeezed into the sitting room, and the kitchen table. Elsie had found some old puzzle magazines and she put them out on the table each morning. He genuinely enjoyed these, and much later, when he'd given up the puzzles, he still went about with a pencil stub tied around his neck. The pencil and string were for Elsie's convenience – the pencil was always rolling off the table and he would never find it for himself – but Ernest came to like his string, putting it on each morning like a watch. Sitting on his chair in the sitting room, he listened or semi-listened to all and everything on the wireless, smiling, nodding, shaking his head. He didn't like the dog though, didn't like it prancing around him.

There was no doubt that his new surroundings confused him. From cradle to now, he had been buoyed up by the kind hands of women – yes, even Bertha with her unaccountable weak spot. Here, in this strange place, he dimly sensed that these hands, though soft enough, did not seek to buoy him up. Overall though he didn't seem unhappy or dissatisfied. He helped out occasionally with the wood, and though he was fussy in his eating, he enjoyed his tea, which he liked very sweet, and his pint pot.

And somewhere inside his head, a steady half-tune was beating and repeating: *I am very lucky, very lucky indeed, these two strange birds will see to me.*

He even took a couple of trips with Rene on her new scooter, which he seemed to enjoy. Margaret Cuff saw Rene and Mr Massey driving past her shop window on the scooter and worried he might fall off, his shirt had ballooned right out and he didn't seem to be holding on. The fine weather held and Rene drove him down to the beach at Gunwalloe on her day off. The sand was grey-gold and the breeze rushed with iodine. There were a couple of old men taking the air up near the sea wall and a boy chased the waves on a feather-footed piebald pony, no one else. She tempted him down to the sea – 'Not far, Uncle, just a little bit further now' – and found a clutch of glossy mermaids' purses to take home for Elsie, while Ernest filled his pockets with stones. They had chips and tea to warm them for the journey back. 'This is grand,' he said, and giggled. Rene wasn't really sure he knew what he was about but, that evening, when he was settled in the sitting room with his pint pot, he said:

'Grand times today, Rene. I never went to the seaside before.'

Elsie was jealous, despite the mermaids' purses. Jealous because Rene had promised to take *her* to Gunwalloe and because Ernest got Rene all to himself. It would have been foolish to say so, and she didn't. Besides, it was still early days and she thought they would bring him round. If he was used to cooked food at breakfast, he would soon lose the habit; if he put his feet up on the fender or the table, he would learn, with a good number of brisk, sharp 'Uncles' to keep them down. They would soon teach him their ways. She was sure he was easier than Bertha would have been. It couldn't be much harder than training Jugger or the other dogs, except he was an old dog and a man.

She didn't mind him rising late: it gave her and Rene a bit of time together, and there was precious little of that. But it was hard trying to change his habits. Used to being eased out of his coat and shoes by Bertha, he would come in from his walk and settle down to doze in a soaking-wet jacket. Elsie didn't care too much if he caught cold, but she hated the muddy tracks on the floor and the rug.

He didn't come round to their cooking either. 'Then he can go hungry,' she said to Rene, but it wasn't that simple, for he took to slipping into the kitchen at odd times, looking for things to eat. It was sweet stuff he liked, and Elsie noticed that they were getting through a rate of jam and treacle and sugar. He seemed to survive on sugar and smokes, for he was always smoking. Sometimes he lit a second cigarette when he already had one going, left forgotten in a saucer or on the edge of a table: there were little burnt-out worms of ash everywhere. 'We need to keep an eye on him,' Rene said, but he wouldn't keep their hours, coming downstairs in the middle of the night – they worried he would do himself a harm while they slept. You needed owl eyes, thought Elsie, and it wasn't just at night. One early December morning, she came into the kitchen to find him clinging to the stove, watching his sleeve flame brightly. His legs were splayed out uselessly beneath him (he had been trying to light a cigarette). Quick and cool, Elsie grabbed the flowers from the jug and poured the flower water over his arm. Fire out, she took the cigarette from his mouth carefully, trying to avoid contact with his beard, and switched off the gas. 'Now, Uncle,' she said. Thankfully he was willing to be helped up, and she managed to bundle him out of the kitchen and back to his chair – though he leant against her heavily, which she disliked. His shirt was singed and he sniffed at it with some distaste. But there was no other damage; it could have been so much worse. BE VIGILANT. Elsie found herself thinking, Remember, always be vigilant. She went back to her work, but by the time Rene came home that evening, she was quivery and upset and nothing Rene said could really reassure her.

And it wasn't just watching he needed, it was coddling. Rene found it quite easy to indulge him, some of the time: she would unlace his boots and get him dry socks, give him another biscuit, another spoon of sugar – it didn't cost her much. But Elsie had never had a cosseting way and she hated to pamper him. 'It's him who should be thanking us, Bert, we do everything for him.' Rene admired Elsie for her conviction and was happy to do more than her share, but it was Elsie who spent the days with him and her manners didn't make things any easier. She could just about muster, 'Will you have an egg for your tea, Uncle?' or 'Shall I bring the other lamp?' But Ernest wasn't used to questions. At the factory, he had always known what he was supposed to do; at home, Bertha had always known what he needed. Here it was different. Sometimes he looked at Rene and the tears bubbled in his eyes, then he would *pat, pat, tap, tap* her hand. Elsie was another matter, and though he used her name greedily, her big shadow seemed to perplex him.

Their first Christmas with Ernest was a qualified success. On Christmas Day itself, Ernest woke gratifyingly late, though Rene and Elsie were forced downstairs very early by his snoring. After breakfast, they all went for a walk and took a big flask of tea. It was a pleasant day: not sunny, but fresh. Ernest was in his jaunty mood, humming to himself, sure-footed and spritely; he only complained once about the tea (not enough sugar), but he ate more than his share of treacle bread. They went further than they planned – perhaps both women had hopes of tiring him out, and sure enough, when they got back to the cottage, he settled into his chair and dozed off, listening to the carols. They had a rabbit stew for lunch – Elsie had made it the day before, she didn't want to waste precious time with Rene cooking – but she did roast potatoes and sprouts in honour of Christmas, to go with the pudding and pies. It all went off quite well and Ernest wasn't too much of a bother. He hadn't said much, but then he never did.

But on Boxing Day morning they found him slumped asleep at the kitchen table, with a half-empty tin of treacle beside him. It was a new tin and the treacle was everywhere: on the table, on the floor, on his nightshirt. But the worst of it was in his beard and hair. It took them more than an hour to clean him up. They had to soap his beard and hair and he complained the whole time he was at the sink, clutching the green-and-gold tin of treacle to his chest. Eventually, he was finished and Elsie guided him into the sitting room and settled him into his chair. He was in a better temper by then: 'Oh Elsie, Elsie, Elsie, oh, a cup of tea, oh Elsie, oh.' Back in the kitchen, she could still hear him, going on in his sing-song way; her name lingered in the narrow corridor like a shadow he wouldn't give up. Wordlessly she joined Rene in the clearing-up, but when it was all over and the treacle put away, well away, she sat down at the table and burst into tears. The whole day was ruined now, she thought, and Rene would be back at the dairy tomorrow, the holiday over.

January came in windy and wet; the only exercise Ernest would take was an amble about the uneven patch of garden. He rarely stayed out for more than half an hour and he usually timed his little expeditions outside to coincide with Elsie. No sooner had she gone outside than he would come tripping after her. He followed her about, always at a distance, but always paying close attention, she thought, to whatever she was doing. That was how he got interested in the old shed, or perhaps it was she who led him to it. She'd made a resolution to clear it out that winter, and as she went in and out of the flimsy structure, filleting the shelves, sanding the workbench, he became curious. Soon he forgot to keep his distance, he would follow her right into the doorway and cast his eyes around – for once he seemed uninterested in her. Elsie fixed the roof and did all she could to make the shed clean and comfortable; she even put a faded cushion on the chair at the workbench. She said nothing to encourage him – it would be tempting fate – but the shed worked like a charm. Soon he was pottering in and out at all hours, moving things around, muttering and smoking.

The shed should have been a victory for Elsie, and it was a relief to get him out of the cottage, but she never knew when he was going to come back in or call her out to him. He often lingered at the kitchen window on his way back inside. He would look in on her in the kitchen. Sometimes he would raise a hand and she would unwillingly respond in kind. Other times, he just stood there, staring, staring at her, or that's how it seemed. And there was no order to his days. He had worked forty years to a factory siren and been managed by Bertha well into his pension; there was something perverse about his resistance to routine. Quite soon Elsie became convinced he liked making a mess of all her plans.

He always came back from the garden or the shed with twigs and leaves, nails and tubs of glue, a padlock, an old tap. Some of these he displayed to her as trophies, but he was also secretive, hiding little piles of stuff under his chair or bed. Sometimes he brought her things, gifts of a sort, but of what sort she didn't like to think. He would lay these out in tidy desolation on the kitchen table: bulbs, tiny half-grown beets and once a sad white onion.

As the months went by, Ernest, never talkative, started to turn sullen. He used their words, but they got turned in the coming-back. *Would I?* he said, over and over, when he was asked if he would like tea, his pint pot, his paper, *would I?* Quick and nimble, Rene at least gave the appearance of being willing, but Elsie's awkward enquiries seemed to make him chary.

'Will you have the jelly now or later, Uncle?'

'Will I?'

Sometimes it was like he was just trying the words out, practising; but he could also sound coldly wondering, teasy, sour. And there was something else: a spry, occasional malice. You could never quite be sure. At the beginning, Elsie dismissed it as he seemed biddable enough, but as time passed she sometimes caught a twist in his mouth, a sudden chill steadiness in his eyes. She wanted to ask Rene but couldn't. Rene was so busy working, so busy making sure everything was all right – some evenings she could barely keep awake through supper. Be vigilant, Elsie thought to herself, be vigilant.

They never called him Ernest to his face, it brought him too close; *Uncle*, with its measure of formality, kept him at a distance, and *Uncle* was literally untrue, which helped. Ernest had no such qualms: he used both their names familiarly, shortening them to achieve ever closer proximity. *Ren*, he would say, and sometimes *Ri. Ri, where are my slippers?* And he loved saying *Elsie*, any excuse. That's a lovely name, he had said to Elsie when he first took her hand, and now Elsie became one of his favourite warbles or mumbles as he wandered about the garden or pottered about the cottage, always leaving a trail of sugar in his wake. Elsie would have said he was trying to wear out her name – if that hadn't sounded like a joke. She was always looking for the right word for him. Sometimes she spoke of him as *the visitor* or *our visitor* (never *lodger* or *guest*); sometimes she thought of him as an intruder, but *trespasser* was the word she finally settled on, her private name, her thought. He was a trespasser at Wheal Rock, trespassing in their lives, and they had invited him in.

Over the years the two women had evolved a rather clear division of labour. Rene laid the table, Elsie fed the animals. Elsie was in charge of housekeeping, Rene shopped, though both women cooked. Elsie did woodwork and Rene fixed machines, Elsie had charge of the garden and growing – but Rene was often around to help. They took it in turns to do the weekly laundry, which they both disliked. And Ernest had to be fitted in now. Early hopes that he would do his bit were long gone; Ernest was work, and a lot of work at that. Most of this was interchangeable, with Elsie doing the days and Rene doing the evenings and weekends, but some tasks were strictly allocated. It was Rene who gave Ernest his medicines and his pint pot; both women bathed him, without fail, twice a week. Rene handled his money, and £3 from his pension became part of the Wheal Rock weekly budget. But he cost a lot more than that. Twelve bottles from the Co-operative Store in Penryn were delivered to Wheal Rock every Thursday, at a cost of £1. 3s. 6d, along with his pouches of tobacco. This also came out of Ernest's pension, but was allocated separately for his 'personal' needs. These were his official rations, but a good deal more money (including some from Rene's purse) went on his drinking habit, most of it whisky and rum. Not that he was particular. He drank nearly a bottle's worth of brandy in the sitting room one Sunday afternoon early on – before they learnt not to leave it out. And over the months he found and finished cooking sherry, drinking sherry, port and a bottle of nettle wine. They got better at hiding it and he got better at finding it. When they ran out of hiding places, they stopped drinking, but he didn't. And when he didn't have enough, he kept asking for more. These were the only times he became visibly angry, though he was never a shouter. On these occasions he could also be itchy, snappish, wheedling. Rene bore the brunt of it because it was she he asked (much to Elsie's relief). They soon learnt to comply: he was better drunk (though he was never quite drunk) and it was easier to get it in than force him to do without. Rene wondered if he would have survived without the drink. Even with his generous allocation, he also consumed meths, turpentine and surgical spirit on occasion, when he was in the shed. These were all routinely replaced, though there were sometimes dark jokes about who should be paying. Every house needed a supply of spirit, Elsie said, like rat poison.

'Do you make your own jam?' Ernest asked one sticky August morning, looking with purpose at a batch of preserve jars Elsie was getting ready to boil. And Elsie, trying to be friendly because he had settled himself at the kitchen table for the long haul, tried to talk to him about jam and preserving. He seemed interested enough, and he certainly appreciated the smell of the strawberries stewing. So normal did he seem that morning that she decided to take Jugger for a proper walk up to the wood; she could clear up later. She couldn't have been more wrong. Returning in the middle of the afternoon, she found him in a stupor on the kitchen floor. There was a thick coating of jam round his mouth and beard; he had also downed half a bottle of the sterilizer.

It was difficult to know which he craved more, the booze or the sugar. He piled jam so thickly on to his bread it made them queasy – then he would lick it off. They found him time and time again with a pink stain of jam around his mouth, and sometimes with lumps of it in his beard. He was always on the lookout for something sweet, and sugar most of all. They gave up noticing what he tried to put it on: toast, potatoes, cabbage, sausages. Sometimes when he stood up, sugar fell from him like a bonbon – you could almost hear it fall – it crisped under the feet and you could never brush it away. He cost them a fortune in sugar. They hid the bowl but he always found it. They stopped using a bowl and used a mug instead, but he found that too and so it went on. And always, always, the little snail trails of sugar.

At the weekends Rene took full charge of Ernest, minding, coddling and above all trying to tempt him out for walks. And then Elsie would go and sit in the empty sitting room, in his chair, uncomfortable, pulling recklessly at the threads of the cushion. It seemed to be the only place in the cottage where she didn't see him. But she couldn't ignore the sticky windows, or the jackdaw caches of paper and pins, or the precarious cup on top of the wireless. Her eyes would wander, looking for the little burnt-out worms of ash. And everywhere the sugar trails, making handles sticky and uninviting and the very floors uncertain.

* * *

The first time Rene found him in their room, she wondered if it was a mistake. He was staring at the tallboy. 'This isn't your room, Uncle.'

He turned to look at her, slow, heavy-eyed; he had pulled his dressing gown on over his clothes.

Quietly, firmly, she clasped his wrist and steered him from the room.

'I thought you were having a sleep,' Rene said. 'Lots of rest, Uncle. Remember what the doctor said?'

Ernest said nothing. Rene closed the door of their bedroom. They stood on the landing, uncomfortably close.

'I'll go out to the shed,' he said.

And she followed him downstairs. He hovered beside the coats and jackets that hung on the door, yet when he eventually declared he was ready he was still wearing his slippers. She chose to ignore it – the ground was hard outside.

He paused in the doorway, turned to face her slowly, then looked at her, intent and clear-eyed.

'You're very close,' he said, and then he turned and trotted off, his thick socks pulled up over his trousers.

Rene chose to think that his presence in their room was, if not quite a mistake, then not exactly deliberate. It couldn't be calculated, surely? She was glad that Elsie was out, and Rene thought not to mention it, there was no need to say anything, unless it happened again.

But it did happen again. One Sunday morning, Elsie went upstairs to dig Nib out of the bed and found Ernest.

It was a shock: he had pulled the door to behind him, and when she pushed it open, she saw him staring into the open top drawer of the tallboy, Rene's drawer. Elsie had never looked inside it (though she had some idea of the contents). He was holding a creased cigarette card in his hand. She stood, frozen, in the doorway. He had the advantage.

'Leave me be,' he said. 'I'm doing no harm.'

Elsie didn't speak.

He turned round to look at her then, standing his ground on unsteady tiptoe.

'What you got to hide?'

Another flash of spite, and it was as if the whole room soured. Elsie wanted to snap the drawer against his bony fingers – that would stop his nosing soon enough. Instead, she steered him out of the room and half pushed him downstairs. The cottage wasn't made for forced manoeuvres of this kind. Together, they could only just occupy the landing, and she had to press him down the stairs in front of her, hoping he wouldn't topple them both. They each disliked the proximity and he protested loudly in semi-fluent gibberish. The commotion brought Rene rushing in from the garden.

Sometime later, Elsie steeled herself to look in on him, slumped in his chair. He looked up at her dimly, half asleep.

'Elsie?'

She did not reply.

'Is it teatime yet?'

'Not long now,' she said mechanically.

He seemed to have quite forgotten earlier.

'Is it stew? I like the stew – you make it, don't you? Elsie's stew.'

'Not long now,' she said.

But he hadn't finished with her yet, and he hadn't forgotten earlier.

'I know her. I know her,' he said, sing-song clear. 'Do you know her? I don't think you do, Elsie, I don't think you do.'

He was looking at her again, very intently.

'Who?' she couldn't help asking. 'Who is it you mean?' Her voice sounded quivery to her ears, nervous.

He had something clenched in his fist, a card of some kind.

'You don't know her, do you, the girl on the card, the actress?' He smirked, opening his hand. But it was only the back of the card – a pretty pink-and-green pattern.

'That's Rene's,' Elsie said.

'Rene's,' Ernest said, as if he were copying her.

Elsie was sure she could see greasy fingermarks and reached out to take the card, but he moved it away quickly, turning it over, studying it.

'You don't know.'

Elsie said nothing this time.

'Mona Verity. She was a big name in the pictures, you know. But you don't know, do you?' He taunted her with a smile, handing her the card. 'You don't know. You better ask your Rene. See.'

Elsie grabbed the card and fled the room.

Back in the bedroom, she looked down at the pretty pink-and-green pattern. Without turning it over, she put it back in the top drawer of the tallboy.

She spent the rest of the afternoon designing a scheme of deterrence. If she had to let him into the cottage, she could at least keep him from their room. She opted for small, sturdy hooks for the door – allowing her to maliciously rehearse his vulnerabilities. His poor eyes and twisted hands would not be able to manage. One set was placed too high for feeble arms, the other set too low. It was not very practical – it slowed *her* up no end. But it was worth it.

He seemed to give up on the door after that. Elsie didn't pause for victory; he would find another way of riling her, she was sure of it. This time silence was his weapon. When she called him, he refused to answer. *Would you like your sandwich now, Uncle?* No reply. *Are you upstairs, Uncle? Do you want your pint pot?* Nothing. *Where did you put your boots?* Everything was met with a silence. Before, she had been irritated by his mumblings and shuffling, but the quietness was worse – unnatural. When she didn't know where he was, he could be anywhere, everywhere, and she always had to go looking: she needed to know where he was, to be sure. So she would put on her boots and go out to the shed, or up to the gate to see if he had gone further afield. When she found him – *Oh, there you are, Uncle. Didn't you hear me?* – he looked up at her with that spry meanness and she knew, or nearly knew, that he had heard her perfectly and just wanted to make her life that bit more difficult. Elsie talked about it to Rene, but Rene was sure that his hearing wasn't good. Ernest never kept his quiet in the same way when Rene was about.

He started to go out walking on his own again, sometimes for an hour or more – it was difficult to know to what purpose. Elsie felt relief at first – to have the cottage to herself – but she quickly started to fret that he would get lost or meet with an accident. To leave him on his own was also a worry: she couldn't be sure what she would find on her return. Once she'd found him sitting in the dark on top of the kitchen table, stringy hands clamped round his knees, legs crunched impossibly in front of him – she had nearly screamed. It had taken her an age to get him into the sitting room and then she had scrubbed her hands raw, trying to rub the table clean. Elsie knew such things were not meant, but other things were, she was sure. One step forward, two steps back. He eventually learnt to take off his own boots, but he often left them lying across the kitchen doorway like a tripwire – she'd nearly gone flying a half-dozen times. It was a war of attrition: she gave him gristle to struggle with in his lunchtime soups (he was proud of his teeth); on one occasion she nicked his fingernails when clipping them (she wouldn't touch his feet). But it was mean and Elsie wasn't proud of herself. Besides, he was far more ingenious than she.

Returning from an appointment in Camborne one day, she found that he wasn't in the cottage, and no sign of the bottle and sandwich she'd left for his lunch. She followed a snail trail of sugar from the kitchen to the sitting room and back, then she went out to the shed – no sign of him. Then upstairs to his room – empty, he rarely went upstairs in the daytime now. She opened his window to get rid of the stale, smoky smell and looked out into the late-afternoon brightness. It was nearly five o'clock. He could have been out for ages, she had no way of knowing, and he could have got a long way: he was sprightly enough, for all his complaints about the 'arthritics'. She went downstairs, started on the tea and went out to feed the animals. She checked the shed again and looked down the lane – still no sign. She hoped he'd be back before Rene, she didn't want her worrying.

Elsie hadn't told Ernest she was going out; now she wondered if he wasn't paying her back. In the kitchen, she checked the hooks for missing items. The only outdoor clothes he ever seemed to want were scarves and gloves – usually theirs – and he wrapped himself up in these whenever he got the chance. Rene laughed to see him in green gloves and navy scarf, but Elsie didn't and once she found him nursing one of her hats like a kitten on his lap, with greasy, sticky fingers.

When Jugger started barking, she thought Rene must be back and hurried out, but when she got to the gate she saw it was him. For a moment she was relieved – at least he was back, and in one piece by the looks of it. He was a good way up the lane, standing on the corner by the old chimney. He started to wave in her direction, but his hand slipped down quickly as if he thought better of it.

They were about a hundred yards apart and neither seemed to have any appetite for getting closer. Nor did Jugger, who had stopped barking now and stayed close to her side.

'Where's Rene?' he called. His voice was surprisingly hale. 'I was looking for Rene.'

Elsie said nothing.

They stood for some moments, not quite looking at each other.

When he started towards her in that jerky, mechanical way, she felt momentarily like running back into the house, but she took a deep breath and stood her ground. He had no coat, just a shirt and that skimpy cardigan; his hands were in his trouser pockets and it gave him a jarring, jaunty look. Even from a distance she could see that his boots were clogged with mud. As he got closer she could see that he was wearing one of her scarves. Did he think she'd mistake him for a friend? Jugger whined.

Closer still and she watched him take his hands out of his pockets and lick his fingers. Soon his fingers would be all over the scarf, probably had been already.

'Is it teatime yet?' he asked as he came close. 'I was going to take me tea with me . . . but I only took the sugar . . .'

Elsie kept her mouth tightly shut – a spoon of his medicine.

Back at the cottage, he sat down heavily at the kitchen table and she struggled to unknot the scarf; she could see a stippling of fingerprints, smears of sugar. His boots were filthy.

'Wash day,' he said and giggled again. 'Wash day. And Elsie doesn't like doing the washing, does she? Poor old Elsie.'

She continued to ignore him and knelt down to unlace his boots. The laces were sodden and she fiddled with the knots. He tapped his other leg cheerily on the floor, spreading mud, enjoying her discomfort, still half singing her name. She kept picking at the knots on the boot, hating him. He was completely uncooperative, kept his foot rigid; finally she managed to pull the first boot off. But as she reached across him to place the boot out of the way, he sent out a sharp, hard kick with his tapping leg. The kick narrowly avoided her face. A howl came from behind and she saw Ernest smile. It wasn't Elsie he was after, not like that anyway. It was poor Jugger, who squealed and sprang back into his basket and then lay down quivering, nursing his muzzle.

Elsie told Rene what had happened when she came home that evening. Usually ready to give Ernest the benefit of the doubt, for once Rene didn't wonder or wait. As soon as Elsie had finished speaking, she marched into the sitting room and told Ernest that he was never to touch Jugger again. Elsie heard a few limp denials but they didn't last long, Rene wasn't going to be fobbed off.

Neither of them trusted him to keep his word and there was some relief for Elsie in that for it brought them together. They kept Jugger close – Jugger was delighted – and carried his basket up to their room at night. Sometimes he slunk up on the bed when they were asleep and Elsie pretended not to notice.

They were still able to glean a little time for themselves at the weekends. Ernest still woke late and Elsie no longer cared about his lazy habits. Rene would tiptoe downstairs when she woke and made the tea. Then she would bring a cup upstairs for them to share along with the *Helston Bugle*, which she brought home on Friday nights. Elsie loved the paper, the funny snippets about people she would never meet, the rituals of show and fair, the team photographs of sports in which she had no interest. They both avoided big, nasty stories. It was a pleasure they both shared, quietly – very quietly – taking it in turns to read aloud. There were occasions when they got through most of the paper before they heard Ernest stirring and grumbling. Other times, they would go downstairs before he woke and share breakfast, just the two of them, and the spoilt, skittish Jugger – it was such a treat. But neither of them could avoid a sense of dread when they heard him on the stairs, and Jugger cowered.

* * *

That year, the cold weather settled early in November and Ernest stopped his walks. As the frosts set in, even the shed seemed to hold little appeal. It was more than a year since he had arrived in that taxi. Day after day, he sat in the sitting room – only Rene seemed able to tempt him out into the garden. When she was working away, Elsie made a point of taking a brisk walk with Jugger every morning after she had done her chores (and settled Ernest with his morning bottle). She didn't like leaving him alone, Lord knows what nonsense he might try, but she needed to get shot of him, even if it was just for half an hour.

One Friday morning early in December, leaving Ernest with his beer bottle and syrupy tea, Elsie closed the cottage door quietly behind her and set off with Jugger for a walk in the wood. Everything was rimy. In the lane the air was like a soft, damp handkerchief; even Jugger's barking sounded muted. The mist lingered in the bare trees and the chimney was half hidden in the grey. When she reached the corner of the lane, Elsie stopped and leant back against the chimney, caught her breath and sucked in deep breaths of ordinary air – air that Ernest hadn't smoked or breathed first. She was glad that it was Friday: Rene would be home that evening, drawing her back just a little towards the ordinary.

She had scraps for the family of firecrests living in the chimney and she urged Jugger off ahead into the wood before emptying the crumbs carefully on to a narrow ledge. It had taken her a while to identify the little birds, with their orange crests so carefully painted – strangers who had been blown off course, they had decided to stay and she was glad. In the wood, she busied herself throwing sticks – much to Jugger's surprise and delight – and he rushed back and forth through the springy ferns. In the thickets, the holly was thriving and there were so many berries. Somehow, Ernest or no Ernest, she and Rene must come here together on Christmas Eve and gather some. She tentatively started to make plans for Christmas while Jugger splashed in the stream, and only turned for home reluctantly.

By the time she reached the chimney, she knew something was wrong. A terrible squawking was coming from the coops; Jugger barked nervously in reply and rushed past her towards the cottage, before she could stop him. Elsie quickened her pace – for all her size she covered the ground quickly – the squawking getting louder and more urgent. At the gate, she heard Jugger howl and then the dog came rushing back towards her to cringe and quiver against her legs.

Ernest.

Elsie marched on into the yard.

He was standing beside the open door of the coop, trying to twist the neck of one of the chickens; it was limp with fear and its eyes blinked uselessly. Feathers everywhere, fluttering. He started spitting and coughing. 'Hungry,' he mumbled. 'Making so much noise.' There were more feathers in his mouth, and blood, and she shuddered. She grabbed the hen and quickly, sharply, wrung its neck, while he stood teetering in front of her, blank-faced. The coop was in chaos: three hens dead on the floor, the wings of two were horribly torn and one had been partially plucked. The rest were huddled miserably, fearfully, at the back of the cage – they would do themselves a damage. She picked the dead hens up gently and took them out. Trying not to look at Ernest, she turned her attention back to the coop. Clicking and whispering, she patted out the straw the way she always did, and rescued a bit of the morning mash from the floor. Back outside, Elsie spied Samson, the cock, who was always ready to make a bid for freedom, and two of the hens, Tessy and Moira, huddled by the kitchen door. She went to get them, propping them under her arms. Back in the henhouse with you.

Ernest had started mumbling: 'Hungry,' he kept saying, 'here chick, chick, chick, chicky, here chicky, chicky, chicky, chicky.' She stood staring at him, catching up with her anger now the worst of the crisis seemed over. He finally met her eyes and a fleeting smile passed across his face, and then he went limp, with no warning, reaching for the wall as if he was going to fall. She steeled herself to steer him inside.

Much later, she took him his lunch. He was still mumbling to himself and there was a trail of feathers across the floor, feathers and sugar. Elsie felt sick as she cleaned it up; she knew she should tell Rene, but when it came to it she couldn't.

No thanks, I can manage.

* * *

'We'll end up living in the shed,' Rene said once. 'And I'm sure we could make it very comfortable.' Both of them started laughing, but in a nervy, skittish kind of way. It was early Sunday evening and they'd just finished bathing Ernest. They had left him in the kitchen while they dragged the bath out into the back garden and tipped its grey and suspect contents on to a patch of weedy ground. Elsie had once hoped that his dirty bathwater would kill the weeds, but if anything they were flourishing more strongly than ever – as if they recognized and relished common cause.

While Ernest fumbled with a stringy towel and an old nightdress in the kitchen, they kept outside, braving the cold to be clear of him. Rene was perched on a rickety old stool, with her mug of tea, smoking; Elsie stood next to her, leaning against the wall. She'd left her cup in the kitchen but she didn't want to go and get it.

It was the first time they had laughed in weeks, Rene thought, and that was something. But there should be other things to laugh about, other things to do. She glanced up at Elsie by her side: her face had gone quite blank – the brittle gladness of a moment ago disappeared.

'Oh Elsie. I meant it as a joke.'

'Oh, I know and it wasn't such a bad one,' she said, smiling bravely.

But Rene could see she was upset.

'It won't be for ever,' she said, trying to be consoling.

'Won't it?'

She sounded sharp, and Rene leant forward to squeeze her hand. Elsie nodded briskly, reassuring, but her hand stayed dumb in Rene's hand. They shouldn't spend their scant time alone like this, nearly arguing, about Ernest of all things. And Elsie clearly felt the same.

'Perhaps we should get a tent,' Elsie said, and the dark moment passed.

And when they went inside a few minutes later they were cheerful enough. He wasn't in the kitchen, and Rene hoped he might have gone upstairs.

'Uncle?'

But he hadn't gone upstairs; he had gone into the sitting room and she found him at the window, trying to paint out the glass – Lord knows where he'd got the paint. She called Elsie and they managed to stop him before he could do much damage, but Rene was troubled. 'What were you doing, Uncle?' she asked when she'd finished cleaning up. 'What's the matter?' He didn't say anything then, but later in the evening he looked up from his pint pot and pointed at the window.

'Blackout,' he said. 'Blackout.'

II.

Trouble

'Uncle?'

Tentatively, but without fear, Rene touched his forehead: cold, but barely colder than usual.

She held the candle closer to his face. His eyes, thank God, were shut, but one of his hands was clenched against his cheek and the chilblains on his fingers were still shiny. He had the special stillness of the dead, but the event was recent, she felt sure. At least he was in his bed, she thought, even if he didn't look exactly peaceful. The room was growing lighter in the dawn; she looked down at his face again and noticed the odd little bow in his lower lip, how thick his eyebrows were.

The mirror she had in her hand was blotched and murky. She put the candle down on the little stool beside the bed and blew on the mirror's surface, rubbed it clean, trying to shine it up before holding it to his mouth. Her breath felt like the only warm thing in the room. She remembered Dad all those years ago: her mother's hands shaking, the tears dripping on to the little compact.

Her own hands were shaking; she reached down and held the mirror close to his mouth, waited. It was an old mirror with a metal surround and a smooth, curved handle – small and heavy – she couldn't remember where it came from. She looked down at Ernest again, holding the mirror as still as she could, then she counted slowly to ten, and then to ten again. How long could she hold her breath? She and Lily swimming through the tide of people in the foyer at the Palace with their mouths clamped shut, Lily going red in the face, she about to explode into giggles; Vicky guiding her to their seats at the Imperial, the fizzing, popping purple drink in her hand – ahead of them on the screen was the man who swam to and fro, to and fro, across the Channel, endlessly it seemed, for ever.

'Bert?'

She turned to see Elsie watching her cautiously from the doorway of their bedroom. She was very pale. Rene counted to ten again quickly, retrieved the mirror, examined it; her hand had stopped shaking. She was quite calm now.

She turned and nodded to Elsie.

'He's gone.'

'Bert, are you sure? He went still that time before, in the kitchen, do you remember? It must have been an hour before we got him awake. It could be that, couldn't it, it could be . . .' She babbled on nervously, still standing in the doorway of their bedroom.

'Elsie, he's gone. The mirror's clear and he's cold – properly cold. Why don't you come in and have a look? He doesn't look so bad.'

But Elsie stood where she was and shook her head.

The morning light was coming in more strongly now, showing up the mottled wall and the ugly stain left by the leaking roof. Smoke still hung heavy in the room; Rene manoeuvred herself round the bed to open the window, struggling slightly with the catch. A gust of cold, damp air brushed past her. She thought of pulling back the curtains, but it didn't seem right somehow. From where she stood at the window, he looked more peaceful, his clenched hand barely visible; she could see the mug on the stool that did for his bedside table and the plaid-patterned slippers they'd given him at Christmas, nearly as good as new.

Elsie was still watching her; she had stepped forward a fraction but seemed unwilling to come closer.

'Let's go down,' Rene said.

Elsie nodded but she didn't move. Downstairs Jugger was scratching on the kitchen door, but she didn't seem to hear.

'Elsie, what's the matter?'

No reply.

'Elsie, what is it?'

'You're going out.' It was half a question.

'Yes, that's right.'

'But where? Where are you going?'

'Elsie, it's Wednesday, remember, I'm going to Margaret's.'

'Margaret? But surely you don't have to go. Not today. Couldn't you telephone her, tell her about him? Please don't go. I don't want to be on my own here, not with him.' Elsie looked towards the bed unwillingly.

'Elsie dear, it's Wednesday. I always go and help Margaret on Wednesdays, you know that – she's expecting me.' Rene paused, nodded encouragingly. 'There's nothing to worry about. I won't be long. Why don't you come downstairs? I'll make the tea. I don't need to go just yet, we can sit awhile.' Rene smiled, trying to take Elsie along. 'I'll take Jugger, or I could leave him with you? Whatever you prefer. You could go for a walk, a nice long one, get some fresh air, if you don't want to stay here. And I won't be long, I promise.'

Rene inched her way out of the room and on to the landing and briefly touched Elsie's arm. 'That's better,' she said. 'Will you come down?'

'I'll get dressed,' Elsie said.

Elsie closed the bedroom door behind her as if Ernest might still be watching. Then she went over to the window, pulled back the curtain and opened the window as wide as it would go. Across the lane in front of the cottage, the field was churned with mud – it had been grazed long into the wet, late summer and there was some trouble with the drainage. On the far side, over by the ditch, she could just make out the orange gleam of a pheasant as it paraded beside the hedge. In the next field the ponies were standing altogether in their favourite place – under a sweeping horse chestnut. She drank in the cold, clean air. Everything looked so fresh, no mist today. She longed to go outside – Rene was right, a walk was the best idea, a long one. But first she would have to go downstairs.

After she had dressed, she lingered at the door, unwilling to open it, unwilling to face the landing and what lay beyond. Downstairs she could hear Rene talking to Jugger. She listened, trying to make out what she was saying, her hand hovering on the little round handle. She could still feel the cold air, in her lungs, on her shoulders, Ernest was always complaining about the cold.

'Elsie?'

Rene was calling her.

'Coming.'

She steeled herself, opened the bedroom door and went out on to the tiny landing. His door was open – oh, why hadn't Rene closed the door? The staircase was ahead, just a step away, but her feet would go no further. She took a deep breath. Count to five, she said to herself and then. One, two, three, four, five. Her feet didn't listen, but her eyes were pulled into his room, like a magnet, towards his bed. He was lying there as he so often did, propped on his pillows, except that he was quiet; no mumbling, what a mercy. The curtain was still drawn, but a fine stream of light rippled on the wall above his bed. She looked at his face more carefully, and all of a sudden something moved close to his face. She froze again and her heart started banging in her ears.

She took a deep breath and tried to steady herself. Rene had checked and she trusted Rene. Rene had put her hand to his forehead and the mirror to his mouth. Elsie shivered and took another deep breath. She looked at him again, properly, steadily, she wouldn't let herself be caught out. On the stool by the bed lay the mirror – Rene must have left it there – and somehow it drew the morning light across his face, gleaming and watery. It was a trick, an illusion, he really had gone. Elsie grasped the doorknob to balance; it was sticky, she was sure she could feel the sugar. She retrieved her hand, wiped it on the wall, closed the door and went downstairs.

They sat for a little, drinking tea, eating toast and a plum jam that had somehow eluded Ernest. Rene was still wearing her mac – a sign of her resolve, perhaps. Once they'd finished eating, she got up straight away to take the plates to the sink; Elsie went out to feed the chickens and the rabbits. There were three eggs, one from Tessy, who was usually a poor layer. It was a good sign, she thought.

When she came back into the cottage, she could hear Rene talking on the telephone. She had her special phone voice on, and it echoed down the passage from the sitting room.

'Thank you. Yes. It's Miss Rene Hargreaves, Wheal Rock, Camborne 2165. You will pass on my message? Thank you. Goodbye.'

'Who were you speaking to?'

'The doctor. Dr Evans is out on a call at the minute. He will have to come here and see Ernest later, after his morning surgery.'

Elsie was looking upset again.

'Why does Dr Evans have to come here to see Ernest?'

She had never liked Dr Evans.

Rene was buttoning her coat. It was time for her to go but she didn't want to rush Elsie.

'You understand, Elsie, don't you? Dr Evans needs to come here and then he'll arrange for the body to be taken away.'

'I can't speak to the doctor,' Elsie said.

'You won't have to, love. Don't worry. I'll be back long before he gets here. But I thought it better to ring now. You need to report a death.'

'You're sure you'll be back before he comes?'

'Of course. I promise.'

Rene took her favourite peaked hat from the hook and pulled it down as far as she could, half covering her ears.

'I must go now.'

'I know.'

Rene opened the door, and Jugger, who had been standing quivering and hopeful in his basket, yelped with delight and bounded outside.

'Here, Jugger, come back. Here, boy,' Rene called after him half-heartedly, and the dog paused by the gate and barked again. She went after him.

'Bert. Before you go . . .'

Rene turned back; Elsie was pale again and shaky-looking.

'What's the matter? What is it?'

'There's a key, for his room, do you remember?' Elsie spoke very quietly, her voice hardly more than a whisper. 'It's on the kitchen windowsill. Please go and lock his door. Please.'

If Rene was shocked, she didn't show it. She got the key, then went upstairs to lock the door of Ernest's room.

'Take the key with you. Take it with you, Rene. I don't want to go in and I might and I don't want to.'

So Rene left the cottage with the key to Ernest's locked door in the long, loose pocket of her mac. Jugger was jumping about in front of her, but she didn't try to stop him – he could come if he liked. She climbed over the gate carefully and plodded through the squelching mud, keeping close to the fence. Jugger barked excitedly, then disappeared into the ditch. She heard the heavy *splat, splat* of his paws; he knew where she was going. By the time she'd reached the wobbly plank that bridged the ditch, he was waiting for her. She hopped over the stile and finally she was on solid ground; she strode out, sure-footed and brisk and preternaturally alert, her fingers tapping in her loose pockets. She liked this walk. The field finished in a narrow lane that led straight to the backyard of the post-office shop. She leashed Jugger, tied him up and told him to sit. He ignored her of course and barked cheerfully as he tried to shake out his muddy fur.

She went through to the shop, past the store and the cool-room, taking off her mac as she went; Margaret was already waiting. The delivery van arrived just a few minutes later, so she didn't get a chance to tell Margaret about Ernest – they were too busy helping with the unloading, carrying crates and boxes into the storeroom.

Rene didn't stay long after Mr Lyons left. She would have liked to stop for tea, but she didn't like to think of Elsie there on her own, working herself up. Margaret didn't seem at all surprised to hear about Ernest, after the first little cluck of shock. Rene left with all manner of messages for Elsie and kind promises of help – such a good friend.

As Jugger bounded across the field and she put his leash back in her pocket, her hand touched the key to Ernest's room. She hoped the doctor wouldn't keep them waiting too long. She couldn't bring herself to feel sorry.

Dr Evans didn't get to Wheal Rock till three o'clock that afternoon and then he was accompanied by a young colleague, who was staying with him – a Dr Carter. Dr Evans drove a smart grey Austin and popped in for some tobacco at Mrs Cuff's shop on his way. At the cottage, Evans waived the offer of tea and the two men went straight upstairs. Evans – who was heavily built and above average height – made the examination with some difficulty, talking all the while to Carter, who had inched himself round to the window but could get no closer than the end of the bed. Evans asked Carter to feel Mr Massey's feet and legs to gauge the rigor mortis and suggest a time of death. Carter winced as his hands moved over the old man's bony feet and ankles, but Evans said nothing – in their own homes the dead took some getting used to. He turned to look at Massey's face again, a little yellower than might be expected, perhaps. A pity his hand was clenched in that way – it must have made a rather upsetting sight for Miss Hargreaves.

Carter pulled the blanket back down over Mr Massey's feet: the time of death was probably about twelve hours before; Evans nodded his agreement. He had a last look round and then the two men squeezed out of the room and inched down the stairs. Dr Evans asked Miss Hargreaves if he could use the phone.

There was quite a gap of time before the ambulance came, and the two doctors sat together on the uncomfortable sofa in the sitting room. Miss Hargreaves made them some tea. When the ambulance arrived, the men had to prise the skinny, set body out of the tiny room and down the narrow stairs – no easy task, and Carter and Evans had to help; the operation left poor Carter looking rather green. The two ladies, rather sensibly, remained in the kitchen.

The doctors followed the ambulance in the Austin. Mrs Cuff saw the little procession as she walked over to see her friend Mrs Marrack.

★ ★ ★

After the strange day they had had, the two women spent a quiet evening. Neither of them had much appetite, most of the stew went back in the pot. After supper, Rene conjured a quarter bottle of brandy and they sat on the uncomfortable sofa in the sitting room, sipping a little too quickly and watching the fire. Things seemed too easy and quiet, not enough to do. Both of them were uncomfortably aware of Ernest's chair. It was the best chair in the house, but it seemed unlikely it would have any further purpose. There was a nice play on, but neither of them had the attention. Nib had stretched herself out on Elsie's lap and Jugger lay deep asleep on the peacock rug. In recent months, neither animal would come into the room if Ernest was there.

'I can't feel sorry,' Elsie said.

'What?'

'I can't feel sorry about Ernest.'

'Nor can I. Nor do I. It's strange, that's all. But you shouldn't have to feel sorry. There's no need.'

'No, I suppose not.'

'Imagine, four whole days ahead, just us together. I'm so glad I phoned the farm, Catherine was very kind about it.'

'So you'll go back on Monday?'

'Yes. That'll be all right, won't it?'

'Oh yes, of course.'

'You'll want to be rid of me by then, won't you?'

The brandy was starting to do its work; Elsie smiled and stretched out her legs, a tiny mew of protest from Nib.

'What'll we do? Let's make a plan for tomorrow. If it's not cold we could go out on the scooter. You'd like it and I wouldn't go too fast, I promise.'

Elsie had so far refused to get on the scooter. She worried enough about Rene on it.

'I don't know.'

'Or you could ride the bike. And I could ride the scooter. We'd look a bit silly, I suppose, but it would be fun.'

'I don't know.' Elsie looked awkward.

'Elsie, what's the matter?'

'I don't think we should be talking like this.'

'Oh, Ernest wouldn't mind, I'm sure. What's it to him?'

Elsie smiled, a little nervously, and Rene continued half to herself: 'I'm not doing a proper funeral, just a burial, there's no point. A funeral costs too much; no one would come down here anyway.'

'You wouldn't have it in Manchester?'

'Goodness, no.' Rene sounded surprised. 'I'm not doing that. I don't want to draw it out, I want it over.'

Elsie seemed relieved, she smiled and stretched again; Rene poured the last of the brandy out slightly clumsily and the glasses clinked together.

'Now, Elsie, it's time to decide about tomorrow. Tomorrow is our day. No scooters, no bikes. A walk, a good long one over to Coate's Wood. We haven't been there together for such a long time – the paths should be all right. We could set out early. And then we could have the rest of the stew for lunch, or if it's fine we could take sandwiches. And there's that concert on in the evening, or we could make a start on the new puzzle.'

Rene was in her stride now, thinking ahead, making plans.

'Elsie, what's the matter?'

'I don't know, it doesn't seem quite right.'

'Elsie, you *can't* feel bad – you said it yourself. And I don't think either of us should feel sad either. We did what we could – more than that, we did our best. And besides, he wasn't . . . he wasn't a nice man. I don't think he was a good man. There was something mean-minded about him, Margaret said we . . . said he was mean-minded. She saw it too.'

'Margaret?'

'She met him too, remember?'

But that wasn't what Elsie was thinking about.

'You told Margaret about Ernest?'

'Not like that. I wouldn't. But there were a few things he said, and that time he kicked Jugger, I told her about that.'

'Oh.'

For Elsie hated the idea of anyone else knowing about Ernest, knowing what it had been like; it rubbed off on them, on her. She still hadn't told Rene about the chickens, the blood and the feathers, wiping his mouth, him spitting and coughing, spit and feathers on her, the blood on her cardigan. She mustn't think about that. She must try to concentrate on Rene.

'It doesn't matter. Anyway,' Rene was saying, 'Margaret said she thought we were a pair of saints. Lord, I'm so hungry. It must be the brandy. If I don't eat something soon I'm sure I'll fall over.'

Elsie followed Rene to the kitchen, very willing to be diverted. But she didn't feel happy about Margaret. A pair of saints, Margaret had said, but she was a Methodist, and they didn't have saints. How could Margaret know? She had thrown the cardigan away. It had just a trace of blood on it, she could probably have got the mark out, but she couldn't even bear to wash it.

The next two days were glorious. They took long walks on both mornings and quite exhausted Jugger, throwing stick after stick for him in Coate's Wood. Back to Wheal Rock by eleven, when Rene would make her telephone calls. After lunch they settled (as far as it was possible to settle) on the sofa in the sitting room, just them. Just them, alone with no one to interrupt them – they had quite forgotten the habit of it. They played Patience as they had done for so many years – each with a tray on a stool in front of her – and together they made a start on the new puzzle. It was strange to be playing in the daylight, but it was also luxurious – Thursday afternoon, Friday afternoon – and they were on the sofa, idling. In the evenings, there was a new serial – it was nearly a week in but they caught up easily enough with no Ernest to distract them. On the Friday evening, Elsie brought out a bottle of ancient, vinegary sherry that she had hidden in their bedroom and two spindly glasses. They drank half of it – making faces as they did so at the bitterness – and played a silly game of dominoes. Nib watched them curiously from the windowsill and Jugger thumped his tail whenever they laughed. And when they had run out of silliness they made tentative plans for the following day. If the weather was fine they would make the long-delayed trip to Gunwalloe – on the scooter – Elsie had agreed. And they would get fish and chips in the village – it was too early in the year for a picnic.

They should have gone to bed early, they were planning to make an early start, but they were too excited. It was partly the trip, so long deferred, but more than that, it was the sheer luxury of being their only company; no threat of interruption, no one to mind or fret about. When they finally went upstairs, they took cocoa and a half-forgotten detective novel that Rene had got from

Boots. It was a cold night and they wrapped themselves up close in the extra blanket while Elsie read aloud. It was a poor story, and the killer didn't seem very clever at all – it was a wonder the policeman didn't catch him sooner – but they both enjoyed it all the same.

They slept late the following morning and weren't dressed and downstairs till just before eight. A fine, clear day, and they quietly made their preparations for Gunwalloe; they were both looking forward to the day ahead. It had been so long postponed – Elsie had wondered if it would ever happen.

They were just about to put on their jackets when they heard the sound of a car coming up the lane.

It all happened very quickly. Rene was at the sink and she saw the car through the window. A police car.

'Oh my goodness,' she said.

'What is it?'

'A police car. I hope nothing dreadful's happened.'

Rene had turned very pale and was rooted; Elsie knew she was thinking about the children.

It was Elsie who opened the door.

Two policemen and a WPC. The two men looked like father and son.

'Miss Hargreaves?'

'No.'

'Miss Boston?'

Elsie nodded.

'May we come in?'

Elsie nodded again and stood back. They crowded into the kitchen, looking around. Rene was still standing by the window, aloof.

'Will you sit down?' said Elsie awkwardly.

'Thank you.'

The WPC sat down and the two men remained standing.

'Miss Hargreaves,' said the grey-haired policeman, addressing Rene.

'Yes.' Her voice was little more than a croak, her face as white as chalk.

'Our visit concerns Mr Ernest Massey. You are the niece of Mr Massey, are you not?'

'Ernest?' Rene said. She sounded confused.

'Dr Evans decided that a post-mortem was required to ascertain the cause of death. You do know what a post-mortem is?'

'Of course.' Rene sounded a little hasty, but there was a bit more colour in her face now. Elsie nodded too but no one was looking at her.

'Well, the post-mortem showed that your uncle died from poisoning.'

'What?' It was Rene who spoke. Elsie reached forward to clasp the corner of the table; she was unsteady all over again, just as she had been that morning on the landing. He hadn't gone after all.

'According to the pathologist, the cause of death is beyond reasonable doubt. Sodium chlorate poisoning. Sodium chlorate is a key component in many weedkillers. I imagine that you keep weedkiller.'

There was something rude about the way he said that, Elsie thought, but Rene didn't seem to notice. The WPC looked like she wanted to giggle.

'He can't have been poisoned,' Rene said. 'It's impossible.'

'As I'm sure you will appreciate, Miss Hargreaves, there are a number of possibilities that we will need to consider. Mr Massey may have poisoned himself – deliberately or by accident – or, and we are under obligation to investigate this, he may have been poisoned by another or others at present unknown. We'll need to ask you and Miss Boston some questions. We will also need to have a look around the cottage and take some photographs. We'll try not to make a mess.' This last was said in an over-cheerful tone and was addressed to both of them.

Elsie was led into the sitting room by the WPC while Rene remained to be questioned in the kitchen. Elsie heard the sound of heavy feet tramping up the stairs, heard them in Ernest's room, and then, after a gap of some minutes, in theirs. It was just like before, someone messing in their room, nosing; she could swear she heard drawers being opened. The last two days were as nothing. Elsie felt faint – the blood was all running away from her head. She leant forward on the sofa and put her hands down beside her; they felt shaky. 'Are you all right, Miss eh Boston?' the WPC asked; she didn't sound unfriendly. Elsie nodded, trying to listen to the voices in the kitchen.

She could hear nothing but a mumbling from the policeman, but she could hear Rene's voice quite clearly. It was her telephone voice and louder than usual. Yes, of course he was happy here, why wouldn't he be? No, he wasn't the kind of man who would harm himself. Yes, she knew exactly what was being suggested. She sounded almost rude.

'Ahem.' The young policeman appeared in the doorway of the sitting room. He had his hat off and a large camera strapped about his neck. They would have to move now, the WPC said, he needed to take some photographs here. 'Shall we go outside?'

There was no way out except through the kitchen. Rene was sitting with her elbows on the table, hands on her chin – she looked irritable – but she caught Elsie's eyes and gave her a quick smile as if to say, *Please don't worry*. Elsie and the WPC passed outside into the garden; they went up to the gate but no further – it seemed to set a natural boundary. So they stood there in the cold, she and the WPC, and all Elsie could see was weeds. And then Elsie started to get confused. They were called back into the kitchen: it was her turn to be asked questions now. She wanted Rene to sit with her but they didn't let her stay, said she couldn't. And then there were questions about saucepans and was he happy and mugs and weedkiller and what were his habits and she tried to answer, tried her best, but it felt as if her hands were getting in the way of her mouth, sticking, sticky as sugar. Upstairs there were more footsteps – this time she was sure they were his. She started to cry and then Rene came running.

'Leave her alone. Can't you see she's upset? Can't you see?'

And then she and Rene were separated again and they were asking Rene some more questions, this time in the sitting room; she heard Rene's voice saying loudly, 'Of course we have weedkiller, why wouldn't we have weedkiller? We have a garden, don't we?'

And then the older policeman came back and told her that they were taking Rene to Exeter police station to answer some more questions. Something about a box of things they were taking with them. And then Rene was already outside, already gone, looking back at her through the kitchen window. Then she had turned away and Elsie saw the car door open and it looked as if Rene was being pushed in. The car started up and she was gone.

* * *

It was Mrs Cuff who telephoned Elsie, the day after the police took Rene to Exeter. She had never done that before, hardly knew Elsie if truth be told, but Rene had telephoned her from the police station and told her what had happened. She had been arrested, arrested for murder. Rene hadn't seemed especially bothered about this, she was sure it would all blow over, but she was very worried about Elsie: 'Please ring her, go and see if she's all right, please.'

Mrs Cuff rang Wheal Rock immediately but with some trepidation.

'Rene?' Elsie's voice sounded muffled.

'No, Miss Boston, it's me, Margaret Cuff from the post-office shop. I was just ringing to find out how you were. This is such a business with Rene, but I'm sure she'll be back at Wheal Rock soon and –'

'They've taken her, they've taken her away.'

Mrs Cuff did her best to reassure her, but Elsie was not in a state of mind to be convinced.

'I'll never see her again. I know it. She'll never come back.'

And so it went on. Until Margaret said:

'I'd like to call round if I may, Miss Boston – Elsie. I hope you won't think it's an intrusion, but I'd like to . . . I'll come in the afternoon,' she finished briskly. It didn't do to talk too long, it would only make things more complicated.

Mrs Cuff telephoned Mrs Marrack and Miss Penn, and just after five the three of them walked up to Wheal Rock. Neither Mrs Marrack nor Miss Penn had made the journey before, so there was curiosity to be satisfied as well as neighbourliness. They took with them a flask of soup, some milk and cheese, a mutton pie and half a bottle of sherry. They were not sure what Miss Boston might need, or what help they could offer – there was no real precedent for any of them. Seen from a distance with their black shawls and baskets they could have been visitors to a bereaved house, or perhaps, given the slight hesitation of step, well-wishers making a first call on a new neighbour.

Elsie saw them coming through the dusk, Mrs Cuff leading the way, like three witches, but carrying baskets instead of brooms; she had been half expecting something like this. She wished they hadn't come, but it was kind, very kind. She went out to meet them.

They petted the dog while Miss Boston made tea, and then Mrs Cuff persuaded her to come and sit with her in the sitting room. She wanted to get as clear a picture as possible of everything that had happened. Mrs Marrack and Miss Penn made themselves busy upstairs. It was a sensible distribution of tasks as Elsie was more at ease with Mrs Cuff ('please call me Margaret') and Mrs Marrack and Miss Penn could make themselves useful. They folded up some washing and gave Mr Massey's room a general tidy-up. They peeped into the other bedroom but didn't linger – neither of them liked a pry. Later, on Mrs Cuff's instruction, Miss Penn made Elsie a sandwich and sat with her while she ate it (she wouldn't accept a sherry, which Miss Penn thought was a pity). Mrs Cuff joined Mrs Marrack in the kitchen and they tidied up, washing up some dishes, a couple of cups and a mug.

In the village, there was shock that such a kind lady could have been whisked away in a police car to Exeter without any warning. In tears she was, apparently (though not handcuffed), and Miss Boston quite hysterical. The three ladies saw no reason to keep all of the detail to themselves. No one thought they could have done Massey any real harm. Miss Hargreaves wouldn't hurt a fly. Rene had made herself useful, men and women both liked her; Elsie they weren't so sure of, she kept to the background, not easy in herself or chatty like Rene. She was reckoned to be fragile, despite her size, and Rene protective of her, for it was as a couple of sorts that they were thought of by their neighbours; there was thought to be unhappiness in the past. The village too was protective, even at its margins.

Village kindness did not extend to Ernest Massey. In the early months, he had occasionally come into the post office on Rene's prompting and mumbled hello to Mrs Cuff; more often, he had lingered outside, twisting his hands in his pockets. As Mr Cardell said, 'His eyes couldn't hold your own.' The general judgement was that he was a little cakey; some also thought he was mean-spirited – pressed for more detail, all they could say was that it was a feeling they had.

The first distinct rumour to gather in the days after Rene had been arrested was that the old man had committed suicide. This was shocking, and some people were quite upset. In the unsettled atmosphere, other rumours: chief among these was that Massey's death was a self-administered accident. Mrs Cuff and Miss Penn were strongly persuaded of this possibility.

At this stage no one doubted that Rene's arrest was a terrible mistake, that everything would be resolved, and she would soon be home. When the news came that she had been transferred to Holloway (there was no room for her at Exeter), things began to get more complicated. Mrs Cuff and her two friends were still regular visitors to Wheal Rock: there was still concern for Miss Boston's health. For others, out of sight was out of mind, and the matter half forgotten. But when Mr Prynne was overheard by Mr Marrack saying that there was no smoke without fire and that he didn't know what to think about that reporter knocking around in the village, Mrs Cuff, Mrs Marrack and Miss Penn took matters into their own hands. They called a meeting at the church hall to discuss 'recent events, Miss Hargreaves, Miss Boston and what we should do'. On the strength of the meeting – well attended – various letters were written and dispatched and a collection was made. Nearly everyone gave something; a few of the contributions were very generous, one in particular. It came from the only stranger who attended the meeting: a middle-aged woman, very smartly dressed. She sat on her own at the back of the hall. She didn't say anything during the meeting but she seemed very interested in everything that was going on. Mrs Cuff hoped she wasn't a reporter.

Mrs Cuff had volunteered to do the collection and as the meeting came to an end she made her way slowly through the hall with her tin. People really were very generous, even the smallest sum was a token of goodwill. She hesitated before approaching the smart woman at the back – it was a little awkward asking a stranger – but she found herself being beckoned forward. The woman had clearly been waiting for this moment because she reached smoothly into her bag and took out a cheque. She put this, unfolded, into the tin. The cheque was for a considerable sum and it had all been written up beforehand. Mrs Cuff didn't know quite what to do, she was quite taken aback by the amount and she didn't want to make a fuss. She went back up to the front to help Miss Penn and Mrs Marrack and resolved to thank the woman properly at the end of the meeting. Unfortunately, by the time Mrs Cuff could get outside, the smart woman had slipped into a waiting taxi and then she was gone.

Elsie didn't come to the meeting – it would have been quite wrong – but she was touched by the kindness of neighbours and quite overwhelmed by the sum of money that was collected. She tried to thank Mrs Cuff, who said that she must call her Margaret and seemed to understand.

Elsie used most of her share to purchase a greatcoat. Some time ago she had seen an advertisement in the *Exeter Mail*, and now she telephoned Abley's Menswear to ask them to set one by. By arrangement, Mr Marrack picked it up for her in Helston. It was an extravagance of course – she had never spent so much on a garment – but it was a wonderful coat and it fitted so snugly. And it was not perhaps quite the indulgence it seemed. The trial date had been set and Elsie was making her plans. She wanted a big coat to wrap herself up in.

Elsie would have to travel all the way to Winchester for the trial, a long and complicated journey that filled her with dread. Mrs Cuff – Margaret – said they should travel together (she was being called as a witness too) and Elsie had gratefully agreed. She was daunted about spending so much time with anyone other than Rene, but it was less daunting than travelling alone.

12.

Letter from Holloway

Dear Elsie,

You must not come and visit me, I insist. I am managing here quite well.
I read and keep to myself most of the time. We sometimes get to listen
to the wireless in the evening, but it is another station and I miss our
programmes. But you mustn't think of coming, Elsie. It is far too far
for you to come, even with Margaret, and I know how you feel about
London.

Poor Jugger. His poor flat ears when I was taken – that was what made
me cry. He must have known something was wrong. You always said I
was too soft with him and I'm sure you're right, but I bet you've kept his
basket upstairs all the same. I know he will appreciate your walks – you
always were the bigger walker.

Remember the night we set off to see the White Horse? Such a long
way. Such a long time ago but it keeps coming back. The brandy made us
silly, didn't it?

We cycled for an age with those muffled lights. And then how we
walked and walked! I was so worried someone would steal our bikes,
but you said I had to trust you. I'm sure you remember that. You said
you would find the right path. It was still moonlight and so warm and
the land seemed to swirl about us. Oh Elsie, we weren't young then, but
it felt like we were. Do you remember we found that old packet of
cigarettes?

You must thank Margaret for sending me the cigarettes, it's very kind
of her. I'm smoking too much I know, but sometimes the time seems to
drag so. The food is dismal, though I promise you faithfully I am eating –
you are not to worry. All the tasty things we used to keep in our
cupboards! But that was before Ernest came and ate them or broke the
jars. He broke a lot of things.

Elsie, please believe me when I tell you that everything will be all right – I'm sure of it. They've made a silly mistake and have to go through with it now but in the end they'll have to let me go – it's just too stupid.

Writing this now I can almost see you, sitting in the kitchen. You'll have your spectacles out on the table but you won't have put them on, you never really feel you need them, do you? If you use the bicycle, remember the brake is always stiff. Travel to the court with Margaret – it's a long journey and it would make her happy, and me.

A hug for Jugger and look after yourself.

Your Bert

At Winchester

13

The Eagle Hotel

At the train station, it was Elsie who bought the tickets, studied the timetable and checked the connections with the sleepy ticket-man. Margaret was surprised. She watched as Elsie strode briskly down the platform and climbed the steps of the passenger bridge – as if her case weighed nothing – she was halfway across the bridge before she looked back. Margaret followed, tripping awkwardly along the platform with her box case banging her shins. This wasn't the Elsie she knew. But then Margaret couldn't know the force of what urged her forward, or the journeys Elsie had made, all those journeys, from half-forgotten stations like this, most of them with Rene. SEE YOUR OWN COUNTRY FIRST.

The train wasn't busy and they had the compartment to themselves. 'We can both sit by the window,' Elsie said – she always sat by the window if she could, ever since that first trip north with Rene. Margaret settled herself down in the other window seat, though there was nothing to see from the window: everything was rubbed out by the rain. Big, hard drops burst heavily on to the glass of the window, over and over. Margaret got out her library book and tried to read, and Elsie got her book out too. 'What will you talk about on that long journey?' Miss Penn had asked, and Margaret had smiled and said nothing. Elsie didn't want to talk; she put her book down and just sat watching the window, watching it like a picture: the rain exploding silently on the glass, over and over.

Margaret tried to keep her eyes on her book but it couldn't hold her attention – she was too preoccupied with thoughts of the next few days. Rene's trial was her main concern of course. But there were far too many other novelties: the long journey that she and Elsie were making to Winchester; the hotel in the town where they would be staying and taking their meals; Elsie's state of mind. And though she wouldn't have admitted it to Miss Penn or Mrs Marrack, or even to Belinda, she was concerned about how she and Elsie would manage together for all this time.

For the moment there seemed little cause for concern; wrapped in her greatcoat, Elsie kept her eyes on the window. After a while she gave up on the rain and pressed her nose to the glass, trying to get a glimpse of what lay beyond. It was a largely wasted effort, but just occasionally there was the shimmer of water and light in a flooded field, a glimmer of movement as if something stirred beneath.

At twelve, Margaret got out the picnic lunch she had made for them both: very plain, just sandwiches and a slice of cherry cake. They would be getting their main meal in the evening – at the hotel. As usual, Elsie ate slowly, chewing carefully. It had been months since she had shared a meal with anyone, and she thanked Margaret warmly – though she still stumbled to call her by her first name.

Time passed; the train squealed slowly to a stop in another half-forgotten station, Elsie rubbed at the glass and pressed her nose hard to the pulsing window, trying to catch the name on the sign. She peered again then sat back, quite lost for a moment, then she bit her lip.

'Elsie, are you all right?' Margaret asked.

And Elsie turned and nodded briefly. Margaret knew better than to say more.

What a day.

The rain did not relent. If anything, it was heavier by the time they reached Winchester. When the taxi arrived at the stand, they could only climb in by taking a big step to cross the gushing stream in the gutter. Elsie managed it easily in her big boots – for once they didn't seem so out of place; but Margaret faltered and caught a bad splash on her nylons.

'Cathedral crypt's already flooded,' the taxi driver told them, but he cheerfully pointed out the town sights: the barracks; the ruin of the Westgate; the famous statue with its sagely pointing finger. Coming into the centre, they got snarled up in the remains of the market-day traffic and were finally stuck on a handsome stone bridge. Through the streaked balustrades Margaret and Elsie watched the water fast and foaming; heard it too, gushing hard beneath.

The taxi eventually stopped outside the Eagle Hotel, a somewhat shabby Georgian building with a porch of fine black columns. This was where they would be staying during the trial. It had once been a coaching inn; there was still an old tethering point and a cobbled yard to one side. 'Here we are,' the driver said, and both women fumbled for their purses. And then it was all a bit awkward as the driver got out to retrieve their luggage and Margaret slipped out of the back seat and Elsie shuffled awkwardly after her. And then they weren't sure whether to wait for him, and then he strode up the stairs to the door anyway, so they followed him and went clumsily through it and wiped and wiped their feet on the heavy mat. The driver hovered and Elsie tipped him for a second time. But then he was gone, the door closed in a soft heavy hush and the sound of the rain finally stopped. They both felt quite exhausted.

Margaret recovered first and went over to the reception desk to make the arrangements. Elsie waited gratefully in the empty lobby, trying to catch her breath. She had never been anywhere like this. She had stayed in numerous bed and breakfasts, but this was a proper hotel. It was the warmth she felt first; it came forward like a welcome, touching the tips of her fingers and breathing ever so gently on her nose. Beneath her feet, there was carpet as far as the eye could see. She stretched herself cautiously into the warmth and took in the even spread of the light – how bright it was here, so different from the relentless grey outside.

The trial was due to start the next day and Elsie and Margaret wouldn't be called till the end of the second day at the earliest. But nothing could have kept Elsie away. Once she knew the day that the trial was starting, she wanted to be in Winchester. If Rene was going to be here, Elsie wanted to be here too. Unlike Margaret, who could foresee all manner of troubles for the days ahead, Elsie hadn't thought much yet about the trial. It was the thought and excitement of seeing Rene that preoccupied her, and everything else was a blur. Perhaps she really did lack imagination.

The warmth and the carpet – a dry, dusty green – extended into the lift and along the second-floor corridor where they had their rooms. Margaret insisted that Elsie have the better room – larger by a fraction and with a nice view of the square. It was agreed that Elsie would knock on Margaret's door at a quarter to six to go downstairs to the dining room, and they parted with mild relief on both sides.

Alone in her room, Elsie switched the light on and off a few times and took off her coat. She was thankful to have her own room – she wouldn't have wanted to share with anyone apart from Rene.

It was a big bed with all manner of complicated coverings and four rather floppy pillows. Nib would have been on them in a minute, looking for a niche. There were pictures on the walls – engravings of the town – and over by the bay window were a big armchair and a little round table and a lamp; she switched this on too. Unable to settle, she unpacked her clothes and put them in the wardrobe. She did this slowly, unfolding everything, hanging what she could and pressing everything else carefully into the drawers, on top of the pretty daisy-knotted paper. Then she hung her damp coat from the top of the wardrobe, put her neat navy bag (borrowed, like a number of items for this trip, from Margaret) under the bed, and placed her book – a detective – on the bedside table. She looked around the room again as if to assess her impact. The window and the armchair beckoned, but she was still too fidgety so she opened the heavy door of her room and went down the corridor to explore the bathroom.

If anything, the bathroom impressed her more than anything: the great white bath and sink; the tall, shining taps; the thin rectangles of pale soap. There was also a basket of bath cubes, each individually wrapped in blue and gold paper and smelling, she quickly discovered, eye-prickingly exotic. There was a radiator, blazing hot, and along the wall a bank of gleaming copper pipes. These were part of the new plumbing system, but, to Elsie, they were, along with the bath cubes and the hot radiator, just more magic. She turned on the hot tap of the bath experimentally. The water came immediately; no cough, no splutter. It gushed hot within moments. She turned the tap off and then on again. It had been a long time since she'd seen a real bath in a real bathroom, far longer since she'd used one. She had certainly never seen a bathroom like this. Just for a moment, she thought that she'd have a bath, then and there, even if it was the middle of the afternoon. There was no one else about after all. She would powder one of the cubes into the hot gushing water and pop back to her room to get the towels and the dressing gown that Margaret had found her and . . . But the plan died as she thought it – she was just too shy. What if she saw somebody as she came out of the bathroom with her hair all wet? Passing people in the corridor in a dressing gown in the early morning or the evening might be all right – but three o'clock was a funny time to take a bath, even if the water was hot. She decided she would wait.

The bathroom and bedroom door both had the same notice: IN THE EVENT OF FIRE, MAKE YOUR WAY OUTSIDE USING THE MAIN STAIRCASE. DO NOT USE THE LIFT.

Back in the bedroom, she moved the armchair closer to the window and pulled the nets back carefully so she could look out. Finally, she sat down.

Her window looked out on a pretty little square of comfortable if shabby houses; there was a garden of some kind in the centre. Most of the houses had outside lamps, which shone a feeble yellow light in the wet winter afternoon. The houses looked very tall and thin to Elsie, and forlorn with their empty plant pots. But she didn't find the scene as a whole so. She was too excited about seeing Rene. She breathed experimentally on the window, blurring the view, then wiping it clear. Soon, in just three days, maybe two; perhaps Rene was here already. The thought of seeing Rene was everything; it made her happy, just the thought of it. Beyond that the trial was a blank, a blur. The only other thing she could see was she and Rene travelling home to Wheal Rock. For Rene would soon be free, she was sure of it, and then she and Rene would travel back together, and Mrs Cuff – Margaret – would come with them too; she had been so kind, so helpful, from the first.

Outside in the square the light was beginning to fade, though she could still see the rain. In the garden, the branches of the birches reached up like a plea of ancient hands. There was ivy everywhere; it gloved the trees' long fingers, leaving just the tips bare. She blew again on the window, blurred out the picture, rubbed it clear. She felt oddly comfortable. It was not just the warmth and the light and the carpet, or even the thought of Rene, who must soon be close by. Wheal Rock had been lonely without Rene, and when Rene had been transferred to London, so far away, quite out of reach.

The garden in the centre of the square was bounded by iron railings; Elsie could see the padlocked gate quite clearly from her window. Inside the circle of trees floated a green lawn surrounded by a fringy shore of gravel. Among the thin, stretching trees, she picked out an old, wizened apple – it seemed left over, forgotten. If the rain kept up like this, the roots would surely rot.

When Margaret opened her door to Elsie at quarter to six, she was relieved to see that Elsie had followed her advice on clothing. She was wearing Rene's smart leather ankle boots – nearly new and only a little small – and a soft, navy sweater that Margaret had lent her. There was nothing to be done about the slacks, thought Margaret, but the sweater and the neat brown boots did something to bring Elsie closer to the ordinary.

They were first into the dining room and that helped too: there was no one to observe them as they were shown to their table, or hear their shoes on the shining wooden floor. The elderly waiter settled them gently at a table between two windows and padded back to the kitchen. The pause gave them a chance to get their breath, for they were both daunted by the room. It was a very grand room, large and high-ceilinged. The tables were dressed in long, heavy linen and gleamed with glassware and silver cutlery. Each table had a vase of pale, crêpey daffodils, quite wilted in the heat, but even the half-dead flowers added something to the grandeur. There were pictures on the walls, as neatly spaced as the tables, more engravings of the town. The waiter returned with the menus then padded away again, his soft-shoed feet quite silent on the floor. It was very quiet, dauntingly so. It made you think of breaking things, Margaret thought. Occasionally, very occasionally, a brief swell of laughter came in from the bar.

Elsie and Margaret studied the menu cards in front of them carefully, keeping the quiet. When the waiter returned, Margaret asked for tomato soup and roast chicken, but Elsie paused for what seemed like an age before blushing deeply and ordering curried prawns and salmon mornay. She kept her eyes firmly on the menu card as she spoke, but her voice was clear enough.

'Gosh, Elsie, are you sure?' Margaret asked, when she was certain the waiter was out of earshot.

'Oh yes,' Elsie said. 'Quite sure.'

And she was. She ate everything, slowly and thoughtfully, with interest. Rene wouldn't have been surprised, not even if Elsie had ordered French snails (which weren't on the menu), but Margaret was a little taken aback. They both ordered the trifle from the trolley to finish though, and this seemed to make things easier. They even made a little small-talk, and though it was mainly Margaret talking about Belinda and the shop, it did well enough for the purpose.

Other diners came in as they ate: most were men and none were young; a few brought drinks with them from the bar, but any noise was left behind at the entrance, like an overcoat or a pair of gloves. No one seemed very interested in anyone else, and Margaret didn't feel they caught any awkward attention. It had all gone better than she could have hoped.

They were just finishing their tea when a large group of men came in, laden with drinks from the bar. One of them, unsteady on his feet, grabbed hold of the wooden menu stand for balance and nearly toppled it over. A very thin young man with long hair jumped forward and grabbed the stand just in time. A couple of the others whistled and applauded. They were a big group, ten or twelve of them; they didn't wait to be asked but settled themselves at two tables close to the entrance, pulling them together with a good deal of noise and some laughter at the expense of someone called Colin. His name carried across the room. They were directly in Margaret's line of vision and she couldn't avoid looking at them, couldn't avoid listening.

They quietened down and were polite enough when one of the elderly waiters came to take their orders, but they burst out laughing as soon as he had turned away; a man sitting alone at a table tutted disapprovingly. Margaret didn't care for the look of them and she didn't want to walk past them, certainly not with Elsie. There was something tricky and unpredictable to them. The man who had nearly fallen over was now talking in a very animated way to nobody in particular, and nobody in particular seemed to be listening. They were all brushed up with drink and a buzzing, fizzing energy, their eyes darting this way and that.

'Shall we go now?' Elsie asked.

She sat, apparently content, with her broad back to all the noise and excitement behind her, seemingly oblivious.

'Margaret? Could we go back upstairs to our rooms now? I'm feeling very tired.'

'Yes, of course. I'm tired too. It's been a long day.'

There was no reason to delay. They had finished their tea and Margaret had promised to telephone Belinda.

They both stood up. Margaret was ready to go in a moment, but Elsie took an age to gather her things. She got the bulky room key and a voluminous hanky into her trouser pockets after a fashion, but there was nothing she could do with her purse but carry it awkwardly in both hands – she was quite at a loss without a jacket and had never carried a woman's bag. Margaret felt sure that at least one of those noisy men would notice them, would notice Elsie's trousers or how long she stood at the table, trying to fill her pockets, her awkward hands clasped around the purse. They were just a nudge from looks, from an ill-concealed remark. For all the drink, the men looked pretty sharp-eyed.

Finally Elsie was ready and they were on their way – Margaret in front, Elsie behind – moving among the white tables. None of the 'ordinary' diners looked up for more than a moment, and Margaret's spirits lightened: the ordeal would soon be over. Her own shoes didn't seem too noisy this time, but Elsie wasn't easy in her boots and skittered a bit behind her. Margaret glanced again at the group, they were just ahead: the men were more settled now, most of them seemed to be listening to a joke one of them was telling. She hoped it was a long one. Taking a deep breath, Margaret walked past the tables with the broad shadow of Elsie in her wake. Despite herself, she glanced briefly at them as she went by, noticing, to her surprise, that there was a woman in the group, very striking, with bright, blonde hair and a hard, lined face. None of the men looked up, they were still absorbed in the story, but the woman did. She looked up at Margaret, clocked eyes with her for the briefest moment, before her eyes passed on, swift and shrewd, to Elsie, where they stayed.

* * *

A couple of hundred yards away from the Eagle, two men in early middle age sat quietly in the lounge of another hotel. The Musgrave was the smartest and most comfortable hotel in the town; a couple of the rugs were threadbare, and the sporting portraits were not of the best, but the furniture was good and, better still, comfortable, and the roaring fire kept the worst of the weather at bay. Thomas Walker and Marcus Quillet were old friends from Oxford with a war in common. They were now meeting in a professional capacity to prosecute the only murder trial of the Winchester Assizes. They had enjoyed a good dinner, a brisk catch-up about the relative states of wives and children, and some restrained reminiscences about 'old times', but now it was time for business and they had turned their attention to the case that started tomorrow: *Regina* versus *Miss Irene Hargreaves* for the murder of Mr Ernest Massey. Both men were reading from the files. QC Marcus Quillet was a slight man with a sharp face, his greying hair cut short like smooth fur. He had put down his glass of whisky and was fully absorbed in what he was reading. Something about the set of his nose and pointed chin suggested the muzzle of a fox. Solicitor Thomas Walker sat opposite him. He was big and broad, and most of his clients thought he didn't look like a solicitor at all – this was nearly always a compliment. He too was reading, but hadn't forgotten his whisky. The case appeared straightforward in many of its aspects, but both men felt a certain unease. This didn't centre on the murder so much as on the life of the accused and her long-established friendship with another woman. The manners and behaviour of the victim presented other difficulties; the state of the cottage where the three of them had lived likewise – there was some pretty unsavoury detail. Still, they were preparing carefully and had decided on their general approach.

The only other occupant of the lounge was the defence counsel for the same trial: Patrick Clifford. Quillet, who knew Clifford from the circuit, had asked him to join them for dinner, but Clifford had politely declined. He was fighting a heavy cold, he said, and would make poor company. He sat at a desk, close to the fire, immersed in his papers.

The fire wheezed and crackled cosily enough in the lounge, but the sound of the river outside was relentless; so was the *thud, thud* of the rain. The Musgrave promised riverside views.

* * *

At Wheal Rock the rain fell lightly. Nib slept peacefully in her usual place: curled in a perfect circle in the cleft between Elsie's and Rene's pillows – nothing would break her routine. The absence of two familiar humans did not interest her particularly, given that another (unfamiliar) human had brought her food that very evening. She had accepted it and a saucer of milk from Belinda, who had cycled over to see to the animals and check that everything was all right. Jugger had been delighted to see her, thumping his tail and jumping up. She had put on his leash and taken him for a walk in the lane, but soon – far too soon, in his eyes – she had gone. And Jugger, confined to the kitchen, was left more fretful than before. True, there were periods when he sat beside the outside door, listening quite sensibly, with his head cocked to one side and an occasional hopeful thump of the tail. But as the night progressed his confidence diminished. Any little noise could raise his hopes – a squeak or squeal in the dark outside, all manner of cottage creaks – and had him scratching desperately at the door. In between, in the silence, he knew that he was really and truly alone and he howled and howled.

Belinda had offered to keep him with her at the Cuffs', but Elsie had said no. It was better Jugger was at Wheal Rock, she said: it was his home, the place he knew. That was what she told Belinda and she was persuaded it was true; but it wasn't only that. The truth was that she didn't want Wheal Rock to be without a dog at night. She thought it very likely that he would fret and that was a pity, but it didn't alter her thinking. She didn't like to think of him upset, she was not hard-hearted, but she also thought that if he did howl, at least it might keep the foxes away.

14.

The Green Hat

In the morning the rain had stopped and there was a passage of blinding sunshine. There was some optimistic talk that the weather was on the turn. This was what the receptionist at the Musgrave ventured to say to solicitor Thomas Walker when he handed in his key. The receptionist asked if she could arrange a taxi, but he refused: the courts were only a ten-minute walk, most of it along the river.

The Winchester Crown Court buildings were in Market Street. They were plain stone buildings and unadorned except for a rather grand fan of shallow steps that led up to the main entrance and a line of statues that were niched along the second-floor facade. The statues had been cleaned recently, but the rest of the building had not, and this made the statues appear more than ordinarily interested in the goings-on below. As Walker and Quillet came through the gates, the large courtyard was full of puddles and bright blue sky but virtually empty of people. At the bottom of the steps, there was a prolix, handwritten sign: *Please watch your step, both the stairs and lobby are very slippery.* Disregarding the message, Quillet quickened his pace, but it was the more careful Walker who nearly lost his footing as they entered the lobby. The marble floor was an ice rink of footprints and brown splash.

The lobby was large and busy, with people standing about, waiting: witnesses and would-be jurors, nervous and self-important.

At the desk, a clerk was having an agitated, whispered conversation with a caretaker. The clerk had clearly had enough of the man with his mop and metal bucket, and seeing Quillet and Walker approach, he turned to them with relief.

'Morning, gentlemen, and how may I be of help?'

Formalities concluded, the clerk pointed out the cloakroom, gave them a lengthy set of directions and gestured them towards the marble staircase.

At the bottom of the stairs, Quillet and Walker passed a loose knot of a dozen or so men. They were noticeably at ease, milling, chatting. It was the same group that had disconcerted Margaret so much in the hotel dining room the night before, but they were quieter now. Some of them looked the worse for wear. Their jacket pockets stuffed with notebooks and pencils, these were the 'gentlemen' of the press: assorted reporters from London, Birmingham, Bristol and a couple of locals. The woman with the hard face and bright, dyed hair was there too.

The lobby began to thin out as people were called upstairs, and after a few minutes the press followed.

'Gentlemen,' said the blonde woman sardonically, 'shall I lead the way?'

'You can lead me anywhere, Babs, you know that,' said the man who had nearly fallen over the night before.

And they followed her up the stairs to the courtroom.

The lobby was nearly empty now, and the caretaker finally settled down to work, squeezing out the mop with feeling and wiping at the slippery brown floor. Outside it had started to rain again.

A young man dashed through the door, tripped on the metal bucket and nearly went tumbling on to the hard marble. He was quite young enough for the caretaker to give him what for. It was the youthful Colin of the night before. He had been delayed by a nosebleed and he was furious: this was his first murder case and he was very likely going to be late. He rushed through the lobby and on up the stairs, hoping to reach the courtroom before the doors closed.

★ ★ ★

The courtroom was high-ceilinged and chilly. There were no windows and the panelling extended fully around the chamber and halfway up the walls, with the doors in the same dark wood. In some lights the doors could not be seen at all. There were faint gleams of jewelled colour in the crest above the bench, and a glint of gold in the inevitable faded Latin – no other colour. In the press gallery, the reporters sat quietly, notebooks at the ready, waiting. The room was nearly full; Colin Mackenzie, cub reporter for the *Western Herald*, had just squeezed into the public gallery. He shouldered himself carefully out of his raincoat, wrapped it in a ball and stuffed it under the seat. He looked across at the press gallery but didn't catch anyone's eye, then he got out his notebook and pencil and waited too. At least he was close to the dock: he'd get a good view of the accused if nothing else.

She came in soon after, with a sour-faced WPO. She was wearing a grey sweater with a blouse underneath: the wings of the collar were just visible. The sweater was pulled up high, as if she wanted to hide the blouse, or at least the collar. Standing, her hands rested on the dock and the sleeves of the sweater were pulled right down and almost completely hid her hands. Young Colin Mackenzie observed her intently from his vantage point. Was he disappointed by how ordinary she looked? Did he think her features 'sharp', as some of the papers later suggested?

Her hair had been recently cut. Elsie would have worried that she was thinner; Margaret would have admired her poise. Thomas Walker, solicitor for the prosecution, who had been somewhat concerned about the appearance of the accused, was relieved. You never knew with women of her kind. She was certainly conspicuous, he thought, with her short, grey Eton crop, but not exactly masculine. She was far too slight for that, though there was something about the way she held herself, the clothes, or at least the way she wore them; perhaps from a distance?

Walker cast a careful eye over the jurors as they entered. The seven women and five men looked solemn and uncomfortable as they edged into their seats. There were a couple of likely spokesmen: the obvious contender was a man in his later fifties, alert, smartly dressed, a rigid bearing; the other was a young man, some way off thirty – he looked like a grammar-school boy but there was something steely about him. One of the women jurors was, he thought, strikingly pretty. There was no obvious troublemaker.

Walker turned back to see that Clifford's solicitor was making his own assessment of the jurors, and the two men smiled briefly at each other. Did the number of women constitute an advantage to Clifford, Walker wondered, or the Crown? It all depended on the accused.

Rene watched as the jurors began to make their promises to the judge, one after the other, earnest and prim, hands flat on the Bible. Not one cast a look in her direction. Keeping her head high, she made a careful survey of the courtroom, trying to get her bearings, picking the doors out of the panelling; the walls above were so white and bleak. In the gap between two jurors promising, she heard hard shoes echoing in a corridor. And outside now it started to rain again, for somewhere close by was an overflow pipe: she could hear the water gushing down and hitting the ground with a hard, fast *spat, spat*. It was the only sound now. The jurors had finished with their promising. It was time to begin.

Marcus Quillet, a little less foxy in his wig and gown, rose to outline the prosecution case of *Regina* versus:
'Hargreaves.'
No one was happy about the 'Hargreaves' – it was irregular. Legally of course she was Mrs Phillips – Irene Roberta Phillips, widow of Alan Phillips – but hardly anyone who was relevant here knew her by that name. Rene Hargreaves was the name she had gone by for more than twenty years. Both judge and prosecution had acceded to Clifford's proposal that Hargreaves was the best option in a difficult situation, but it didn't stop Quillet feeling awkward the first time he spoke the name aloud.
'Miss Hargreaves is a woman of powerful loyalties who felt her obligations very keenly, perhaps too keenly.'
He would show that Miss Hargreaves's divided loyalties were the heart of the matter, the heart of the murder.
'For murder,' he said, pausing for effect and looking directly at the jury for the first time, 'is what is being talked about here.
'Murder by poison.'

Quillet's eyes remained on the jury.

'As the prosecution will demonstrate.'

Rene stood up straighter, pressing her fingers down hard on the ledge of the dock. She had known the word was coming, and wondered what it would be like to hear it, spoken out loud in front of so many people. Hearing it now, she didn't wilt, but it was a shock to hear it three times in quick succession. It seemed to linger, not quite an echo, long after Quillet had moved on.

'Miss Hargreaves's connection with Mr and Mrs Massey stretched back over most of her life. Mrs Bertha Massey was a close friend and help to Miss Hargreaves's mother, whose own health was fragile. Miss Hargreaves, her brother and her mother all lived in Mrs Massey's house after Miss Hargreaves's father died. Miss Hargreaves lived there till she married; her mother lived there until her death. When Miss Hargreaves's marriage to Alan Phillips broke down, she left her youngest son in Mrs Massey's care when she left Manchester. Mrs Massey reared him as her own. Miss Hargreaves was indebted to Mrs Massey for this, and there was an agreement between the two women that Miss Hargreaves would care for Mrs Massey in her old age, if and when the need arose.'

After his opening statement, Quillet kept his manner mild. Thoughtful and grave, he turned frequently to look at Rene; his eyes were not without sympathy. Miss Hargreaves had left the family home because she was overwhelmed, he said. Alan Phillips was a charming and affectionate man, but he was a gambler first and foremost, and serious gamblers do not make good husbands and fathers. Miss Hargreaves did her best, but with three very young children, her mother dead and no sister . . . He trod lightly over the matter of the children.

But there was no going lightly for Rene. Mr Quillet seemed far too kind. He said she had been overwhelmed, as if a great wave had come and washed her away down the street, all the way to Lambourn. She looked up at the crack on the ceiling, unwilling to trust her eyes anywhere else. The truth was that she had abandoned the children: she had set two of them on a train and waved them goodbye, she had handed the other one, the youngest one, over to Bertha. Her throat was thick and tight. *Abandoned* was not a word she ever spoke out loud, but it was the word. Mr Quillet made everything sound far too sensible. Once she had thought it was the war, the war and Elsie, dear Elsie: everyone had ended up so far from where they started. But that wasn't good enough. There were women who ran from their husbands with their children, there were women who fled and returned, women who wrote letter after letter asking, begging, for forgiveness – she wasn't any one of these.

When Rene finally looked round the room again, she could see the press with their notebooks, busily writing, a group of men and one woman. Bright blonde and with the lines running hard down her face, she seemed the busiest of all with her pencil. Rene looked away; she didn't want to think about what they might be writing. She needed to listen carefully to what Mr Quillet was saying. The jurors were all watching him, enthralled by the scene, but the usher looked bored – he yawned and hastily tried to cover his mouth. Rene tried again to catch Quillet's thread: she made herself stop looking round and fixed her eyes ahead of her, trying to settle herself. Straight ahead was a plump woman in a green hat who appeared to be looking at her, though it was difficult to tell. Her hat was quite a thing: close-fitting but such a bright shade of sheeny silk, and there were roses – in the same green – wound round the side of the hat. Yes, the woman was looking at her, Rene thought, but the attention didn't seem hostile.

'Mrs Phillips reverted to her maiden name, Miss Hargreaves, and decided to make a new life for herself on the land. The exigencies of wartime assisted her. It was as a land girl that she first made the acquaintance of Miss Elsie Boston, the woman with whom she now shares the remote cottage in Cornwall, known as Wheal Rock. Theirs is an unusual friendship; the two women have lived together for the past twenty years. Miss Hargreaves is exceptionally protective towards Miss Boston, who is ten years older than herself and vulnerable. Miss Boston is very reliant on her friend.'

Quillet slipped over the matter of the 'friendship' lightly – no one wanted to get too entangled there – but it could not be ignored.

Indeed, it formed a central plank of his case. The press continued writing busily.

'Mrs Bertha Massey's death must have come as a shock to Miss Hargreaves. Mrs Massey was ten years younger than her husband and no one had really expected him to survive her. Nevertheless, Miss Hargreaves felt obliged to take Mr Massey in because of a promise she had made long ago to his wife . . . Mr Massey came to live with the two women at Wheal Rock. No one would deny that he was a difficult man to care for, and he certainly required a great deal of supervision . . .'

Quillet was talking about Uncle's habits now. She hated having to hear it all again, getting tangled up in his stale breath and clammy hands. She felt the eyes of the court, the furtive, grudging interest. Two of the female jurors cast tentative glances in her direction. There was more than curiosity, she was sure.

'No one would deny that Miss Hargreaves and Miss Boston tried to do their best with Mr Massey in very difficult circumstances. However, his presence at the cottage took a toll on both of them. Committed as she was to caring for Mr Massey, Miss Hargreaves's strongest bond was, as I have said, to Miss Boston. And she gradually came to feel that Mr Massey's presence in the cottage was incompatible with her bond to her friend. Working extremely hard just to make ends meet, Miss Hargreaves was acutely aware that much of the daily caring for Mr Massey fell to Miss Boston, who was feeling the strain of it. Indeed, Miss Hargreaves came to fear for the vulnerable Miss Boston's health, and visited the doctor on her account. Late in 1961, his behaviour took a further dip. Up to this point, I am sure that we can all sympathize with Miss Hargreaves's difficulties with Mr Massey. But around this time, her goodwill evaporated and she took the decision to deal with Mr Massey in her own way. It was at this point that she took the decision to poison Mr Massey, a decision which required substantial premeditation. The pathologist's evidence will demonstrate just how premeditated and deliberate. The poison that she used, sodium chlorate, is highly unpalatable and could only have gone undetected by the recipient if it was administered in tiny quantities over a period of time.

Miss Hargreaves always served Mr Massey his breakfast before she went out to work. She sometimes served him supper and always took responsibility for his drinks during the evening. She also took a cup of tea up to his room before bed. She had ample opportunity.'

Rene had to admit that Mr Quillet's case against her sounded very reasonable. Some of it was true. She *had* felt a deep obligation to Bertha, and not just for the obvious things. If it hadn't been for Bertha, she might not have left Manchester, might never have joined the Land Army; never met Elsie. And yet. No one knew just how cleverly Bertha had worked to secure her gratitude: those neat little stitches sewn over and over, so strong. And somehow, through the rain, very quiet but very regular, came a faint tapping, the sound of Bertha on her mother's sewing machine. When she was working, that whirring *tap tap* could be heard through every wall of Bertha's house. For it never became 'Mr and Mrs Massey's house', it was only ever Bertha's – Mr Quillet was quite wrong about that.

The woman in the green silk hat was looking at her and Rene looked directly back. Their eyes met; the woman didn't turn away. It was an open look, curious, not hostile. They were probably about the same age, and not as different as they might have been. The woman was smartly dressed in a tailored, brown velvet jacket, with neat silver buttons, and Rene caught a glimpse of a bright green blouse underneath. The clothes weren't just smart, they were expensive, Rene could tell, even from a distance. Her hair didn't reach her chin but it was thick and curly – no one would have noticed that it was short. There was something familiar about her.

Rene turned her attention back to Mr Quillet. It seemed that he would never finish speaking.

'Protection of her vulnerable friend was her primary motive. The prospect of modest financial gain also had a role. Mr Massey changed his will just after his arrival at Wheal Rock to make Miss Hargreaves his sole beneficiary. The sum of money involved was modest, but it should not be ignored, given the impecunious state in which they lived. However, it was her bond with the vulnerable Miss Boston that was primary, a bond that led her to take

Mr Ernest Massey's life, take his life, moreover, in a planned and premeditated way.'

Vulnerable was the word Quillet used to describe Elsie. Rene didn't like the way it sounded, but he must have liked the word because he used it a good deal. 'Miss Boston was a vulnerable lady and Miss Hargreaves saw that Mr Massey had become too much for her,' he said. 'Miss Boston's vulnerability,' he said, 'was never far from Miss Hargreaves's mind.' He used it like it was a word for something else. *Touched* was the word Rene used if someone wasn't quite right; or sometimes *poor*: poor Eric with his puppet limbs at Mrs Crawford's shop. Did Mr Quillet really think, Poor Elsie? And Rene felt angry all of a sudden. She pressed her hands down hard on the edge of the dock, stood up as tall as she could, and looked out steadily across the courtroom.

Quillet finally concluded his outline of the case.

The judge announced the break for lunch.

Two WPCs took Rene down to the cells. Morris, the older, sullen one, went in front. Rene was cuffed to a nervous, young WPC whom everyone just called Maureen. Watch yourself, Morris said, for the steps were steep. The damp chill made her shiver and the cuff rubbed slightly on her wrist, but she and Maureen worked out a rhythm of sorts: very slow and steady, lots of stops. Morris was well ahead, and Rene could sense her irritation at their slowness. All of a sudden, Morris came to a sudden stop.

'Oh lordy,' she said.

She was half a dozen steps from the bottom. Rene and Maureen stopped behind her and peered over Morris's shoulders. Maureen squealed.

The narrow corridor beyond was six inches deep in murky water; it lapped against the pale tiled walls and the metal padlocked doors of the cells. And it hadn't finished rising yet. At the end of the corridor, the water was pushing up hard from a drain: above the metal grille, it foamed and spun.

'Anyone here?' Morris called, and her voice echoed and tremored along the corridor.

There was no reply.

An old metal chair, posted beside one of the cell doors, stood its spindly ground while the lights on the walls flickered alarmingly.

For some moments, they didn't move, just stood on the steps watching the water, half hypnotized by the sound and the flickering light. It was only when Maureen began to sniff and snuffle that Morris came to herself and ordered them back up to the next landing. Then they all made their way slowly upstairs. And Rene was led back to the empty courtroom, out through the judge's door and into the warren of rooms behind. Morris alerted a clerk about the water below, but there was quite a delay before somewhere suitable could be found for Rene. Various offices on the first floor were considered. The first was deemed too big; in the second, there were glass panels on the door and this was thought unsuitable. WPC Morris went off to take her lunch. For another ten minutes, Rene stood awkwardly clasped to Maureen in the corridor, while there was much toing and froing of police and middle-aged suited men and women. The fingers of Rene's free hand went *tap, tap, tap* on the wall behind, but Maureen had gone quite dull and limp after the excitement of the flood, as she called it.

And finally a room was found: poky but with a large, uncluttered desk, three chairs and a solid wooden door. And a window. Without thinking, Rene made towards it, drawing, pulling, Maureen in her wake. Reaching it, Rene used her free hand to prise apart the pleated blind, and awkwardly rubbed her knuckles on the misted-up window. There wasn't much to see: an empty street in heavy rain in a town she didn't know. But it was a pleasure to be looking out, to meet the light at eye level.

One person had ventured out: an old woman who was standing in the middle of the pavement as the rain poured down. She was standing quite still and seemed to be talking to her wheeled wicker basket. A car drove by, slow and stately; it splashed the woman but she didn't seem to notice. Rene continued to look out on to the street, the limp girl locked to her wrist forgotten. She wished there were more people. She didn't usually mind the rain, but she resented it now for keeping people inside, robbing the street of its everyday business. If there were more people, she might see someone familiar; if there were more people, she might see someone she knew. She knew she was being silly, but she kept looking all the same. And of course it was Elsie she was looking for. Elsie must be here by now, she thought, Elsie wouldn't be put off by the rain.

One flight up from Rene, in the dining room reserved for the Law, lunch was being served; it was a bit of a squeeze fitting in three courses.

At the Crown and Two Chairmen, the press called in the pints and talk was lively. The news that Miss Hargreaves was Mrs Phillips, the spinster was really a widow, and a mother to boot, occasioned a good deal of speculation. Rene's trousers were another talking point, that and the Eton crop. Cub reporter Colin Mackenzie had managed to tag along again. They were all soaking: coats and hats were sodden, hair flopped in oily licks on to cheeks. Only the lady reporter – Babs – had been able to preserve her hairdo from the rain. It was generally agreed that the defendant was 'a bit nervy', a bit 'above herself', and, perhaps predictably, 'a bit of a chilly customer'. 'Skinny as a whippet,' Mackenzie nearly said, and stopped himself. Ruder and cruder were reserved for the evening. In the same pub, the woman who had caught Rene's attention sat at a quiet table and sipped a gin and tonic, the green hat on a seat beside her. Close up and without the hat, she looked older, her short hair flattened by the rain; she watched the antics at the bar very carefully.

At the Eagle, Margaret and Elsie ordered sandwiches and tea to be sent to Elsie's room. If only it would stop raining.

Back in the courtroom, the usher circulated photographs of Wheal Rock: a sequence of ten large grey images, each one sleeved in plastic. The jurors busied themselves with the photographs, relieved perhaps to be looking at something else.

There was one of Ernest's tiny bedroom, the bed stripped, pillow and blankets neatly piled. The picture had been taken by the window to include the half-open door. You could see on to the landing and the door of Elsie and Rene's bedroom, which was firmly shut. There was a photo of the sitting room with the uncomfortable sofa and Ernest's unwieldy armchair and, over by the window, the little cupboard, the cream, curved edge of the wireless, a biscuit tin. There were two photos of the kitchen, taken from different positions, and it was here that the tidying-up the police had done was most obvious. The table had been pulled closer to the back door and the chairs were pushed underneath it tightly. Jugger's basket had been removed. The only sign of life was the jumble of long macs, coats and scarves on the door; all the everyday angles of living were gone.

Rene looked over towards the jury, who were absorbed in the photos. What did they see? What were they looking for?

She looked down at the photograph of the shed, its shelves stacked tight with bottles and tins, the huge can of Corry's Slug Death and a jumble of things she barely remembered: an abandoned bellows, a clutch of mousetraps, a plastic box full of padlocks, plant pots, paintbrushes. The tin of sodium chlorate peeked out slyly from behind tins of varnish and coils of fat rope. Next to the shelves were the little table and stool that Elsie had set up for Ernest – the pile of curling, damp magazines was still there. And a mug and two glasses. There were close-up photographs of these: watermarked, printed with fingers and dusty sediments. Rene winced at the state of the glasses.

She passed to the outside photos with relief: there was Nib, sitting like china in the window of the cottage, no sign of the yard. A shot taken from the field which included part of the old chimney. How far away it all seemed.

'Call Dr Evans,' the usher said.

'You were Mr Massey's doctor?' Quillet asked, his manner brisk.

'Yes.'

'You were also Miss Hargreaves's doctor?'

'I was. And Miss Boston's, though you understand I never saw her as a patient, she was physically very strong.'

'I see. And you were called to the cottage after Mr Massey's death?'

'Oh yes. I think it was Miss Hargreaves who called my surgery that morning, my wife took the message. I was already out on my rounds so –'

'Yes, thank you.' Quillet was eager to get on.

'Dr Evans, when you look back on your visit to the cottage that afternoon, was there anything about the visit that struck you as abnormal, anything that suggested that this was *not* an ordinary, a natural, death?'

'Then? No, nothing – well, nothing to speak of.'

'Dr Evans?'

'There was a slight yellowing of Mr Massey's face. It was rather marked under the eyes.'

'And this isn't normal?'

'It certainly could be. But it could also point to some pressure on the liver and the kidneys and poor function. Again, this could be quite normal, given the subject's age and habits, but such yellowing is also, can also be, a sign of toxicity.'

'So the yellowing of the skin could be a sign of poison?'

'Yes, it could, though –'

'But you didn't suspect this at the time.'

'There seemed no reason to suspect anything.'

'But you ordered a post-mortem examination, did you not, Dr Evans?'

'Oh yes, but I considered that appropriate because I hadn't seen him for some time.'

'I see. And was there anything about the behaviour of Miss Hargreaves – or Miss Boston, for that matter – that struck you as odd or suspicious?'

'Nothing at all. Neither of them appeared upset, but I think that was pretty unexceptional given the circumstances.'

Rene was finding it more and more difficult to attend to what was being said. She knew how much it mattered, but it didn't stop her drifting. She kept trying to call herself back: with every question she focused anew. There was nothing difficult as such; she just kept losing the thread. In the morning it had been easier, she had been on her mettle. Hearing Quillet quoting from her statement and mangling her speech had kept her alert. But this afternoon it was just Mr Quillet and Dr Evans. Listen, she thought to herself, they're talking about you, about you and Elsie and Uncle. Listen, it's important.

'Dr Evans, I wish to ascertain Miss Hargreaves's attitude to Mr Massey in the months before his death. Did you get a sense of how she felt about him during this period?'

'She was concerned for his health. She was also worn down and irritated by his very difficult behaviour – that was very clear. But her main concern was how Mr Massey's continued stay at the cottage was affecting Miss Boston.'

'She said this to you directly?'

'Oh yes. She came to my surgery in Helston. I had been treating her for a chest infection. I assumed that was why she made the appointment, but she told me she was feeling much better. That was when she told me that she was worried about Miss Boston.'

'So she made an appointment with you to talk about Miss Boston?'

'Yes.' Evans came to a stop, unsure of the impression he was giving.

'Well, I asked her if Miss Boston was ill.'

'I see. And what did Miss Hargreaves say?'

' "Not exactly." Those were her words. "Not exactly." And then she said that Miss Boston was struggling to cope with Mr Massey. She was quite run-down by him, those were her words. She also told me that Miss Boston had been having terrible trouble sleeping.'

'Why do you think she told you this?'

'She was extremely worried about her friend – unnaturally so, one might say. It can happen in these cases.'

Quillet let that pass.

'And you had some direct experience of Miss Boston, I understand?'

'Oh yes. I saw her on three of the occasions when I attended Mr Massey at the cottage and on an earlier occasion when I attended Miss Hargreaves herself.'

'And how did you find her?'

'Fragile certainly, not one of life's best adjusted . . . if you take my meaning, but harmless of course, completely harmless. Miss Hargreaves was certainly very protective of her.'

'Perhaps you could explain what you mean by that, Dr Evans?'

'Of course . . .'

And now nothing could stop Rene listening, though she dearly didn't want to hear. 'Not the best adjusted.' Poor Elsie.

And as the smug doctor went on talking – he too used the word *vulnerable* – it came to Rene that Elsie would find out that Rene had gone to see Dr Evans. She had spoken to a stranger about their situation, about Ernest; worst of all, she had spoken about Elsie, she had offered her up to somebody else. TITTLE-TATTLE LOST THE BATTLE. And to Dr Evans of all people, whom Elsie particularly disliked. She looked down at the photograph in front of her: Nib sitting on the narrow ledge of the window. The cat seemed smaller than before, as if Wheal Rock itself had moved further into the distance.

When Dr Evans finally finished speaking, the judge adjourned till the following morning – though he did not release the jurors. He had a practical matter to consider first, he said.

The reporters dispersed briskly to write their copy.

The accused was taken directly to the police van that was waiting in the flooded car park; a blanket was held above her head to keep the worst of the rain off. Released from the long-suffering Maureen, she sprang nimbly from the kerb to the second step of the van. WPC Morris was not so lucky: she partially lost her balance and ended up with her right leg deep in an oily puddle.

In his office, the judge considered the progress of trial and weather. The latter, for the time being, concerned him more. One of his clerks had spent most of the afternoon on the telephone to the meteorological service. The forecast for the next few days was for more heavy rain and local flooding, probably severe. He was disheartened if not altogether surprised, but the usher brought him good news shortly afterwards: everyone who might be called had now reached Winchester. This made his task easier – he didn't want to delay the trial if it was at all possible. The usher also told him that the pathologist, Maurice Vanstone, had arrived, and the judge asked him to be shown up – they shared a distant family connection. Vanstone was soon upstairs, splendidly dressed in oilcloths; he was due to appear first tomorrow and he corroborated the weather reports. He had driven, very carefully, from his home some ten miles away and believed that the roads into the town would be impassable by morning. The centre was already flooding.

Clearly they would need to make some arrangements. The judge offered Vanstone a drink and consulted briefly with the usher. The jurors would be found accommodation close by, and a clerk and a secretary could be sent to do any shopping that was required. Witnesses should be reassured that the trial would go ahead and any necessary variation of travel arrangements or other general expenses arising from the weather would be reimbursed.

Pleased with how things were developing, he sent the usher to arrange matters with the jurors, and invited the two barristers and the solicitors to join him for a whisky in his room.

After a couple of drinks, the mood lightened and a list of essentials was made. Walker, inspired by Vanstone, had the idea that they should kit themselves out with sou'westers and the like, and someone was even dispatched to phone Runcorn's, the fly-fishing shop, to see what protection they could offer. The caretaker was instructed to improvise a 'wet' cloakroom in the downstairs hall. A young clerk was dispatched to the far end of the high street to pick up the wet-weather wear. Outside, the rain was now torrential. It bounded the vision at every point, like a great grey curtain. Meanwhile, down in the cells, the water lapped on the step where Rene had stood with the hapless Maureen, murkier than before.

15

From Spinster to Widow

Weedkiller woman. Miss Rene Hargreaves, aged 55, was charged with the murder by poison of Ernest Massey, aged 82, a charge she vigorously denies.

Western Press

Miss Hargreaves, a small, slight woman with a grey Eton crop, stood throughout the day's proceedings. Wearing trousers and a dark pullover, she followed events intently, though there were occasions when she appeared distressed. Prosecution counsel, Marcus Quillet, QC, laid out the case against her . . .

Daily Herald

Elsie awoke into the warmth of her room at the Eagle the following morning and listened: it was raining steadily. It was still deep dark outside – she thought it must be about five. She grappled with the flex and found and fiddled with the switch for the bedside light. Then she picked up her book, *Death on the Line*, and started to read. It was a good one: all the characters were stranded on a train because of a snow drift near the Lakes – more bad weather – and the passengers were being murdered. It was gory too: she had just passed page 70, but two had been done away with so far, one with a stocking, another with an antique paper knife. It wasn't a patch on *Murder on the Orient Express* (which she adored), but it was good fun, as Rene liked to say, and it was pleasant reading quietly in the warmth with the rain doing its worst in the dark.

The rain didn't sound like rain at all, she thought, more like wind – or no, a wind-*machine*: a wind-machine that kept blowing and blowing from the same point, never changing. As for the sound of water, you could only hear it at the edges: a sudden *glug-sloush* through the guttering, a stubborn drip-beat on to her window ledge – that was all. But it was the rain rather than the book that eventually won her attention, wind-machine or not, and once she saw that it was getting light, she got out of bed and went across to the window.

She quite exclaimed at what she saw: for overnight the square had become a lake. Road and pavement were now fully underwater – the kerb had gone. The trees seemed to be floating in the square. The 'lake' itself was grey and opaque, except where the street lamps left their sad yellow marks. In the garden at the centre of the square, the apple tree had become a bush – its trunk already covered by water – and the other trees had shrunk by a good foot. For some minutes, she simply watched the scene in pleasure – a wonderful pink shone through the mottled sky as the sun came up, and the room was so cosy and warm. Then she decided, all of a sudden, that she was going to go out for a walk. She hurried to get ready, wrapping her trousers tightly round her legs before she pulled on her big boots. She tied a belt over her coat to try and keep herself dry, tied a knot in her hair and crammed it under her mackintosh hat.

Downstairs, it was quiet. There was no one at the reception desk, and the porter who sometimes loitered by the doors was nowhere to be seen. From somewhere in the lounge a clock chimed six. Elsie pushed out of the heavy doors into the sound of the rain. She stood on the top step of the porch, which was still well clear of the water, and surveyed the scene. The early colour was nearly over, but it had left traces of light in the water. She went carefully down the hotel steps on to the pavement and felt the water rise and lap around her boots – it reached well over her ankles and the road would be a good deal deeper.

Elsie set off carefully round the square. She kept close to the railings of the houses, her eyes on the waters below. Water could always be treacherous. The rain grew heavier; it pitter-pattered on her hat, running off the edges of its black shiny surface at all angles. A stream rose from somewhere close to the back of her neck and dripped cold and heavy down her spine; another ran heavily down her arm; a third made its way along the curve where her nose met her cheek before dripping down on to her chin. But she kept going, walked all the way round the square twice, the second time more briskly, never losing her rhythm or her balance. Then she made her way back to the hotel and pushed hard on the door.

The girl who was sitting at the reception looked up in surprise at the early and unexpected visitor: a tall, broad figure in a very long coat and a floppy black hat. It couldn't be a new guest, the weather made that extremely unlikely, and it was too early for casual traffic for the dining room or the lounge. The visitor seemed quite at ease, standing on the mat, stamping vigorously and shaking out her greatcoat. The girl at the desk was just a little unnerved. But then the big dark figure took off the hat and made to wring it out and the receptionist realized it was the odd lady in number 20. She was here for the trial with that nice Mrs Cuff.

'Oh, Miss Boston,' she said.

Elsie looked up, clearly surprised, nodded very briefly and made quickly for the stairs.

It was after breakfast that Elsie asked Margaret if she wouldn't mind fetching some of the newspapers from downstairs.

Elsie had known that there would be papers. Court cases were a staple of the locals, she read them herself; and though she took no interest in the national press, there was no reason why they would be any different. The newspapers would be upsetting: she would see Rene accused of murder (Margaret had worked hard to prepare her). Reading about Rene in the court and particularly about Ernest would be unpleasant and hurtful, but that didn't mean she didn't want to do it. She was desperate for news, news of Rene. Yesterday had been so dreadful: sitting by the window, the whole day spent indoors (Margaret had prevailed on her to keep inside), staring into the square, staring into the rain, fretting about Rene. Only when it got dark – and she was sure that the trial was over for the day – had she been able to calm down, drink some cold tea and read a part of her book.

Margaret had been wondering about the papers too.

'Are you sure, Elsie?'

And Elsie nodded, so Margaret went down to fetch the papers from the lounge, so they could read them in the privacy of Elsie's room.

> Miss Hargreaves, a small, slight woman with a grey Eton crop, stood throughout the day's proceedings. Wearing trousers and a dark pullover, she followed events intently, though there were occasions when she appeared distressed. Prosecution counsel, Marcus Quillet, QC, laid out the case against her . . .

For a moment, Elsie felt jealous, jealous of this unknown reporter who didn't sign his name. He had seen Rene just yesterday, had spent the whole day with her in the courtroom.

'Widow not spinster' ran the headline.

> 'Miss' Hargreaves is not a spinster as she had previously claimed but the widow of a Manchester man, Alan Phillips, and the mother of their three children. Miss Hargreaves left her husband and children before the war. Mr Phillips died of tuberculosis, a year later.

Elsie paused uncomfortably at that chilly little history of names and places – it shone such a bright, interrogating light on Rene. Poor Rene, she had done so well to keep her married life private all these years – and now the reporter made her look like a liar. What would Margaret think when she found out that Rene had been married and run away, leaving her children, leaving her husband? What would Margaret think when she discovered that Rene was a widow but had never said anything about it – Margaret, who was a proper widow, with a widow's pension. She looked up, cast her eyes quickly in Margaret's direction, but she was busy reading.

Elsie read on:

> Miss Hargreaves lives at Wheal Rock, an unmodernized cottage in a remote part of Cornwall, with her female companion, Miss Elsie Boston.

Elsie was brought up short by that: *her* name, which she hadn't been expecting. And then another headline: 'Vulnerable Companion'. She was getting confused now, the print under the headline was swimming. Outside, she could hear the rain and she listened to its dismal beat with some relief. *Vulnerable Companion*. She wanted to stop reading but her name summoned her on.

> The court also heard from Dr Philip Evans, who was called to the remote cottage after Mr Massey's death. Dr Evans explained that Miss Hargreaves had visited his surgery a few weeks earlier because she was concerned about the welfare of her friend, Miss Boston, who was struggling to cope with Mr Massey . . .

Elsie pressed her short, neatly cut nails into the newspaper and scratched against the soft, thin paper; a couple of shreds gave way silently, little flaps of skin. She turned the paper over briskly – now only the polished surface of the table could see. Then she tried to read about the thieving of milk and a horrible drowning.

'Elsie, are you cold? You look cold, can I get you something?' Margaret was watching her, she looked concerned.

Elsie spoke up as best she could: 'Oh Margaret, would you take the newspapers away now? I have such a headache, I don't think I can read any more.'

'Of course.' Margaret gathered the papers together quickly. 'Can I get you an aspirin?'

'What?'

'An aspirin for your head. I have some in my wash-bag next door.'

'Oh, that's very kind, but I have some. It must be all this reading – and I woke terribly early. I may lie down.'

When Margaret had gone, Elsie took an aspirin, lay down on the bed and closed her eyes. Her head was pounding but she knew the tablet wouldn't help: it wasn't that kind of pain.

It was quarter to nine.

In the lobby of the court, yesterday's skating rink had been replaced with a pair of heavy, jute mats which were holding up well so far. To one side of the wide cloakroom counter, the floor had been lined with thick layers of newspaper and there was already quite a collection of umbrellas and boots and galoshes. The Water Authority had promised to arrive by eleven to pump out the basement – the flooding had nearly reached the first landing of the staircase and showed no sign of slowing. The caretaker stood by with his mop at the ready; he had a young washer-up from the staff canteen to help him, armed with another mop and a sack full of rags. The boy had been told to keep his eyes on the two buckets, which were steadily filling with a quick *drip, drip* from the cracks in the ceiling above. Luckily these were over by the barred side door. Ventilation was poor and the damp atmosphere held on to every smell: there was a heady whiff of breakfast fry and strong sweet tea, fresh tobacco and late-night booze along with the tang of various chemical compounds: mothballs and Coty, Camay and hair oil.

There were noticeably fewer nerves than yesterday, and fewer people, but the overall effect was brighter, noisier, as everyone coped with the weather and soldiered on.

Walker and Quillet arrived punctually, having made good progress through rain and flood. They cut quite a dash in their different ways. Thomas Walker made the more dramatic picture: striding through the lobby, tall and broad, he wore braced, dark green waders, with a voluminous matching coat and hat – all purchased enthusiastically from Runcorn's Fly Fishing. He looked even less like a solicitor and perfectly at ease, joking with the cloakroom attendant as she struggled to attach his waders to the hanger. Beside him, Marcus Quillet looked unremarkable with his gumboots, short waterproof jacket and large umbrella. But when he eased out of his outerwear, revealing a suit untouched by the weather, his neat, dry appearance seemed little short of magical. Both men paused to talk to Patrick Clifford, whose cold was much worse, and the three men made their way upstairs. The men and woman of the press had done their best to equip themselves for the weather with more limited funds and most of them had invested in cheap umbrellas.

Overall, the judge should have been pleased with the execution of his plans; all arrangements had been made: hotel rooms booked and umbrellas purchased for the jurors, various calls made to re-assure witnesses that the trial was going ahead and that any extra expenses incurred directly 'or indirectly' from the weather would be honoured. There were a couple of little confusions, it was true. Two witnesses for the defence had turned up in error to the court-room today. The first of these was Major Veesey from St Keverne, bluff and gruff but not disgruntled to discover that he wouldn't be needed till tomorrow. He had only met Miss Hargreaves twice but had been happy to stand as a character witness. He hoped he could do something to help – clearly there had been a terrible mistake. Dressed to attention, in his best tweed, he was rather looking for-ward to seeing Miss Boston, though he fully appreciated the circumstances were inauspicious. If all went well, he had hopes of asking her if she would come back to his garden. Over by the desk, in one of the few chairs provided, was another familiar face: Leo Hargreaves, brother of the accused, professional magician and all-purpose bad penny. He looked much older – partly the effect of his clumsily dyed hair – but just as sly and hopeful. He lingered in the lobby for a good hour after discovering his mistake.

The courtroom seemed darker this morning, though all the lights were on, and the atmosphere was stale – some of the smell from below had carried upwards. Young Colin Mackenzie from the *Western Herald* was sitting with the other reporters in the press gal-lery, notebook at the ready; his long legs were already uncomfortable. The benches were narrow and pew-like and the whole courtroom had a top-coat of church.

Rene took her place in the dock. Avoiding the press, she glanced carefully around the public gallery. She recognized various people she had seen yesterday. The woman in the green silk hat was sitting in the same place, the hat just as bright, the jacket just as smart. She was reading when Rene came in, but after a few moments she looked up and the two of them exchanged the faintest nod of acknowledgement – she was familiar from somewhere, it was the strangest thing. The courtroom felt colder that morning. The room itself reminded her of the register office where she and Alan had got married, the same heavy panelling. That room had had no windows either. She could hear the rain here though, somewhere nearby. Looking up, she saw a balcony above the press gallery which she hadn't noticed yesterday; she was relieved to see that it was empty – she didn't like the idea of people sitting there, watching her from above. She looked further up at the ceiling and traced a crack that ran all the way to the door. Another one, deeper, and fractured by tributaries, ran from the door to just above the judge's bench.

The morning was given to a series of sober-suited professionals, witnesses for the prosecution. The first to appear was the pathologist, Maurice Vanstone. Vanstone had conducted the post-mortem examination and concluded that Massey had died of sodium chlorate poisoning. He had also identified traces of sodium chlorate in a glass and a mug that Massey regularly used.

Was there any chance of another cause or contributing cause? Quillet asked.

No.

Quillet persevered: he didn't want to make things easy for the defence.

'It was well known that Mr Massey was a heavy drinker. Could this not have contributed to his death?'

In Vanstone's opinion, no. The examination certainly revealed signs of alcoholic degeneration, but these were not nearly so extensive as might be expected given his reported intake of alcohol. Mr Massey's drinking wasn't doing him any good, but it didn't kill him. Indeed, Mr Massey was in pretty strong health, all things considered. Sodium chlorate poison killed him, the post-mortem confirmed it.

How was this administered?

In small quantities over a relatively prolonged period – possibly weeks.

And how could he know this?

Sodium chlorate was almost uniquely unpalatable in anything other than the smallest quantities.

Quillet asked him to elaborate.

In the interests of the case, Vanstone had tried a home experiment: he had put a dessertspoon of sodium chlorate in a cup of tea, mixed it carefully and tasted – very gingerly. He had done the same with the other beverages that Mr Massey consumed regularly and pronounced the mixtures in all cases to be undrinkable. From this he concluded that Mr Massey had been poisoned 'little and often', as he put it, over some time. This was of course a common method in poisoning, when the killer had the opportunity to interfere with the preparation of consumables. When questioned by Clifford, Vanstone was willing to concede that Massey's sense of taste could well have degenerated somewhat on account of his age, but he insisted that Massey could not have consumed a significant quantity of sodium chlorate on one occasion, in error. It was simply too unpalatable.

(In his experiments, Vanstone never considered adding more than a couple of teaspoons of sugar to his sodium chlorate mix. Though both Rene and Elsie had described the sugar frenzies in their police statements, Massey's marked predilection for all things sweet was virtually ignored.)

Rene remembered the photographs of the shed, the tin of sodium chlorate, the padlocks, the mouse traps, the fat coils of rope. And then into her nose crept a smell she would never forget, an odd, eye-blinking smell that misted ever so gently into her lungs. It was the smell of the Free Library, or rather the smell of the old hospital, the smell of operations. Except that Mr Vanstone wasn't a surgeon and Uncle hadn't had an operation, not of that kind. She shivered. Mr Clifford stood up and began his questioning. Mr Kemps, the solicitor, had been very impressed by Mr Clifford. He had called him *your barrister* and sometimes *your man*: *He's a good defender, your man.* Rene did not feel remotely proprietary towards him and he certainly didn't seem very interested in her. They had only met briefly for the first time the day before: 'Chin up,' he had said, 'don't worry.' Watching him now, Rene found it odd to think that he was asking these questions and making all this fuss on her behalf. He was very like Quillet, except for the handkerchief and the thick throat.

After Vanstone stood down, a WPC, sergeant and inspector followed (in that order). The first two had come to Wheal Rock; Inspector Miller had interviewed her at Exeter. Quillet's line of questioning demonstrated that there was agreement among the three about Miss Hargreaves's demeanour – a word that sounded like an insult in itself. Miss Hargreaves had appeared quite affronted by perfectly straightforward questions, and her replies on occasion had been dismissive and bordered on the rude. Each of them had been left with the strong feeling that the accused was a little prickly, sharp; in the words of one, she 'thought herself very clever'. In the words of another, 'she behaved as if she had something to hide'. The press wrote busily in their notebooks. The judge told the jury to ignore both the last remarks.

Rene began to feel a change in the courtroom, some new mood settling, a more probing interest. When Clifford got his chance to cross-examine the police, he couldn't dislodge it. She was aware of a more insistent attention coming from the gallery; it plucked and pinched at her cheek.

The next witness was the solicitor whom Mr Massey had instructed to make Miss Hargreaves his sole beneficiary. Though money was not the primary motive for the murder, Quillet was keen to emphasize that Miss Hargreaves had made the appointment to change the will barely a week after Mr Massey's arrival at Wheal Rock. Clifford was able to ascertain from the solicitor that Massey seemed content with the changes and clearly understood them. Nevertheless, Clifford couldn't seem to dislodge a growing sense that something in this death was underhand.

The rain beat a steady rhythm outside, the witnesses proceeded briskly. Next came Dr Lane, a man of about forty, fine-boned with steely, blue-grey eyes. Rene remembered him from Holloway – he had seemed friendly enough at the time – and kept her eyes on him.

'Dr Lane, would you share with the court your assessment of the prisoner?'

'Yes, of course. I had two lengthy interviews with the prisoner, Miss Hargreaves, while she was at Holloway. Overall, I found her friendly and cooperative. I –'

'You did not examine her physically?'

'There was no need. She had already been examined by two medical doctors. Their notes were very thorough.'

'And you are not a medical doctor.'

'No, I am not.'

'For the benefit of those who may not be familiar with the procedures of psychiatric medicine, could you explain briefly the form your questioning took?'

There was just a hint of scepticism in Quillet's tone.

'Of course.' Lane smiled politely before continuing. 'Well, I asked her about her early life and her current circumstances in some considerable detail. Her responses enabled me to evaluate her state of mind.'

'Her responses?'

'Her responses to my questions were, in my opinion, quite normal.'

'Quite normal?'

'Normal.'

Dr Lane wore horn-rimmed glasses, which he took off when he looked at his notes.

'Did you question her about her friendship with Miss Boston?'

As one, the press pricked up its ears.

'Yes, of course, but I do not consider her friendship with Miss Boston to be relevant to the case.'

'You don't. I see.'

Quillet sounded surprised and also perhaps a little relieved; the press were a little disappointed. Colin Mackenzie, uncomfortable in his pew with his long legs, stole a glance at the accused, whose eyes remained fixed on the doctor in the witness box.

* * *

'Just one further question, Dr Lane.'

Making up for his heavy cold and lack of impact so far, defence barrister Patrick Clifford was out to get the court's attention.

'Yes.'

'In your opinion, is Miss Hargreaves capable of murder?'

A brief pause.

'In my opinion, no.'

'Thank you, Dr Lane, that will be all.'

The judge rose. Miss Hargreaves would begin giving her evidence after lunch.

16.

In the Dock

Standing in the dock with her hands resting lightly on the ledge, the stance of the accused was almost identical to that of yesterday. She was wearing the same grey sweater, pulled up high at the neck and pulled down long at the sleeves. And yet something was different, Walker thought. Perhaps she was standing up straighter; perhaps her chin had a slight upward tilt? Yesterday, she had said she preferred to stand, and it had sounded polite and unremarkable; this morning, when she had declined a seat, it had taken on an edge. Now, this afternoon, when she must stand and had no choice in the matter, she was compliant, except she was not. She spoke her oath out clear and plain enough, but Walker was bothered by her manner, though he couldn't resolve the feeling into anything more precise, certainly not a judgement or even an interpretation. Casting a quick glance at the jurors, he saw something of the same in a number of their faces.

In his coverage for the *Western Herald*, Colin Mackenzie made no comment about Rene's accent. Had that voice that so startled Ainsley at Starlight changed twenty years on? Could you still taste the smoke?

'Miss Hargreaves' – Quillet's voice was soft, he was determined to go gently – 'Miss Hargreaves, were you fully apprised of the state of Mr Massey's health before he came to live with you?'

'Pretty much.'

'Who informed you?'

'I saw it myself.'

'When was this?'

'When I visited Manchester after . . .' She trailed off.

'After Mrs Massey's death?'

'Yes. But even before. Aunty was worried that Uncle was on the slide. She was worried what would happen if she went first.'

'Went first?'

'Passed on. I told her I didn't think it was likely to happen. I was wrong about that.'

'And did you yourself see any signs at that point that Mr Massey was on the slide or in decline – would that be the phrase?'

A brief pause.

'He did seem confused sometimes, but I didn't think much of it then.'

'Moving on to the period just before he came to live with you. Did you speak to his GP in Manchester?'

'Yes. Yes, I made an appointment with Dr Finch so I would know about his prescriptions. He was very helpful.'

'"Very helpful." I see.' Just the trace of a smile from Quillet. 'So you felt you were, so to speak, well prepared.'

'Oh yes.'

'Did you know about his drinking at this stage?'

'I knew he liked a drink. I didn't know what it was going to be like.'

In the press gallery, heads were down, hands were writing busily. She had everyone's attention now.

'Miss Hargreaves, I must ask why you extended this invitation to Mr Massey. Mr Massey did not make this request himself; he had always lived in a busy city and you were expecting him to settle to a very different sort of life. It must have been clear beforehand that your life and Miss Boston's would be considerably disrupted. Why did you invite him?'

'He had nowhere else to go.'

A pause that became a silence.

'Miss Hargreaves?'

'Yes?'

'Is there anything else you wish to add?'

'No.'

'I see.'

'In your statement you said you discussed the situation with Miss Boston before you volunteered the invitation. Did Miss Boston require any persuasion?'

'We decided.'

'You both decided?'

'We decided. Yes.'

Quillet was still not satisfied.

'Do you think now that you underestimated the difficulties?'

'No, no, I don't think so.'

'Do you think that Miss Boston underestimated the difficulties?'

'I don't think so.'

'You don't *think* so. You must have talked about it together. After all, you run Wheal Rock on what has been called' – a pause, a studied consulting of notes – 'a "partnership basis", a description that will do as well as any. Miss Boston would surely have been part of any decision about Mr Massey?'

'Of course.'

'Of course you talked about it together or of course she was part of the decision?'

'Both.'

There was another silence, longer this time.

Colin Mackenzie noted a sharpness 'creeping' into Rene's responses at about this point; he wasn't the only one to register this. Was it the same as the sharpness the police reported: the sharpness of one who thought she was very clever, with 'something to hide'?

'Miss Hargreaves, can you confirm that you are the sole beneficiary of Mr Massey's will?'

Quillet was on more familiar ground now.

'Yes. Uncle – Mr Massey – signed things over to me, we went to the solicitors. He had three insurance policies. I shall get the money from them, but I don't know how much.'

'Do you know why he made you his beneficiary? He had a nephew, after all, with a young family.'

'It's what he said he wanted.'

'I see.'

Rene would have got a total of £131 5s 8d from the policies, rather less than the £314 paid to Marcus Quillet; double what Elsie had in her post-office account.

'This sum would have made a considerable difference to you, and Miss Boston.'

'Yes,' she said. 'Look, I don't know why he wanted me to have his money, but he did, he said so. I know it gives me a reason, I know it looks like I had a motive, but I didn't poison him.'

'So you insist. But you must admit that you made sure Mr Massey visited the solicitors to change his will in your favour barely a week after his arrival in Cornwall.'

'He said he wanted to sort things out.'

'Yes, I understand. But was there such a hurry? Really? He had just made his move from Manchester, in somewhat distressing circumstances.'

'He said he wanted to.' She sounded irritated.

Quillet waited. Writing hands caught up; heads came up; a little shuffling and stretching among the public, a yawn and cough. Then it went quiet again; Quillet continued to look at Rene all the while.

The accused looked at the jurors. 'I know it looks bad, I know it does. But I didn't poison him and that's that.'

But then she turned back to face Quillet.

'I didn't poison him, and if I had done, I'd have made sure there wasn't anything left in the glass. I'd have made sure everything was cleaned up properly.'

And there she was again, too clever by half, too conceited. It didn't help.

'Miss Hargreaves, when did you realize that you and Miss Boston could no longer cope with Mr Massey?'

'I'm not sure I follow.'

Quillet was happy to clarify. 'Miss Hargreaves, you were sick with a serious bronchial infection in the early weeks of November. When Dr Evans called to see you, he found you fraught and tearful as well as sick. When you visited him just a few weeks before Mr Massey's death, you told him you were concerned about Miss Boston. Did you not?'

'Yes.'

'This was the main topic of your discussion?'

'Yes.'

A silence.

'It sounds as if you were both finding it very difficult to cope with Mr Massey, but that in addition, and particularly, you were very anxious about Miss Boston – you made an appointment to discuss it, after all.'

'We were both feeling very strained at that time. We had both been ill.'

'You and Miss Boston?'

'Yes.'

'And when you both recovered, things returned to normal?'

'No. There was no improvement.'

'No improvement in Mr Massey's behaviour?'

'He was more and more difficult to . . . look after. We didn't, I didn't think we could look after him properly any more. I was working away all day and Miss Boston had her hands full with the house and the animals.'

'Had Miss Boston told you that she couldn't cope with Mr Massey? Had she said this to you?'

'No, no, of course not.'

'Of course not? I find it surprising that she made no complaint, no appeal to you. She was spending most of her days saddled with a senile, intractable, alcoholic old man, a labour no one in their right mind could relish. I must ask you again, Miss Hargreaves, did she ever say, "I can't do this any more" or "This is too much for me" – words to that effect?'

'No, she didn't. She wouldn't.'

'She wouldn't, you say, but she is considerably older than you, and you must have been concerned for *her*, when you were working away, as you call it.'

'Of course I was concerned.'

'About Miss Boston?'

'Yes.'

Quillet knew he must tread carefully.

'Because you felt responsible for her.'

A pause.

'I felt . . . concerned.'

She was cool now, Miss Hargreaves, 'a chilly customer' – just as the reporters said.

'Miss Hargreaves, I put it that you were a great deal more than concerned. This was, after all, your close friend . . .'

The accused said nothing but continued to look Quillet straight in the eye.

Quillet had hoped to avoid stating the terms of their relationship, but he had no choice now if he wished to press his point.

'This was your companion, with whom you had made your life for the past twenty years. Her well-being was your prime concern.'

Opting for the oblique to avoid the lurid, he sounded curiously soft.

'Dr Evans has told us that when you visited him at his surgery you were, I quote, "extremely worried" about Miss Boston, that you told him that Miss Boston was "quite run-down" by Mr Massey.'

'I was concerned. I may have said that.'

'Miss Hargreaves, do you think that it is possible that someone else poisoned Mr Massey?'

'No.'

'But you must have wondered how it happened?'

'Not at first. I just thought he'd died – he was old, he'd been ill with his chest. It wasn't a surprise.'

'But you've known for some months now that he didn't simply die but died of poisoning, administered over a relatively long period. Remember, we are not talking about a single event here. You must have wondered how it could have happened, surely? You must have some ideas of your own? You're clearly a woman who knows her own mind.'

A silence. But Quillet didn't want to let go.

'What do you think happened, Miss Hargreaves? Could somebody from outside Wheal Rock have poisoned Mr Massey?'

'Of course not.'

'Or Miss Boston? Do you think that Miss Boston poisoned Mr Massey?'

'Of course not. She could never have done such a thing.'

'Well, yes. I think we can all agree on that. So what do you think happened?'

'He did it to himself.'

'He took his own life?'

'No, no. He wouldn't do that – he wasn't unhappy. I mean, he did it by accident.'

'Mr Vanstone has shown that the poisoning must have occurred over a number of days at the very least, and probably over more than a week. That doesn't sound like an accident.'

'Yes, yes, I know that. But I don't think you appreciate. He had very odd tastes. Very odd. There was an occasion when Miss Boston was making jam when he drank most of a bottle of sterilizing liquid. He drank methylated spirits quite regularly in the shed. Of course we tried to keep such things out of his way, but we couldn't always. I said all this in my statement. The sugar.'

There was distaste in her voice. She spoke haltingly, as if she too could taste these bitter, noxious substances, as if their residues still bothered her and got in the way of her speech.

'No further questions.'

Outside, the rain continued to fall. Rene's look swept around the courtroom; regaining her balance, she soon found the woman in the green hat. And then a rather odd thing happened: the woman nodded, as if she was pleased Rene's ordeal was over, as if she approved of what she had said. Just a little nod but it was certainly there. What was it that made her familiar? For she was familiar, a face from the past.

17

Land of Water

The following morning Elsie and Margaret waited in the hotel lounge, watching from the window for the 'taxi' that would take them to the court. The rain had stopped, though the water level was some inches higher than the day before. The scene was peaceful. Underneath an overcast sky the dark water rippled gently; the reflections of the tall, thin houses glimmered softly in the water. The town was adapting to its aqueous form: the trees in the little square were content to grow shorter, the streets had yielded gracefully, everything was now riverside. It was quiet, some had left and many were staying indoors, unable or unwilling to leave their homes. Those few who ventured outside were well prepared. There were a number of men in waders, clearly on errands; one had a little child on his shoulders. Everyone moved slowly – no one was willing to take a chance with the water. Seen from a distance, these careful semi-pedestrians also seemed becalmed. A woman passed underneath the hotel window, she was inching along in long boots that were too big for her and carried a floppy, black Labrador puppy. Voices seemed muted or muffled by the water.

The change from yesterday was the smattering of dinghies and little rowing boats, and this added to the sense that the town was coming to terms with its liquid state. Some of these boats were already working as taxis and delivery vans; a number were assembled by the taxi sign, just opposite the hotel. A trip up to the market square cost tuppence, a return trip threepence; rates were negotiable, but there was little of the usual chat. Instead, there was the occasional, soothing sound of one boat lightly knocking against another.

Elsie and Margaret stood by the window, watching, fascinated. The water looked so dark, yet how it gleamed, changing as you looked. Even through the glass of the window, they could hear it lapping, soft and insistent, some way below. After a time, they spotted a slightly bigger boat; the oarsman rowed smoothly past the houses, skirted the taxi rank and turned across towards the entrance of the Eagle. As he got close to the hotel, the hotel porter in his battered green suit and gumboots appeared out of nowhere to catch the rope. Boat temporarily secured, the porter hailed them cheerfully from the window.

'Oh well,' said Margaret, but it might as well have been *oh dear*. She was nervous of the boat, just as she was nervous of all this water. But there was nothing to be done about it and she followed Elsie through the heavy door towards it. Elsie paused only for the briefest moment on the top step – still a good six inches clear of the water. Then she stepped, decisively, into the deep water and sprang, surprisingly lightly, into the boat. Without a pause, she stepped carefully down to the prow and sat down, looking straight in front of her.

Margaret hovered on the top step, unwilling to exchange one element for another, despite the gumboots which the hotel had found her. Finally she took the plunge, looking down at the water and reaching her hand out blindly to the boatman at the same moment. She didn't lose her footing in the water as she had feared, but as she stepped on to the boat, she wobbled a little before she managed to sit down. 'Easy does it,' the boatman said, and Margaret sat down rigidly, determined not to move till they reached the courthouse.

The boatman took up the oars and soon he was rowing slowly up the street – the same street that Elsie had gazed up the morning before. Then it had been misty and luminous in the lamp light; this morning it was clear. Elsie sat still at the prow, looking ahead, her hands wrapped in her coat. She had been very quiet since the episode with the newspapers yesterday. Margaret certainly thought the newspapers were to blame and Elsie had avoided them this morning, but she didn't want to ask. Besides, it wouldn't be surprising if Elsie was worried about her visit to the court – Margaret certainly was.

The boat slid gently through the water with just the occasional bump of the oars on the street below. The houses looked taller and more imposing from the boat, and gloomy, unmarked by pavement and kerb, the dark water lapping just below the ground-floor windows – the levels were higher here. And through one ground-floor window, Margaret glimpsed a whole room badly flooded, could just make out a little table topped with ghostly lace floating in the centre of the room. It made her shiver. They passed a set of traffic lights without seeing any other transport and made their turn towards the centre of the town. It was still very quiet and Margaret wondered where all the people were. Had they abandoned their houses, or were they somewhere inside, trying to battle the water with sandbags or dragging furniture upstairs to protect it from the flood?

They saw just one person: a tall, elderly man taking short, splashy strides through the water – almost as if he were trying to march. He wore a green tweed jacket over a pair of braced green rubber waders. He had a matching tweed hunting cap and carried a rifle – not casually slung, but cocked and at the ready. For a little while he paced himself with the boat, walking alongside them. Boatman and man in green nodded to one another, and the man in green raised his cap to the ladies but said nothing.

'Not planning to shoot the fish?' asked the boatman, smiling.

'It's not the fish,' the man replied, looking very serious, 'it's the rats. They're everywhere.'

Margaret saw Elsie start at this. It was the only movement she made. She sat quite still at the prow of the little boat, oblivious, it seemed, to the strange world that lapped around her.

They were travelling up the high street now, where the awnings of shops drooped forlornly below the flowing italics of Bluston's Gowns and Morley's Hardware and Teague's Quality Grocers. The big glass window of the gown shop looked like an abandoned fish tank, with odd shoes lying at strange angles on the floor.

They passed the cinema, battened down rather pointlessly with sandbags, and the All Day Coffee Bar, which had fared better than some, with its stools and red tables stuck to the floor. Up ahead in the market square, trestle tables had been weighed down with chains and sandbags and improvised into a series of rickety paths for those who dared. One of these led to the bus station at the bottom of Antoch's Hill – the route to the new shops at the top of the town; another led from the entrance of the Lamb Hotel (where most of the jurors were staying) up to the court. Planks and crates created further paths or bridges. It was a good deal busier here, and there were a few boats too, plying their trade across the market square and up to the council offices and the court.

Margaret knew they'd arrived when she saw the tall iron railings rising in front of her. She looked up at the great stone building and saw the bright statues, staring blankly, bearing down. The boatman rowed through the gateway into the courtyard, aiming for a pair of large trestle tables – this had become the official landing platform for anyone arriving by boat. A wide plank bridged the twenty feet or so from the landing platform to the top of the courtroom steps. It was supported by all manner of odd bits of furniture, some of it on loan from the market, the rest raided from the court buildings: document chests, desks and the like. A group of new arrivals was making its way along the bridge: one by one, and very slowly and carefully they went (the plank was wide and solid enough, but some of its moorings looked a little flimsy); there was a man in waders on hand to walk the more nervous along the 'bridge'. Margaret was glad to see him. She watched as one by one they reached the steps and solid ground.

And there at the top of the steps was the hard, blonde-haired woman that Margaret had seen in the hotel dining room on the first night. She was watching them intently as they made their approach to the landing platform. Or rather, she was looking at Elsie, motionless in the prow of the boat, her coat draped around her, staring at the watery world about her like one of those blind statues perched in the building above. The blonde woman kept looking, making no attempt to disguise her interest.

Elsie woke from her trance and made a deft job of getting out of the boat and on to the platform – it was a big step up – then she walked along the planking with confidence. Margaret followed cautiously in her wake, wondering at this physical ease that was so out of place with her usual diffident manner. And all the while the blonde woman was watching Elsie quite openly, even as they drew close, then she pulled out a notebook from her coat, wrote something down quickly, turned and went inside. Margaret knew who she was now, one of those reporters who had written so spitefully in yesterday's papers.

It was busy when they got into the lobby, and the peculiarities of some of the wet-weather wear on show saved Elsie from immediate attention. The flooding had made any manner of outdoor get-up permissible, and parts of the lobby looked more like the deck of a trawler than the anteroom of justice. But there was a deal of good humour and no one seemed to mind. It appeared you could arrive in anything. But you were expected to revert promptly to ordinary (smart) clothes immediately after, and that was the rub. Margaret took off her coat, slipped out of the boots with relief and put on her smart shoes. Then she joined the queue to the cloakroom counter. She looked around and was glad there was no sign of the blonde-haired reporter. Elsie stood patiently behind Margaret; there was a little ordeal when the girl at the counter asked for Elsie's coat but she flatly refused to take off either this or her big boots. As they climbed the curving, marble staircase, Elsie ahead now, Margaret was sure she could feel the looks from some of the people below. The waiting room was empty, with one exception: Major Veesey. He spied Elsie immediately and nodded his pleasure at seeing her, but it wasn't the time to speak to her, he knew. He was glad to see she had a friend with her.

In the courtroom the panelling and pews still exuded that top-coat of church. Most of the congregation was back too, sitting in the same place. Rene picked out the usher with the shiny brow, the sharp-eyed young man in the jury stand; there was the woman in the green silk hat. They looked straight at each other – it was a kind of greeting.

An attentive observer would have noticed that Miss Hargreaves seemed a little nervy or excitable; someone might have noticed how carefully her hair was combed, how neatly turned the pullover, her fingers tapping on the dock. For Rene was excited. Today, she would see Elsie. Elsie was probably already here, waiting somewhere in the building. She did hope she wasn't too nervous. Yes, she would see Elsie. No wonder the rain had stopped.

But before she could see Elsie came news, and the news concerned Leo. He had arrived a day early, but now, just when he was needed, he'd disappeared, vanished into thin air. Solicitor Thomas Walker was disappointed. It was a pity that the brother wasn't here, he might have made a point of comparison. Did they look alike? he wondered, turning his eyes on Rene, unable to make up his mind – how did she look exactly? After a bit of a delay and a deal of paper shuffling, Leo's statement was read aloud to the court. It contained a lively report of how Elsie had sent him packing from Occanby, which came as news to Rene. There was also a lurid account of a Christmas card in which Rene had complained bitterly about Ernest. This sat oddly with his finale.

> . . . I know that many people find my sister strange and she can sometimes seem hard-hearted, but she is the kindest person you could ever hope to meet. She has helped many people in her life, she's always thinking about other people. I wonder sometimes if she hasn't been taken advantage of over the years.

Rene was unsettled by his words, spoken by a silver-haired matron with a soothing wireless voice – a clerk of the court – but they sounded like Leo all right, he had always liked colouring things up.

After the non-appearance of Leo, it was the turn of Margaret Cuff.

'Call Mrs Margaret Cuff.'

Dressed in a royal-blue coat and matching hat, she bobbed at the judge as if he were the Queen. Not quite the friend he might have expected, Walker thought. Still, she was pretty, with the pinky-white colouring he particularly admired.

'Mrs Cuff, you are well acquainted with the accused and I understand you have employed her at your post-office shop on a regular basis?'

'Oh yes, she is my good friend.'

'Mrs Cuff, did it surprise you when Miss Hargreaves arrived that morning and told you that Mr Massey had died?'

'Not really.'

'Why? Could you explain?'

'He was old. They'd had the doctor out to see him a good few times through the winter. His chest. And everyone calling it a mild winter. Mind you, I don't think he got enough fresh air – Miss Hargreaves said she just couldn't tempt him out.'

'I see. So you weren't surprised.'

'No.' Mrs Cuff sounded very cheerful. 'Well, it wasn't out of the blue.'

'Miss Hargreaves said that?'

A pause.

'Oh no. I think that was me.'

'You're not sure?'

Another pause.

'It could have been Miss Hargreaves. It's the kind of thing you say, isn't it?'

'Is it?'

If Quillet was enjoying himself, he gave no sign; his manner remained mild and polite throughout.

'Mrs Cuff, if we could return to the morning in question, is there nothing else you can remember?'

'Sorry. Oh yes, the snow. Miss Hargreaves was hoping the snow wouldn't come till the evening, because the road might get blocked – I think she was a bit worried for the doctor.'

'Did she mention Miss Boston at any point?'

'She said she wanted to get back as quick as possible because she didn't want Elsie, Miss Boston, to deal with the doctor on her own. I offered her a cup of tea. We always had a cup of tea when we'd finished, but she said she'd better not stay.'

'Nothing else?'

'No.'

'Can you recall at exactly what time Miss Hargreaves arrived at the post office that morning?'

Mrs Cuff was confident about this.

'Quarter past six.'

'You're sure?'

'She was always there by quarter past six. The delivery came at half past. They'd always phone from Helston if they were going to be late.'

'Do you remember looking at your watch or at the post-office clock?'

Mrs Cuff didn't follow.

'Is there anyone else who can confirm the time? Was there anyone else in the house that morning?'

'My daughter, Belinda, but she was asleep.'

'Thank you, Mrs Cuff. That will be all.'

Mrs Cuff seemed surprised that there were no more questions and a little uncertain as she came down from the witness box; she gave a quick, smiling nod to the judge and another to Miss Hargreaves.

* * *

'Call Miss Elsie Boston.'

The court used the short intervals between witnesses to rearrange themselves in the narrow seats, a little inconspicuous stretching, a few faint murmurs but nothing that really amounted to speech. But now, as the gap lengthened, both public and press became restive. There had already been one disruption this morning. A number of people cast surreptitious glances in Rene's direction, but she stood as before, looking out across the court.

'Call Miss Elsie Boston,' the usher said again.

There was a further delay and then Walker heard the sound of footsteps in the marble corridor outside. The heavy footsteps grew louder, then they stopped. The courtroom was completely quiet now, waiting for the proverbial pin. Walker heard the door being opened and felt the attention of the courtroom begin to focus behind him. Unable to turn around and look himself, he saw some of the jurors make brief, guarded glances in the direction of the door. Everyone who looked, looked away then looked again.

She remained poised on the threshold for some moments, looking blindly across the court, oblivious to the usher, who tried to coax her forward. A current of cool, damp air followed her through the open door. Perhaps she became aware of the attention, because quite suddenly she dropped her head and started looking at her hands. The usher coughed politely but to no effect. Her hands had her attention now. They were clasped together and she was looking at them as if she expected to find something there. But she looked so deep, as if her hands were not quite her own. Like she had lost a coin in a well, thought Colin Mackenzie.

'Miss Boston,' the usher said quietly, almost confidentially.

She looked up then and seemed to see him for the first time. She took a step forward and stopped. Then, as if bracing herself, she stood up tall, fixed her eyes on the witness box and began a somewhat clumsy progress across the court towards it. She cut quite an extraordinary figure as she pressed through the court in her greatcoat and big boots. And her fixed stare gave everyone the chance of a better look. Walker registered the tightly buttoned greatcoat and the tightly bunned hair. The hair was scraped unflatteringly tight across her head. There was something pleasing about her face, he forced himself to admit, her features were good and she looked younger than her years. Yet her looks bothered him far more than Miss Hargreaves's. She didn't walk quickly but she strode out, almost as if she were still outside in all that water. Her eyes never wavered from the witness box. She looked neither to right nor left and certainly not at the thin, short-haired figure in the other box. Inevitably, perhaps, there was a price to pay, and she knocked a big pile of papers off the prosecution table. She didn't register this minor catastrophe, or the little hum set off by it – sharply curtailed when the judge sent a clerk scurrying to help. She never looked back and finally climbed into the box. *As the crow flies*, young Mackenzie wrote, in his tidy shorthand.

Asked to swear her oath, her voice rang out surprisingly clear and strong: 'I swear by Almighty God that the evidence I shall give will be the truth, the whole truth and nothing but the truth, so help me God.'

Like her friend and companion of so many years, she sounded foreign, but it wasn't clear the two of them came from the same place. Walker stole a quick glance at Miss Hargreaves, who was steadfastly looking straight ahead. It was difficult to know exactly what fell in her line of vision.

Walker didn't see the tips of Miss Hargreaves's fingers tapping lightly on the edge of the dock. Whether this signalled an impatience with court proceedings or the declaration of a different rhythm, it was impossible to say. Walker and Mackenzie, solicitor and journalist, both missed a look that passed between Miss Boston and Miss Hargreaves soon after Miss Boston had entered the chamber. In the right-hand pocket of Miss Boston's tightly buttoned coat was the letter she had been sent from Holloway. She had kept this letter about her since she received it, some nine weeks ago.

Patrick Clifford, whose cold was improving, kept his questions to particulars where he could; he judged this would make things easier for Miss Boston. She managed quite well at first: she could explain the routine of her days with Mr Massey and how she fitted in her duties to him (as she called them) with her other work. She was extremely clear about the division of tasks between herself and Miss Hargreaves. Miss Hargreaves laid the table. She fed the animals. She was also in charge of housekeeping. Miss Hargreaves shopped; both women cooked. These divisions also extended to the care of Mr Massey. Miss Hargreaves gave him his morning tea; Miss Boston provided his breakfast and lunch as well as other drinks through the day. Miss Hargreaves took over the care of Mr Massey when she returned from work, serving him his supper and his various drinks. She always made him a cup of tea to take up to bed. It was Miss Hargreaves who gave Ernest his medicines; both women bathed him, 'without fail', twice a week.

The distribution of the gardening was not so clear. Miss Boston was the gardener of the household, but Miss Hargreaves helped her from time to time. Ernest was to have done his share, but didn't. Elsie was going to concrete the path, she said, and Rene bought the weedkiller.

'Miss Boston, it was you who asked Miss Hargreaves to purchase the sodium chlorate, was it not?'

'Yes.'

'Did you and Miss Hargreaves make a habit of keeping a supply of weedkiller?'

'Oh yes, of course.'

'Had you run out of weedkiller? I understand that you asked Miss Hargreaves to purchase a large tin?'

'We still had a little left in the old tin but I wanted to concrete the path as soon as possible, as soon as the weather was suitable. It needed a good deal of work.'

'And a good deal of weedkiller.'

'Yes, it did.'

'Thank you.'

Miss Boston was also able to give a clear, if halting, account of the events preceding Mr Massey's death. The afternoon before he died, she had found Ernest slumped in the shed, almost in a trance, and had finally managed to raise him and help him back to the sitting room. He would take no food or drink – though she had tried to persuade him – and when she checked on him later, he had fallen asleep. In the evening, when Miss Hargreaves got back, they both tried to persuade him to eat but he picked at his stew and was only really interested in the prospect of his pint pot. As soon as *The Archers* was finished, he went out to the kitchen to get it. But he took his time coming back and Miss Hargreaves had gone to see what was the matter. Miss Hargreaves had called her into the kitchen and she had rushed through to find him slumped at the kitchen table. They got him back to the sitting room with some difficulty, thinking he could sleep in his chair, but he seemed to revive. They all listened to the news and a quiz. By this time, Elsie thought he was quite back to himself, and he carried his bottle and mug out to the kitchen as usual.

'And did Mr Massey request anything else to eat or drink?'

'No.'

'And, to the best of your knowledge, did Mr Massey seek out or consume further food or drink that night?'

'To the best of my knowledge, no. But you could never be sure with him – sometimes he went downstairs at night, rummaged around.' She came to a sudden halt.

'Did Miss Hargreaves make a cup of tea for Mr Massey that evening?'

'I suppose so.'

'You're not sure.'

'Yes, I'm sure.'

'Why is that? Did you see her?'

'It's what she always did.'

'I understand it was her routine, but you didn't see her make the cup of tea yourself?'

'No.'

'Had you . . . gone upstairs by this time?'

'No. I was outside.'

'Outside?'

'I went outside, so I could go to the toilet.' Elsie looked uncomfortable.

'And did you see Mr Massey's mug, his pot, in the kitchen at any point?'

'No.'

'And you didn't wonder where it might be?'

'No, Miss Hargreaves always washed his things in the evening.'

'That was her job?'

'In the evening, yes, it was.'

The judge announced lunch. Miss Boston would continue giving her evidence at two. Mr Clifford thought that the morning had gone well, considering. Mr Quillet was glad he had chosen not to ask any questions so far.

Elsie saw Rene disappear through a door she hadn't even noticed. She had to follow everyone else, pressed down the staircase to the lobby and towards the door. She needed to get away, to get outside. It was only when she passed on to the top step of the building that she remembered the flood. It was bright sunshine now and calm. Down in the market square, the water glimmered silver and blue;

closer up, in the courtyard, it was dark with just the odd gleam of oily rainbow. In between were the high iron railings they had come through this morning. If only she could leave now. It was a long way back to the hotel through the water, but she had her boots. But she couldn't leave. It wasn't over yet, and Rene was locked somewhere in the dreadful building behind her. She couldn't leave without Rene. Dear Rene, her hair looked so shiny and nice and she liked the new pullover, but she was so thin. She knew she hadn't been eating properly – whatever her letters said. Poor Rene. She so hoped that everything would be all right.

Elsie turned around unwillingly and went back through the big door into the lobby. There, she was immediately caught up in a hubbub of people. Momentarily, she was distracted by a thin, sharp-faced woman who eyed her intently; a woman with impossible, silver-bright hair. Elsie turned away, belatedly remembering Margaret, looking round for her, but it was hopeless in the crowd. Slowly, very slowly, she made her way back up the stairs to the first-floor waiting room.

In her office-cell, Rene sat at the desk, looking at the plate of sandwiches. The bread was grey-white and the ham was thin as paper. She was handcuffed to another prisoner officer, Susan Lyle, who was noisily stirring her tea. Susan Lyle made Rene all too aware of her confinement. There was no aimless wandering about the room as there had been with Maureen, no idle gazing out of the window. Officer Lyle had accompanied Rene on her long journey from London and she knew Rene quite well, but that didn't mean she liked her. Quite the reverse. Rene didn't understand it – they had been quite friendly when she first arrived at Holloway. Her thoughts settled quickly on the morning. It hadn't started so badly with Leo's statement, and Margaret had been so kind, and then Elsie. Poor Elsie. The awful gap after her name was called, the sound of her big boots in the corridor outside. How oddly she had stood in the doorway; it had felt like an age. And then that slow journey across the courtroom, the minor turbulence she left behind, the pile of papers knocked from the desk. She had expected Elsie to be ill at ease, but she was not prepared for how severe and strange she looked, that unrelenting grey bun – what had she done to her hair? Everyone in the courtroom had been looking, that was what it felt like anyhow, and their eyes were catching.

Rene saw again the big, awkward figure standing in the doorway, looking deep into her hands. Just for a moment Elsie had looked up and found her, found her so easily, without looking round. It was just a moment, but they were good at small smiles. But then it was past and all Rene could see was the absurd bun, the boots, the heavy man's coat she'd never seen before (it looked – impossibly – new). She had never looked so out of her depth.

Back in the courtroom, Rene watched Elsie make her way back to the witness box: she was still wearing her coat and boots. She tried to catch her eye again but couldn't, Elsie was too preoccupied. She moved more slowly this time – perhaps Margaret had told her about the papers falling – and looked even more out of place. *Clumsy*, the word came to Rene clear as a whisper; she wanted to bat it away but she couldn't. *Clumsy* wouldn't go away, and it was succeeded by other words: *strange* and *odd* and *poor*. They were words she had caught from other people, but for now they were the only ones she could hear.

Quillet trod very carefully.

'Miss Boston, you said in your statement that you were, and I quote, "obliged to give up my own occupation" when Mr Massey came to live with you, and that "since that time I always remained at home to look after him because he could not be left."'

'Yes.'

'You also said that you became "tied to the house" and that this was affecting your health. Was Miss Hargreaves aware of the burden that caring for Mr Massey placed on you?'

'Of course she was.'

'You told her then.'

'I told her.'

'Do you have anything to add to that, Miss Boston?'

A pause.

'She knew it wasn't easy for me. It wasn't easy for either of us.'

'But for you especially? Surely?'

Elsie said nothing.

'All I meant, Miss Boston, was that you had a far greater burden of care of Mr Massey.'

'We both did our share. It was very fair.'

'I see, yes. You also had the main responsibility for Wheal Rock. I understand that this is the distribution between you?'

'It is now.'

'Now?'

'Since I retired. I explained to Mr Clifford this morning.' She sounded fretful.

(Bored on his bench, Colin Mackenzie wrote in tiny longhand, *Miss Boston is no Mrs.*)

'Of course you explained everything to Mr Clifford, of course you did,' Quillet said soothingly and turned to the jury.

'Miss Boston had the chief responsibility for the care of the rabbits and chickens, the gardening – the two ladies grew much of their own produce –'

'We grew what we could. It wasn't easy.'

'I'm sure it wasn't. A busy schedule for somebody who has just turned sixty-five, and with none of the modern household appliances that members of the jury might be familiar with.'

Elsie looked up and took in the jury properly for the first time. Taken together they did not bother her so very much; one or two did not look at all interested, but anything was better than the attention of the men in wigs.

She looked down again.

'And to this was added the considerable labour of looking after Mr Massey. It must have been difficult trying to keep everything up.'

'I managed. We managed, nothing suffered.'

'Yes, of course, but when Mr Massey arrived, it must have put considerable pressure on your housekeeping?'

'We had his pension . . .'

'Miss Boston, no one could doubt the difficulties of your shared situation; it can't have been easy. Besides, your circumstances were already very constrained prior to Mr Massey's arrival. Were they not?'

Silence.

'Miss Boston, your lives couldn't have been easy *before* Mr Massey arrived. I'm sure you must agree.'

Elsie raised her head and looked carefully at Quillet; she looked puzzled.

'I don't understand you,' she said.

'Miss Boston, excuse me if I was unclear. What I mean is that you and Miss Hargreaves lived on a very limited income and things can't have been easy.'

'Our kind of living is never *easy*. It's always hard work.'

'Yes, yes, of course, but you were struggling to manage before his arrival.'

'We managed.'

'Yes, of course – you were doing the best that you could.'

'We managed.'

Perhaps Quillet heard something stubborn in her tone. But he didn't hear her pride. There was more to Elsie's *managed* than getting by.

His manner remained thoughtful, punctuated with nods and frowns of concern: he tended to adopt this mode when the witness was plainly disadvantaged.

'You were doing the best you could . . .'

Elsie said nothing.

'I'm sure we can all agree that these were conditions of nobody's choosing. Would that be a fair assessment?'

'No.'

'Miss Boston?'

'It is not a fair assessment.'

'Miss Boston, I intended no offence, but you must accept –'

'We were rich . . .'

The words appeared to come out of nowhere, nothing to do with anything. There was a smattering of laughter which dissolved into the damp chill and interest of what might come next. Rene's hands were cold and clammy; she found all of a sudden that she was breathing very fast. She looked down into the gallery and found her mooring: the woman with the green silk hat. The woman was watching Elsie very intently, and suddenly Rene knew who she was.

Elsie looked up and faced Quillet, fully stubborn; suddenly it seemed she knew exactly where she was.

Quillet was momentarily at a loss.

'Miss Boston, you had no electricity.'

'We had no need of it . . . it was a good life.'

And Quillet seemed to pick up on the tense at least: she was not just intractable, something had been lost.

'Yes . . . well. But I'm sure that there must have been times when you wished he'd never come to live with you both at Wheal Rock.'

'Of course I did, we both did. He spoilt things.' Elsie looked down, the boldness was passing. 'It was a good life, and he spoilt it.'

'Miss Boston, there must have been times when you shared these feelings with Miss Hargreaves.'

'Yes. Yes, there were.'

'Perhaps you could oblige the court by telling us about one of these occasions. What exactly did you say?'

There was a silence.

Then it seemed to Rene that she was no longer standing in the dock, but sitting in the gallery, tightly pressed in the back row, trying to see Elsie with all the rows of people in front of her and there was no room to get a clear sight of her. She was all alone and Rene could do nothing. Rene's heart was banging against her ribs. And then ahead of her, she saw the woman in the green hat, Vicky, the much-loved, disappearing Mona Verity. Vicky, who had let Joan Bennett escape and had now returned to help her rescue Elsie from the box.

The silence lengthened.

'I did it,' Rene said.

The sound of her voice surprised her.

'I did it. I killed him,' she said again, louder this time and slower.

A murmur went round the courtroom but it didn't get far, blotted by the panelling and the damp.

'Miss Hargreaves,' said the judge, 'do I understand that you are changing your plea?'

A certain rustling expectation took its place. The press finally had a little of what it wanted.

'Yes, yes, I am.'

'You are saying that you poisoned Mr Ernest Massey?'

'Yes, I did. I poisoned him but I didn't mean to kill him. I wanted him to get sick. I wanted them to come and take him away.'

The judge nodded the two barristers over; Rene's solicitor exchanged glances and raised eyebrows with Thomas Walker. Rene stared at the empty place where Quillet had been standing; even her fingers had frozen. She knew that people were looking at her. She had the attention, she and the men in wigs. No one was looking at Elsie now.

The conference went on and the audience grew restive. Both were interrupted when Elsie climbed down from the witness box and tramped back across the court. The usher tried to stop her, the judge looked up from his conference. Everyone was watching by the time she reached the door. She fumbled with the handle for some moments, then the door clicked open and she was gone.

A few minutes later, the judge called an adjournment. Rene was led away and the room began to empty. The handsome landing soon filled with people, uncertain what to do next. The jurors were sent back to their room and served tea by a sullen girl who had hoped to be on her way home by now. They were fidgety. Some thought they would now be dismissed and were relieved or disappointed accordingly. Further down the corridor, Patrick Clifford and Marcus Quillet, having finished with the judge, shared a whisky before returning to talk to their respective solicitors. It was only then that Clifford went to the office where Rene was being held to explain what would happen next.

The press adjourned promptly to the Crown. More whisky, a few predictable jokes, mainly at Miss Boston's expense, speculation about the likely sequence of events. Young Mackenzie had his bit of excitement now – the accused had not disappointed – but he was tired and confused. It would be simple now, Babs said, the jury would have a straight choice between murder or manslaughter. She was pretty sure it would be murder. The reporter from the *Mail* joined them, and the talk soon turned technical; Mackenzie had neither the will nor the grasp of legal procedure to follow. 'Keep up, cub,' Babs laughed. Much later in the evening, Mackenzie came up with a line that pleased him, though not one he could use: 'The whippet jumped the gun.' Can a cub call a woman a whippet?

* * *

The following morning was grey and mild. The levels were falling; the rule of water was ending. The courtyard was no longer a lake, more of a shallow pond. In the lobby, some continued to dress for the flood; most trailed mud and dirt in from outside. The floor was filthy and the caretaker was fighting a losing battle with his mop.

Upstairs the court reassembled and Rene was questioned again. She confirmed what she had said the day before. She had poisoned Ernest, yes, she had given him a small amount of sodium chlorate on a good number of occasions; yes, she had added it to various drinks that she gave him over some days, maybe even a week. But she hadn't meant to kill him, of course she hadn't, and she wished things had turned out differently. She was questioned about her intentions in some detail, and Quillet reflected on her changed manner – for the first time, compliant. She spoke as clearly as she had before, but she sounded regretful. He would not have trusted stagy contrition, he doubted it was in her, but she certainly seemed genuine now – probably the relief. When the questioning was over, Rene sought her ally in the gallery and found her. They nodded at each other fractionally and Rene saw the trace of a smile – Vicky's was the only friendly face she saw that day. Neither Elsie nor Margaret was anywhere to be seen.

In the end, the jury took just three hours to reach their verdict. Maybe they wanted to make up for the time wasted by the defendant. There was very little discussion. Not guilty of murder; guilty of manslaughter.

When the verdict was announced, Miss Hargreaves collapsed and had to be carried unconscious from the court.

The usher brought the news to Miss Boston and Mrs Cuff, who were sitting in the waiting room. He spoke to Mrs Cuff, who was very shocked. Miss Boston sat quite still, looking into the distance. It was left to Mrs Cuff to explain, and she waited until the usher had gone. And then all she said was:

'Come on, Elsie dear, we'd best be going. We must go home now and then we'll see what's best to do.'

* * *

An eighteen-month sentence to be spent at Holloway was announced a few weeks later. It parted them for longer than they had ever been parted – Rene was determined that Elsie would not see her in prison. But they were both practical in their different ways. The distance had to be endured and it would come to an end; eighteen months could be measured: it was not so very long.

The newspapers were kinder than they could have been, particularly to Rene. 'Little grey-haired woman whose life has been touched by tragedy' – the *Daily Mail*'s final verdict. Massey, or Old Nosey, got the harder time, punished perhaps for everyone's unsavoury curiosity. The physical details about the two women obtruded though – mannish, trousers, crop, masculine – plenty of coded smirk and sneer there; and Rene's confession confirmed her as the 'weedkiller widow' if not the 'weedkiller killer'. Elsie seemed to present more of a problem, and they couldn't resist some mirth at her expense.

'Miss Elsie Boston, long-term companion of Miss Hargreaves, shared her philosophy of life with the court,' sneered the *Daily Mirror*. '"If you have all you want, you are rich," she said, "I did not want anything more."' The other newspapers also enjoyed 'we were rich': headlined and twinned with a picture of the ungainly Elsie on the steps outside the court, beside a story that punished with its details of a pinching day-to-day. This same pattern was repeated in a number of the papers, national and local; but it was beyond Colin Mackenzie to make anything of it: he was too young; Miss Boston was too old.

But judge and press did not constitute the real, the long-lasting, punishment.

Their lives were so very ordinary, except perhaps in one or two respects.

There was little outright hostility to Rene or Elsie but, slowly and carefully, the two women had to be taken to the vantage point from where the court collectively perceived them. It was not a deliberate tactic, and it was undertaken without relish, but common sense was relentless. It was also differential: Rene may have been a chilly customer and too clever by half, but Elsie, poor Elsie, was made to look a bit of a fool. *We were rich*.

What did Rene and Elsie look like from the top of common-sense hill? In summary: odd, most certainly odd, and probably lesbians, odd and poor and gradually ground down by a situation that tainted them. The court knew how they were trying to do their best, but in the end they had had to 'make do'. They were certainly respectable, but no one would *choose* their life. Quillet and Clifford, prosecution and defence, were both convinced that Rene and Elsie wouldn't have chosen it either, if there had been any alternative. Theirs was, by definition, a second-best life. The two women had never had to think this. And perhaps Elsie's clumsy 'we were rich' was a general retort to the trial, not an answer to Marcus Quillet's insinuating question; perhaps she sensed an attack. They were both proud of their ways, for all that they were quiet and kept their own company. It was true that over the years they had left much unsaid. People they had lived among had thought they were both widows, or cousins, even, on occasion, sisters, and neither Rene nor Elsie had seen any need to put them right. Since they had taken that train to Cumberland all those years ago, no one had heard them mention Starlight. Mrs Cuff was one of a handful of people who knew Rene had been married. Over the years, for the most part, this uncertainty had served them well; now it had all been blown away.

In their answers to the court and in the police statements the two women gave, their relationship took a number of forms: there were various chords, but no single one prevailed. There was a little history of semi-formal requests and permissions, granted or withheld. 'With my approval, Miss Hargreaves went to Manchester and brought Mr Massey back to live with us . . . I don't know what Mr Massey's income was, but I, being responsible for the housekeeping, was given the sum of £3 per week by Miss Hargreaves, for his keep.' Perhaps these requests and permissions were in keeping with their rather precise distribution of labour. There was also the relationship between a Miss Hargreaves and a Miss Boston; though

'Miss Hargreaves' was also the name of Rene's choosing: 'I have always been known as Miss Hargreaves since that time.' She was also, of course, Bert. If many tasks were divided, many things were shared in the easy familiarity of a life lived together, hands in each other's pockets, the morning cup of tea shared in bed, 'as is our custom'. Coats, gloves, scarves, also shared. But animals were not. Jugger was Rene's dog – a present from Elsie, his arrival coinciding almost exactly with Massey's. The chickens and rabbits were Elsie's, as was Nib, the black cat who sat like china on the windowsill in a police photograph. Yet this division was part of a we: *we agreed*; *our present address*; *when Mr Massey came to live with us*; Miss Boston and Miss Hargreaves, Wheal Rock . . .

The *Exeter Mail* would title one of their stories about the trial 'The Old Man with Curious Tastes', though there was rather little interest in Ernest's eating habits. Did his tastes include feathers? Wasn't it the women tending him who qualified as curious?

Curious was like *remote*. In this case, *remote* didn't measure yards or miles, just two women living alone, two women in some ways remote from the values of the court. A big house, a great house, ten miles from the nearest public road was never remote, but well appointed in its parkland acres. It was not the cottage that was remote.

'She is fond of reading and also has some rather masculine interests' – part of Dr Lane's report, which he didn't repeat in court. In his *Who's Who* entry for the same year, Lane's own interests included shooting, fishing and fell-walking. Were these masculine interests? Lane declared on his best authority that Miss Hargreaves was not capable of murder. Was he surprised by the turn of events?

One person was not at all surprised: Prison Officer Susan Lyle. Neither the confession nor the temporary disruption of proceedings surprised her one bit. In her view, it was typical. Miss Hargreaves was the kind of person who didn't care what trouble she caused. And Susan Lyle was pretty sure they hadn't had the whole truth, even now: Miss Hargreaves had told too many stories, she'd seen that sad look before and she wouldn't be taken in. Susan Lyle was the guard who had accompanied Rene in the van on her journey from Holloway. Lyle could have forgiven her for lying about being married, it was a long time ago. She could have forgiven her for leaving her husband and lying about that – at a pinch. No, the biggest, the worst lie was that she became a husband herself. She knew about Bert and Elsie and it made her sick. Officer Lyle felt betrayed because she had liked Rene. She remembered thinking it, how normal she had seemed, how nice, before she knew about Elsie (and Bert).

One of the newspapers chose to reproduce the sketch that the court illustrator made of Rene. He was more observant than most, though he had to work from memory. His sketch showed the long, narrow jaw, rather fine; the nose slightly sharp, not large; skin weathered rather than lined. And her hair of course: the grey Eton crop. If Elsie had seen it in some other circumstance, she would have thought it a very good likeness.

* * *

Settled on his homeward train the evening after the verdict, solicitor Thomas Walker watched the land flatten, before the light disappeared completely. He was looking forward to getting home, though he would miss his evening conversations with Marcus – they had been the highlight of the past days. It was raining heavily again and there was a wind up. The rills made surprisingly steady traces on the glass of the window before being blown suddenly away. At Wichley Halt they seemed to wait an age. With his fellow passengers he shared an unwilling tension – everyone wanted to yield to day's end. But finally they moved off, the train picked up, and as the man sitting opposite him dozed, Walker gazed out once more into the dark.

A painting came into his mind; it was a long time ago, he'd been a young man. The Ravilious exhibition, his first visit to London after the war. It was one of the chalk horses viewed from a third-class train window. *Train Landscape* was its name. The horse was the first thing you looked at, high up in the left-hand window of the train carriage; but it was the large 3 – nearly the same colour as the horse – in the foreground that your eyes really fixed on: once you'd seen it, it was somehow the pivot of the painting. He still wondered why it was a third-class carriage. The horse had also bothered him. With its arched neck and carefully raised foreleg, it was elegant but stagy. It was clear to anyone that the horse wasn't going anywhere, but somehow it still managed to look like a wish.

Epilogue
Homecoming

The woods are lovely, dark and deep,
But I have promises to keep

Robert Frost, 'Stopping by Woods
on a Snowy Evening'

*Dear Elsie, there was no getting to the phone today so this is
just a note to say I will be arriving at Penryn at four tomorrow
and will take a taxi. I know it will be dear but I cannot wait to
be home. Your Rene*

Rene took a train from London on the morning she was released
from prison. It would take her most of a day to reach home.

Paddington. A shock of recognition. She stood for some moments
under the clock in the chill early morning, trying to get her bearings. This was the station where she'd bought her ticket to
Lambourn, all those years ago, the station that had taken her
to Starlight and Elsie.

She had dressed as smartly as she could, with a dark green jacket
over the blouse she had worn in court and brown lace-up shoes. She
carried her own big bag. She didn't like the cheap board suitcase
she'd been given by the prison – it let her down, she thought – but
at least it wasn't heavy. It was odd being on her own. After she'd
checked her ticket she took a walk about the station. She was early
for her train, which added to the sense of freedom, and she liked the
feeling of walking about, not quite knowing where her feet would

go. It wasn't a demanding liberty: the arched horizon of crossing tracks and wires was as good as the open road for now.

Everything seemed bright and colourful and dirty. Over by the great mouth of the cloakroom counter were black and gold posters for Petter Oil and the red and green livery of Swan Vestas: USE MATCHES SPARINGLY. The posters were pasted all round the counter window and then spread out along the walls. Most were familiar, but one showed a man and a dog waiting at a busy road crossing. TRAIN YOUR PETS, it said. The dog sat beside the man on the pavement, looking very patient and rather like Jugger. Rene walked on past a smart tea room and the ticket office, continuing on till she came across a fancy grocer's shop where she lingered at the window. She'd counted out the money she needed for the journey and she wanted to buy something nice with what she had left. Eventually she decided on a tin of shortbread, Elsie loved shortbread, a half bottle of brandy and a fancy box of chocolates. The chocolates were so pretty. There were just six of them, arranged like the petals of a flower in a white oval box. Each one had a dainty sugar flower on top too, rose and violet.

After she'd made her purchases, and still feeling oddly light-footed, she walked back to the departure board on the main concourse to check the platform again. As she stood watching the board, there was a sudden outbreak of clickety-clacks and times and places began to disappear. For some minutes there was nowhere; everything seemed suspended; odd strings of letters flittered across the board and the tiles clicked as one departure after another was spun away. The ripples of sound grew quieter and louder as journeys moved along the board; others appeared from nowhere. Rene held her breath, finally the clickety-clacks slowed and stilled, and she saw the train to Penzance again – it had moved some way across the board. Time to go.

She was first into the carriage and she popped her case up on the rack, settled herself in a seat by the window and placed her bag with her lunch (courtesy of HM Prison Holloway) and purchases carefully on the seat beside her. She prayed no one would come and sit next to her. There were still fifteen minutes to go. Looking out of the glass, she noticed that some young women, just a few, were wearing trousers, though the cut was very different from her own. She wouldn't have worn them herself, she didn't like the style, but she liked the way they were striding out. One was wearing plimsolls. How young they were. She wondered if Jessie dressed like this, in trousers, perhaps in plimsolls; she hoped that she was striding out too, somewhere in this city, striding into the future. Finally the whistle went and the train smoothed out of the station and Rene took out her cigarettes from the generous pocket of her jacket, and a book, borrowed from the prison library. They continued slowly for a time, passing into a long tunnel; she lit a cigarette and watched the flame flare and gleam in the glass. Blowing out the match, she caught sight of herself in the window, drawing on the cigarette, her face pale and angular above the dark of her jacket. She watched herself carefully for a few moments, assessing. Elsie would say she was too thin and she would probably be right. But I don't look old, she thought, old-fashioned perhaps, but not old, not yet. The train passed out of the tunnel and started to pick up speed.

The first part of the journey wasn't too bad. She dozed a little over her book, the train stayed quiet, no one tried to talk to her. All in all, she thought, she hadn't handled her time at Holloway so badly. She'd done what she had on her land-girl training, thrown herself into it. Quick to grasp the rules (official and unofficial), she had rarely needed reminding: almost a model prisoner. She had worked in the library and helped some of the young girls with their reading and writing. She felt sorry for them, some had been in twice or three times already, some would be back within the year. She had also worked in the grey, sunless plot called the garden, trying to grow carrots and potatoes in the waterlogged ground – she doubted even Elsie would have succeeded. Throughout her time in the prison, her highlight of the week had been the television they got to watch on Sunday afternoons. A group of them were taken to the smaller of the two 'recreation' rooms, where the chairs were already put out in semicircular rows. They always got to see a film and sometimes part of a serial as well; they'd had *The Moonstone* and *David Copperfield*. She always made sure she sat at the front, right up near the screen, because not everyone paid attention.

Rene carried on with her book and a man came round with the trolley and she had some tea. It was only when the announcement came that they were approaching Plymouth that she began to get excited. Up till then she had tried not to think too hard about where she was going. She knew that Elsie and Wheal Rock were waiting at the end of it, she could see Elsie standing at the window, but she couldn't quite believe it. But as the train left Plymouth and Devon and crawled across the homely Tamar, the journey caught up with her. At last she was going home. And then as she looked out of the window, everything outside started to come vivid. The tide was well out, and in the sandy sludge of the river she could see waders, probably redshanks, though it was hard to be sure, looking for food. Easier to see but less well adapted were the old folk, picking cockles and God knows what, slow and awkward in the sticky sludge.

At Truro, she changed trains for Penryn and she stood in the corridor from then on. She could have sat down – there was plenty of room – but she was too keyed up, her fingers were tapping, drumming in her pocket. After a while, she pulled down the window and stuck her head out. The quivery, yellowed trees of a few hours ago were gone; so were the empty and faded fields. Here, everything was still green. They passed neat fields with row after row of fat cabbage and potato plants. Above, the sky was so blue, with just a few white whispers of cloud. They went past a cluster of fruit farms, apples mainly, the orchards busy with pickers. The train chugged on, slower and slower; she knew all the stations now and the order: Penwithers Junction, Perranwell, Ponsanooth and, last, Penryn. Each stop seemed to take an age: the train would squeal to a halt just outside the station, and a brief lull of warmth and summer sound would come wafting through the open window. Rene would look out, often she could see the platform, almost within reach. Then the train would inch forward into the station. After that there was the brisk click of a door, a pause and then a tinny slam; at Perranwell she heard the hulking of luggage from the van; at Ponsanooth there was no one, nothing at all. Rene crossed each station out in her mind as they left it: Penwithers Junction, Perranwell, Ponsanooth. When they came into Penryn, the train was still moving when she opened the door.

She was the only person who got down and she felt light with her half-empty bag and her cardboard suitcase. The station seemed deserted.

She stood on the platform for some minutes after the train eased away. Along the bank the willowherb was in full flower, staking out territory with its fine lily leaves; along the tracks all manner of things were thriving, buzzing, crawling. Ragwort sprouted from the sides of the platform, the flowers were such a pretty buttercup yellow – but Elsie said it was a weed: if you let it flower it would run right through the garden. A ladybird landed on the sleeve of her jacket and she carefully blew it away. She was quite unprepared for the heat: here it still felt like summer, as if she'd travelled back half a season since leaving Paddington. A chaffinch hopped along the rail; proud, with his blushing chest, he twittered his song and then paused, waiting for a reply. Rene whistled back, but she was out of practice, her mouth full of air and too much puff. The little bird stopped in his tracks and looked around, his bright eyes blinking, then he twittered again and flew away.

The little bird's flight brought her back to herself: she remembered the taxi and walked slowly up the platform. There was no one in the tiny station and she left the building, ticket still in hand, and followed the sign to the road. Down a narrow lane, rather overgrown, and into the little car park – it came back to her now. And there, waiting for her, was the taxi, the driver reading his paper patiently, waiting for her – dear Margaret.

The taxi was the worst part of the journey. She'd travelled these roads many times, on buses and on her bike, and once, like this, in a taxi – with Ernest. She knew all the signs and turnings but nothing was quite where she expected. Well-remembered distances felt shorter, or longer, and while the taxi kept a steady speed, she sometimes had the feeling she was being pressed forward, almost against her will. She didn't fully get her bearings till they reached the crossroads that led to Rosenys. Here the taxi driver stopped to wait for a cattle truck which was rattling down the hill. Rene wound down the window and felt the faintest trace of a breeze on her cheek, smelt the furze; she could catch her breath more deeply now. From here she could surely count every turning, every house, every gate. The truck approached them at some speed and drove past, rattling and empty. They set off again, the taxi grinding a bit on the hill. But even now she wasn't quite sure of herself, for the taxi was already halfway up the hill before she remembered Upper Rosenys – her punctured bike on that cold evening, Kat's van – or thought of looking back.

And besides, she was nearly home now and her fingers were drumming. As they skimmed through Rosenys, Rene kept her eyes on the road, looking to neither left nor right, blurring her sight; she didn't want to see anyone before Elsie.

Soon they were out of the village and she had a glimpse of the chimney, their chimney, across the field; quickly, very quickly, the driver had reached the turning: there was the sound of rushing water and the flash of white gatepost. Then they were heading up the track, a little narrower, a little stonier – the driver was wary and took his time – and through the wood, still green and heavy with summer. And just a couple of hundred yards down, they came out of the wood and back into bright sunlight, and there was the chimney again, their landmark, and, just beyond it, the cottage. It was nearly as she remembered it: small and square with its skittery extensions. The little window in their bedroom was open. She was nearly home.

She paid the driver and waited for him to disappear, then she walked up to the gate. She stood there with her bags, as she had at the station; just for now she could go no further.

Rene saw Elsie's work first, how busy she must have been. The garden had been extended a little way on to the moorland at the back. It was still rough and a bit straggly, but she could see that Elsie had finally succeeded in tempting the dog rose down out of the old crab apple tree and on to a little ruin of wall – there were still a few pink flowers. There were also a new bed and new plants: glossy evergreens that had been carefully pinned and staked. Rene couldn't be sure what they were, but they stood out in the garden, so neat, so straight. They didn't look like the usual cuttings and clippings Elsie picked up on her walks. Unless she was mistaken, these new additions had been bought. Rene had never known Elsie to buy plants or seeds – it ran against her very nature. There were so many signs of Elsie's work – Rene's sharp eyes spotted various gleams of metal and wire which meant other, more improvised repairs. She had whitewashed the big shed (Ernest's shed), the chicken coop and the lavvy. Everything looked very fresh and neat.

Rene continued to stand by the gate; she felt warm and a little heady, it wasn't just the heat. She looked down and saw the front gate was unbolted. She remembered too clearly standing here when she'd arrived in the taxi with Ernest. She and Elsie had stood talking across the gate for some minutes, quite forgetting him. *You could have opened it for once*, she'd said, but Elsie was always cautious about things like that. This afternoon the gate was unbolted. Elsie must have remembered: she had left the gate unlocked today, because Rene was coming home.

Finally, Rene let herself look up the path to the kitchen window. And there was Elsie in the window, still as a picture. How long had she been standing there? They smiled at each other through the glass and she saw Elsie raise her arm very slightly; Rene did the same, and they smiled again. It was only then that Rene noticed that Nib was sitting on the windowsill, just as she had been in the court photograph: a perfect china cat. Rene pushed the gate and walked up the path to the cottage and here was another change: the old path was gone. The old path – rough-scored, boot-made, rain-made – was gone, and in its place was the long-planned concrete path, neat and narrow and lightly gravelled. How had Elsie managed that? she wondered, but she didn't have time to think about it because suddenly from inside there came the sound of barking and squealing and she heard traces of Elsie's voice: 'Down, Jugger, down. Let me open the door. Silly dog. Down, boy.' And she knew she was home.

They couldn't speak at first. Rene sat down at the table and Elsie lit the kettle and brought out a cake. And of course Rene stood up to get the plates and a knife – and was told to sit down. She did as she was told and took out her cigarettes, saw that Elsie had already put out the shell ashtray. Jugger stood in front of her, his whole body wagging. Whining and panting, he looked at her for a moment with his dark, liquid eyes, then jumped up so that his paws were on her lap – how neatly his nails were trimmed. He barked just once, leant forward and licked her face. Oh Jugger. He trotted around the kitchen after that, his long feathery tail wagging, quite getting in Elsie's way as she put out the rest of the tea things. But when she sat down, he took his cue, lay down beside Rene with a contented sigh and placed a proprietary paw across her foot.

They had each imagined something like this: the two mugs side by side, Elsie cutting slices of plum cake, Rene pouring the tea before Elsie would have – they both smiled at that. It was only what they had done so many times. Even when Rene leant back on her chair to reach the sugar and Elsie said, 'Oh Rene', still worried the chair would topple over. There were plenty of things to talk about: Rene's long journey on the train, and how was Margaret, and who was helping her with the deliveries, and where had Elsie got the posts for the fence, and how good the berrying had been. Plenty of things to talk about and each of them eager to make any one of them last, but not one of them took. They agreed and accorded and yes-ed and of-coursed, but they weren't in harmony. Elsie was wordier than usual, still speaking the paragraphs she'd composed so carefully for her weekly letters (she had dreaded the monthly telephone call). Rene felt as if she was interrupting. Elsie's words seemed to come too slow, but her voice was so soft, she had forgotten. Her own voice sounded harsh and loud to her ears.

Things got a little easier when Rene got up to clear the cups: Elsie rose too, almost on cue, and fetched the bowl she used for the dry feed. And for a few minutes there was nearly a simple silence as Rene cleaned the tea things and Elsie measured the feed out for the rabbits and mushed up some peel and crusts for the chickens. Cups and plates clean, she left the tap on and felt the soft, cool water running over her hands, heard Elsie closing the door behind her as she went out into the yard. Rene almost followed her before she remembered that it was only what Elsie usually did.

She sat down at the table and lit another cigarette, uncertain what to do next. Jugger came and laid his head gently on her lap and she patted him and stroked his silky ears. He soon grew restive under the attention, raised his head and sniffed delicately, almost showily, at the air. He looked at her again and whined, hopeful for crumbs. Rene cut him an edge of cake and she rubbed the thick fur at the base of his neck. He took this attention very much as his due – and she smiled, wondering if Elsie had been soft with him in her absence. But she couldn't keep still for long so she went upstairs.

She had half expected the door of Ernest's room to be closed, but it wasn't. The little stool they'd used as a table was gone, but the bed had been made up with a pretty cover and there was other linen neatly piled on it. There was a strong smell of lavender. There was no sign of Ernest's candle stand, but the room was full of stuff she'd never seen before: a nest of rickety 'occasional' tables, a faded loom chair that had taken too much sun, a barometer. She stood on the landing, looking into the room, oddly satisfied by the jumble of it all, picking out some familiars now: a handsome standard lamp too tall for the sitting room, and Elsie's navy trunk where she still kept her old chequebook and her gun. These were things that had been squeezed into the shed when Ernest came. Now they were back where they belonged, though goodness knows how Elsie had managed it.

And their bedroom door was open of course. It was just as she remembered: the tallboy with its secrets, the little casement window, the high bed. There was a straw sun hat lying on the bed and roses in a jug on the tallboy. Outside she could hear Elsie, murmuring to the animals, humming; Rene wanted to call down but she couldn't quite, the distance seemed too far. She noticed a new curtain in the casement window, a pole had replaced the pins they'd used before. She watched the curtain stirring gently in the breeze for some moments, liking the pale stripes of blue and grey.

By the time Elsie got back, Rene had arranged the presents and two glasses on a tray in the sitting room. So they sat down on the uncomfortable sofa, nibbled at the shortbread and sipped, wincing, at the brandy. And Rene drank it all in: the wireless in its place of honour on the cupboard, the green cushion on the window seat, the flaunting peacock rug; it still looked a little extravagant on the dark flagging but Rene had always liked it, even if it was a little out of place.

There was no sign of Ernest's chair – Mr Marrack had it now, Elsie said.

'I hope you don't mind, Rene, but Mr Marrack's been so helpful, everyone's been so helpful, and I thought, well, we didn't want it, did we? So I asked him. I had to press but he took it in the end and I think he was rather pleased. It's very much a man's chair, don't you think?'

After this bubbling from Elsie, Rene opened the chocolates and they each had one, not sure if they really liked the silky, flower-flavoured cream. 'They taste like scent,' Elsie said uncertainly, and Rene poured some more brandy and they sipped the taste away.

'Oh Bert, I've been so worried all day. Silly things, such silly things. About the station and the train and the taxi and had I got the day wrong. I even telephoned Margaret. I'm sure she thought I was a fool.'

Rene reached forward, tried to squeeze her hand, but Elsie moved her hand away, then brought it back and touched hers quickly, awkwardly.

'Margaret's been so helpful, Rene, so kind. I don't know what I'd have done without her. We must find a way of thanking her, now you're back.'

Rene agreed – all those cigarettes she'd sent her – and asked about Belinda and the shop, but they still couldn't find their ease. Her own voice no longer sounded strange to her ears, though Elsie's words did. She had wondered if it would be difficult for her to find the tracks of their old life. It hadn't occurred to her that Elsie might have trouble finding them too. She had been here all this time, after all – alone, it was true, but knowing that Rene would return, knowing when. Yet it was Elsie who seemed to be the chief culprit in the making of this mood. She had little bubbling overflows when she sounded quite herself, but then she would fall silent and snuff the talk, their talk, quite out. She grew quieter and quieter and stiller and stiller, sitting so upright, her glass forgotten on the tray. She looked so uncomfortable – more than that, horribly awkward, her palms placed face down on her knees, her mouth slightly open. So awkward, so rigid; for a moment Rene couldn't help remembering the courtroom. She had determined never to think of it, never to remember, but for a moment she saw Elsie standing in the witness box, so severe, so vivid, her hair drawn back, buttoned up in that greatcoat: *We were rich*, she'd said.

'Oh Rene,' Elsie said.

That was all she said.

'What is it? What's the matter?'

'Oh Rene,' Elsie said again, but this time it sounded different, easier, like a sigh of relief.

'Oh Rene, I'm so sorry. Everything you had to go through and you were all on your own, so far away.'

'I managed, Elsie, it wasn't so bad. I managed and I'm home now, that's what matters . . .'

'No.'

Elsie raised her hand shakily towards her mouth and swallowed.

'You didn't even let me visit and I know why. It was because you were thinking about me, how much I'd be upset.'

'It was a long journey. I know how you feel about London.'

'Everything you had to go through. Always so kind.'

She picked up her glass quickly and sipped at the brandy. Rene could see that her hand was shaking.

'And it should have been me. I should have been in prison.'

'What?'

'It should have been me. I did it. I killed him, Rene. I killed Ernest and you took the blame.'

'Elsie –'

'Please let me finish or I'll never get through. It wasn't an accident and I didn't want him to get ill. I meant to kill him, Rene, I really meant to. I wanted him to die.'

Rene leant forward to take her hand, but Elsie brushed it aside, shaking her head – she wouldn't accept any more help, not just now.

'I wanted him to die. I did it very slowly, very carefully. I worried that he'd guess, that he'd realize, he was so clever, always watching when you didn't even know he was there.'

Elsie put down her glass. The sun was coming through so brightly now on to the peacock rug, it made everything else look faded.

'I never thought anyone would find out, not even you. I never thought the police would come, and when they did, even then I felt sure . . . And then they took you away and I didn't know what to do. You were so sure that they'd made a mistake, so confident that it must be an accident, I couldn't say anything.' She came to a stop and looked down at her hands.

'Listen, Elsie.'

Elsie looked up, barely able to meet Rene's eyes, dropped them again.

'Please, you must listen. You said nothing and that was the best thing you could have done, believe me.'

'I don't know why they were so sure it was you anyway. Why did no one ever think it was me?'

This last held the faintest trace of resentment.

'Elsie.'

'Dear Bert, everything you had to go through. Always so kind.'

'Elsie, stop.'

Rene reached forward and took Elsie's clenched hand, squeezed it hard. This time Elsie didn't shake her away. Rene felt the heat in it, the strain, tried to prise her fingers open. She still wouldn't look up.

'Elsie, you must listen to me. Please. I don't want you to feel sorry. You'd been through enough with him. You had a far worse time with him than I ever did – you two, you never . . . well.'

Rene gave up trying to prise her fingers open and squeezed her hand again.

'I don't think Holloway was any worse than what you had to put up with him, day after day.'

Elsie looked at her properly, carefully, for the first time.

'You knew that I did it? But when, when did you find out?'

'I think I knew in the courtroom, I'm not really sure. Everything was so confused.'

She could still smell the violet – the violet was stronger than the rose.

'Oh Rene. Is that why you said it? Is that why you confessed . . .'

The word seemed to hang in the air.

'Elsie, please listen. What I'm saying is, I think I knew in the courtroom but not for sure. Afterwards of course, well, I had plenty of time to think about it. But it was so dreadful in court. All those questions, all that attention, I hated it. And then to see you go through it too. That horrible man, going on and on with his questions, so sly . . .'

'I don't understand.'

'I don't think I understand exactly what happened. I just wanted it all to be over. I didn't think beyond that. Once I got to Holloway and I had a chance to think everything through, I worked out very quickly that it must have been you.'

'But Bert, you had to go to prison, all that way.'

'Elsie, you need to understand. I'm glad you did it, really I am. That's the most important thing. I'm glad. I'm glad you did it, you must see that, even with everything that came after. I'm still glad. God, Elsie, he could still be here. Think about that.'

Elsie shivered.

'You don't think he still is, do you?' Rene said.

'Oh no,' Elsie said, 'he's gone, quite gone. Didn't you see the room upstairs? There's no room for him there.'

It was impossible to know if she was being serious.

'Where did all those things come from? The barometer and the tables?'

'Major Veesey – and Margaret gave me the tables. Do you like the picture?' Elsie asked, suddenly sounding shy.

For Rene hadn't noticed the painting. It was on the wall above the wireless and it showed a branch that had been cut from a pear tree. The leaves had a sheen of grey and the pears were a lovely yellowy colour. It was framed too.

'Are they Bartletts?' asked Rene, thinking of Starlight.

'Do you think so?' Elsie said eagerly. 'I thought they might be, they're just the right shape.'

'It's a lovely picture.'

'I'm so glad. I wasn't sure what you would think. I bought it in Helston.'

The picture had been done very carefully. You could almost see the leaves starting to dry out. The pears were plump, ripe bells and there were tiny dents and bumps on them.

'You didn't notice the path,' Elsie said.

'Of course I did. It looks very well.'

It was an hour or so later, they were still sitting on the sofa, but comfortably now, easily. Nearly dusk but it was still hot; Jugger lay on the floor at Rene's feet, his tongue lolling.

'How did you manage it? You can't have done it all on your own.'

'Mr Marrack got me the cement and helped with the mixing and he got the roller. I did all the rolling myself. I got it so smooth but all manner of things got stuck in the cement when it was drying, twigs and leaves and –'

'But you can't see any of that now. It looks very smart.'

'Oh yes, the gravel covers it all nicely. Except.' Elsie began to laugh.

'What is it?'

'Jugger's paw-prints are in the concrete up by the door,' Elsie said.

Jugger thumped his tail proudly.

'It's a place where the gravel will never settle.'

'I'm sure he knew that.'

Jugger jumped up and barked again.

'It's better now though, isn't it? We were always planning to do it.'

'Oh yes, one of those things, but now it's finally done. You did a good job.'

'Margaret came and helped with the stones and the gravel, she had her nieces staying – from Bristol. I let them do some of the raking. They made a bit of a mess but I put it right.'

'We should go for a walk before it gets dark.'

Jugger thumped his tail again.

'He could do with a swim,' Rene said.

Jugger squealed.

'Aren't you tired, Bert?'

'Quite exhausted. But I so want to walk, it's been such a long time.'

Jugger barked his agreement.

'Silly dog,' Rene said.

Rene went upstairs to change into an old shirt and lighter trousers; Elsie made up a bottle of squash. They took torches with them and the remains of the shortbread.

Elsie showed Rene Jugger's paw-prints just by the door as they went out (Jugger himself was already halfway up the lane). She made to cover them over with some gravel that had accumulated in a dent beside the drain.

'Oh, leave them, Elsie. I like to see them there. It's his mark.'

So Elsie rubbed the gravel away and then they walked down the little path together. They slipped through the gate and Elsie bolted it; Rene remembered the long, loose clang of it.

'We're going to the wood then, I suppose.'

'Of course we are. Why did you even ask?'

'Does Jugger know?'

They both looked ahead to the dog, who was bounding giddily to and fro across the lane. From time to time he stopped and turned back and barked, urging them on.

'We're coming, Jugger. Good boy.'

'He looks as if he's been on the brandy,' Elsie said.

The light was fading more quickly now. Looking across the fields, they could just make out the roofs of the village where the swifts were still flocking their hectic patterns.

They walked up the lane quietly now and easy; side by side they dwindled into the darkening.

★ ★ ★

The next morning Elsie took Rene into the garden to show her the new plants. They walked about, cups in hand, Elsie picking out this clump of daisies or that lavender as if they were old friends. Rene sipped her tea, savouring the luxury of being outside in the open air; it was another warm, summery day. She admired the new frame of runner beans, the neat tub of cos lettuces, bunched like posies and ready to eat. The new bed she had noticed yesterday was a scaffold of strings and sticks. The glossy evergreens were osmanthus, Elsie told her, and the flowers would smell lovely, like vanilla, if they came. You could never be sure of course with this ground. Rene admired the shiny leaves and tried to imagine it in flower: the smell of the confectioner's shop amidst the bitter-sweet of garden and moorland. Elsie had bought them from a catalogue, she said.

A catalogue?

That didn't sound like Elsie at all.

So they meandered through the garden with their tea, taking their time, enjoying the idleness, Rene remembering the springy ground underfoot – the water was never far below. Nib followed them at a curious distance. At the wall they paused to admire the struggling dog rose and Rene noticed the fuchsia with its fine, pink candles – another new addition. She lit a cigarette and leant back against the wall, looking towards the cottage; Elsie started to prink and pull at some erring shoots.

'So all's well here, I see.'

'Pretty well.' Elsie's tone was matter of fact, but she looked pleased.

'You've clearly managed very well without me.'

'Oh Bert, how can you say that?'

There were none of yesterday's eggshells, but Elsie wasn't ready for teasing yet.

'I only meant,' Rene said and then stopped. 'I only meant that everything looks so well and I'm glad.'

Elsie smiled.

'I've so enjoyed getting things ready this last month, knowing you'd be home soon to see it.'

'And here I am.'

'Yes. Here you are.'

They smiled at each other. Rene dragged at her cigarette, coughing slightly.

'I've been doing quite a bit of gardening work,' Elsie volunteered.

Of course, thought Rene, now she understood all the little signs of prosperity: the new plants from the catalogue, the curtain, the picture of the pears in the frame.

'Major Veesey?' she asked.

'Yes. I decided to go back to St Keverne, it isn't so very far. He still pays me too much.'

They smiled at each other again – the major's generosity was a little joke between them. But Elsie didn't want to be distracted, there was something else she needed to say.

'I don't want you to think that I've been spending too much money.'

'I wouldn't think that.'

'I haven't used any of our savings.'

'Elsie.'

'And I've only used my share of the help fund money. Yours is all in the post office. I wouldn't have spent any of your share without asking.'

'I wouldn't have minded if you had.'

'People were very generous,' Elsie said; she felt awkward about the money.

'I know, I couldn't believe how much it came to in the end.'

'Apart from Mr Prynne, of course.'

'Well, that didn't surprise me, he never liked us.'

No smoke without fire, Mr Prynne had said to Mr Marrack, no smoke without fire.

* * *

'Oh yes, I nearly forgot. A letter came for you last week, Margaret brought it over.'

'A letter?'

'Yes, I've got it upstairs.'

'A letter for me? Who's it from?'

'I don't know. Local – a Camborne postmark. I'll just go and get it.'

Rene could hear Jugger barking in the kitchen. He couldn't understand why she was outside and he wasn't. She followed Elsie indoors.

Dear Rene,

It seems odd to call you Rene but I can't call you Miss Hargreaves – the last time we met you were a little girl! I do hope you don't mind me writing, it is meant in a friendly way.

You realized who I was I think – Vicky McCrane. I did hope you would. I should explain how I come to be writing. It is quite a story. As it turns out I live very close to you – in Upper Rosenys. I dare say you'll remember that you visited the Fox and Hound with Kat. Kat and Jude saw your name in the paper when you were charged, and when Kat said she thought you were from Manchester I wondered if it might be you. I even went to a meeting in your village – they were raising money for you and your friend.

In the end I came to the trial and as soon as I saw you I knew. I felt I owed you a good turn – it was you who led me to the pictures. Well, I wanted you to feel that somewhere in the gallery there was a friendly face, albeit one in a dreadful hat. I'm so sorry the trial ended the way it did. People can be so foolish.

I've lived in Cornwall for many years now, I moved here just before the second war. At first I was living near St Ives. I knew a good number of people when I was Mona Verity, all very bohemian I suppose, but I grew tired of that so I left and moved to Upper Rosenys – which, as you know, is a rather particular place. It does me well, though I live very quietly and I am on my own now. Do you remember the day we met Eric Stoller? Such a long time ago. One minute we were climbing along the walls and the next we were in that garden – it was like magic.

Anyway, I just wanted to say how glad I am that you'll be home now with your friend. I do hope that you don't mind me writing to you in this way.

Best wishes to you and to Miss Boston,

Vicky McCrane

Rene finished reading. It was quiet in the kitchen, but outside she could hear the birds chattering. Elsie was watching her, careful, concerned.

'Who is it from? Is it from the people at the pub?'

'You mean Kat and Jude? No, it's from someone I knew a long time ago.'

Elsie looked wary.

'But it was such a long time ago . . . Her name is Vicky McCrane. I can hardly explain. I last saw her properly when I was seven.'

'Seven! I wonder why she decided to write to you now.'

'She wanted to send her best wishes to both of us . . .'

'Oh. That's nice, I suppose.'

'Yes, it is. Very nice.'

'Does she want to meet you?'

'I don't think so.'

'Would you like to meet her – Miss McCrane?'

'No, I don't think so . . .'

Rene put the letter down on the table; Elsie smoothed back her hair and tried not to look at the letter.

'Here, you can read it if you like,' Rene said.

'Oh, I don't think I should.' She looked uncertain.

Rene picked it up and made to hand it to Elsie.

Elsie looked at the letter in Rene's outstretched hand; she briefly touched the tips of Rene's fingers and squeezed them tightly. Then she smiled.

'Oh no, Rene, it's your letter. It was addressed to you. I'm glad it's a nice one though.'

* * *

Elsie wasn't that easy with the children. It had started when Margaret's nieces visited from Bristol and tried to help with the path. Soon after Rene returned, Mrs Marrack's two came over to Wheal Rock with Belinda one Sunday 'to see the dog' and stayed all afternoon. Rene had taken them on a walk, had nearly got lost, but they were back for a late tea and Elsie made biscuits to go with the cake. They came back on their own the following Sunday and brought a friend from the village with them. Now there was a little trail of children who came up from the village, it had become a pattern.

They came after school or on Sundays, unless the weather stopped them. They came across the fields. Friday was open house and there was always lemon barley, or sweet weak tea to keep the chill off, if it was cold. Elsie's size could be intimidating, especially when she was out in the garden, in her dark trousers and black wellington boots. She didn't really walk fast, but her long strides covered the ground quicker than you'd think. Inside, even though she dwarfed the stove and the red-and-white Formica table, she was softer, slower. Mrs Jack Spratt to Rene's Mr. It was all quite cosy. The children were old enough to find the two women both ordinary and odd.

The children often brought a little something: a bag of sugar, a cake, a bunch of pinks. These they gave to Elsie, but they preferred to spend their time with Rene. She showed them the best trees to climb in the little copse, the best places for berries and mushrooms, and she taught them to bird call – sometimes the copse seemed full of giddy birds. There was always a dog loping around her legs, floppy-eared. She seemed to take a pleasure in passing on this hard-learnt lore to country children. Elsie was different. She was kindly. She always remembered the children's names, and took careful note of who liked the rabbits and who liked the chickens. Grouped together three on a stool, they were like baby blackbirds, she thought, all stretching necks and beaks; and their mouths, all gaps and sprouting oversized teeth, bothered her. But they were trying to be friendly. Jenny with the jewel-green eyes brought a pink plastic box with her one wet Sunday. 'This is where I keep all my treasures,' she said, sitting down next to Elsie. And she took each little trinket out of the box and showed them to her, one by one. Elsie complimented her painstakingly.

'Have you never seen treasures?' the little girl asked eventually.

'Not like these,' said Elsie, truthfully.

'You dig too deep,' Rene said later. And Elsie said nothing and turned away; she was a little jealous of Rene's easy ways, and perhaps she wondered too about the reminding those eager little faces did. Rene did not dig deep, she trod lightly on the sandy soil, easily wind-blown, and if her eyes got stung, she didn't seem to notice, the soil would settle again, leaving little or no trace of her footsteps.

The children never came on Saturdays though, for on Saturday afternoons she and Margaret Cuff always went to the matinee in Helston. Rene would stride across the fields, hands tapping, and knock on the door of the post-office shop. Then she and Margaret would walk up to the bus stop to catch the one o'clock bus. The bus went past the turning for Upper Rosenys. Rene had written a note to Vicky to thank her for her letter.

On Saturday afternoons Helston was always full of shoppers, and when they reached the bus station she and Margaret had to join the mill of people. There was just one picture house on the high street, there had been another but it had closed down. Inside the Regal though nothing had changed, the brush of the seats, the smell of smoke and the little metal ashtrays; she still loved to step into the dark. Elsie wouldn't come to the cinema, Rene had asked her but she always said no, she liked to keep to her wireless and the books from the library.

When the programme finished, Rene and Margaret always had a cup of tea at the Florin, then they would walk up to the bus station. By then Rene would be thinking of Elsie at Wheal Rock, waiting, waiting, at the window.

Some months after Rene's return, little Jenny came skipping up the new path and knocked on the open door. Rene and Elsie were sitting at the table, drinking their tea. Jenny was a little shy and not quite sure who to look at or speak to, and then all in a rush, because she was nervous but she knew them after all:

'Mum said, was it all right if I took my tea with you today?'

And Rene said, 'Let Elsie look after your hairpin, Jenny. You wouldn't want to lose it if we went for a walk in the fields.'

Historical Note

This novel began while I was trying to find out about the life of my mother's mother, Rene Hargreaves – a black sheep if ever there was one.

Like most ordinary people, Rene's life would have been nearly invisible in the official sense – but for her encounters with the criminal justice system and the rigours of wartime documentation. What I found suggested a partial chronology for Rene and, to a lesser extent, Elsie; the police records also revealed some tantalizing details about their life together.

Still, there were very few incontrovertible facts: Rene left her husband and three young children before the outbreak of the Second World War; she met Elsie Boston in Berkshire, working at Starlight Farm as a land girl; Elsie's farm was lost somehow during the war and the two women became itinerant workers; they settled in Cornwall at some point in the late 1950s. Rene was tried for the murder of Ernest Massey and convicted of his manslaughter. The two women lived together till Elsie's death. My mother was named for a film actress of the day.

Many names – of people and places – have been changed, but not Rene's or Elsie's. Even here, things are not quite as simple as they seem. Rene appears as Irene Roberta on her marriage certificate; in other official documents she appears as Renee, Irene and Rene. In the 1911 census, Elsie's full name is given as Elsie Clare Boston; much later, her police statement gives her name as Clare. The press reporting the trial alternate between Clare and Elsie. I settled on Rene and Elsie because I liked the names, perhaps because they were less formal. And, of course, records cannot always be trusted. Rene's death certificate gives her occupation as 'widow of — Hargreaves' – hardly a helpful summary, given that Hargreaves is Rene's maiden name and her husband died a good forty years before she did. On occasion, I have quoted from police statements and other reports, including newspapers; sometimes I have altered these.

Elsie did write the following as part of her police statement though:

> When I was a young girl, I went to live at Starlight Farm, Lambourn, Berkshire, with my parents. When I was about thirty years of age my father made the farm over to me by deed of gift.
> In May 1940, Miss Hargreaves came to the farm as my land girl and I have known her ever since.

It should be clear that *Miss Boston and Miss Hargreaves* is a fiction and not a speculation and it should be read as such.